ALSO BY ARI BARAN

The Penalty Box Series

Game Misconduct
Delay of Game
Home Ice Advantage
Goaltender Interference

Home Ice Advantage contains descriptions of anti-Semitism (challenged), an anti-Semitic slur, racism (challenged), an emotionally abusive family and undernegotiated kink.

HOME ICE *ADVANTAGE*

ARI BARAN

HARLEQUIN

ISBN-13: 978-1-335-00441-3

Home Ice Advantage

First published in 2024. This edition published in 2026.

Harlequin Enterprises ULC
22 Adelaide St. West, 41st Floor
Toronto, Ontario M5H 4E3, Canada
Harlequin.com

HarperCollins Publishers
Macken House, 39/40 Mayor Street Upper,
Dublin 1, D01 C9W8, Ireland
www.HarperCollins.com

Recycling programs for this product may not exist in your area.

Printed in U.S.A.
1 2 3 4 5 6 7 8 9 10 HDC 29 28 27 26

I.

FALL

CHAPTER ONE

September

On the day of Ryan Sullivan's forty-fifth birthday he discovered that his wife had gotten him a divorce.

Embarrassingly, it took him until the afternoon to realize it.

He had left early in the morning to get to the game with his peewee hockey team. That kept him occupied for a few hours. It was his first coaching position and he'd been taking it *really* seriously. Sure, it was only peewee, but eleven- and twelve-year-olds were a real handful on the best of days. To make matters worse, Ryan had been mediating a season-long dispute between the parents of his 1C and the parents of a kid who thought *he* deserved to be the 1C. He'd kept their ice time pretty even, but that didn't matter to hockey parents who looked at the lines beforehand and kept track of matchups and deployments.

After the game, Paul, the father of Jaxon-the-2C, confronted Ryan outside of the locker room. Ryan had to talk the guy down, spinning a tale about PP1 time and reassuring him that really, *no one* was scouting this early, and it truly was not a knock on Jaxon's hockey skills that Wyatt had been taking more offensive-zone draws, but simply that Jaxon's defensive responsibility was stunningly well-developed for his age and—well. At least Paul hadn't punched the locker room wall this time.

Ryan had been so busy with the parents that by the time he got out to the parking lot, it was over an hour later than he normally would have been on his way home. He took a moment, alone in his car, to rub his eyes. When he was on the ice with the kids, he fucking loved every minute of it. He'd always considered himself a people person, but the parents…man, the parents were something else.

And holy shit, did Ryan know about *parents.* Ryan had four brothers who had all played pro hockey in some form or another, and their dad made Paul look like a family therapist in comparison.

By the time he had gotten out of the rink, stopped by Dunkin' to get his third cup of coffee, braved the shitty weekend traffic on the way home and narrowly avoided getting sideswiped by some asshole doing 80 mph with nowhere to go, the headache was building up behind his eyes. The news radio was still talking about the fact that yesterday the Boston Beacons, who'd already fired their general manager in the offseason, had fired their head coach in the middle of *training camp,* which didn't bode well for the season. If anything, the headache intensified.

It didn't get any better when he actually got home.

He parked in front of the house the same way he always did because the garage was where he'd set up all of his hockey equipment and the skate-sharpening machine and you could only fit Shannon's car in the other side anymore.

He keyed in the door code and the lock whirred uselessly in place.

Ryan frowned and tried it again. Another long, sad whirr. He waited for the lock mechanism to reset before trying again, slowly this time, to make sure he hadn't typed it wrong.

The combination didn't work.

Ryan tucked his coffee into his elbow as he shifted his bag around and fished for the cell phone in his pocket. "Shannon?"

"What do you want, Ryan?"

"Did you…change the locks?"

"What do *you* think?"

"It seems kinda like you changed the locks."

"Really? Wow, look at the brain trust we got over here today."

Ryan took the phone away from his ear and stared at it. This kind of venom in Shannon's voice wasn't entirely out of the blue, but he couldn't figure out what he'd done today. "Shannon, why did you change the locks?"

"Why didn't you stay at the rink so my fucking process server could find you?"

The pieces of the puzzle fit together with the sudden clarity of figuring out the right move on the ice ahead of anyone else. Except this time, he was trailing the play. "Shannon, are you *divorcing* me?"

"No shit, Sherlock. I've only been trying to talk to you about it for the last goddamn month."

Ryan stared at the phone again. "You have?"

Shannon hung up on him.

He thought, for a second, about all of the teammates and friends he'd known who had gotten divorced and how you probably weren't supposed to lock your spouse out of the house without warning. He thought about equitable distribution and how humiliating it would feel, telling a judge, *well, she locked me out, so...*

He had never really wanted to move to New Hampshire in the first place, but it was close to Shannon's family. The thing was, he'd never even been particularly fond of the house in the first place. It felt like more work than it had been worth, the constant negotiations with Shannon about how much of his awards and medals and memorabilia he could keep anywhere except the basement. About how much space in the garage he was allowed to use up for his workshop.

Maybe…he could just let her have the house.

Every time they fought, it was a reminder that they had started dating when they were eighteen years old and had just kept going, even though it became clear, the longer things went on, that they had really different priorities.

Shannon had wanted the big house in Newfields to be close to her family. And at the time, Ryan had wanted what Shannon wanted. She'd deserved it after years of living far away from her family and friends, in the kinds of places she never would've chosen if she hadn't married a hockey player.

It wasn't until later that Ryan had realized exactly how much he hated living in New Hampshire in a house that was far too goddamn big for two people.

He called her again.

"*What*, Ryan?"

"Shannon. Just to be clear. You're really divorcing me? Really, completely, seriously divorcing me?"

"Yes, Ryan."

"But…what about all of my stuff?"

"We can figure out a time for you to come and pick it up. But I'm over this. I told you I didn't want you to start coaching. I've waited years to have a life without fucking *hockey*—"

"But that is my life, Shan. It's always been my life."

"Not like this. Not like you get. Or did you forget that I made birthday brunch reservations for today—"

"You knew I had a game!"

"You couldn't have gotten the assistant coach to do it, Ryan? It's your *forty-fifth birthday.* It's peewee fucking hockey! I'm sick of always being reminded where I stand in your priorities and how as long as it's something hockey related, I'm at the bottom! And it's clear you don't understand this at all. We don't have anything else to talk about right now. I'll text you times and dates if you want to pick up your stuff."

Ryan thought about asking her to throw down a bag of clothes to him or something, but the back of his neck felt hot and sweaty. He hadn't fought much on the ice when he was a player, but the few times he'd gotten angry enough to do it, he'd felt like this. Like a teapot whose lid was about to explode with the force of the pressure built up under it.

Instead, he said, "Okay," and hung up again.

He stood there in the driveway—not *his* driveway anymore—and looked at the house. It was an ugly McMansion, and he could admit that now that Shannon had kicked him out. He couldn't quite figure out what he was feeling. It wasn't sad and it wasn't angry. Maybe *resigned* was the closest word for it. Maybe this is what it felt like to not care about losing anymore. He'd never felt like that in his life.

Ryan walked back to the car, slung his bag of hockey gear back into it and sat down in the driver's seat. He wasn't sure how long he sat there, but it was long enough that he could see Shannon peeking out at him through the curtains, probably wondering what the hell was going on and worrying that maybe he'd try to call her again.

His phone rang, and he almost threw it across the cab. *No, Shannon, you don't have anything else you could say to me.* It wasn't Shannon's number, though. He didn't have it saved as a contact and didn't recognize it at all. It was a Boston area code, though, which didn't bode well.

"Hello?"

"Ryan Sullivan?"

"Uh, yeah? I'm Sully."

"This is Joe Conroy, the general manager of the Boston Beacons."

Ryan blinked.

Joe Conroy was a legend. Ryan had grown up wearing his jersey. Conroy had played for Boston for years. Had his jersey retired at the Spectrum. Had been hired after Boston's last general manager was unceremoniously fired in the dumpster fire of the last season. Ryan knew him socially, but not enough for a phone call like this.

"Hello?" Conroy asked, and Ryan realized he had probably been silent too long.

"Sorry. Sorry, I was just—surprised."

"Well, you're going to be a hell of a lot more surprised than that by the time we're done. Do you have some time to talk?"

When he looked up at the house, Shannon glared at him from the upstairs window. Ryan pressed the ignition and said, "All the time in the world."

At six a.m. on the dot, Eric Aronson's phone rang, the same way it did every morning.

Usually, he was awake already and just getting out of the shower of his tiny South End apartment. Today, he'd woken up even earlier than usual. It had been three days since Joe Conroy fired Harrison Leclerc, the Boston Beacons' twenty-ninth head coach.

Eric had worked with Leclerc for three long years, and he wasn't *expecting* to be given his ex-boss's job… but the fact was, he'd earned it. He'd earned it for no other reason than he'd bitten his fucking tongue and hadn't decked that fuck right in his prissy mouth every time he'd wanted to, which was often.

His phone screen said *Mameleh*, which wasn't a surprise, because his eighty-two-year-old mother was the only person who would ever call him at six in the morning, even on days when he was half-expecting the most important job offer of his life.

"Good morning, Maman."

"Good morning, Éric," she said, her voice a little wheezy.

The weirdest fucking thing about being in his forties—the age Maman and Papa had been when they'd had him—was realizing that his parents were aging and that they weren't going to live forever. It had been a really rude awakening. A smack in the face when his father got sick two years ago and Eric had moved home in the offseason to help his mother take care of him until his death.

With his father gone, now it was the insidious little reminders, like how breathless his mother sounded when she'd been going up and down the stairs. That instead of the tall, sturdy woman who had terrified him and his friends when they'd been teenaged hooligans, she was now wizened and weak. Knowing that when he spoke to her, he was speaking to an old lady. Eric still felt as rootless and immature as he ever had, but the fact that his dad was gone, and his mom was *old*—it didn't feel real no matter how often he saw the evidence right in front of him.

"Are you getting enough sleep?" she demanded.

Eric thought about reminding her that she asked him the same question every time she called, but instead, he said, "Yes, 'Man."

"Why are you up so early?"

"Because you called me at six a.m., 'Man."

"You were awake before that. I can tell."

"Can't get anything by you," Eric said, smiling as he poured his coffee. Probably to an outsider, it would have sounded short, annoyed. Impatient with a meddling old woman. He couldn't accurately convey how far from the truth that was.

"What happened with that shande?" She slipped out of the French they usually used and into the Yiddish that emerged when she had particularly strong feelings about something. Today, it was her disapproval of Harrison Leclerc. "They fired him, didn't they? So how is training camp still running?"

"They fired him. The rest of the coaching staff have been sharing the responsibilities until they hire a new head coach, which they'll have to do soon, because the season's right around the corner."

"Why haven't they offered you the job?" She sounded annoyed, more annoyed than she usually did these days.

"I don't know, 'Man. I mean…they're not obligated to give me the job."

"You've been there for four years. You're *good* at your job, tateleh. You're better than that man ever was."

Eric thought about Harrison Leclerc—so sure of himself, so serious about implementing his system, about making sure that everyone played the right way—and the way things had come to a head in such an abrupt manner.

Leclerc hadn't just gotten himself fired. He'd gotten into a screaming match with Caleb Cook, the Beacons' hotshot sophomore who wasn't such a hotshot after he'd had a disappointing rookie year yo-yoing between the big leagues and the Beacons' minor league affiliate. At one point, it had looked like they were going to come to blows before Eric and another player got in between them.

"Well," he said, "that man is a prick, unfortunately. But so am I."

"You are *not* a prick. The boys like you."

She was stubborn, and she was loyal, he had to give her that much. "I know, 'Man. But that's not enough to get the job. Hey—are you okay? You need anything?"

"No, I'm fine."

She wouldn't have told him anyway, even if she did need something. It had been hard for her after his father died, alone in the too-big house in Côte Saint-Luc. Eric did what he could. He had hired a caretaker to look in on her a few times a week, but his mother was wily and would pretend that she had gone out for errands when Cecile arrived.

When it was too much for her to make it to the grocery store, she would accept the deliveries he scheduled through an app, but that was about it. There wasn't much he could do this far away, and as ever, he wondered whether he was doing the right thing, working a job that took him all over the continent but so rarely home to her.

"Okay, well, you just let me know if you change your mind," Eric said, making a mental note to order her a Sunday delivery with some cupboard and fridge staples.

"And you let me know what's going on with your job. I'll come down there and give them a piece of my mind if I have to."

He laughed at the mental image, all five foot seven of Rosa Aronson, showing up at the Spectrum to give Joe Conroy a piece of her mind. "I'm perfectly capable of taking care of myself, but your support is appreciated. Love you, 'Man. Hang in there, okay?"

"Yes, yes," she said, and he could picture her dismissively waving her hand at him. "I love you too, Éric."

Eric poured his coffee into the thermos. He had lived in Boston during the season for three years and he had never understood the local obsession with Dunkin' Donuts. It tasted like sugary, watered-down milk.

If it was up to Eric, he would have walked to work every day. As it was, he'd had to buy a car so that he could make it to the practice facility on time. Sometimes he walked it anyway, just to be stubborn, but on days like this he couldn't really afford to be late.

It was stupid, to be so concerned about it when he probably wasn't even going to get it. If they were going to give him the fucking job, he probably would have had a hint of it beforehand. They would have called him in for interviews, given him some kind of an idea, anything. His mother's faith in him aside, Eric was starting to feel less hopeful and more frustrated.

Sure, the Beacons hadn't had a great record over the last three seasons, but that wasn't surprising given that their stars were aging or injured, their goalie had knee and hip issues and they hadn't drafted particularly high *or* well for the last ten seasons.

That wasn't anything that Eric could help. He'd done his job as best he could. Showed up to work every day. Argued with Leclerc when he felt that the man had overstepped. Done his best to soothe the ruffled feathers of the young players on the team.

He paused outside of the facility to take a picture of the letters emblazoned over the door: Beacons Ice Arena. It was stupid and almost sentimental, marking a moment that might even be insignificant. But he did it anyway.

Inside, Eric was pleased to find that a lot of the guys were already there and either on the ice warming up, or in the locker rooms getting dressed. Whatever else you had to say about the team's record last year, Eric had made sure they had a good culture. Everyone showed up and did the work. If Conroy didn't name a head coach soon, though, they were going to start running into issues.

His phone buzzed in his pocket, and he fished it out. The screen said *Conroy*. Eric swallowed down his nerves, swiped and answered. "Yeah?"

"Aronson, can I talk to you in the office?" Conroy asked briskly. Even though his name was synonymous with Boston now, he still sounded like he'd rolled off of the fields in Sudbury, Ontario.

"Sure. Be right up."

"The office" was located up the stairs from the ice level, a space the coaches and general manager shared in the practice facility. It served its purpose of demarcating the line between the public and the staff, particularly when they needed to talk to players alone after practice.

Or, in this case, talk to an assistant coach who was hoping that he would be a head coach before practice.

"Sit down," Conroy said, when he opened the door.

Eric didn't want to. He'd always hated sitting in the chair across from the desk and not behind it. It felt a little like being back at school in Boisbriand, getting chewed out by a teacher because he'd gotten into another fight or had been slacking too much on his studies in favor of hockey.

He did it anyway. Sat silent without fidgeting, just raised an eyebrow and waited for Conroy to break it to him.

"I want to preface this by saying that this isn't a reflection on your work performance or the trust that the organization has in you at all," Conroy said, and all of the tension in Eric's body released at once, like his strings had been cut. Here it was. "We're just thinking of going in a different direction."

"I understand," Eric said, like someone else was using his tongue. "Is the new hire already under contract?"

"We're still in the preliminary stages of negotiating the deal; it's not set in stone yet. But we wanted to talk to you about it so you could be prepared to work with him, because it's looking likely that he will accept, and we can get things really started before training camp is over."

"Who?" Eric asked. It was blunt, and he couldn't

quite keep the annoyance from his voice, but he was justified in that, he felt.

Conroy was in his sixties now, but he was still a handsome man, lean and distinguished looking. His steel-gray hair was carefully cut and maintained; he wore clothes that looked like his wife had picked them out for him. He'd made the graduation from the ice to the front office without looking back, while Eric was still hanging in the middle, not quite a player, not quite more, no matter how hard he worked.

Conroy said, "Ryan Sullivan."

Eric said, *"Tabarnak."*

If anyone else had tried to process the last twenty-four hours of Ryan's life, they probably would have been confused as hell, too. In slightly less than one day, he had turned forty-five, his wife had locked him out of the house, and he was driving to Boston to formally interview for a job as the thirtieth head coach of his childhood Original Six hockey team. It was a lot to wrap his head around and not solely because of the fact that he hadn't even coached his peewee team for a full season.

The logical thing to do would be to say *yes* to the offer. It was insane to even consider turning down an opportunity with only thirty-two positions available, positions that only opened every now and then and were often more like a game of musical chairs played by the same rotating cast than actual hiring opportunities. He probably wouldn't have the ability to do this again, if ever, and if he did, it would likely be years in the future. He'd probably have to put his time in in juniors, maybe jump straight to the minors if he was lucky. There wouldn't be a head coach's chair gift wrapped and waiting for him.

And the thing was…it was *Boston.* He'd grown up loving the Beacons. He'd grown up dreaming of playing for them. He'd had the jerseys, the pajamas, the ticket stubs, the binders full of hockey cards, the whole nine yards.

Still. There was a reason he'd left home and hadn't come back, and there was a reason he felt bad about it. Ryan had grown up in Southie. Ryan's dad and four older brothers and their families all still lived there. Ryan had let Shannon talk him into moving to New Hampshire because of her family, but to a lesser extent, he'd agreed because of *his* family. Newfields was only three hours away, but three hours was enough when none of the Sullivans ever left the Boston city limits.

He shouldn't let them prevent him from taking a huge opportunity. And this was the Beacons. This was—if the interview went well, anyway—the chance to take the Beacons and make them into something *better.* Something amazing.

Ryan had played hockey for a long time, and by the end of his career, he was basically coaching already. The younger guys coming up were so different from him, from the way he'd had to learn to play. He could see the benefits they'd had, with the newfangled training regimes and parents who understood the importance of skating clinics as early as possible, but he could also see the blind spots.

The opportunity to put all of his ideas together, to make a team that was *his* and that really focused on development…it was tempting. It was really tempting, no matter how close to his family he'd have to live.

In his gut, Ryan knew he would accept the job. He was a ship at sea otherwise. The rest of his life was going to involve hockey, somehow. It had been his single-minded obsession to the exclusion of almost everything else from the time he'd first gotten onto skates. And at his age the options were basically coaching, a front office position or nothing.

He didn't have to ever work again, but if he didn't, what was he going to do, go home to Newfields and beg Shannon to take him back?

He had *some* pride.

Strangely, he didn't feel nervous at all. If Joe Conroy had called him like this, they'd already made up their minds. Really, all he had to do was make sure that it was the kind of position he'd actually want, that he'd have the freedom to run the team the way he wanted to run it without too much front office interference. What Ryan had planned wouldn't work if he wouldn't be allowed free rein.

The traffic, expectedly, was terrible. Everyone complained about Boston drivers, but New Hampshire was way, way worse, and the combination of the two was just asking for a headache. By the time he parked his car at the Spectrum, he wasn't the half hour early he generally preferred, but he did have time to swing by the Dunkin' near the front gates. Shannon had always teased him about it, but Ryan liked his coffee sweet, and the Dunkin's in New Hampshire just weren't the same.

He'd been in the Spectrum—the old one across the street—many times as a kid, watching games, even playing mites on ice exhibition matches during the intermissions. He'd pounded the ice in the new Spectrum many times during his long career. He'd looked up at the blue glass and red brick above North Station more times than he could remember. The halls and the seats and the stands were so familiar. He knew his way around the warren of hallways around the locker rooms.

But it was different now, walking into it and heading for the office, knowing that he might have a chance to do something really innovative here.

It was stupid, but he reached out and pinched the skin and tendon on his own wrist. The sharp pain of it a reminder that yes: he was, actually, here.

After all of the internal buildup the actual interview was almost anticlimactic. In the room were Joe Conroy, Gilbert Underhill, the president of hockey operations, and Andy Chernoff, the team's owner. It was pretty funny to find that Ryan had been right from the beginning. The whole interview was more their sales pitch to him rather than the other way around.

"Do I get to pick my own staff?" Ryan asked, halfway through.

"We have assistant coaches under contract for the next year and we would like to finish out their contracts so that the team isn't paying treble, but if you absolutely can't work with them or if they don't fit your vision, you have carte blanche."

Ryan had done his research before heading in. The staff was a strange one: the assistant coach responsible for the forwards was Eric Aronson, a guy who, like Ryan, had also gone undrafted. Aronson had had a long and relatively successful career, but he'd never won the Cup in Calgary. Even though he'd set all kinds of franchise records for the Stampede, most of them were for games played and penalty minutes; he'd been suspended multiple times and had at least two separate biting scandals.

The assistant coach on defense wasn't much better. Peter McCaskill was one of the last of the old breed, a stay-at-home defenseman who was lucky to crack twenty points a season, a man who'd done more of his work with his fists than on his feet.

"Is it going to be an issue that none of them were offered the job?" Ryan asked.

"It won't be if they want to stay in our employ," Underhill said, with a shrug.

Ryan thought about everything he knew about Aronson and thought maybe this was a little optimistic.

By the time the hour finished, Ryan had a new job, a handshake promise that he'd have free rein in that new job and a *lot* of shit he needed to get done before reporting to training camp the next day.

His mind raced through all of it: hotel reservations and apartment tours and cheap furniture and lists of personnel and tape from the training camp days he'd missed and what he was going to say to a new team who had no idea what to expect both from him and from the season in general and what he was going to say to the guys whose job he'd snatched right out from under their noses. The vague guilt that he was leaving behind the boys on the peewee team mingling with the faint relief that he wasn't going to have to finesse their parents anymore.

In the back of his head, he could hear Dad's derisive, booming laugh. *You?* You're *the one they picked for this?*

Ryan had spent a lot of his forty-five years proving people wrong. Not least among them his family. This was no different. For the first time in a long time, Ryan felt the prickly-skinned feeling of excitement before a big game, the eagerness to compete that fizzed through his bloodstream.

He *was* the one they'd picked for this. And he was going to work damn hard to show them they'd made the right choice, the same way he'd done his entire life.

Still, it felt weird to accept it. To know that all of this was weird and that it was going to happen and that he and the Beacons' front office were the only ones who knew about it. In the past, he would've called Shannon to tell her. But hockey was the last thing she probably wanted to hear about, and Ryan was the last person she probably wanted to hear it from. She had already had him served with the divorce papers, when he was coming out of the hotel in the morning, and had followed up with a curt text message, Fill out the forms the process server had for you. Send them back to me immediately.

He had done it, because he wasn't an asshole, but it had stung a little.

Once he was back in his car, he buckled his seat belt, slipped his phone into its holder, called Murph.

"Hello?" Murph asked, picking up on the second ring.

Ryan could hear the sounds of a rink in the background: the scrape of skates on ice, kids and parents yelling. Of course Murph was probably out with his family. "Hey, bud. Bad time?"

"Nah, it's cool. Tara and I are at Sophia's game. And then Mason's playing after. But I have a minute if you have the time."

Somehow, he felt better just hearing Murph's voice. The two of them had known each other for years. First in the general way you knew everyone who played hockey, growing up in Boston, even though Murph had gone to the expensive Catholic prep school with its own varsity team and Ryan had gone to public school in Southie. They'd played against each other in tournaments and Ryan had always been both annoyed and impressed by him. Murph's size and strength and skill in comparison to Ryan's sheer bloody-minded fucking willpower. Back then, Murph *had* been a whole foot taller.

It didn't mean anything until what should have been their draft year. That was when he'd really gotten to *know* Sean Murphy, beyond the vague outline of a gigantic redheaded menace with more freckles than skin.

Ryan went undrafted and went to college; Murph was picked third overall by the Desperadoes and went to college. The Desperadoes had let Murph do his time in school and grow into his body while Ryan left school early with a chip on his shoulder and something to prove. And then, when Ryan was really starting to consider whether or not he should hang up his skates after a couple seasons of grinding along in the minors, the Desperadoes' general manager took a flyer on him.

From the time he'd made it down to Dallas, they'd been inseparable. Practically lived out of each other's pockets for months. Were referred to by their teammates as *SullyandMurph*, an inseparable unit. Were the best men at each other's weddings. They'd won a Cup together. Had their jerseys retired together. They still talked almost every week.

Everything that had happened to him—Shannon kicking him out, the job offer—had happened so fast Ryan hadn't even had time to think about it. As soon as Murph started talking, everything felt easier.

"You wanna sit down?"

He could almost see Murph's expression, the way

his eyebrows would have crawled up his forehead to his hairline. "Maybe I should find somewhere a little quieter. Sounds like you got some big news."

"I can wait."

Ryan listened to the noise recede a little into the distance. Murph and his family still lived in Dallas. His kids played peewee hockey in the rink Murph and Ryan had helped open together. That had been their thing, growing the game down south. Sometimes Ryan wondered what his life would've been like if he'd stayed in Texas after all instead of buying the offseason home in Newfields as soon as Shannon had asked.

Maybe less lonely. Maybe not.

"Joe Conroy called me yesterday."

Murph let out an ear-splitting whoop, and said, "You're *shitting* me, Sully. *You're* gonna coach the Beacons?"

"I didn't even say what Conroy called about!"

"Sully, come on. Why the hell else would Joe Conroy be calling you? After firing his head coach?"

"Well, you were right. I'm gonna be the new head coach of the Beacons."

"Holy shit, brother, that's *incredible*. You're going to be great. I can't wait to—wait." Ryan could hear the excitement in Murph's voice, and he could almost see the smile. But then the good mood faded. "Hang on. What'd Shannon say? She can't have been very happy about that."

Ryan was relieved, for a second, that he hadn't started the car yet. "Well…about that. She kicked me out. We're getting divorced."

For once, he had shocked Murph into silence. For once, he couldn't imagine what his facial expression looked like, whether he was pitying or sympathetic or just plain disbelieving. They sat like that for a while until Murph finally said, “Well, shit. I’m sorry.”

“It’s…okay.” Ryan was surprised to find that it was true. He had been in survival mode from the beginning, but now that things had started to slot into place, he still wasn’t—as upset as he probably should have been. It was like they’d been building toward it for so long that when Shannon actually ripped the Band-Aid off, all Ryan felt was a numb sense of relief. “It actually happened before I got the job offer, if you can believe it.”

“Hey,” Murph said apologetically, “we have a lot to talk about, but this ain’t the place for it, and I really do have to get back to Sophia’s game. Can I call you back tonight?”

Ryan looked out at the parking lot. A woman was getting out of her car to scream at the guy who’d hit her from behind backing out. That was Boston for you. “Yeah, of course. Tell Mason to keep his head up.”

“No advice for Sophia?”

“Man, you know I can’t tell goalies shit.”

He hung up to the sound of Murph’s familiar laugh.

Ryan thought about McCaskill and Aronson, about whether Murph would’ve moved back home if he’d asked for help with the coaching staff. But that was stupid: Murph had his family and a life in Dallas, and Ryan was more than capable of managing this minefield on his own.

Without another pause, he pressed the ignition and backed up out of the space, looping a safe distance around the screaming.

CHAPTER TWO

September

The more Eric thought about it, the angrier the new hire made him.

Ryan fucking Sullivan? Was Conroy kidding him?

If they were going solely by hockey careers, then Ryan Sullivan was a *name*. He was more than a name. He was a story. A guy who'd been told his whole life that he was too small to play hockey, who'd forced his way into the league and made it in a huge way.

Not only had he been a longtime alternate captain for the Desperadoes, he'd helped lead them to a Cup, scoring the game-winning goal in the Cup-clinching game. He'd had all of the hardware, the MVP award, scoring awards, sportsmanship awards…you fucking name it, Sullivan had won it. He had been inducted into the Hall of Fame in his first year of eligibility, because of course he was.

Eric remembered playing against him, too. He'd been an annoying little pest even back then, running his mouth at every opportunity and hiding behind Murphy whenever anyone took offense. Sullivan would fight if he had to, but the thing was that he almost never had to. Anyone looking at him funny found Murphy in their face first.

Fine.

Maybe Eric was jealous of the fact that Sullivan had all of the glory Eric had never managed to win with the Stampede. Even if he was jealous, it didn't matter. The fact was that the highest level Sullivan had ever coached was peewee, while Eric had been in Boston this whole time, trying to wrangle the power play into something that actually had a breath of life even after losing three or four of the most important players the team had had over the past decade.

And here Sullivan was, handed the job like he'd been handed every other good thing in his life, while Eric was still asked about the times he'd lost his temper and done something really stupid on the ice. His mother would have said that whining didn't solve anything, but he wasn't whining, he was just *pissed off.*

Hey, Sullivan texted him and Petey, can we set up a time to speak before I have to do press conferences?

Petey wrote back immediately, sure thing, boss, because that's the kind of guy he was.

Eric didn't answer, because that's the kind of guy *he* was.

Eric thought about letting his mother know what had happened. That he'd worked his ass off to develop good relationships with his players, that he'd bitten his tongue during three years of Leclerc, that he'd done the best he could and that it hadn't mattered. That, once again, his temper and the fact that he hadn't won shit overshadowed his more recent accomplishments. That it had all come back to bite him in the ass. She would've said something sympathetic, but she wouldn't have understood the deep-seated rage. Maman just wasn't like that.

He couldn't avoid Sullivan, either. Sullivan was coming in to take over the next day of training camp, and when Eric hadn't answered by the close of business that night, he had taken matters into his own hands. I'll see both of you in the coach's office before training camp. Be there by 6:30.

"Be there by six thirty," Eric said mockingly to his empty apartment. No one answered him back.

As much as he wanted to show up late just to piss Sullivan off, Eric was also aware that even if he was currently keeping his job, that wasn't a given. He was in the last year of his contract, so it wouldn't even be that much dead money for Chernoff to keep paying through the end of the season if Sullivan decided to bring his own man in.

So even though he felt like punching something about it, Eric showed up at the practice facility bright and early, although he didn't bother putting in the effort of actually forcing a smile onto his face. It probably would've looked more like baring his teeth, anyway.

Sullivan was already in the office, it seemed, judging from the light sneaking out under the door. Petey waited outside, slouched against a wall with his eyes closed. Didn't matter if they were at home or on the road—Petey wasn't a morning person, and no amount of coffee could shift the martyred look or sleepy eyes off of his face.

"Bon matin, Roney," Petey said.

"Maudit matin," Eric muttered back, ignoring Petey's laugh.

"Ready to meet the new boss?"

"Fuck off."

Petey opened the door first, and Eric followed him in. He hadn't been sure what to expect, but it didn't look at first like Sullivan had changed much since Leclerc had vacated it. The whiteboards hung in the same spot; the same desk sat in the same place. Of course, he'd just been hired; there probably wasn't *time* to change anything. Sullivan sat behind the desk, looking down at an iPad and a shitload of papers spread all over the leather blotter that Leclerc apparently hadn't bothered to take with him.

When he heard them come in, Sullivan stood, and Eric got his first close-up look at the guy in over five years and his first close-up look at him out of hockey equipment in even longer.

The first thing you noticed was that he was short as fuck. The kind of guy who was officially listed at five-eight but was probably closer to five-six. The second thing you noticed was that despite the fact that he was short, he was anything but small. Built like a bulldog, with a barrel chest and broad shoulders and ridiculously huge legs. His thighs were so distracting Eric had to force himself to look up. He had come dressed for practice in a hoodie and sweatpants in Beacons black and gold, not quite sized right for the proportions of his body.

The third thing that Eric noticed, anyway, was that despite the fact that there was nothing about his face that was classically good-looking or anything, Sullivan was…shit. There was only one way to describe it, and that was: Sullivan was hot. Silver fox, broken nose, light brown eyes, smiling mouth and stubborn chin hot. Something about the way he held himself, like he had too much energy to be contained in that small of a space. Some answering thing in Eric thrilled to the surface, itched to contain him.

Not that it mattered if Sullivan was hot. It didn't matter what he looked like, because Eric fucking *hated* him.

There was a second where they just stared at each other, wordless. And then Sullivan opened his mouth and Eric hated him even more. Hated him and his stupid fucking Boston accent.

"It's good to meet you both," Sullivan was saying, and Eric fought the urge to shake his head like a dog escaping from a bath and trying desperately to clear the water from its eyes. "I know things are probably going to be a little awkward given the way we started off, but I want you both to know that I'd like this to be a collaborative environment."

Eric's face made expressions he couldn't entirely control, no matter how he desperately tried to rein them in. *A collaborative environment.* Fucking hell.

To make matters worse, Petey was nodding along with this little speech like it was exactly what he'd wanted to hear. Petey's playing career had ended after one too many concussions, and Eric had worked with him long enough to know that he still suffered from some of the effects of post-concussion syndrome.

He'd tried a variety of therapies and eventually found that microdosing psychedelics worked better than any traditional treatment. Whether it was his natural personality, the psilocybin, or a choice he'd made, Petey was probably the most aggressively chill person Eric had ever met. While it normally meant that they got along well, right now, it made Eric want to shake him and yell, *now is not the time to be agreeable, you stupid fuck.*

"Is everything clear?" Sullivan asked, and Eric realized, belatedly, that they'd been staring at each other again and that his face was probably doing the thing where his eyebrows drew in above his glasses and people assumed that he was angry with them.

In this case, at least, the assumption was correct.

"Crystal," Eric said, drawing out the word as sarcastically as possible.

Sullivan gave him an odd, quizzical look, and then smiled at the two of them. "I'm going to go down to the locker room to talk to the boys before we start camp for the day. I'd like you to be there with me."

"Makes sense," Petey agreed, and Eric wanted to draw his finger sharply across his throat in the international sign for shut the fuck *up*.

Instead, he said, "Lead the way."

Ryan wasn't sure how well the speech had gone. He was used to giving speeches; he'd given a shitload of them in Dallas. They'd come naturally and hadn't flopped like a lead balloon. But the thing about giving speeches in locker rooms was that everyone was on the same page, everyone wanted the same thing: to win. In the locker room, he was a respected teammate and comrade, not an interloper who'd taken a job that probably both of them wanted.

Well, maybe not McCaskill, a middle-aged veteran with a paunchy belly and sleepy eyes who seemed about as easygoing a guy as Ryan had ever met.

Aronson was a different story.

They had played against each other not infrequently over the years. Aronson was a couple of years younger than Ryan, but they'd both taken a while to crack a major league roster and had come up right around the same time. They had never played in the same division, though, so at most it was three or so times a year.

There had been one contentious playoff series that the Stampede had lost. Ryan had never really looked at Aronson while they were playing. He'd been just another guy on the ice, a pest who lived to get under other players' skins, who never shut the fuck up, no matter what.

Looking at Aronson now, Ryan was surprised he'd never noticed him before. Whatever the issues with his personality, Aronson was…noticeable. He was tall. Not as tall as Murph, but definitely a lot taller than Ryan, with the kind of body players got sometimes when they still worked out regularly but weren't working out for a playing season, gangly and muscular but not bulky.

It was his face, though, that was hard to look away from.

Aronson's nose dominated his face, strong and pronounced, but the rest of his features seemed almost too big, too. Huge dark brown eyes and an equally broad mouth, twisted in a smirk or down in a frown. Your attention went right to those eyes, too, because his glasses magnified them, huge-lensed wire frames. Heavy eyebrows with the same sarcastic tilt as his mouth, just pointed in the opposite direction. He had what seemed like a perpetual five-o'clock shadow on his chin and jaw and a mop of unruly, wavy black hair that was just a little bit too long.

He was wearing the same thing they all wore, Beacons sweats in preparation for practice. He looked, a little bit, like a looming crow.

Ryan realized, too late, that Aronson was staring back at him. He frowned. He was just sizing up the coaching staff he had to work with, there wasn't anything wrong with that. Ryan had to shake himself a little, weirdly unsettled by the whole thing.

He couldn't afford to be distracted right now, either. He had the locker room to talk to. This would be establishing the rapport he hoped to have with the players for the rest of the season. Maybe beyond, if it worked out for him and he liked the work and Conroy wanted to remove the *interim* tag from Ryan's title, not that he was going to do anything except ignore the pressure and do his best to focus on the day-to-day. And then after practice, he would have to meet with the media for the first time.

Growing up in a hockey town like Boston, Ryan was used to the kind of scrutiny a head coach received. It probably wasn't as bad as it was in Toronto or Montreal, but it was definitely way more intense than Dallas. Ryan was pretty much prepared for the skepticism he'd end up facing, but he had to be on top of things to do it. Getting distracted worrying about Aronson wasn't it.

As Ryan packed up his shit to head down to the locker room with McCaskill and Aronson, his phone buzzed in his pocket. He checked it. The banner said *Dad*. Ryan sighed: he could ignore it, but that only meant his dad would keep calling, and today was not the opportune time for that shit.

"Dad," Ryan said, "I don't really have time to talk right now, I have to go down to the locker room to meet the guys."

"I won't keep you. I know how busy you are," Dad said, and Ryan's skin crawled when he heard the tone. Oh, Dad was pissed. He wasn't yelling and his voice wasn't loud, but he was *pissed*. "Were you ever gonna tell your father that you're coaching the Boston fuckin'

Beacons, or was I always gonna have to find out fifth-hand from Christopher down the block?"

"I was going to tell you, it's just been kind of a crazy couple of days, I've barely had a chance to breathe." He could see Aronson watching him from the corner of his eye, those heavy eyebrows raised. Like he was either skeptical or making fun. Ryan's skin felt itchy, like he was going to snap, either at his dad, or at Aronson. He didn't like it one bit: it wasn't the frame of mind he needed.

Dad hissed out a breath between his teeth, and said, "So you're back home now, eh?"

"For now."

"You gonna come *home* to see us?"

"I don't know. Probably sometime soon. Dad, I really can't talk. I'm headed down to the locker rooms and then I gotta meet the media."

"You do what you gotta do, Ry. But I gotta say that if you don't come home, the family's gonna be real disappointed. *I'm* already real disappointed. All we ever wanted to do was celebrate your success."

Ryan exhaled. For a second, he wanted to laugh. *All we ever wanted to do was celebrate your success* sounded like a threat when it came out of Dad's mouth. A lot of things did. Particularly when Ryan knew what was waiting for him if he went back home to hang out with his brothers and their families. Dad wouldn't know about the impending divorce yet, and that was another thing he'd have to put off as long as humanly possible.

He'd gone for a four-mile run this morning before heading to the practice facility and he still felt as fidgety and defensive as he always did when he got too close to Southie.

Aronson was still watching him, quizzical and judging.

Bizarrely, Ryan felt the need to explain. It wasn't any of Aronson's business. He *hated* talking about this shit, even with Murph, who implicitly understood because his family was the same way. Something about the way Aronson was looking at him just slipped right under his skin. "My family. They're all, uh, hockey guys, too. But I'm the one who's gotten the furthest, so…it gets complicated."

"You don't have to explain to us," Aronson said hastily, looking away for the first time to exchange a glance with McCaskill.

"It's not going to be an issue," Ryan said firmly. "I'm setting my phone to silent."

To his surprise, Aronson laughed. He had a nice laugh, like his voice: deep and somehow bigger than his body. "Might as well chuck it in the toilet at that rate."

"I'll take that under advisement," Ryan said dryly.

Aronson, his brown eyes dancing, held the door open for him. "After you, boss."

And for the first time, Ryan walked into the home locker room of the Boston Beacons as their head coach.

Eric surveyed the room as they went in. The boys looked both interested and apprehensive, which was about to be expected considering the way that Harrison Leclerc had gotten fired.

An entire shitty season last year hadn't been enough to do it. An entire season of Caleb Cook underperforming hadn't been enough to do it. The management group had looked at the injuries and the loss of personnel and said *we're gonna roll it over into next season.* Of course, it was difficult to roll it over into the next season when your head coach was screaming and spitting in the face of one of your franchise players. Even a slow-to-move front office couldn't ignore that. The incident had been the last straw for Leclerc, and he'd been summarily tossed on his ass.

And honestly, good fucking riddance.

Eric had also done what he'd could to diffuse the tension over the last few seasons, but it hadn't been good enough. He wondered sometimes whether the guys blamed him for that, whether they blamed him for the dismal record, too. Whether they wished he'd been fired along with Leclerc. It was easy to see the affection that the d-men had for Petey, because he was the kind of guy who was easy to be friendly with.

Eric wasn't.

He looked around the room at his guys. Caleb Cook and Kai Williams, inseparable as always, watched the trio of coaches with interest and suspicion. Travis Sinclair, one of the veteran forwards, threw him an ironic little salute from his spot on the outside end of the horseshoe. Davit Kancheli, the baby goalie they'd had to call up and throw into the starter's net after Kristian Rajala retired following his hip surgeries. All of them probably had expectations for the season and most of them were probably in the shitter, as it were. There was only so much he could do about that.

It was an awkward time to come into camp. Before cuts were made. Probably one of Sullivan's first jobs would be meeting everyone and then getting to know them and then having to tell some of them they were going back to their juniors teams or Europe or the minor leagues. And that would be some of their only interaction until next fall.

He glanced sideways at Sullivan, standing at attention in front of the guys. He thought about Sullivan's phone call with his father, how frustrated he'd seemed after hanging up. Eric could almost see Sullivan's entire body vibrating with concealed energy, like he'd wanted to punch a wall or go running down the hallway. He turned all of that now on the room. It wasn't quite a smile but the hint of one trembled on the edge of his mouth.

"Good morning," Sullivan said. "As some of you might know, I've been hired to take the reins as the interim coach for this season. Before we started camp for the day, I wanted to talk to you a little bit about my vision for the season. What I'd like for this team to become, if we have the opportunity to continue working together beyond this year."

Eric had played hockey for a long time, and he had coached for a shorter but not insignificant amount of time. All in all, he'd been listening to coaches giving fucking *speeches* of varying sorts for the last thirty-five years at least. Most of them left him cold or weren't particularly effective. He remembered the Stampede's coach trying to rally them after they'd gone down 3-2 in the Western Conference Finals against the Desperadoes.

It had been so flat he'd almost felt like laughing.

No one was laughing now.

Gradually, as Sullivan spoke, all of the faces in the room turned toward him. The murmured conversations ceased. The players listened, rapt, as he talked to them about how he wanted to approach this differently, build something sustainable. How he was going to learn right along with them, and how he wanted them to play hockey, and the structure of their personal style within the larger game. To learn how to make the right reads.

About learning to think in concepts rather than relying only on mechanical systems, and the freedom to make the calls they saw fit.

Sullivan talked about how he was going to mess up and he hoped they'd talk to him about it, and how he anticipated the players also messing up, but that he would rather see a mistake in the service of trying something new than no mistake and not trying at all.

He didn't raise his voice. He was steady and calm and confident, and it was hard to look away from him. There was something about his face. The sincerity and genuine excitement so visible. Sullivan was just magnetic.

It was fucking *infuriating.*

It was petty, but the better Sullivan sounded, the more Eric wanted to strangle him and shake him by his obnoxious little neck.

In the center of the room, Sullivan was giving an impassioned speech about how the wins didn't matter this season as much as learning the right habits did, as much as learning how to play as a team. And that if they all trusted each other and learned to play as a group the way he envisioned they could play, eventually the wins would start coming. He talked about playing defense in the offensive zone and offense in the defensive zone. He talked about being a dynamic 200-foot force.

Sullivan talked about how the most rewarding parts of the latter half of his career hadn't been winning the Cup, but mentoring younger players, learning the game and helping to teach it to others. That he might not have had the title, but that he'd been doing this for years, and if they trusted him, he'd repay that trust in what he could give them.

Sure, it *sounded* good.

A lot of bullshit sounded good if you wrapped it up in a pretty bow, if you ignored the fact that the roster was the roster and no amount of sweet-talking it could whip aging veterans and baby rookies with barely three seasons between them into shape. Of course Sullivan thought that he could just waltz right in and make things better, of course he hadn't understood that the last season had been such a grinding misery.

He hadn't ever had to try.

Things had just been handed to *him*.

Belatedly, Eric realized he was glaring and that it was pretty much at odds with the rest of the room, which was just now breaking out into applause. And then even more so as the guys started to get up to come and introduce themselves to Sullivan and shake his hand.

Sullivan accepted all of the greetings the same way he did everything, with his pleasant, beaming smile, like there was no place he'd rather be than right here. Like there was no one else in existence except the person he was looking at right then. For the first time in ages, the room crackled with energy, and the boys seemed excited to be there.

Petey looked at him with raised eyebrows.

Eric mouthed *I'm fine* back at him.

"Come on," Petey said, "you better get it together, bud. We're about to go out on the ice and get the full Ryan Sullivan experience."

"Jesus fucking Christ. Can't think of a better way to spend *my* fucking Wednesday."

Petey's eyebrows went up again, but all he had to offer was an exceptionally mild "'Kay."

Eric got his shit together and went out onto the ice to do his goddamn job.

***

Ryan hadn't had the usual amount of training camps that guys generally did, because once it was clear he wasn't going to make it very far in the top junior hockey leagues in the States, and he definitely wasn't going to be drafted by any of the Canadian juniors teams, and then when he wasn't going to get drafted, period, he focused on going through the NCAA. And that meant that after his handful of development camp invites, he had to go back to school, if he wasn't going to play his way into a pro contract. He certainly couldn't afford to pay out of pocket at the rest of the training camp.

Even then, he had always been one of the first ones cut, and it wasn't due to his effort or talent, it was solely because he was *small*. He remembered the coaches and general managers who'd said shit like *come back a little stronger, put on some more muscle, and then we'll see how ready you are*. Ryan had always known that despite his size, he was more than tough enough to stick it out in a full major league season, but no one had given him the chance.

He knew where the guys were coming from. He knew how frustrating it felt, even when you knew that it was in your best developmental interests. He knew how frustrating it felt when you knew that it wasn't. And now that the camp was winding down, he had to sit down with most of the juniors players to let them know they would be headed back to their teams. It was tough, especially when he would have made a different decision than the front office but had his hands tied. He tried to offer some encouragement and specific advice about things they could do to get ready and his phone number if they ever had questions.

In at least a few cases he talked to the kid about his own experience: the Beacons had drafted a few undersized but highly skilled wingers, and he'd had to say *look, at least you were drafted. That's a huge vote of confidence. Now you just have to prove them right for taking that risk, and a rebuild year is probably not the best time.*

"Never gets easier," McCaskill said, turning his sleepy-eyed gaze on the kids who were packing up their lockers. He'd told Ryan to call him Petey almost immediately ("everyone does") but Ryan still didn't feel like they were there yet.

"No, it doesn't," he agreed. "Feels worse the younger the kids are, though. You try telling a ten-year-old there's not a roster spot for him and see how much of a monster *you* are."

"Couldn't pay me to do it," McCaskill said, and laughed. "Glad I never went that route myself."

"Oh, great," Aronson muttered from the corner, where he'd been flipping through iPad tape, "are we going to get regaled with tales from the peewee trenches now?"

Stung, Ryan turned to look at him. Sometimes he thought that he was probably looking at Aronson too often. He'd catch himself doing it and have to stop. It wasn't his fault Aronson's face was so expressive, like a puzzle Ryan was always one step away from solving.

Aronson looked back, the same way he always did, eyebrows raised over the wire rims of his glasses in a challenge. He'd wait for Ryan to get embarrassed and look away first.

Ryan thought about asking him what the fuck his problem was, but aggressiveness wasn't the way to build bridges, not when he knew that Aronson was probably still stung by not having been offered the job. He couldn't blame the guy for being pissed. But that didn't make it any easier to put up with withering sarcasm every time Ryan did literally anything.

It didn't make it any easier when Aronson looked at him like that and Ryan felt like he wanted to crawl out of his own skin, which was something Ryan had never really felt before.

Instead of saying what he actually wanted to say, Ryan said, "We don't have time for reminiscing. Now that we're cutting through the chaff, I want to start really focusing on getting the guys used to the way I want to hold practices going forward. I've sent you both my general outlines, but I'm interested in hearing what you all have to say."

"It'll be different, but I think it could be fun to implement." McCaskill chewed on the end of his pen, the cap twisted and bent with the imprints of his teeth. "We have a lot of vets, Sully. I'm not sure how that's gonna go over immediately."

Ryan thought about asking Aronson whether he had any opinions, but one look at Aronson's thundercloud of a face, the eyebrows drawn down again in a scowl, put him off of that idea pretty quickly. No sense in picking a fight this early. They would be doing the drills Ryan's way whether Aronson liked it or not, although Ryan would take his concerns into consideration, of course.

"You're the boss, Coach," Aronson said, after a moment.

Aronson was still looking at Ryan in that particular piercing way that he had, and Ryan felt his hackles rise in the same way that they always had in games, when an opposing player thought he could try to intimidate him just because he wasn't as big. Ryan shook it off. What the hell was his problem? This wasn't a game. This was a collaborative working environment, and he couldn't just battle Aronson in the corners if he didn't like the way Aronson was looking at him.

On the ice, it was a different story.

Ryan split the still-oversize roster up into groups with mixed d-men and forwards, set them in drills against in a few different areas, took one for himself and assigned the assistant coaches to the others. Their new skills coach—Heidi Hughes, a USA Hockey women's hockey legend, a former team captain married to her Canadian rival—worked with the remaining group.

The players took to it right away. They did high-intensity repetitions of each drill. That morning Ryan had them working on a variety: the 2v2 rush, a 4v4 in-zone, a high 3v2. Ryan wanted to see how they adapted, because the small-area work was a big change from the repetitious single-focus drills they'd been doing before.

Unsurprisingly, Cook and Williams were the two standouts: they had what Ryan was looking for in the team he'd like to mold. Not just a killer instinct but intelligence. Even in the drills, you could see them thinking two or three steps ahead, moving their bodies into a position in anticipation rather than reaction.

Somewhat surprisingly, Travis Sinclair also adjusted well. The book that Ryan had on him hadn't been particularly impressive: he'd had a lot of injuries that he'd played through and a lot of injuries he couldn't play through despite his best efforts; his point totals reflected the time he'd missed. But Ryan wondered whether this was a case of a guy not being given a chance to play to his strengths by a previous administration. Or a guy who was finally healthy and might have something to prove. He made a note to try Sinclair out as the other winger on what would inevitably become the Williams and Cook line.

After the practice ended and before the players left for their homes or hotels, Ryan pulled Cook aside for a talk in his office. A look flickered over Cook's face. Worry or frustration, Ryan couldn't tell. Cook's expressive face showed everything, even if it was opaque. With his curly blond hair and huge brown eyes, he looked a little bit like a comical Renaissance cherub. One of the scowling ones shooting arrows at suffering saints. He was small, too. An inch taller than Ryan, and that wasn't saying much.

Even before Cook had been drafted by the Beacons, Ryan kept a half an eye on his career. It was hard not to with a player with that much talent, who also reminded him so much of himself. Not only that, a sure sign that things were changing. Ryan had been undrafted, but Cook was a later first-round pick.

"Hey," Ryan said, "don't worry about it, bud. I'm not doing anything except checking in, because you had kind of a rough start to the camp."

Cook looked at him warily. "It was okay."

Ryan couldn't help it—he laughed. Cook relaxed almost immediately, like he knew they were on the same page.

"I don't wanna talk shit about anyone," Cook said, when Ryan had gotten control of himself. "I really tried last year; you know? But it didn't—I just didn't know what he wanted from me."

"I've been there. Sometimes you just don't see eye to eye with a coach. I don't expect you to always see eye to eye with me. But I just want to make clear from the beginning, that if you have an issue with your usage—or with anything, really—you can feel free to come and talk to us about it."

"Really?" Cook asked, doubtful.

"Really. Like I said. I'm learning, too. And if things aren't working for the individual players, they're not going to work for the team. And I won't always know if they aren't working if you don't tell us. I mean, if we're getting blown out every game, I'll know. The analytics I'll know. But the more subtle things, I won't."

Cook laughed again. "Man, Coach. It sounds kinda too good to be true."

"It doesn't have to be."

"Uh, forgive me for saying so, but I've been disappointed before. I'm gonna withhold judgment."

The kid had balls; Ryan had to give him that much. Again, Ryan was reminded of himself at twenty, still stuck in Division 1 hockey and bitter as hell about it, determined to prove everyone wrong. If he had anything to say about it, Cook wouldn't have the same experience. "That's absolutely fair. Just give me a chance, and be honest with the staff, is all I'm asking."

Cook surveyed him, eyebrows raised. "I can do that."

Ryan held out his hand and Cook shook it. It was a firm handshake, nothing to prove. Ryan only wished he felt the same about training camp.

CHAPTER THREE

October

Eric somehow managed to get through training camp, even if he wanted to *scream*. If playing against Sullivan was annoying, coaching with him was infinitely worse. There was, after all, a limit to how many times Eric could say to him, "Look, I know you coached peewee for a while, but this isn't peewee anymore. This is *the* big show."

There were only so many times Sullivan could stare back at him and say, "There are translatable skills. I'm not trying to teach them how to do a perfect face-off in conditions that aren't replicable in a game, Aronson. We're trying to teach them how to trust their own judgment and make snap decisions in an actual game."

On the ice, too, Eric was constantly aware of Sullivan's presence. Even though he was small enough that he'd get constantly lost in a crowd of giant hockey players, Eric could practically sense him anyway, see his crooked smile and intense expression. The stupid little repetitive habits he had that were so annoying: a hand constantly running through his hair, his teeth digging into his lower lip. Sullivan was so enthusiastic when he talked that he practically vibrated with it, and everything about him made Eric want to grab him and shove him down on the ice. Just to get him to shut up.

Not for any other reason.

Really the worst part about all of it was that the players were already responding. It was a novel approach, Eric had to give Sullivan that much. It was different from any training camp Eric had ever been in before, either as a player or a coach. He couldn't say for sure if it was better. They didn't have a regular-season record to base it on. But the players from Cook to Sinclair to Rodion Afanasyev, a defenseman who was pushing forty but stubbornly hanging on for the last few years of his contract, seemed engaged, having fun.

It wasn't that Eric was bitter that they hadn't seemed to be having fun in *his* practices. Again, this was training camp. It was about preparing for the season, not about having fun.

Eric actually looked forward to the beginning of the preseason games, mostly because whatever high-and-mighty ideals Sullivan might have had about the practices, they would have to translate on the bench.

The thing about coaching in the major leagues was that it was complete chaos. You were both a general keeping an eye on things from afar and an NCO right in the thick of it.

It was your responsibility to make sure that the lines were called and changed appropriately, that no one was stuck out on too-long shifts. You had to make sure you were telling the boys to switch up the tactics if they were getting jammed in the neutral zone and the passes weren't getting through. You had to keep an eye on things to be able to make the appropriate coach's challenges—

whether for offsides or goaltender interference—and you had to judge whether it was worth risking a power play if you got it wrong. You had to keep an eye on the pulse of the team in case they needed the time-out, in case things were collapsing quickly.

Basically, things were always moving. It was like watching a car's engine churning, but more chaotic. Things didn't run in their neat, expected paths, on carefully defined grids. You had to be ready for anything.

"Have you ever done this before?" Sullivan asked, as they sat in his office before the game. Petey sat slumped in one of the chairs nearby, catching his usual pregame nap anywhere and everywhere he could.

Eric looked away from Petey, who clearly wasn't going to answer. "Coach a pro game? Or run a major league bench?"

"Both."

Eric narrowed his eyes, trying to figure out Sullivan's angle. His face was as open and pleasant as ever, his light brown eyes focused and interested. Eric wanted to punch him. "Never headed the bench myself. I was down in Providence with Leclerc, and I came up to Boston with him. But Petey's got seniority, and the few games Leclerc missed with an illness, he was the one who got to step up."

"They didn't offer him the job?"

"I think he made it clear that even if they were considering it, he didn't want it. And besides, we aren't the direction the management wanted to go in," Eric said. It came out belligerent, like a challenge. He had his arms crossed over his chest, equally aware of the defensive posture.

Sullivan didn't take the bait. Just looked at Eric

again. It was really fucking unfair that he looked the way he did, the laugh lines crinkled at the corners of his eyes and mouth, the way his lip curved in a half smile. Eric had to get over it: it didn't matter that Sullivan was attractive when—

Sullivan said, "I've never done this, either. I mean, a hockey game's a hockey game. I had my peewee team, and I did a bit of unofficial coaching myself in the late years of my career. But it was different doing it from the ice and in the room."

Eric snorted. "I'll say. Don't tell me you're fucking nervous."

"I'm not *nervous,*" Sullivan said, and rolled his eyes. "I don't get nervous."

"I'm not *nervous,*" Eric repeated, in the exact same intonation, just a little mocking.

"I'm just—what is your problem?"

"I don't have a problem, it's just that you're pretty damn full of yourself, huh?"

"What are you trying to say?"

Petey opened one eye. "I need to put you boys in a get-along shirt?"

"No," Sullivan said, and he took a deep breath. "I was just trying to…have a conversation. Not get my head bitten off again."

Petey turned a baleful eye on Eric, who frowned. "Don't look at me like that, Peter McCaskill."

Petey closed his eyes again, a distant smile on his lips. "Peter McCaskill, eh? Careful, I'm gonna think my mother showed up to sit on the bench as well. Since she's the only one who ever calls me that."

Sullivan had evidently decided that he wasn't going to get what he wanted out of either Eric or Petey and started gathering his papers and his iPad. "Your mother could probably have helped improve the team's record last year," Sullivan said primly, as he headed for the door.

Petey's eyes flew open. He turned his entire body toward Eric, like he was making sure he wouldn't miss a single second of Eric's head slowly expanding and exploding with fury. Petey had a much higher-pitched laugh than you'd expect from such a big man, wheezy and delighted. When he finally caught his breath again, he managed, "The old dog's got some bite in him after all," and promptly started howling again.

Eric took a deep breath, and then another. He wondered what kind of a fine he'd get if he pushed his head coach off of the bench and onto the ice in the middle of the game. For a brief second, he regretted the fact that now that he wasn't playing anymore, he couldn't just throw down. Couldn't just sink his teeth into a problem. Petey was laughing at him, which was how he knew that if he showed exactly how much Sullivan infuriated him, it would only get worse from here. He took another breath.

"You better get it together, Petey," Eric muttered, standing and stalking out of the room to the sound of Petey's whoops behind him.

Ryan's head was a mess, and it wasn't because he was nervous, whatever Aronson would have liked to imply. The problem was that he had a billion pieces of information knocking around in there on the best of days, and it was even worse now that he was preparing to go out on the bench for his first professional coaching game. He took a second to close his eyes, shove the extraneous bullshit into the background and try to focus on the things that really mattered.

Namely: the roster was mostly rookies and prospects, the few stragglers he hadn't sent back to their juniors teams because he wanted to see what they could do against men, so he wasn't expecting much. Secondarily, he needed to see if he could keep up with the pace of major league line changes and matchups. It was a home game, so he had last change, and the ability to control them more easily than he would have otherwise. But that didn't mean shit if he wasn't at the absolute top of his game.

As they went down the hall toward the bench, Williams swung by to check in with him. He wasn't particularly tall, but in his skates and Ryan in his shoes, he loomed above anyway. Williams was a handsome kid, almost the polar opposite of Cook. Cook was as white as a white kid who'd grown up in small-town Manitoba could be, and Williams hailed from New York, with a Filipina mother and a Black father.

Where Cook was blond, Williams had dark, thick hair; where Cook's complexion was pale and splotchy red, Williams's skin was a deep brown. And where Cook was a tiny spark plug, Williams was solid and steady, deceptively strong. He had a sense of humor hidden underneath his serious face but was already shouldering more responsibility than a twenty-two-year-old should have had to, and it showed.

"All ready, Coach?" Williams asked.

"Sure," Ryan said, and laughed. "Might as well get thrown into the deep end."

Williams looked sideways at him again, like he was trying to gauge whether or not Ryan was actually freaking out. It was a very funny gesture, like a kid who'd only had a couple of shortened seasons would be able to do anything about it. Apparently, whatever he saw eased his mind. "Well, I'll try to make it as easy as possible for you."

"That's *really* not your responsibility," Ryan said, but he couldn't keep the corner of his mouth from tipping up in a smile. Say whatever you wanted to about the Beacons' overall level of talent after last season's trade deadline massacre and sudden retirements—and the stats writers who published roster summaries and playoff odds certainly did—but it was a good group of guys.

In response, Williams held out his gloved hand to fist-bump. Ryan obliged, and Williams dropped his hand lower for the extended version. It immediately hit him, the memory of developing secret handshakes with his teammates over the years, reenacting them over and over in hallways exactly like this all over the continent. He hadn't expected to have that as a coach. They bumped low, raised it and knocked elbows, that indescribable sense of knowing where the other guy was going even if you'd never done it before.

Williams smiled. "You still got it, huh, Coach?"

"That's what they tell me," Ryan said, and headed out to the bench.

After all of that, the lead-up to the first game was almost anticlimactic. Ryan found that coaching, no matter where you were doing it, was like riding a bike. You didn't just forget because you had suddenly upgraded from a $100 beater to a $10,000 full-suspension mountain bike. Once he got into the swing of things it was easy: he called the line changes, he consulted with

Aronson and McCaskill about tactical adjustments and he tried not to overthink things too much.

They were playing the New Jersey Scouts: the team hadn't made the leap last year that their fans had hoped, but they had qualified for the playoffs and even though they'd gotten knocked out in the first round, they'd taken it to seven games. They were icing the majority of what would be the opening-day roster, probably because they had signed a bunch of free agents over the offseason to complement their homegrown talent who were beginning to come into their own.

It was strange, too, looking over at the bench and seeing Danny Garcia behind it. Ryan remembered playing against the former enforcer in the later years of his own career. Specifically, being knocked on his ass repeatedly by him. He didn't have time to worry about Garcia, though, because the game was starting.

The talent gap was evident.

Williams struck first, scoring on a clean win off of the face-off, but the Beacons were simply outgunned. They made a valiant effort, but they went down 2-1 fairly early and never quite recovered.

Ryan tried to take mental notes for things he'd need to fix later on himself: the rhythm of the line changes was definitely something he'd have to adjust to, working in the feedback from McCaskill and Aronson another. In the peewee league, the team had him, an assistant coach, and the developmental coach, but Ryan had always been the one calling the shots alone on the bench. It was still, ultimately, his responsibility. But Aronson especially had a lot of thoughts he didn't hesitate to offer, and Ryan had to fight back the urge to shove him away.

Aronson in particular had a way of getting up in your personal space when he was annoyed that made Ryan's hackles go up, stomach lurch. As though it would've ever gotten physical in a professional setting? Ridiculous. Ryan had to get it together and talk to the team.

Afterward, Ryan gave them a few minutes, but stopped briefly in the locker room to talk to the guys. He told them the things he'd liked: their hustle, their effort, the fact that they were still skating hard even when they were down. He told them the things he'd like to work on: the neatness of the passes, or more specifically, the lack thereof, playing a bit smarter off the puck, working on positioning. Taking the best shot rather than the available shot. He didn't focus too much on the negative: half of the guys who were playing tonight wouldn't be on the opening-night roster.

It wasn't any easier after the preseason got in full swing. Even though they were in the Atlantic Division, the Beacons mostly played New Jersey, Philadelphia and the New York Liberty during the preseason. Each team had their strengths and weaknesses—Aiden Campbell, the Libs' goalie, was in his last contract year looking pretty rough, for example—but the problem that Ryan had run into was the Beacons' roster. They had a lot of rookies on D, they had a lot of underperforming veteran wingers and their center depth outside of Williams was weak as hell.

"Conroy told me we had some leeway with the deployment of the older forwards, but he wants to showcase them as much as possible for trades," Ryan said, as the three assistant coaches went over the tape after their last preseason loss to the Cons, who were the reigning

Cup champions. "But I'm not sure about some of these guys."

Aronson raised one eyebrow and looked Ryan up and down with a skepticism that made him want to scream. "What happened to *I'm gonna work with everybody*?"

Ryan exhaled and counted, internally, to ten. "We're still going to work with them. Especially if we have to scratch them during the season, I expect both of you out on the ice with me after practice is over to get extra reps in and make them feel like we're still taking them seriously."

Aronson said, "Whatever you say, Coach."

Petey leaned back in his chair, arms folded behind his head. "I'd like to keep some of the rookies up with the big club rather than send them to the minors. We can have Granlund and Johnson anchoring the first two pairs, but I think it'll be beneficial for the boys to get the time up with us. If we can."

"That would mean keeping Lockwood as a seventh D. He'd be sitting a lot," Ryan said. It wasn't a challenge so much as an observation.

"Right," Petey agreed. "But he's a team-first guy. If we talk to him, he'll understand. We can rotate him in if one of the kids is having a rough game, but we're focusing on development above everything else. He's not going to be part of the long-term future here."

Ryan nodded and looked up at the depth chart handwritten on the whiteboard. The neat columns and rows of forwards and defensemen arranged by position and their place in the organization, color-coded so the eye jumped easily from line to line.

"Jesus," Ryan added, whistling. "I wonder if I can

pull Conroy's arm and convince him to trade for a veteran C."

"He won't want to give up the assets," Aronson said, his eyes half-lidded, his fingers steepled in front of his mouth. "This is a rebuilding year, even if he refused to say it. Anything anyone would want isn't something we could afford to give up."

"We'll see how it goes once we start hitting the midseason injury grind. There aren't a lot of great depth options beyond Williams and Novák. I can shuffle the lines to a certain extent, but…" Ryan trailed off and rubbed his eyes. "I think I've narrowed down my final roster for opening night. I'd like both of you to look at it tonight and let me know if you have any differences of opinion tomorrow."

Aronson snorted. "How much of our opinion's actually gonna be taken into account?"

Ryan frowned. What the hell was Aronson's problem, anyway? Ryan hadn't been anything except polite, and Aronson hadn't been anything except snarky and disparaging about the small-area drills, about Ryan's more philosophical ideas regarding the way they should coach. About pretty much everything he did. Maybe it sounded worse in Aronson's deep rumble of a voice, because of Aronson's accent, not as thick as it had been in his youth but still tinged with French, especially on the vowels.

Ryan counted to ten again. "All of it will be taken into account."

Aronson unfolded his lanky body from the chair. He reminded Ryan of a praying mantis constantly about to strike. Probably about to bite Ryan's head off. But that was a bad analogy because that was only after sex. "I'll believe it when I see it. Give me the list."

Ryan gave him the list, and wondered if he scowled deeply enough, whether that would convey the depth of his annoyance. All it did was earn him another scowl in return, like Aronson was determined to win the battle of the glares.

Petey, whistling an off-key tune that Ryan vaguely recognized as the Doors, loped up to Ryan's desk to take his sheet as well. He scanned it quickly and then handed it back. "No notes."

"No notes?"

"'S what I would've done."

"Traitor," Aronson muttered.

Ryan considered whirling on him, snapping, *what is your problem*. Instead, he said, "Great. See you tomorrow. Lots to do." He turned back to the whiteboard so he didn't have to watch Aronson leaving.

They were starting off the season at home against the Arizona Scorpions, which suited Eric perfectly fine. Not only were the Scorpions perennially tanking, which meant it was a low-stress season opener for a rookie head coach and rookie half of the lineup, it gave him a little more time in the morning to get ready, to scroll through his timeline on Twitter while he was making his morning coffee. Today he frowned at some of the news, then whistled.

"Petey, did you see the Railers shit today?"

"Roney, if you think I read the news, you are sadly mistaken," Petey replied, his face buried in his coffee mug.

"It's a new investigative report. John Wilde."

Petey stared at him blankly.

"You know? The guy who broke the national team

scandal last year? The one who's been covering the Thomas charges? The one who wrote about *your* head trauma class-action lawsuit?"

"I," Petey said, "am just vibing. I don't read the news; it gives me a headache."

"Well," Eric said. "This one's gonna give you a migraine." He flipped through his phone again to pull the article up. He could feel his ears heating up as he thought about it, the fury on several levels: as a person, as a coach, as a guy who cared about the players on his team. "An anonymous player filed a lawsuit yesterday, alleging that during the Railers' last Cup run, he was sexually assaulted by one of the team's assistant coaches. And that the team knew, and that they covered it up so it wouldn't disrupt the playoffs."

Petey peered over his shoulder, and frowned, which was about as expressive a look of disapproval as he ever wore. "Jesus. That's fucking awful, ain't it?"

By that time, Sullivan had come back into the office. He'd already been on the ice that morning, skating before anyone else had gotten there. Eric had scowled at him from the upper levels, annoyed that Sullivan still had all of the power and grace of his playing days, like he hadn't lost a step on his stride even though it had been over five years since his retirement.

"Did you guys see the news?" Sullivan asked.

"Roney was just showing me," Petey said. "Because I don't read the news."

"Probably for the best. Fucking awful," Sullivan said, frowning. "I'm just—Jesus. Even to file anonymously, that poor guy's going to go through so much shit on top of what he's already gone through. And Terrance was coaching them at the time already…"

Richard Terrance had a league-wide reputation, well-earned, as one of the winningest coaches of all time. He was a fucking legend. He'd brought two Cups home to Long Island, and he'd managed one of the rarest feats in the coaching world: longevity. Despite the team's decline in fortunes, the general manager of the Railers had kept him employed. When he eventually did retire there was no question that he was a Hall of Fame candidate.

"If any of the boys have questions, I think we should say something," Sullivan was going on, frowning off into the distance. "That if any of them have issues, they should feel comfortable coming to us. You know?"

Eric rubbed a finger against the bridge of his nose, exasperated again, because Sullivan was *right*. It was fucking annoying when he was right, even about this. "None of us are anything like that, though."

"I'm not saying—but just, you know. A general statement. I think it's important. Jesus, I gave the same speech to my peewee kids. Fucked up you can't even trust adults to handle this better," Sullivan said, frowning at the printed depth chart.

Eric felt the urge to play devil's advocate, to say maybe Terrance didn't know. He knew enough about the American legal system to know that a complaint was just allegations, that they still had to be proved in court. And he also knew enough about hockey players to know that no one was going to put themselves through this particular wringer if it wasn't true.

The complaint had been detailed. And the complaint had alleged that Terrance had known.

Instead, Eric said, "We can all say something. I don't know how long this is going to go on. I can't imagine the Railers' ownership settling something like this."

"Hell of a note to start the season," Petey said, shaking his head.

"Can't control what's going on in the rest of the league," Sullivan said, "can only control how we handle our guys."

Eric frowned at his phone again. He thought about how he had been at the age the kid had alleged the assault had occurred. He thought about himself, desperate to make the team, willing to do almost anything to achieve the dreams that had dangled just out of reach for so long. He thought about himself, queer and not even with a foot out of the closet like he was now, and how vulnerable that had been. He thought about himself now, in his forties, responsible for the kids he had been all of those years ago.

He thought about someone abusing that trust, and he felt, again, a rush of fury and the regret that he couldn't just go on the ice and beat the shit out of someone. It wasn't fair.

Sullivan was looking at him again. "Aronson? You good?"

"Yes, Coach," he said, flexing his fingers into fists and open again. He stood and, together, the three of them went out to talk to the boys.

Ryan's first game of the regular season wasn't as difficult as he was expecting it to have been. The preseason really had prepared him for what to expect, and it didn't hurt that the Scorpions, frankly, sucked. Granted, the Beacons weren't far behind in the fancy stats race to the bottom, solely based on the roster, but playing the Scorpions you'd never guess that the Beacons were anything except a team full of hot-shit, young-gun talents fully prepared to take the league by storm.

At a certain point, he gave Williams, Cook and Sinclair a little break, and didn't ice them as much in the dying moments of the third. There wasn't any point in running up the score when you were already winning 6-1. Cook already had two goals on the season, and the announcers were practically orgasming over the fact that after having ten goals last year before ending up in the minors, he was now on pace for 164. It obviously wasn't sustainable, but it sure as hell was a fun stat.

"You're really gonna turtle *now*?" Aronson demanded. He leaned forward into Ryan's space, looming over him. There wasn't much of a difference in their height with Ryan standing on the bench to be able to actually see what was going on.

"It's not turtling," Ryan said, somehow very aware of how big Aronson was, how little space they had crammed together on the bench. For some reason, it made him feel a bit breathless. "It's the first game of the season, and it's sportsmanship."

"That wasn't like you as a player," Aronson said. They had to yell so they could be heard over the noise of the game and crowd and the players on the bench. "The Ryan Sullivan I played against would've gone for the throat. He would've gotten that last point if he had to break his own damn legs to do it."

"I'm *not* a player anymore. I'm a coach."

"This is going to come back to bite you in the ass, Sullivan."

Ryan exhaled again. As was becoming more common than he'd like, he had to take a deep breath and count to ten. He thought about saying something like *well, you'd fucking know about biting, wouldn't you?* But he was going to be the bigger person. If not literally. "Not curb-stomping the Arizona fucking Scorpions in the season opener is not going to come back to bite me in the ass, Aronson."

Aronson shrugged and turned away from him, and Ryan hoped that wasn't caught on the jumbotron. He hadn't been expecting, when he accepted the job, that the hardest part wasn't going to be managing the bench or dealing with the players or even schmoozing with donors and season-ticket holders but getting along with his assistant coaches. Well. Assistant coach. Petey was, as ever, a fucking delight, and so was Heidi.

Aronson, on the other hand, was a demon.

After the game, Ryan stood in the hallway, fist-bumping the guys as they came down the hall. Cook and Williams, the first and second stars of the night along with Davit Kancheli, came through last. Cook was beaming, his rosy cheeks a brilliant red, and Ryan hoped that this would be the start of getting the monkey off his back.

He didn't have much to say in the locker room after the end, except to note that they had played a good game, and that they should keep the momentum going against tougher competition. It was getting easier to come up with the remarks on the fly, the same way he had read the lineups for the room during his later playoff series. The secret was just getting the rhythm of it.

There was a day between games, and the team didn't have an on-ice practice. It was a gym and video day. Ryan took the time to go over tape with Laurent Martel, one of the veteran wingers who'd been underperforming last season and hadn't shown any signs in the preseason or the first game of changing that. Martel was a little standoffish at first, his shoulders hunched.

"This isn't a criticism," Ryan said. "We're here to *coach.* We're here to help you improve. I think if you work on a few specialized drills with the skills coach, you'll start seeing an improvement."

"I did those drills in juniors," Martel mumbled.

"The thing is, you're always learning. If you think you aren't, then you're stagnating. Like I said, this isn't a knock on you. Just a few things we noticed. And I'm just asking you to keep an open mind." He met Martel's gaze and held it. Martel looked away first. "Good? Good."

After he was done with the forwards, he dropped in on Lewis Segal's session with Kancheli and their backup, Lucas Olsson. The goalie coach was a veteran himself, and he had a particular way of getting through to them that Ryan didn't even bother trying to interpret.

Goaltending had always seemed a bit like magic to him, completely dependent on the whims of the stars and seasons, and the fact that Segal seemed to be able to break it down into a science was good enough for him. He stayed just long enough to make sure that Kancheli and Olsson seemed comfortable and engaged, and then moved on.

The worst part was knowing that after the practice, he'd have to go to his father's house. There wasn't a way to put it off any longer. It was a Friday night, the team was going on the road the next day, and he had promised that he would come home to see everyone before he was thrown back into the busy schedule of travel and games. Some of it wasn't bad: Ryan was genuinely fond of his nieces and nephews, and there were a lot of them. But the rest of it…

It was with an impending sense of doom that Ryan took his car and drove from his hotel near the Spectrum to Southie, where his dad still lived in the big row home where the Sullivan crew had grown up. The blue shiplap house had been in the family for generations, and each son to inherit had put his own touches on it; if the house hadn't been passed down that way it probably would have sold for well over a million dollars, because the neighborhood was changing as surely as his father hated that it was.

Dad hadn't made substantive changes to the house itself, but years ago he had added fencing around the stoop to prevent people from sitting on the steps and smoking cigarettes or shooting up, and he'd hung hundreds of pictures of his sons playing hockey and their draft day portraits in the living room.

Ryan did not feature prominently in the gallery.

By the time he found street parking and walked briskly to the house, it looked like Mark Junior, Kevin, James, and Eddie were already there with their wives and kids. Ryan and Shannon had never had kids: there had been a few miscarriages, and then he'd been on the road so often that they had just sort of mutually agreed to stop trying. At one point, Shannon had been pretty broken up about it, but she'd eventually stopped asking him about a timeline to have a family. Even then, it had always made both of them feel out of place to come home to Ryan's father's house, surrounded by an entire horde of Sullivan children that Shannon would never have. Now it seemed almost like a relief that they hadn't.

Ryan took a deep breath as he unhooked the gate to the steps and walked up, paused outside for a long second before he opened the door.

Inside, the house was chaos. Each of the Sullivan brothers had at least three kids, and when all of them were in the house together it got real loud, real fast. Ryan was immediately mobbed by tiny bodies, ranging in age from two to ten. The teenaged niblings hung back, probably dying to pick his brain about the team—they all played hockey, of course they all played hockey—but way too cool to want to look like that's what they were doing. Ryan hugged everyone, patted some heads, greeted all of the kids in turn and tried to pick himself up from the foyer floor where they'd knocked him.

"Well, look who decided to take time out of his busy schedule and pay a visit," Dad's voice boomed from the living room.

"Hi, Dad," Ryan said, trying not to sound too resigned. With a niece attached to each leg, he limped into the room to pay his respects.

The living room was set up exactly the way it had been when he'd left it, a rough horseshoe of overstuffed couches and his dad's reclining chair in the middle like a throne. Next to him, on the closest couch, sat Chelsea, Ryan's stepmother. It did feel strange calling her that, because she was three years younger than Ryan, but she had been in the picture since very shortly after his mom had passed away. He had been twenty-four and never really warmed up to her. She knew enough not to try actually mothering anyone, but her sudden presence at family events had been a shock. Right now, she turned a tired smile on him; he smiled back, but it wasn't a real one at all.

Ryan's older brothers and their wives were all arranged in varying configurations on the other couches. There was a hierarchy about who sat where, but it depended on whether you were in Dad's favor or not. Ryan would have to take a few minutes getting the lay of the land before he sat anywhere himself. Based solely upon distance from the recliner, Eddie had done something to piss Dad off, and Jimmy had clawed his way back to his position as the golden child. The interfamilial politics were ruthless enough to make a Targaryen sweat.

"I had to find out from Christopher down the block," Dad was telling Jimmy's wife, Andrea. "He didn't even call to tell us, can you believe it?"

Andrea shot Ryan a brief, sympathetic look and said, "I'm sure it all happened very fast, you know how those things can be—"

"Don't be stupid, Andy," Jimmy interrupted her, shaking his head. "Ryan's always been like that. A secretive little shit, huh?"

"That's right," Dad agreed, taking a sip of his Sam Adams and replacing it in the cup holder. "Didn't even tell us when he went running away to college. Broke his mother's heart, he did."

Ryan winced; Chelsea winced too but didn't say anything. "I'm sorry I didn't get a chance to call," he lied. "I really didn't have the time at all."

"Hey," Eddie said, suddenly. "Where's Shannon?"

He had known it was coming, but he'd hoped it would have come a little later in the evening. Maybe after he had had a chance to have a beer himself. "Well. We're actually getting divorced, so she didn't come back to Boston with me."

That shocked them all into silence, and everyone's eyes turned slowly to him.

Finally, Dad said, *"Divorced?"*

Ryan wondered whether he could get away with not talking about it at all. He was still standing in the middle of the room like he was facing a judge and jury, arrayed in the half circle around his father. "She wasn't happy. I wasn't happy. It's probably better this way." As he said it, he was surprised to find that it was true: he *hadn't* been happy, in god knew how long.

"Divorced," Dad muttered. "Divorced! I never thought I'd live to see the day that a child of *mine* was getting divorced."

"Mark," Chelsea said, "be kind. I'm sure Ryan's very upset about it."

"He doesn't seem very upset about it, Chelsea."

Ryan glanced at his watch. He probably had to suffer through another hour or two of this, and then he could go. It was like this every time he came home, and every time he thought maybe it would be different, his family proved him wrong. Well: he didn't have a choice. He was here now, and they weren't going anywhere. Ryan took a seat on the couch, as far from Dad as he could get, and prepared to be grilled.

Guess where I am, he texted Shannon, even though he knew it was a bad idea. Being back here made him miss her, the solidarity they'd had even in that very specific misery. All your favorite people are here.

Don't talk to me unless I reach out first. Or go through my lawyer. You have her contact info, Shannon responded almost immediately.

Ryan sighed, locked his phone, and looked down at his hands. It was stupid to have hoped she'd still be there when he needed her: she wasn't his wife anymore, even if they hadn't signed the papers yet, and it was at least 95% his fault that she wasn't. The realization was unpleasant, along with the realization that he'd been avoiding thinking about it as much as he could.

That was it, though: he was alone, and he was at home with his family. There'd be no getting out of it now.

CHAPTER FOUR

October

Sometimes, even though he generally hated most people, Eric wished that he had a better social life in Boston. It was partially his own fault for being busy all of the fucking time, and also partially his own fault for being a prickly, unapproachable jackass. Once you hit a certain age, it was hard to make friends that you hadn't dragged with you from your youth. And sure, Eric had his hockey buddies, but they were scattered to all corners of the continent, some of them in Canada, some of them in America, none of them in Boston.

Sometimes, he and Petey would go out and grab a beer. As fond as he was of his colleague, Petey was also very…low energy. They had shit in common to talk about, but sometimes Eric didn't want to talk about work. It was a strange conundrum, really. When his mom was trying to set him up with girls, all he wanted to do was talk about hockey. But when he was hanging out with the boys, all he wanted to do was talk about other shit. Or play pool. Or listen to music. Or maybe that was just Eric and his contrary fucking nature again.

Sometimes, against his better judgment, he just went out alone. It was a half-hour walk if he wasn't hurrying to one of the few dive bars in the city that still felt like a dive bar, even if it had the kind of notoriety that meant you also needed to avoid hipsters while you were drinking. The walls behind the bar and in the bathroom were scribbled over with messages and caricatures and other invectives lost to time. It had pool tables, and Eric was competitive enough that if he could bully a stranger into losing a game against him, he would. The drinks were cheap. The bartenders weren't too chatty.

So he walked down Fourth Street, from South End to Southie proper. As he walked, he took a quick picture of the last lingering fall leaves clinging to the trees, the moon in the sky behind them. It was a cliché shot, but he posted it anyway before shrugging his shoulders and heading into the bar.

Whitey's was loud and crowded as it always was, and Eric elbowed his way up to the pocked and scratched wooden bar to order a whiskey and beer. While he was waiting for the bartender to come and take his tab, he glanced down the bar and did a double take. He recognized *that* gray fucking head, unfortunately. But he'd already paid for his drink, and he would be damned if Ryan fucking Sullivan chased him out of *his bar*.

If he played his cards right, maybe Sullivan wouldn't even notice.

Of course, Sullivan looked up and saw him, and narrowed his eyes. Even in the dim light of the bar, Eric noticed the line at the corner of his mouth tighten. A face that was usually laughing twisted into a frown. Sullivan slid off of the barstool and almost immediately disappeared in the crowd of taller, standing patrons. The visual effect was so funny that Eric almost laughed himself, except he had the distinct impression that Sullivan was headed his way, and he didn't want to encourage him.

"What are *you* doing in Southie?" Sullivan demanded.

"I live in South End. It's not that far a walk. This is one of my favorite dive bars. What are *you* doing in Southie?"

"I grew up here," Sullivan said. His face was a little flushed; Eric wondered how long he'd been here, how much he'd been drinking. "I was visiting my family."

Eric wasn't stupid. He could put two and two together about *visiting my family* and then immediately after *drinking at a dive bar*. "So you decided to come and get drunk instead?"

"I'm not *drunk*," Sullivan said, waving his hand emphatically, and Eric grabbed it so he wouldn't smack the arm of a woman who was trying to squeeze by them.

Sullivan looked up at him sharply and flexed his hand; his skin felt very warm under Eric's fingers. He didn't pull away.

Eric let go. "Okay, toasty."

"Oh Jesus, Aronson, you are just..."

The bartender slid Eric's beer across the counter to him, and he took it with a lift of his hand in acknowledgment. "I'm what?"

"A pain in my ass," Sullivan muttered. For once, he didn't have the beaming, optimistic face that he wore around the guys at the rink. Eric wondered if he was always like this when he was alone. Whether there was a darker underbelly to his sparkling personality. Anyone who played the way he had couldn't have been all shitting rainbows and unicorns.

“That’s mutual,” Eric said, and Sullivan surprised him by laughing.

He had a wheezy little chuckle, as breathless as he was after repeatedly running the steps at whatever rink they happened to be playing in before every morning skate. “You really come all the way to fucking Southie to drink?”

“I like to play pool,” Eric said, a little defensively.

“Yeah? Come on. One game.”

It wasn’t a good idea. There was not having friends in Boston, and there was belligerent pool with his boss, who had been drinking. Eric downed his entire pint in two gulps and gestured for another one. “You’re on. Let’s see if you can even reach the table.”

Sullivan’s brown eyes narrowed and for a second, Eric felt the little thrill of competition. The same way he would have done facing him across the red line for an opening face-off while they waited for their centers to duel it out. Sullivan ran one hand through his gray hair, pushing it out of his eyes. He was a bit disheveled, like the wind and alcohol had whipped him out of the tidy persona he usually presented.

Eric thought about grabbing him by the shoulders and shaking him. He would have, if he had any idea what would happen next. “Let’s see if you’re all talk the way I think you are.”

“Oh, shit. Does Ted Lasso actually have a temper?”

“Less crap, more pool,” Sullivan said, firmly, and Eric thought about reaching down to ruffle his hair out of order again.

Eric took his second beer, downed that too, and followed Sullivan to the pool table. He might have been short as hell, but his body was broad and solid enough, muscular enough, that people moved out of his way instinctively.

It was the kind of bar where even though everyone had to have recognized Sullivan, no one actually approached to bother him. The most anyone did was glance at them out of the corner of their eyes, and Eric was aware, once again, that he really could not afford to do anything stupid, like trip his head coach just to see him go tumbling to the tile floor and sprawl in an undignified heap.

Sullivan moved to rack the first set of balls. Even drunk, he moved with a careful and easy economy of motion, although Eric had to snicker a little when Sullivan did need to lean forward so he could reach and position the triangle correctly. Sullivan caught him at it and his head whipped around, frown tugging the corner of his mouth down, and Eric couldn't resist.

"Should I get you a stool?"

"You can break them, and we'll go from there, how about that."

"Which rules? You want to pick stripes or solids?"

"Your choice. Whatever bar rules you usually use. I don't need to worry about who has the best setup."

"Oh, cocky, are you?"

"Competent," Sullivan corrected him, and Eric really should not have found that as attractive as he did, especially because Sullivan was so fucking self-righteous about it. He held the cue stick in one hand like it was a hockey stick, leaning over the table to peer at the angle Eric chose to take to break the rack.

The balls broke with a satisfying crack. To his eye, the stripes were better arranged, but he wasn't going to give Sullivan the satisfaction of *competence* by taking the easy way out. Eric took solids, and let Sullivan have the first go at it.

"I can't believe you voluntarily hang out in Southie," Sullivan said, with a disparaging snort, as he moved around the table looking for the best angle. "If I had the choice, I'd never come back here again."

"It's really not that bad," Eric said. "At all. Where else would you, Mr. Hall-of-Famer Cup Champion, be able to play pool without getting bothered for autographs every five seconds?"

"I can tell *you* didn't grow up here," Sullivan retorted, neatly pocketing his first ball.

"What gave it away?" Eric couldn't quite keep the smirk off of his face, and it only seemed to infuriate Sullivan further. What annoyed him was the equally neat shot and satisfying noise as Eric's ball made its way to the target, too. "Was it the fact that this place isn't as terrible as you think it is, or was it the accent?"

Sullivan didn't answer, just moved around the pool table like a shark, picking his spots, getting a better view of the lines he'd have to pick to get his next shot. As much as he hated to admit it, Eric watched him, the way his shoulders shifted visibly even under the bulky fall sweater he was wearing. The muscle of his stupid, thick thighs pulling against the legs of his pants. Sullivan played pool the same way he did everything else, with an air that would have been cocky if he wasn't so obviously enjoying the competition on its own merits.

The bar was crowded and humid, like everyone else in Southie was either avoiding their own shitty families or had simultaneously decided it was better to be lonely in a group. Even in the space around the tables, Eric kept getting shoved to the side as he waited, pushed around until he set his weight at the center and refused to move.

He had to stand too close to Sullivan, stupidly aware of the heat of Sullivan's body, the way that the hair on his arms stood a little on end where he'd rolled his sleeves up to the elbow. Couldn't help looking at Sullivan's face, the way his mouth twisted in a firm line when he was concentrating, squinting down at the table. Teeth digging into his lower lip. Couldn't entirely ignore the way he'd catch Sullivan watching him when it was his turn, the too-long stare, focused on the wrong parts of Eric's face or body.

They were evenly matched, for the most part. A few fouls set Sullivan behind. A push from behind while he was lining up set Eric's ball careening off at the wrong angle. Sullivan didn't crow triumphantly at him either, just watched, intent, like he was plotting the trajectory of a particularly bad-angle wrister from behind the net. Even though he swayed a little as he walked, he still had a hell of a shot. It was satisfying, watching him play, Eric realized with a little jolt. He had let his guard down, and every time his arm brushed against Eric's or his hip jostled Eric out of place, it threw him off of his game.

In between turns, Eric wove his way back up to the bar for drinks, Sullivan bristling when Eric warned him not to cheat while he was gone.

"Is this what you do with your spare time?" Sullivan asked when he returned, and Eric did a double take because the question had sounded so sincere.

"Nah. I watch a lot of hockey, you know."

Sullivan laughed, and Eric felt the frisson of annoyance and frustration that he always had when Sullivan smiled. "No shit."

They had wound down to Eric's last ball, and the eight ball. He said, "Five ball, right corner."

"Oh, confident," Sullivan drawled.

"No, competent," Eric corrected him. He wondered if there was a berachah for not embarrassing yourself in front of your annoying fucking boss. There were a lot of weirdly specific ones, but probably not that specific. He muttered a little encouragement to the ball, anyway, before he sent it careening into the right corner pocket.

"Goddamnit," Sullivan exclaimed.

"See?" Eric couldn't resist. "And I didn't even take the best setup."

Sullivan's head whipped around with the kind of energy that a hawk had. He wasn't glaring, exactly, but there was a very intense focus, a frustration vibrating out of him. Eric thought, smugly, *good.* Instead, he said, "We ever decide on a bet?"

"No," Sullivan said, and folded his arms over his broad chest. "And at this point, I don't think you should get to pick the forfeit. That's cheating."

"I won fair and square, you obnoxious little—"

"I'll buy you dinner on the road," Sullivan cut him off firmly.

"Are you kidding?" Eric started. The *last* thing he wanted was to spend time with Sullivan outside of work. Especially in an unfamiliar city, where he couldn't escape. Sullivan's whiskey-brown eyes were looking at him. His eyebrows drew down in a frown. He was leaning forward a little, into Eric's personal space. A few more inches and he'd practically be in Eric's arms. Eric wondered how it would feel, his sturdy body pressed against Eric's. He wondered—

No. He had to stop thinking like that. He had to be normal about Sullivan, no matter what he looked like, no matter how oblivious he was to the distance between them. Somehow, Eric's mouth was saying, "Fine, whatever."

"Okay," Sullivan said. For some reason Eric had the distinct impression that he was being laughed at. "It's a bet." Sullivan glanced up at the glowing TV screens over the bar, which were playing the Patriots game. "Ah, shit. It's almost midnight already… I should go."

Eric frowned at the empty glasses stacked up neatly on the table next to him. They had a flight to catch early the next day, and he'd been here in a dive bar, wasting time talking shit with a coworker he hated. "Yeah, same."

He didn't look at Sullivan when they settled the tab. He didn't look at Sullivan when they left the bar and, without further conversation, went on their separate ways. He realized that he didn't even know where Sullivan was staying. Whether he was living out of a hotel, whether he'd already figured out an apartment. It wasn't his business, and he didn't care.

Falling asleep that night, knowing what he knew.

Even the victory felt hollow.

Ryan had always loved road games. You didn't necessarily get the chance to see another city if the timing wasn't perfect, but he liked the excitement of knowing that he was going to be in a new place for a few days.

He'd liked being on the plane with the boys, shooting the shit about nothing or playing cards or pranking anyone who was dumb enough to fall asleep while the majority of the team was still awake. He'd liked the excitement of heavy steps down the bus stairs, knowing you were heading into enemy territory. He'd liked hotels, even when he'd had to have a roommate, enjoyed the crisp clean sheets and heading down bright and early to see what was available at the hotel buffet. He'd liked playing in other teams' barns, especially when they'd win it, savoring the satisfaction of watching faces fall and the crowd go silent.

It turned out that the excitement was still there, just tempered, as a coach. He stood waiting for the guys to corral themselves onto the bus to the airport, watching the rookies goofing off and knocking each other's hats to the ground, some of the older guys texting their wives, the equipment managers hauling the last few boxes of gear before the team would start loading their own bags.

At his shoulder, Jesse Keen, one of the veteran left wingers who'd been there through the previous administration's entire tenure, had his arms folded over his chest as he watched. He was frowning. Keen hadn't impressed Ryan very much in the small sample size.

In the previous lineup, Keen had been a defensive specialist, skating heavy minutes on the penalty kill and rounding out a third line that could do a little bit of everything. He'd never broken fifty points, but he'd been a reliable source of secondary scoring. He had yet to make it onto the scoreboard this season. Ryan wasn't up his ass about it, but he was keeping an eye on the situation. Sometimes this was just bad luck, sometimes it was a confidence issue, sometimes it was some other thing working its way in and wreaking havoc on a guy's game.

"Everything good, Keen?"

"Oh, yeah," Keen said. He had the kind of nondescript face that your eyes skated right over, and thick hair cut in a way that reminded Ryan a little bit of Wolverine. "I mean, would like a little more ice time, if you're asking sincerely."

Ryan blinked at him.

"Joking," Keen said, in a way that indicated that he was not, actually, joking.

Ryan made another mental note to keep an eye on him. He hadn't expected everyone to immediately fall in line to the new way of doing things, but Keen hadn't had a point yet so far that season. He had been smiling that same determined, brittle smile about it, but Ryan had the feeling that ice time was going to be an issue. Same as deployment. He had started the season determined to kill everyone with kindness, but that depended on the personnel.

This was a circular little not-quite-road trip, starting in Columbus, swinging through Pittsburgh, stopping in New York, and then up to Toronto, with some time to head home and do laundry in between.

Columbus was the kind of city that had a bad rap, but that Ryan had always enjoyed. The city was the kind of place you could legitimately describe as up-and-coming, and the Battery's goal cannon was one of a kind. It was especially funny watching the rookies, and some of the veterans, jump. Aronson hadn't specified where he wanted Ryan to pay the forfeit, so Ryan had decided to get it out of the way as quickly as possible *and* before he'd have to pay Toronto prices.

As the team went up the ramp to the plane, Ryan turned to Aronson and said, "I made reservations in Columbus for the night before the game."

Aronson turned an unimpressed brown stare at him. "Columbus? Really?"

"Hey, they have nice places there," Ryan said, feeling a little defensive. "We can't all be from Montreal."

"I feel," Aronson said, his lip twitching in an effort to hide the smirk, "like you're just trying to avoid paying New York or Toronto prices."

"*You* didn't specify," Ryan said, lifting his chin. "Columbus is a perfectly nice town with an underrated food scene."

"Gentlemen…" Petey said, slinging his arms around both of their shoulders, "we have a two-hour flight ahead of us and I get migraines on flights. Can we all agree to chill the fuck out? Eh? Eh?"

"Yeah, sure," Aronson said, flicking his fingers against Petey's wrist until Petey released him.

On the plane, the boys spread out in their preferred places. Ryan took note of the way that groups broke up: Cook and Williams sat together like always, but they'd roped Davey the goalie into their little group and were already pulling out the deck of cards. Some of the veteran d-men congregated around Afanasyev, toward the middle of the plane; they were all taking out their masks and earplugs for what looked to be a group nap.

And the coaches ended up in the front, in a group of four seats separated by a table in the middle. Petey immediately took one side, lifted the chair divider, and flopped down on his back.

"You're going to have to buckle yourself in," Aronson told him.

Petey said, "Bite me."

"My biting days are behind me," Aronson protested, and narrowed his eyes when Ryan laughed.

Somewhat against his will, Ryan settled into a seat next to Aronson, and pulled out his iPad and notes to start reviewing shit ahead of the game. The Battery were another one of those perennial bottom-feeder teams, no matter what big splashes they made in free agency. It was tough to keep players, but maybe not so much now that they'd shuffled the coaching staff around. They were already riddled by injury, with a few stars starting the season on LTIR.

Next to him, Aronson pulled out one of the yellow legal pads he was always carrying around and set it down on the table. Ryan could see out of the corner of his eye the sketchy diagrams and chicken scratch scrawl that passed for Aronson's handwriting—most of it was in French. He couldn't take too close a look, though, because by that time, the flight attendant had come out to the aisle to give them the usual talk about staying seated when the lights were on and buckling their seat belts securely. Some of the older guys were already snoring.

Ryan's ears popped as the plane gained altitude, and he rubbed the side of his head absently. On screen, he watched his defenseman and the fourth line completely losing defensive zone coverage and allowing a goal against in an almost comical series of miscommunications.

Under Leclerc, they had had a complicated system of zone coverage. Petey and Ryan had worked out that they would be better served taking it man-to-man, but that also required practice and training to make sure that the players knew how to make the judgment calls necessary to actually pull it off. That would be a teachable moment before the Battery game. It was encouraging that some of the players had already come to him to ask for extra video review time: whatever you had to say about the talent level, you couldn't fault the effort.

Strangely, Ryan couldn't relax and concentrate on his work the way he had always been able to do. He'd flown on planes like this for the majority of his life, and he couldn't ever remember being so weirdly aware of the guy sitting next to him. Usually it was the unspoken rules of the road: you made sure your arms and legs weren't overlapping, the same way you didn't look where you shouldn't in the locker room. It wasn't even like Aronson's arm was drifting.

Ryan was just very aware of where it was resting in relation to his own arm. He shivered, although the plane wasn't cold.

He frowned at the armrest and Aronson's elbow. Aronson had rolled his sleeves up again, and Ryan could see his forearms, the thick, dark curly hair that went right up to the edge of his wrist. He wondered what it felt like, if it was soft or scratchy or—

Aronson caught him looking, eyebrows lowering. "What are you looking at?"

"Do you still think in French?"

"What do you—" Aronson started, surprised, then stopped. "It was what I grew up speaking at home. But I've been away long enough that it's mostly English." His eyes narrowed. "Why?"

"You write all of your notes in French, so I was just curious."

"It's so nosy assholes like you can't spy on 'em."

"Aronson, we're literally coworkers."

"So?"

"So, we're supposed to be on the same page."

Aronson leveled one of those blank brown gazes at him, eyebrows drawn down over the rims of his glasses. "Are we?"

From his vantage point on the opposite side of the table, hidden beneath the edge, Petey said, "Don't take it personally, Sully. Roney's just like this."

"Like what?" Aronson demanded, the pen balanced in his hand like a dagger.

They couldn't see Petey's face, but the smile in his voice was almost audible. "Nuh-uh, I'm not giving you *that* fight. Come on. Migraine, yeah? Chill. Out."

Ryan realized it was sound advice. He also realized it was easier said than done. He slipped his earbuds in, connected them to the iPad, and turned the volume up. It was easier to listen to the sounds of skates on ice than it was to pay attention to the very bony elbow, still encroaching on his personal space, or the nearness of Aronson's lanky frame, radiating like a space heater.

Thankfully, the flight wasn't long, and by the time they had disembarked, the equipment staff had unloaded all of the bags and the team had made its way through the airport, Ryan felt a little more like himself.

He walked at the end of the line, watching the way the players were interacting with each other, filing things away for future reference. Who was at the center of it all, who was a problem, who was getting jokingly bullied by the older players. While he was watching, he caught a glimpse of Aronson, ducking down to pick up a pebble from the stretch of concrete outside of the arrivals terminal before slipping it into his pocket.

Ryan frowned. What a weird fucking thing to do. He wondered what on earth Aronson would want with the little chip of concrete, which wasn't even really an actual rock. But it wasn't like he could ask. He turned his attention away from Aronson and onto the team. His *real* responsibility.

Eric realized the error he had made in allowing Sullivan to buy him dinner as a forfeit. And then again, the error he had made in not setting any boundaries around it.

First of all, it meant that he actually had to spend time with Sullivan outside of work. Second of all, it meant that Sullivan had picked the city and the place, which meant that Eric had been dragged out to dinner in Columbus, Ohio, of all places, to a restaurant that was half-exposed beams that had been bolted on top of the regular ceiling and half glass separating the inside parts of the restaurant. There were fancy chandeliers made of delicate strung-glass crystals and a large glass wine cellar.

Eric glared at all of it as he followed Sullivan to the front desk. "Really?" he hissed out of the corner of his mouth. The waiters wore bow ties and pale green suspenders and aprons that matched the chandeliers, and the whole effect was ridiculous.

It was the kind of place that, if he was a different kind of person, he'd be documenting for an Instagram post later on. He could see diners beyond doing just that, the flash of phone cameras here and there. Eric, however, wasn't the kind of guy who took pictures of his food unless he was cooking it at home. He had *some* shame.

"The food's great," Sullivan said, with a shrug. He was smiling at the hostess, turning on every ounce of stupid twinkly-eyed charm he had. "Hello, we had a reservation for two under Sullivan?"

The woman, a pretty blonde, smiled back, the kind

of irresistible reflex that people seemed to have when faced with the full force of Sullivan's personality. "Of course," she said. "Right this way."

It was the kind of place that would take your coat for you, but Eric stubbornly kept his on until they got to the seat and slung it over the back of his chair. Sullivan shot him a look, and Eric looked back, all fake innocence. Eventually, Sullivan seemed to decide it wasn't worth it, and sat down without commenting on the coat situation at all.

"You know," Sullivan said. "You're getting a free dinner out of this. You don't have to look like you're facing the firing squad."

"I have to look at those bow ties and suspenders every time they come over here. That's bad enough."

"All right, old man," Sullivan said, but the corner of his mouth was twitching like he was trying not to laugh.

It only made Eric more annoyed, so he covered his frustration by looking down at the dinner options. The menu actually didn't look half-bad, even if it did have ridiculous description choices like *tuna ribbons*.

Eric was still busy frowning at the various options when the waiter made his way over. He was a very young man with the freshly scrubbed look, red cheeks, and somewhat ostentatious earrings of someone who'd made his way from a small town to the big city and decided that, fuck it, now that he was here, he was going to be himself. Eric's initial inclination to be sarcastic at him wilted under the force of his earnest smile.

"Welcome to the Guild House," the server said, "my name is Cayde, and I will be taking care of you tonight."

"Great," Sullivan said, smiling back. "Thank you so much."

"Have you dined with us before?"

"I've been a few times, but this is his first."

"Well, if you let me, I'll explain the menu," Cayde started, and Eric immediately tuned him out.

He kept half an eye on Sullivan and the waiter as they chatted about the raw dishes and the appetizers and the wine list. He pinched the bridge of his nose and frowned at delicate scrolling print. It was frustrating that everything did sound good, but he'd dawdled too long: when he looked up, he found that Sullivan had already ordered several appetizers for the table, and Cayde was smiling widely as he looked from Sullivan to Eric, taking in Sullivan's pleasant, oblivious grin and Eric's thundercloud of a scowl.

"Your partner has picked out some *excellent* options, I assure you," Cayde said cheerfully, as he turned to leave. "The tuna ribbons are my personal favorite."

Eric started to say *he's not my partner* but caught himself when Sullivan looked back at him. He waited until Cayde had moved on to the next table, but before he could say anything, Sullivan cut him off.

"Now," he said, pointing the butter knife he'd been holding in Eric's general direction. As far as threats went, it was vaguely comical. "Do you want to tell me why you've been such a damn buzzkill at practice?"

"I don't know what you mean," Eric lied.

"I'm trying to make the practices fun for the guys. Something that they can look forward to, that's not rote, that's not *boring*. And you're in there glaring at them like—like some kind of bird of prey, and it's not the vibe that I'm looking for."

"A bird of prey?" Eric asked, laughing. "Wow, Sullivan, who would've thought you had some poetry in you."

Sullivan's eyes narrowed and he pointed the knife at Eric again. "Look, I know it's not what you were used to with Leclerc. It's probably not even what you were used to when you were playing. But like I said before, we're supposed to be on the same page, and I need you to work with me if this is going to be effective."

Eric was torn between the boiling frustration that had been simmering in the pit of his stomach since Conroy had hired Sullivan, and the opposing natural tug toward him. It was easy to see why Sullivan had been as vital to the Desperadoes as he'd been. He said everything *so* fucking earnestly, putting his whole stomach into it. Those big brown eyes narrowed, focused and intent. And despite Eric's inclination to dislike him he was charismatic as hell.

"I just—look, Sullivan, it's not just me. It's the older guys, too. Some of them haven't been thrilled about the adjustments. And at a certain point you just can't teach an old dog new tricks."

Cayde brought out some of the appetizers and Eric glared at the tuna ribbons. They were arranged in a flower shape on a bed of smashed avocado and paper-thin slices of radish. They were garnished with micro greens. The effect was ridiculous, the kind of fussy food that Eric had always felt the urge to just push over with his fork.

"What are you talking about?" Sullivan asked. He was frowning, now, his chin jutting out stubbornly. "We both learned that way. That's how we both made it through all of those years of play. I was constantly teaching myself shit. If I hadn't, I never would have gotten as far as I did."

"Maybe *you* did," Eric said. The worst part about the

whole thing was that the tuna was actually delicious. He chewed and swallowed, furious.

"What do you mean, maybe you did? You played a long time, too."

"I'm not—" Eric didn't want to say it here, when Cayde was smiling at them and bringing out more dishes. Didn't want to say the worst things he thought sometimes, about toiling away so long, fighting every other night and bruising his knuckles and blacking his eyes, no Cup to show for it. "I'm not *like* you."

Sullivan looked at him intently, like Eric was one of the roster players on one of his teams, the kind of guy he would have motivated by reading the roster before heading out onto the ice. He leaned forward a little, shifting to try to get closer, his whole body tense and focused solely on Eric. Eric thought for a wild, insane second that Sullivan was going to try to take his hand. Under the table, his foot bumped against Eric's; just the simple contact sent a shock up his spine.

Sullivan flinched, like he had felt it too, but said, "We were both undrafted. We both worked our way—"

"We are nothing. *Nothing.* Alike."

They both had to pause because Cayde hovered at the edge of the table, looking very concerned. "Um, I'm very sorry to interrupt, but I wondered if you might want to put in an order for your main dishes? Or if I could bring you another bottle of wine?"

Eric blinked.

He hadn't looked too closely at the menu. He'd grown up in a kosher household, but once he went away to live with a billet family, he'd fallen out of the habit. It was fucking difficult—almost impossible—to keep kosher when you were one of the few Jews in the league, and the team didn't even think about trying to billet you in an appropriate home.

He'd never really managed to get back in the habit again. But he still thought about it every time he ordered something made with lobster broth, every time he ate pork or a cheeseburger.

His mother wasn't very judgmental about the way he lived his life, but he knew that she was always secretly disappointed. The same way she probably would have been disappointed about other things he hadn't told her, like the fact that he was perfectly fine dating Danielle from shul, but he'd really preferred David.

"I'll—uh—the sea bass?" he said, after a second.

Cayde nodded, and then smiled brightly at Sullivan. "And for you, sir?"

Sullivan frowned and said, "I'll do…the halibut, thanks." He very studiously did not look at Eric, frowning, instead, at the woodgrain of the table.

Cayde glanced from one of them to the other, like he was trying to figure something out. "You know what? I think maybe the occasion calls for some wine, really. Can I show you the list?"

"No, it's okay," Sullivans said, and winked. "We both have to work late tomorrow."

Eric could almost see Cayde's sigh of relief, the way his whole body relaxed, and he realized something kind of horrific. That fucking kid thought they were there *together* together. And Sullivan. Stupid, oblivious Sullivan. He had no fucking clue.

Eric imagined the floor opening up underneath him, swallowing him without a second thought. That would have been preferable to tuna ribbons and a very fresh-faced young queer kid assuming that he was *dating his boss.* His obnoxious, optimistic boss who said shit like *it's not the vibe I'm looking for* and seriously meant it.

"You okay?" Sullivan asked, his eyebrows raised.

"Fine," Eric said, and put his head down and concentrated on demolishing the rest of the oyster mushrooms that Sullivan had ordered for him.

He carefully minded his own fucking business for the rest of the dinner. He didn't argue. He didn't snap. But it didn't help. Toward the end of the evening, Cayde came sweeping back in with a wink for Ryan and a grand flourish: a torte and a poppy cake, to split.

"Complimentary," he said, beaming. "I just wanted you to end your night on the sweetest note you could."

Sullivan looked at him, bemused. Eric kept his mouth *firmly* fucking shut, even when Sullivan, calculating the tip and scrawling his signature on the bill, said, "The waiter was nice, but do you think the conversation was a little odd?"

"All in your head," Eric said, curtly, and counted down the seconds until he could flee.

CHAPTER FIVE

November

The road trip hadn't been as successful as Ryan had hoped. They'd won a few and lost a few. The thing that was both frustrating and heartening was that the team played up to tougher competition, but down to lesser competition. The kernels of what could be? They were there.

When he watched Williams and Cook on the ice, the way they seemed to know where to find each other even without looking, he was encouraged. They had played well in Toronto and New York especially. But when they went down two goals in thirty seconds against Columbus, Ryan had to duck his head into his hand behind the bench to keep his face under control.

They regrouped after the trip to go over the tape, to look at who was underperforming, to consider whether the lines and pairings needed to be shifted. The coaches often stayed late, sharing a beer in Ryan's office while they discussed the details. He wasn't surprised to find himself at odds with Aronson again.

"I thought you *liked* Keen," Ryan said, frustrated. He'd moved Keen up to the second line, temporarily, to see if they could get him going again. He'd also slotted him onto the second power play unit for the same reason. Not the first unit, of course. He didn't want to get *too* crazy.

"Yeah," Aronson said. "I mean, we got along just fine under Leclerc. He knew Leclerc's system. Knew where he was supposed to be and who he was supposed to be covering. But he's exactly what I meant when I said you can't teach an old dog new tricks."

"Conroy wanted us to highlight the veterans for trade deadline day, and to get them cooking however we could," Ryan pointed out.

Petey, who had already done his talk on the defenseman, opened one eye. "There's highlighting, and there's Keen."

"I don't believe you can just give up on *anyone* like that," Ryan said, frowning at the whiteboard. The numbers were there, in black and white. The abysmal effect that Keen had on shot share when he was placed on the second line. His own eye test. "I just need to work with him, get it through his head what we're actually asking and expecting."

"Okay, sure, Pollyanna," Aronson drawled. He was shredding a piece of paper, his long fingers twisting the pieces into little balls. It was the kind of anxious habit that was completely at odds with the way he spoke.

Petey laughed. "Wow, Roney, really showing your age with that reference."

To Ryan's surprise, Aronson's ears turned red. It was…kind of cute? "You know my parents are older."

"Well, the fact remains," Ryan said, frowning again, "we've gotta get him going. It's not like he's going anywhere if he doesn't start putting up points, at least, and we can't waive him."

"Why not?" Aronson asked, flicking a tiny ball of paper at Ryan, who brushed it off of his sleeve. "He's not really doing anything fucking useful out there, and he's not really lighting it on fire at practices."

"Can you imagine how that would go over in the room? Waiving a veteran who's been on the team this long?"

"We've done it before," Petey said. "Last year, when we had to free up cap space. It's not the best way to handle things, but if a guy's a professional, he understands."

"Would *you* call Keen a professional?" Ryan started, and both of his assistants sighed, because he was right. "Look. We don't need to make any drastic decisions today. I'll keep working with him at practice, and we'll see if some time on PP2 won't get him going a bit. I can give him a better center and see if that helps. Can always adjust midgame."

"I just think," Aronson said, a little singsong, "that sometimes you need to be a little nasty to get the point across."

"That's not the kind of environment I want to build here. I want the players to enjoy coming to the rink and I want them to trust that I'm not going to spend all of the time they're here yelling at them for things I know they're working on. I want to be able to meet them on their level and *encourage* them to be better."

"And that's admirable," Petey said, and then closed his eyes again. "But sometimes, you may wanna have a little bit of Roney's bite."

Ryan laughed. "Not literally, I hope." Aronson glowered at them but didn't say anything—he didn't have to. Ryan already knew what it would be. He rubbed his eyes and said, "All right, good work tonight, boys. We'll revisit in the morning."

Even in the loss, there were a few light spots, at least. The guys were still goofing off on the ice during warm-ups. It was Afanasyev's birthday, and Cook, Williams, and Davey had decorated his locker for the occasion: in multicolored hockey tape, the words HAPPY BDAY RODDY were clearly visible. They'd blown up the trainers' vinyl gloves to make bizarre-looking balloon clusters. The stoic defenseman had clearly been bemused by the offerings, but accepted them anyway with a solemn handshake.

On his walk back to the hotel, Ryan thought about whether he should contact Shannon's lawyer to see whether or not he could get some of his stuff. He was staying at a Residence Inn about a ten-minute walk from the Spectrum, but it was starting to wear on him. It was one thing to travel and stay at hotels and another entirely to come home to one every night, to the reminder that you were living out of a suitcase. At least he had a little kitchenette so he could cook, even if the utensils were completely dull metal and flimsy plastic bullshit. It was starting to become the final straw that had him searching for available apartments, although he still wasn't sure where the hell he was going to live.

Ryan wondered what he would even end up taking from the house. Probably Shannon would want to keep all of the furniture. It wasn't like he couldn't afford to buy new—he had made a tidy amount of money over the course of his contracts, and he had invested it well. Even if Shannon took half, Ryan would never have to worry about money ever again. But part of him almost didn't feel it was worth it, if he didn't know how long he'd be here. Ryan might have been confident in his ability to develop a team, to build something solid and lasting and successful, but he didn't know how long Conroy's leash would be.

Walking across the causeway, he was reminded that no matter how busy he was and no matter how many people he talked to in any given day, it was a pretty fucking lonely existence. Especially compared to his playing days, when he would have Murph and his wife over for dinner or go to their house pretty much every day they were home, when he would be hanging with the boys every single night they were on the road. And he was reminded, with a sudden, stinging little shock, that he'd been pretty fucking lonely for…a really long time. Even while he was married.

Part of him wanted to text Shannon or call her and ask, *Is this how you felt too? Is this why you locked me out?* But she had been pretty clear about the fact that he shouldn't do that. Instead, Ryan paused on the walk, looked out over the Charles River and the lights on the bridges, and thought about how he had kind of fucked up his life. He'd landed on his feet, sure. But there had been a lot of things he just…hadn't thought about. Hadn't seen.

He wondered if that was part of getting to middle age. Being able to look back on shit you'd missed out on, shit you hadn't done, and realizing that above everything else, you *regretted* it.

He wondered what Aronson was doing. Ryan knew that he lived in the South End, but beyond that, he didn't know anything about what the guy was like outside of work, where he was mostly glowering, arguing, or snapping Ryan's head off. Ryan wondered if Aronson liked to cook, whether his apartment was as spare and empty as Ryan's would probably be. He had said to Petey that his parents were older—Ryan wondered how old. He wondered if Aronson was getting ready to sleep, whether he was in bed, whether he was—

But all of this was stupid. It didn't accomplish anything. It didn't matter what Aronson was doing or what his apartment was like: Aronson hated him, too. Ryan took a deep breath, and shrugged his shoulders like that alone could clear the weight. He walked back to his hotel room and resolved that, no matter what else happened, he was going to find a new place to live within the next two weeks.

There.

That was a goal, something solid, that he could work toward. The rest of it? That was just noise.

Eric wasn't going soft, he told himself, it was just that if he wanted to keep his job, he couldn't fight tooth and nail with Sullivan *all* of the time. He had to be professional, and he had to continue working with the forwards and coaching the power play. It didn't help that no matter what he tried, the power play remained abysmal. To some extent, he knew that it was the lack of a good quarterback. Having a defenseman back there who could really *move the puck* completely opened the game up for the forwards. But what he had to work with could be considered at best "pretty grim" and at worst "pylons."

If he wanted to keep his job, he had to stop arguing with Sullivan, and he had to get the power play cooking. He honestly wasn't sure which one was more difficult, in the end. Part of him was beginning to enjoy the sparring, look forward to the way Sullivan's brown eyes would flash whenever Eric challenged him. The answering thrill low in his stomach.

His mother had started asking about Sullivan in the morning, like she was actually eager for updates about all of the woo-woo bullshit he spouted after the games.

"Maman, it's just stupid hockey clichés," Eric insisted.

"I think he has a point, tateleh. It's a little different, don't you think? The boys seem to like it. It's not the same old things they usually hear."

"It's just a bunch of stupid nonsense," Eric grumbled, as he got his coffee together. It was more small-area drills at practice today, and he was specifically working with the power play with an exercise designed to cut the amount of time they spent passing around looking for the best shot and starting to just take *a* shot. "He's charming, so everyone just ignores the fact that he isn't actually saying *anything*."

His mother made a noise of assent that was not a noise of agreement. He'd become very used to all of her nonverbal cues over the years, especially when they spoke on the phone, because like many Jewish mothers, she could express an entire book's worth of information in one *hmm*. "Well, he listens to you?"

"I mean…yes, sort of."

"He values your opinion? Petey's opinion?"

"Yes…"

"Then listen, Éric, I know you feel you should have gotten the job, and honestly, I agree that you are qualified and have put in the time. But you didn't. I think maybe you should give this Sullivan more of a chance before you start—and no, I know how you can get when you are upset about something. You are so stubborn, my darling."

Eric thought about protesting, but that would prove her point. Instead, he ran his hand through his hair and frowned at his coffee thermos. "It's just…he's got all of these stupid high-minded ideals and we just do not have the *roster* for it, 'Man. We've got a few kids that maybe that kind of approach will really help, but we've got a roster of fu—of veterans. They're struggling. They're *really* struggling."

"Maybe you just need to give them some more time. It's not like you're making the playoffs this year."

"Wow, *ow*, brutal."

"It's just the truth. But come, Éric, you were never one to shy from a challenge. It doesn't sound like a bad situation. Look at that lawsuit in Long Island, that poor boy there. Things could be so much worse. It's all in how you look at it."

"I'm *looking* at it like Sullivan is a pain in my ass."

"Tateleh."

"I know, 'Man. I know."

They were playing at home at the Spectrum that night, and it was the kind of game that Eric hated to lose. It was a Saturday night game. Against the Colorado Black Bears, one of the top teams in the league. In front of a home crowd, the kind of loud, drunk Boston crowd that he had always despised during his childhood and then during his playing days, even though Calgary and Boston had no particular skin in the game against each other. It was just that old growing-up-in-Montreal feeling, the old rivalry impossible to shake even when he'd been working in Boston for years. But now they were his assholes, and he hated when the team put on a bad show in front of them.

Beforehand, he was aware that it would be a difficult game. Colorado had a dangerous array of assets on both defense and forward, so if you cheated to cover one you were leaving the other to activate. The forecheck could morph immediately from a pretty typical 1-2-1 to an aggressive 2-1-2, and he wasn't entirely sure that some of the defensemen, particularly the rookies, would adjust well to cover it. The defensemen were Petey's problem, of course, but Petey had other shit to worry about, like the fact that the east-west rush Colorado loved so dearly was going to wreak hell on his bottom-six.

Eric had gone over the game plan with Sullivan and Petey beforehand, but standing behind the bench during the national anthem, he didn't feel particularly confident. He could already tell he was fidgeting. Catching himself pushing his glasses farther up his nose, running a hand through his hair. All of the stupid tells that meant that even while he was focusing his brain on the task at hand, the subconscious parts of it were fucking *worrying.*

Petey glanced sideways at him.

"It's a losing season," Eric said, "so tell me why I give a shit?"

"Because you're a competitive bastard and you hate to lose."

"A rhetorical question, Petey."

"Don't ask a question you don't want an answer to," Petey said serenely.

Eric scowled at him, then looked sideways. Sullivan was already standing on the bench, watching the third line standing at attention under the shifting lights that accompanied the anthem. He practically bounced in place, all nervous energy, and Eric immediately felt annoyed that they were both doing these things. He thought about grabbing Sullivan by his broad shoulders and gripping hard, *forcing* him to stay still. If he could force Sullivan into stillness, he could will himself into line.

He forced himself to calm. Exhaled. Took stock of everyone on the bench: the third line was taking the first shift, so at his left, Cook and Williams and Sinclair sat ready to jump onto the ice when the call to change lines came.

The game started out disastrous. Davey let in two quick goals fairly early in the first, and the team was getting caved in on several levels, both possession and shot-share. The team's internal metrics on the iPad were pretty grim. "I think we should have the forwards spread out a little more to counter the rush," he snapped, after Colorado jumped on yet another turnover and took it back into the Beacons' zone.

"That's just asking for trouble," Sullivan said, shaking his head. "The way Colorado attacks, we've got to focus on the main—"

"What are you *talking* about, Sullivan?"

"Listen to me," Sullivan said curtly. He was almost at eye level, standing on the bench. His light brown eyes were alight with anger, for once, not focused on the play on the ice. Below them, the players were studiously trying to ignore the argument, shuffling down the bench as they had to come on and off the bench. "You don't need to agree with me, but on the ice, you need to fucking respect me, and if I say we are deploying the forwards in a particular way, then we are deploying the forwards that way. Do you *understand*?"

The righteous fury flared in his stomach. Respect? Seriously? When had he *ever* been disrespectful, especially to someone who talked a big game about collaboration but didn't seem to be willing to listen when he felt he was right.

There were a number of things he could think of that he wanted to say in response. There were a number of things he would have liked to do in response, namely, pushing Sullivan off of the bench and seeing what would happen if he fell on his ass on the floor and its thick coating of spit and blood and mucous and melted snow.

Instead, he said, "I understand," and tried with all of his might to telekinetically punch Sullivan in the face.

In the intermission between the first and second, Sullivan did what he did best, which was wait ten minutes or so to give the guys time, and then go to stand in the middle of the dressing room and give a speech. He talked passionately about the lapsed defensive coverage, the way that they needed to play *on top* of the opposition, how you couldn't give them an inch or they'd take a mile. It was hard to look away from him when he got like that, stalking around the room like some kind of big cat, doing half of the talking with his hands. It was no wonder the team would run through a wall for him.

"We just need to watch our sticks," Sullivan concluded. "Stay out of the box. Come on, boys. You've got it in you, we just need to execute."

Eric had never been one for speeches, either as a player or a coach. The few times he'd had to talk to the room during intermissions, he'd mostly focused on the video screen and talking strategy. It wasn't that he was envious of Sullivan's ability to just step in front of a group of people and start *talking*, like every game was St. Crispin's Day. If he ever wanted to become a head coach, he'd probably have to learn how to do it, even if it seemed ridiculous.

People didn't respond to him the way they responded to Sullivan. That was a personality failing, maybe.

In the tunnel, as the team psyched themselves up to go back on the ice, Eric went up to Cook and Williams and Sinclair, all of whom were leaning against the wall and waiting. Cook bounced up and down on his skates, a wiggly little dance, and he looked up curiously when Eric approached.

"Hey, Coach?" Cook said, but waited for Eric to go on before following up on the question.

"Boys," Eric said. "Specifically, when the Bears come up on the rush, you gotta cut to the middle immediately. That's where the attack's going to be focused. There'll be the F3 high, but the D2 is the one you're going to really need to cut off to disrupt things."

Williams turned that serious gaze on him, his eyebrows raised a little bit. It was a curious, measuring look, open to what Eric was saying, but wary anyway. "That's not what Coach Sully said."

"Look," Eric said, frustrated, three seconds away from grabbing his hair and yanking fistfuls of it out right then and there. "I want to win. I think you want to win, too. Sullivan's always talking about reads and making your own decisions, so don't you think you can make one goddamn decision if I'm *right*?"

Cook and Williams exchanged a glance, like they weren't particularly sure about this, and Sinclair exhaled a long, slow breath. "I don't wanna get in the middle of whatever—is going on here," he said slowly. "But if it's the right play…it's the right play."

Whether it was Sullivan's locker room speech, Eric's tactical adjustment or Davey the goalie turning on another gear and making a few key desperation saves, the team managed to slowly fight their way back into the game. Williams somehow sauced a ridiculous pass through traffic to Cook for an insanely bad-angled one-timer that nevertheless managed to glance off the goalie's shoulder and into the back of the net. With screams of joy, the team converged on him, and just like that, they were back in it.

Eric could feel Sullivan's eyes boring a hole in the back of his head from his vantage point on the bench, but he did his best not to look. Sullivan wasn't stupid: he could see what the first line was doing, and he could see that it wasn't what he had asked them to do. He was furious, that much was clear, his sturdy little body practically trembling with suppressed frustration.

Eric had no idea what the fuck his problem was, because they were fighting back into the game, weren't they? And it was on the back of the adjustment. Sinclair had broken up three rushes since they'd made it, covering the D2.

By the time Afanasyev, who was practically a dinosaur in hockey years and slow as shit, managed to get a slapshot from the point on the power play that somehow lasered right through, everyone crowding the net to tie it up, Sullivan looked like a bomb about to go off. Eric had never seen him like this coaching before, only as a player. It was the kind of look that meant that someone was going to get a very embarrassing shorthanded goal scored on them.

In this intermission, Sullivan didn't come into the

room at all, he just paced in the hallway while Petey and Eric went over some video with the guys who needed it as the team changed and prepped for the third. It only got worse from there.

In the first thirty seconds of the period, the Black Bears scored in the middle of a nasty scrum in front of Davey's crease. It was one of those situations where the call could have gone either way, probably. Eric wouldn't have challenged: not when they were this close and risked opening up the lead even further. Sullivan, on the other hand, was practically apoplectic, signaling to the ref.

"Don't do it," Eric said, urgently.

"What do you mean, don't do it? Number 67 was fucking laying on Davey's leg. He couldn't get across to cover. I'm making a challenge."

"The review room calls *never* go in our favor. You want it to be a two-goal lead instead of a one-goal lead you could easily catch up to? Our penalty kill's been garbage. There's no way it wouldn't end up in the back of the net."

"Look at Davey, Aronson. Look at his face. We have to let him know that when this shit happens, we'll back him up."

"I don't think—"

"I didn't *ask* you what you thought," Sullivan said, in a voice entirely unlike anything that Eric had ever heard out of his mouth before. It was the kind of voice that made Eric stand a little straighter. The kind of voice that made him feel the prickly about-to-fight feeling he used to love and dread, all at the same time. The feeling that was so close to something else.

Even after the goal was called back, he couldn't

relax. And when Williams scored what turned out to be the game-winning goal on an absolutely beautiful rocket from the right circle and then Davey shut the door for the rest of the game, Sullivan stood with his arms crossed over his chest.

Jubilant at pulling off a gutsy win, the guys cellied on the ice, hugging it out and then skating forward to give Davey his taps and hugs. The baby goalie accepted them all, beaming, his sweaty hair plastered to his forehead, his cheeks red.

Sullivan was already off the bench, heading back to the locker room, and Petey glanced sideways at Eric with his eyebrows raised, as if to say *you done fucked up.* Which was fucking ridiculous: *they had won the game.* Eric headed back into the locker room himself, feeling absolutely murderous. If Sullivan was always going on about reads, then he should have been fucking happy that his concepts had worked. But that didn't seem to be the way it would go.

During the presser afterward, Eric went out to watch, which he usually didn't do. He stood in the back of the room, his arms crossed over his chest, as Sullivan answered questions from the beats.

Usually Sullivan was upbeat and even cheerful during the availabilities, cracking jokes and dispensing his little gems of wisdom to an admiring crowd, all of his charisma on display as the reporters ate out of his hand. Today he was curt and visibly pissed off, particularly when Kayla Lawrence, one of the writers from the *Globe*, asked about the midgame tactical adjustment. Eric couldn't even really make out the answer over the roar of frustration in his own ears, like an ocean wave.

He didn't speak to Sullivan after the presser. He didn't speak to Sullivan during the normal postgame routines, when the guys were showering and doing their cool-down workouts and heading into the kitchen to find out what meals the nutritionists and in-house chefs had provided for them. Eric was going to have to speak to him eventually. This wasn't the kind of shit he could let go. Unbidden, his mother's voice in his ear: *You are so stubborn, my darling.*

He would have to say something. He just had to wait to get Sullivan alone.

Being on a rebuilding team meant that there wasn't the same kind of pressure you'd have on a contender, but that didn't mean that Ryan wasn't constantly aware of the internal pressure he'd placed on himself. The pressure to make sure that the guys were learning, that he was steering the team in the right direction, that night by night, he could see tangible improvements. Overall, he'd been happy with the start to the season. All of the guys he'd wanted to see take steps forward had done it. They were sitting at or around .500 on any given night. The losses weren't blowouts. The team was engaged in practices.

They had even won that night against the Black Bears, which would have normally been something to savor. Colorado was where he'd like to see the team in five years, a Cup contender with no glaring holes in the roster, playing fast, physical hockey, constantly a threat in all three zones.

Ryan should have been happy about it.

Ryan *was* happy about it.

Unfortunately the happiness regarding the result of

the game was drowned out by the argument he'd had on the bench with Aronson and the fact that no matter what he'd tried to do to show the man that his way of coaching was actually getting results—even the results themselves, staring them both in the face—Aronson simply refused to stop…well, Aronson was unable to stop being a fucking *dick* about everything.

Ryan had managed to get through the presser without visibly reflecting that he was annoyed in any way. He had always prided himself on his ability to shrug things off: he'd had to do it a lot over his career. Starting out as a short undrafted nobody had meant he'd taken a lot of shit his first few seasons, on the ice and off it. He'd let it roll off his back and focused on proving them all wrong.

This was—this was different.

Aronson was irrationally, infuriatingly determined to piss in Ryan's cereal. No matter what he did, Aronson disagreed. Disagreed loudly and often in front of the guys. Ryan had tried over the last month or so to talk to him about it, but every time Aronson had pushed his glasses farther up his nose and peered down at Ryan like a bird of prey staring at roadkill, and glared until Ryan eventually gave up.

Today, though. Today Ryan was pissed off enough that he wasn't going to let Aronson glare his way out of it. There was being a dick and there was blatantly ignoring Ryan's preferred systems and telling the guys to do something completely different in the heat of the moment. There was challenging him on the bench in front of the whole team. It wasn't like Ryan was unreasonable or unwilling to listen to his assistant coaches, but this had been beyond insubordination, this had been fucking insulting.

He made it back to the office before Aronson did, and he furiously set about diagramming what he had wanted the forwards to do on the breakout, versus what Aronson had told them to do. It was one thing to see it in the heat of the moment on the ice but somehow worse to have it all laid out there in black and white and red.

He was still scribbling angrily when the door opened. Ryan didn't bother turning around; this late after a game, it was only ever going to be Aronson.

"What are you doing?" Aronson asked. He sounded amused, his faint accent a little stronger the way it always was when he was making fun.

"Drawing you a diagram," Ryan snapped, "because you apparently didn't understand what I was talking about on the bench."

"I understood perfectly. I just thought that considering the aggressive way their D were pinching all night, an adjustment was in order."

"Then you discuss that with *me* first, you don't—"

"Oh?" Aronson said, and laughed.

Ryan whirled around to confront him. It must have looked comical to an outsider: Aronson well over six feet tall and gangly as hell, a lopsided smirk on his face; Ryan at least half a foot shorter, stocky and red-faced with fury. He almost never lost his temper, but even he had his limits, and weeks of this bullshit had caught up with him.

"Because I seem to remember you talking a pretty high-and-mighty game about collaboration when you first got here, and this is kinda dictatorial, *Napoleon*—"

"What the fuck is wrong with you, Aronson?" Ryan demanded. His hands felt white-knuckled, clenched in fists at his sides. "Why the hell do you hate trying to work with me so much? I've never been anything except accommodating, I've never been anything except nice—"

"You've never been anything except a fucking Hall of Fame superstar who waltzed in here and took my fucking *job*, Sullivan. You're nothing except a guy who gets everything fucking *handed to him* when I've worked for years to earn this."

Ryan felt like the top of his head was going to explode in a cloud of smoke and lava, like an erupting volcano. As they argued he could see Aronson's face getting redder and redder too, the taciturn smirk that pissed Ryan off so much vanishing into something more dangerous.

Aronson's full mouth was pressed into a thin line, twitching with fury. The dark brown eyes were narrowed, fixed on Ryan with the kind of attention that really did remind him of nothing so much as a falcon, the kind of mad energy that a bird on jesses had. His whole body leaned into Ryan's personal space, like he could intimidate him into backing down with sheer size alone.

Well. That was his first mistake. Ryan hadn't spent almost eighteen years playing in the league against guys who were taller and heavier to be easily intimidated. He glared right back, even if he had to look up to do it. Ryan couldn't have stopped himself if he'd tried. "Everything *handed to him*? Do you have any idea how hard I fucking worked to make it into the league in the first place? You of all people should understand—"

"We are *nothing* alike—"

"Yeah, it's not my fault you never got the hardware and that you never won *shit*."

As the words came out of his mouth, he was aware that it was a step too far. A low blow considering that the Cup was the one thing everyone wanted, and so few people were able to win. Sometimes it was the difference between a Hall of Fame career and eventually being a has-been everyone talked about in hushed terms, like, what would it have been if he could have just won a Cup? It was even worse because Aronson had almost gotten there with Calgary, back in 2009, and Ryan's team had swept them right out of it.

He shouldn't have said it, but it was too late to back down now.

Aronson stared down at him, his whole body vibrating like if he opened his mouth something absolutely vile was going to come out of it, like if he moved even one inch, he was going to do something violent he'd regret later. Ryan remembered the year Aronson had broken 200 penalty minutes and almost laughed; of course Ryan would be unlucky enough to end up having to share the bench with the kind of guy who had had multiple biting scandals *and* get along with him so badly to the point that they were about to come to blows in their office.

He could feel the sting in the air, almost like electricity crackled between them, like if he said the wrong thing the spark would send the whole room up in flames.

"Aronson—" Ryan started, intending to try to diffuse the situation after all, but the words were trapped on his tongue when Aronson moved forward suddenly, faster than Ryan would have thought possible. The entire weight of his body shoved Ryan back against the whiteboard, and when Ryan opened his mouth to yelp in surprise, Aronson's lips came down hard on his and Ryan's entire brain shorted out.

For several long seconds he couldn't even think about

what was happening in a logical way. He'd never kissed a man before. He had never even considered it. Ryan had kissed a normal amount of girls as a kid, and then he'd met Shannon in his freshman year of college, and after that, he'd only ever kissed her.

Kissing Shannon that first time had felt like fireworks going off in his head, like the world had suddenly aligned into a way that made complete and perfect sense.

Kissing Aronson was like fireworks, too, but it felt like he was drowning, like nothing would ever make sense again. He was insanely conscious of Aronson's five-o'clock shadow rough against his chin, of Aronson's big hands gripping his shoulders, of Aronson's tongue fucking his mouth, of Aronson's furnace of a body pressed up against his, of the way Aronson had him bracketed in against the whiteboard, the metal strip where the erasers would sit digging painfully into his back, all of the pens clattering to the floor as he squirmed.

Ryan was shocked to find that Aronson wasn't just kissing him, but Ryan was kissing him back, eagerly, hungrily. It wasn't something he'd done consciously at all. His body reacted instinctively and before his mind could scream, *what the fuck are you doing?*, his hands had somehow made their way up to grab Aronson by the hair—it was thick and curly and easy to wind his fingers into—and yank his head down so he couldn't escape.

He could hear his own breath in his ears, ragged and gasping, could feel Aronson's wandering hands, grabbing his ass and pulling him in closer, hitching him up so that his feet weren't even touching the ground, pinned between the whiteboard and Aronson's body.

His legs automatically hooked themselves around Aronson's hips—

The whole thing was fucking nuts.

It was *insane*.

And Ryan couldn't have stopped if one of their players had shown up at the door, shocked to find his coaches, well. The only way to describe what was happening to Ryan was *getting mauled* and *loving it*.

Aronson kissed like he used to play hockey, vicious and dirty and competitive. His mouth was hot and anything but giving; the kiss had teeth in it. Ryan was perfectly happy to bite back, and when he did Aronson shuddered and redoubled his efforts, his nose bumping Ryan's, his glasses smudgy from breath and skin.

It was like being on the ice again in the middle of a game, when all of his senses felt heightened and he could react entirely on instinct, like every scrape of a blade on the ice and every flash of color at the corner of his eye was a secret message just for him, a map to a win.

Except now instead of the sound of metal on ice he had the deep groan Aronson made when Ryan let go of his hair with one hand and dragged it down his back. Instead of the bright blues and reds of jerseys he had Aronson's brown-and-gold-flecked eyes, open and furious, his pupils huge and dilated. And instead of the goal horn, he had the hot length of Aronson's erection, grinding into his thigh.

That was what finally snapped him out of his dazed, almost drugged haze. "Aronson," he managed, his voice ragged. "We have to—we can't—"

"Oh, fuck," Aronson said, and immediately dropped him. He was breathing hard, his shirt askew where Ryan had pulled it out of its careful tuck, his hair wild where Ryan had yanked at it. He blinked, then said again, "Oh, *fuck*."

It took Ryan a second to get his balance again. He lifted his hand to touch his mouth, his chin, a little red and raw from the scrape of Aronson's stubble. He felt like he had to go through concussion protocol. "I—uh—well. That was. One way to handle a coaching dispute."

"I didn't mean—" Aronson started.

"What you should be apologizing for is being a *dick* on the bench and messing up my goddamn diagrams—"

"That's what you're worried about *now*? I should've kissed you fucking *harder*."

Strangely, Ryan could feel himself flushing, like he was a teenager again or something. "You *should've* listened to me."

"Oh my god," Aronson was saying, looking at the smudged ink on the whiteboard. His smile twitched, so obnoxious that Ryan wondered what would happen if he kissed Aronson again to shut him up. "You only messed it like halfway up. You want a step stool next time?"

"The fuck do you mean, next time?" Ryan demanded, his heart beating so hard that he could hear it in his ears.

Instead of answering, Aronson took another step forward and leaned down. He took Ryan's face in his hands and Ryan was aware that at any second, he could have slapped Aronson's hands away, hit him in the stomach, pushed him to get him to stop. He didn't do any of those things. He let Aronson kiss him again. It was slower this time, less angry, but no less world-skewing.

Ryan was forty-five years old and apparently learning some really surprising things about himself, like the fact that Aronson, obnoxious, annoying, frustrating

Aronson, had a particular way of kissing him with full-out intensity and then starting to pull away in the exact manner that had Ryan's body leaning into it. Chasing after it. It wasn't until Aronson had stepped back again, smirking, that he realized what he was doing.

"Yeah. Like right then, Sully."

"I—" Ryan started. He realized, belatedly, he hadn't thought about *what* he was going to say. He was still pissed at Aronson for the game debacle, but he was also embarrassed. And hard. And—

"That's what I thought," Aronson said, grinning, and turned on his heel to leave.

"This isn't the last you're gonna hear about this, asshole."

"Oh, I bet."

And Ryan was left to sit there with dry-erase marker smeared all over his sweater, an inconvenient erection and even more inconvenient truths about himself to reconsider.

All in all. It had not been his best day.

CHAPTER SIX

November

Eric fast-walked out of the coach's office and then down the hall. His palms still felt sweaty and his heart pounded in his chest. He was glad that by this time of night no one was still in the arena, because he also had a pretty inconveniently obvious…well, it was obvious what he had been doing. Even if no one probably would have guessed who he'd been doing it with.

He still couldn't entirely believe that it had happened. That it had happened the way it had. He almost couldn't remember exactly *how* it had happened. Only that he had been furious and Sullivan was looking up at him with equally furious eyes and he'd reacted before he could even think about it.

It was always a gamble, with another guy like that. Even if he stared at you a lot, the way Sullivan had done since they started working together, that didn't necessarily mean anything. Even if you thought there was maybe a chance that he was *looking* it didn't necessarily mean that anything physical would be welcome, would start anything except a fight.

Eric had been playing hockey for a long time and

he'd known he was queer for almost as long. It was a weird space to exist in, knowing there had to have been other guys like him playing, but not knowing who they were, not wanting to even risk asking the questions that could lead to finding out.

Once, when he'd been drunk and feeling kind of daring, he'd slipped into a gay bar after a game on the road in Los Angeles. Just to see what it was like. Come face-to-face with one of his teammates. They'd both stared at each other, frozen, neither willing to say anything. He'd beaten a hasty retreat and they'd just never mentioned it again.

This wasn't the past, though. This was the present. This wasn't his teammate, this was *Ryan Sullivan*, and he was being just as stupid. It was a risky thing to do. Sullivan could have punched him, could have had him fired, could have done any number of disastrous things.

Instead, Sullivan had just—

Eric could hear his heartbeat in his ears again, thinking about the way Sullivan had melted under the initial onslaught, the way he'd licked his lips when Eric had taken his face in his hands to kiss him again. The way his teeth had felt digging into Eric's lip. The way his biceps felt under Eric's grip. The way he'd groaned low in his throat when Eric shoved his tongue in his mouth. The way his solid, sturdy fucking body had fit against Eric's.

He shouldn't even be thinking about this still. He should put it entirely out of his fucking head. Sullivan was his *boss*, Sullivan was an asshole he had to work with day in and day out, Sullivan was probably his least-favorite person to see in the entire goddamn world. A smiling, overly optimistic jackass who'd had everything just handed to him.

But Sullivan kissed him back like… Eric wasn't good with metaphors. He couldn't think of anything to compare it to. He couldn't remember the last time anyone had kissed him like that, like there was nowhere else he'd rather be.

Whatever else Sullivan was, he definitely wasn't straight. And whatever else Sullivan was, he was definitely fucking *annoying*. Just because he kissed Eric like it was some kind of religious revelation didn't mean that anything was going to change between them.

He absolutely could not, and would not, touch Ryan Sullivan like that again.

He just had to go back to his tiny, quiet apartment, alone, and forget it had ever happened.

Ryan stumbled out to his car. His head still felt like it was spinning, completely off-balance. But he wasn't sure if he was off-balance or if it was the rest of the world that had been completely knocked off of its axis. Now that he wasn't in that office, with Aronson so close to him, with the promise of Aronson's mouth against his and Aronson's hands on his body, it was like—Jesus fucking Christ, he'd just been lifted up and kissed stupid against his own fucking whiteboard by another man.

There was being kissed by another man and there was being kissed by another man and liking it. Liking it so much that he was still thinking about it, that he could still feel the hot press of Aronson's mouth against his, a memory like a ghost of a touch.

That was pretty fucking gay.

Was *he* gay?

Ryan tried to think about a time in his life when he'd been attracted to a guy, and he was coming up blank. Sure, he noticed when other men were good-looking, but that was just a normal thing to notice. It was just a general aesthetic acknowledgment, right? Didn't everyone appreciate a good-looking person? In youth hockey, sometimes guys would mess around, but he'd never even done that. Had never even considered that someone would be interested in doing that with him. Then he'd met Shannon his freshman year and never even thought about hooking up with anyone besides her after.

But there was really no other way to look at it. Aronson had kissed him, and Ryan's head felt like it was going to implode every time he thought about it, every time he thought about doing it again.

Doing it again?

What the hell was he even thinking about?

His phone buzzed, and because Shannon had impeccable comedic timing, she had written, When do you want to come home to pick up your shit.

Ryan stared at the text message. He thought, again, about Aronson pinning him against the whiteboard. He'd been married for twenty-five years and within the last...god, he couldn't even remember how long, he had barely felt anything kissing Shannon. It had been familiar and comfortable, but there wasn't anything behind it. The reason he felt so rattled wasn't just because Aronson was a man but because kissing him felt—raw. He hadn't realized how much he'd been missing that feeling until it happened.

I'll have to wait until we have a day off at home. So probably not until Thanksgiving.

I won't be in the house. So that's fine. I'll text you a temporary code.

Shannon, you know I'm not going to be trying to get into the house if you don't want me there.

By the time he buckled his seat belt, she still hadn't written back, and Ryan exhaled. He still wasn't entirely sure what had happened to his marriage. It was clear that somewhere along the line they had lost the passion they'd had in the beginning. And that was even before things had started to go *wrong* wrong. But he didn't understand what he had done to earn this kind of treatment. He wondered if Shannon had met someone, if she didn't want him stumbling across something awkward that would hurt her in the divorce proceedings.

But that was stupid, too. He wasn't contesting anything. A fair split was what she deserved for supporting his career as long as she had, even if it had been too much in the end. A boyfriend before the papers were final wouldn't have changed that.

It was weird. He thought he would've been more upset at the thought, but he didn't feel anything. The more time that went by the more Ryan started to realize that the marriage had been over long before he'd realized it. He wondered how long Shannon had known.

He wondered what she would've thought if she'd been a fly on the wall of his office the other night. Probably better not to know.

Ryan pressed the ignition and pulled out of the space. Jesus, he hadn't even had the time to think about the game and what he needed to talk to the guys about tomorrow. All right: that was it. First order of business, upon returning home, would be to lesson plan. Aronson, Shannon, all of it: that had to go on the back burner.

Easier said than done, but no one had ever said Ryan Sullivan was anything except stubborn as hell.

Eric woke up the next day to his mother's phone call and a splitting headache, even though he hadn't had anything to drink. For once in his life, he didn't really feel like talking to her.

He answered anyway and they went through the usual greetings and pleasantries. He told her a little bit about the game, about the win. Even though her eyesight wasn't very good anymore, she watched every match, and she usually had thoughts about them. This time, she wanted to know why he had been arguing with Ryan Sullivan on the bench.

"We just have really different views of the way things should be," Eric said, which wasn't untrue.

"You need to learn how to get along with your coworkers, even if they're wrong," his mother scolded him. There wasn't any bite in it, and she'd been telling him the same thing since he was in primary school and getting detentions for fighting. Except in that situation, there had always been the unspoken exception, like kicking the shit out of a boy who'd thrown pennies at him.

Eric thought about the argument on the bench. The frustrating thing was that Sullivan wasn't even *really* wrong. He'd been especially right about the coach's challenge. Eric wasn't about to tell his mother that, though. Even at eighty-two she had a steel trap memory, and he wasn't going to give her future ammunition. Instead, he went for the tried-and-true tactic of changing the subject.

"What are your plans for today, 'Man?"

"I'm going to meet Hélène Roback for lunch."

"Oh, that should be nice. Are you going to have someone drive you?"

"She'll pick me up; she's eighty-five but her eyes are better than yours, probably. And you know, we were talking earlier this week, and she has a granddaughter who's living in Boston right now, she's doing her residency at Boston Medical Center, and she's a really lovely girl *and* she's going into derm—"

"Maman, *no*."

"I could put you in touch if you wanted. I'm sure she'd love to meet you for coffee. She's a Royal fan, but maybe she could put the rivalry aside for you."

Eric pinched the bridge of his nose above the glasses. He loved his mom dearly, but she had her fatal flaws. One of them was constantly trying to marry him off to whichever daughter or granddaughter of her friends happened to be single and available. It had only gotten worse since his father's death, like she had suddenly realized her own mortality and the fact that Eric would be alone when she died. She was determined to find someone to keep him company before she passed and channeled a good amount of her energy into that.

It was annoying, sure. But Eric knew it also came from a deep place of love and loneliness, so even when he got frustrated, he had to temper it. All his mother had ever wanted for him was to be happy, and this was the last gift she was trying to give him. If he thought about it too much—if he thought about losing her too—it was overwhelming. So he put up with her efforts at becoming his own personal shadchan without protesting too much.

It wasn't like a relationship with a woman was out of the question. Eric liked women, had had short relationships with women. He'd only ever really had short relationships with *anyone*. But women or men, he didn't really trust his mom's taste, which tended to run to "is she available, Jewish and in possession of a pulse."

Sometimes, if he thought about the nebulous future, it was nice to imagine having Shabbat dinner with some faceless, disembodied person, someone who would understand why he'd want to take trips to the cemetery to leave pebbles on his father's grave.

In practice, all of the dates he'd gone on that his mother had set up had either ended disastrously when he'd put his foot in his mouth or fizzled out after the fifth or sixth follow-up when he and the woman inevitably realized that they had nothing in common besides their shared cultural background.

Unbidden, an image of Sullivan flashed across his vision. Eyes wide open, looking up at Eric with desire and a challenge he couldn't resist meeting.

God*damn*it.

"'Man, I have to go get ready for work," Eric said.

"Okay, tateleh. I love you."

"I love you, too," he said, and added, "Can you cool it on trying to set me up with anyone for a bit? I'm still trying to adjust to this new work situation."

"Of course," his mother said, and Eric wanted to laugh: that would last all of a week, probably. She was almost as stubborn as Sullivan when she had something she wanted to dig her heels in about.

Unfortunately, work was no less frustrating. There was no game today, but they were still having a morning practice, which Eric usually loved. There was nothing like being on the ice again, even if it wasn't in a playing capacity. Today he couldn't enjoy it because no matter where he was, Sullivan was always fucking underfoot. It was almost like their playing days again, where no matter what open space he tried to find on the ice, Sullivan was there, blocking the way, being a fucking pest.

The last straw snapped while Eric tried to lead the forwards in one of the small-area drills that Sullivan was so fond of. He buzzed by close, like he was a fighter plane strafing a target. Eric gave him a shove in the shoulder and said, "Watch where you're fucking going, Coach."

Sullivan whirled around, those whiskey-brown eyes alight with a challenge. "Get out of my way, then. Coach."

For a second Eric wished they were wearing pads so he could crosscheck Sullivan. Just a little bit. The players were staring at them, so he didn't do anything else, even though he dearly wanted to flip his middle finger up at Sullivan to let him know what he thought about all of this. Instead, he turned back to the drill and passed a puck to Härmälä so that the team could begin the next phase of the practice.

It didn't get any better, though.

No matter what he did, Sullivan was always there, always in his personal space. It was frustrating and annoying, and it made him think, again, of just picking Sullivan up and slamming him into the wall. It made him think of things he had promised himself he wasn't going to think about, and it didn't get any easier once practice was over and the team had showered and headed home to rest.

The coaching staff usually stayed after the practices to discuss tape and the progress the players had made;

today was no exception. Petey especially had a lot to say about the progress, or lack thereof, with their veterans. Some of them were adjusting. Some of them weren't. The deeper they got into November, the more it became clear who was going to work with the new system and who would need to be on the way out at the trade deadline. Conroy liked to have weekly updates.

There was always something to do.

It was the same there, too. Sullivan was always too close. He shouldered Eric aside like he wasn't the one who'd just gotten into his space. He was close enough that Eric could smell his hair, fresh from the showers. It was infuriating and he could feel his eyebrows drawing down in a deeper and deeper frown.

He didn't say anything. Not in front of Petey.

But then Petey rubbed his eyes and said, "All right, boys. You got my updates, and I got a splitting fucking headache. I'm going to head home to sleep it off. You'll be all right finishing up here without me?"

"Perfectly fine," Sullivan said, grinning a foxy grin, all of his teeth flashing.

All of the hair on Eric's arms stood on end. The premonition of disaster. But he ignored it, fist-bumped Petey as he shuffled out of the room, squinting and rubbing his eyes again.

Once they were alone, Eric turned on him. "What the fuck is wrong with you?"

"You're really shit at staying out of the way," Sullivan said. He was smirking, that little bastard, like he knew exactly how much he'd gotten under Eric's skin, exactly how much he'd been trying not to think about what had happened the night before.

For a second, Eric had a flash of doubt as to where

this was going. Whether all of the incidental touches, the inability to get out of the fucking *way* was an encouragement or another form of torture, a reminder of what he couldn't have.

"You," he said, "are a pain in my fucking *ass*."

Sullivan set the papers he was holding down on the desk. He was still standing so close that Eric could feel that irresistible current between them, like a magnet. It was chilly in that room, always, because it was so close to ice level and mostly cinder blocks on the wall and concrete on the floor, and no one had bothered to make sure the heaters worked efficiently. It didn't matter, because Eric's entire body was on fire just from the proximity.

Sullivan opened his stupid, annoying mouth and said, "That sounds like a personal issue you need to work on," and before Eric could even think about what he was doing, he had closed the distance between them and grabbed Sullivan by the shoulders. At first, he was intending to shake him, like everyone said you should never do with a child, but before he could do anything else Sullivan had looked up at him with that stupid challenge Eric found impossible not to meet.

It was worse this time, because he already knew exactly what Sullivan felt like when he was opening his mouth eagerly to a kiss, exactly the way Sullivan tasted, exactly the way his hand felt winding into Eric's hair and yanking. He already knew, and it somehow still blew even the last kiss out of the water. It should have been impossible, that one person was so fucking annoying and also felt so fucking good under his hands, under his mouth.

Every resolution he'd made not to do this again went up in smoke as Sullivan's hands eagerly explored his body, grabbing his ass to yank him closer. Somehow during the initial onslaught, he'd backed Sullivan up against the desk, didn't realize it until there was nowhere else to push him. Sullivan didn't seem to mind, kept making these stupid noises against Eric's lips, gasps of encouragement, urging him on.

It had been a long time since he'd kissed anyone like this, openmouthed and biting and desperate, like the clash of tongue and lips and teeth was as much the point as any further destination. It was just his fucking luck that it was Sullivan that did this to him, that it was Sullivan who was panting into his mouth, his hands grabbing at any part of Eric that he could reach.

Leaning forward, Eric pushed at the papers, scattering them away, then lifted Sullivan up to set him down there. He tried to pull back a second, so he could see what Sullivan looked like, rumpled and debauched in the middle of all of his stupid plans, but he could only manage a second before Sullivan grabbed him by the shirt collar and yanked him back down. Fine. If Sullivan wanted to play that way, Eric could up the ante.

With the small amount of space Eric had left, looming over him, he managed to get his hand down Sullivan's pants and immediately discovered how fucking easy he was for all of this, already hot and hard in Eric's fingers. As soon as he touched Sullivan, he was rewarded with a long, ragged groan, with Sullivan finally relenting on the bruising kisses. His head drooped forward against Eric's chest, like he was looking down at Eric's hand where it was hidden by fabric.

"Fuck," Eric managed, although his voice sounded strange, too strained and high, "you horny little bastard, this was what you were after that whole practice?"

"Shut the fuck up and just—and just—"

Eric didn't have any words for the way it felt to have Sullivan firmly in hand, thrusting up into his grip, like he would die if Eric didn't jerk him off. He was already leaking, sticky on Eric's fingers. Eric was suddenly furious again, by the fact that this had just happened to him without his really thinking about it, how easily Sullivan had turned the tables on him. Eric might have had the upper hand the last time, but as soon as Sullivan had put his mind to *continuing this*, Eric was thrown off-balance.

He pulled back far enough to disentangle himself, ignoring Sullivan's attempts to pull him back. Yanked at Sullivan's pants and was rewarded when his eyes widened a little, like he was unsure about where this was going, not confident about what he wanted. For a second, Eric wondered, in his stupid, lust-fogged head, whether this was a bad idea.

Of course it was a bad idea. They were at work. They were in the arena. Anyone could walk in. But he simultaneously needed Sullivan's dick in his mouth *and* to prove to Sullivan himself that he had no fucking clue what he was doing, who he was messing with—

And then Sullivan was shifting his hips to help Eric along, his hands gripping the edge of the desk for support, mumbling, "Come on, come on, oh my god, please—"

It was the *please* that did it. Eric knelt. He was tall enough and the desk was low enough that it wasn't uncomfortable for him to be in this position, to reach where he needed to reach. He ran his hand up the length of Sullivan's dick, thumb dragging through the wetness leaking at the tip, rewarded by a groan and another jerk of his hips. With a bruising grip Eric pushed him down again, hands pressing into his thighs where they were trapped by the sweatpants, and then leaned down to take him in his mouth.

The noise Sullivan made when he did it was worth all of it, ragged and wanting and completely obscene.

Eric was aware of so many physical sensations just then. The cold concrete uncomfortable against his knees, Sullivan's hands twisting in his hair, Sullivan's *insane* thigh muscles shifting under his grip, the shape and taste of Sullivan in his mouth, the way it felt completely right and completely wrong all at the same time. Sullivan was noisy in this too, even while Eric was taking him apart with his mouth: incoherent but moaning, wordless but gasping.

Eric looked up and realized he was going to be jerking off to this image for a long fucking time: Sullivan with his thighs spread wide for Eric's body, arms shaking but holding himself up, head thrown back and mouth open, slack and stupid with what Eric was doing to him. He shifted, uncomfortably hard himself, had to press his palm flat against his own cock to keep things under control.

"God," Sullivan was saying, "Jesus fucking god, *Aronson*—I'm going, if you don't want—"

Eric squeezed his thigh to let him know that it was fine, and whether it was just the extra pressure or the fact that he'd been panting for it all fucking day before this, Sullivan came, shivering and with a noise that seared itself immediately into Eric's brain.

He swallowed. Ran his tongue over Sullivan's dick until it stopped pulsing, until Sullivan made a pained little whimper that indicated it was too much. Eric pulled off and leaned back to survey his handiwork and again, the picture it made… Fuck. Sullivan was still panting and red-faced, his eyes closed, his dick wet with spit and come, still hard and curving up toward his stomach, the rumpled pants and boxers pulled down around his thighs.

For a second, Eric felt transfixed, still on the floor but unable to move. And then Sullivan opened his eyes, huge and dark, and held out his hand. Almost against his will, Eric took it. Let Sullivan's strong grip yank him to his feet and into an embrace.

He was furious at himself for being in a position to discover that Sully, postcoital, was a *cuddler*. He molded himself up against Eric's body, mess and all, and kissed him like Eric wasn't dying himself, like his erection pressed between them wasn't painful as hell. He took Eric's face in his hand and angled him into the kiss, mouth salty and warm.

"Fuck," Sully was saying, "that was—*fuck*. Can I—"

"Oh, *now* you're asking for permission?"

Sully looked up at him, eyes heavy-lidded, and said, "Okay, well, do you want me to suck your dick or not? Because I can go home."

For a second, Eric thought about telling him to fuck off. Telling him that of course he didn't want this. That would've been the most obvious lie he'd ever told. Instead, he said, "Do you have any clue what you're doing?"

"No," Sully said, frankly. He was still holding Eric like they didn't hate each other, like they weren't in the arena, like this was all completely normal. For a second, Eric wondered whether Sully was the crazy man, or if he was. "But you clearly know what you're doing. Tell me what you like. Tell me what you want. I can learn."

Eric would have pinched the bridge of his nose again, if his hands hadn't been full of Sully. "This isn't a small-area drill."

"It also isn't fucking rocket science, bud. Come on. I'm not gonna bite you unless you're into that."

The fact was that even if Sully had been inclined to bite, Eric probably would've risked it. His whole body burned with wanting, with anticipation. He disentangled himself from the half embrace, pushed himself away from Sully's body, the warmth coming off of him in waves. He exhaled, shaky, and said, "Get on your knees."

To his surprise, Sully did it, eagerly, slid off of the desk, yanking his pants up as he went. He got down on his knees easily enough, with a little wince: hockey players might have been strong, but they weren't necessarily flexible. And Eric knew from experience that the floor was hard on the knees. Neither of them was getting younger.

Sully looked up at Eric from that position, his mouth still a little swollen from making out, from biting his lip when Eric went down on him, and said, "I'm going to get better at this."

"What do you mean, get better at this?" Eric asked, pulling his own pants down.

"I mean I don't know what I'm doing," Sully said, "but I'm going to—I hate being *bad* at things. I've always been good at learning."

Eric still felt like he should probably be entering concussion protocol. The conversation wasn't doing much to help. "Sully, I mean this in the worst way possible, but what the fuck is *wrong* with you?"

"Nothing," Sully said, grinning that foxy grin again. "I'm just competitive. You get it, I'm sure."

His hands were warm on Eric's thighs, and he licked his lips again, and Eric's brain decided that it wasn't worth arguing anymore. His dick was painful now, straining upward, and he had to take hold of it and stroke it, just to keep himself from making an embarrassing noise. Sully's eyes followed the line of his hand the entire time, dark and hungry.

"Shut up and suck my dick," Eric said.

"Okay, but you were the one with the hang-ups about this," Sully retorted, before he pushed Eric's hand away and took a closer look, like he was examining some kind of a tactical diagram. And then he leaned forward and ran his tongue experimentally over the head of Eric's dick, down the length of it. The whole time he did it, he didn't look away from Eric's face, like he was gauging his responses and adjusting accordingly.

When he finally slid his whole mouth around it, Eric couldn't help the involuntary, pained groan that ripped itself out of his mouth. Even though it was awkward and the rhythm was off as Sully went on by trial and error, it felt so fucking good.

It *looked* so fucking good, Sully's mouth stretched wide around him, the way he'd glance up through his thick, short eyelashes every now and then for guidance. What he lacked in technique he made up in enthusiasm, choking occasionally, eyes watering, but when Eric tried to push him away, he stubbornly kept at it. Thinking about that, feeling it, every part of Eric felt drawn and tight, trembling on the edge.

Sully's hands on his thighs, his ass, his balls, like he was learning Eric's body almost as much as he was learning how to suck a dick. He had to pull away, gasping, and wiped his mouth with the back of his hand. His lips and chin slick with spit, red and swollen, his eyes huge, like he was getting off on getting Eric off all over again.

Eric's dick twitched in Sully's hand and he said, "Well?"

"Gimme a second," Sully panted, "it's, uh, an adjustment. I'll figure it out."

"You can use your hand to—"

"Yeah. Shit," Sully sighed, as he went back down. Finally, he wasn't looking, wasn't analyzing. His eyes were closed, like he was lost in it.

Eric remembered, belatedly, that he was supposed to be offering instructions. He was supposed to be telling Sully what to do. But letting him figure it out on his own felt so satisfying and so right that he couldn't find the words even if he'd wanted to. Could only hang on to the desk for dear life, his legs shaking jelly, while Sully went to work. While he watched Ryan Sullivan, Cup champion and three-time playoff MVP, on his knees, eyes closed, intently concentrating only on Eric. It was too much to handle.

He managed, belatedly, to get his hand into Sully's hair. It had been an unremarkable sandy brown during their playing days and now it was mostly silver-gray, only hints of its original color flashing through. It felt soft under his hands as he shoved Sully's head down. Sully choked but gamely went along with it, gasping around him. That was the final thing that pushed Eric over the edge. The orgasm seemed like it went on for a long time, like an out-of-body experience.

When he was finally able to open his eyes, Sully

had pulled away and was still crouched on the ground, staring up at him. Eric felt slow and stupid, like he was swimming through molasses. Reached out and grabbed Sully's hair again, just to give it a tug.

To his amusement Sully let him do it, although he rolled his eyes and said, "Well, that was, uh, more than I thought I'd get out of you today, eh?"

"Next time if you want a blowjob don't fucking bodycheck me during practice," Eric mumbled.

"Where's the fun in that?" Sully demanded, and Eric's cock twitched again at how wrecked his voice sounded, scratchy and throaty. Eric had done that to him. Sully winced and shifted where he was sitting and groaned when he stood. "I'm too fucking old for this."

Eric, pulling up his underwear and sweats and tucking his dick back into them, snorted. "Yeah, you're practically decrepit. Geriatric."

Sully made a noise low in his throat, an amused little hmm. "You weren't complaining when you were sucking my geriatric dick. And you're, what? Forty-two?"

"Don't remind me," Eric said, and then paused. He felt, for the first time, uncertain. It was one thing to argue with Sully on the bench, another thing to joke around with him after they'd both gotten off. He still felt slow and easy, magnanimous. But this was new ground. He didn't want to follow up about *next time*, and he didn't know whether to—

"So, uh," Sully said. It was still obvious what he'd been doing. His mouth was still red, his chin a little scraped up from Eric's beard. His hair was a bird's nest where Eric had yanked his head around. His clothes were rumpled. "Since we're here. We never did get a chance to go over the forwards' tape."

Eric burst out laughing. He couldn't help it. Of course Ryan fucking Sullivan would wheel immediately from blowjobs to analyzing tape. And, strangely, that made Eric feel more at ease, too. Things hadn't changed so much at all.

"Fine," he said, "but I still think you were wrong about the way you tried the breakout on the 1-3-1 forecheck they had."

"That," Sully said, with a sniff, as he turned back to the whiteboards, "is not a forecheck. That is what we in the business refer to as a neutral zone trap. You know this."

"Well, *you* didn't know how to get the guys around it, so…" Eric paused. He wondered whether he could shove Sully against the boards again. It was a very tempting proposition. But they did have the work to do, and he would have to be careful about how he separated it. "Fine. The trap. We can't just do that same breakout again."

They didn't touch again, even though Eric's skin still felt prickly with the sense memory. It went long into the night, that meeting. But strangely, on his way to the car, Eric felt as wide awake as he ever had.

Ryan was slowly accomplishing his goals. The day after what he had started thinking of as the Incidents, he signed a lease on a two-bedroom apartment in Allston, reasonably close to the practice facilities where he'd end up spending most of his time. He spent several uncomfortable days in there, sleeping on an air mattress. And then it worked out that the Beacons had a three-day stretch of days without games in the middle of November, so Ryan texted Shannon to ask, Can I come and get my stuff tomorrow?

What time? Shannon wrote back, suspiciously quickly.

Lunch. I won't be long. I'll just pack some of it up and then I'll get out of your hair.

Fine. OK.

While it was somewhat short notice, Ryan was able to book a U-Haul and pick it up so that he could make the drive once the Beacons were finished with their morning skate on the first day "off." He assumed that Shannon wasn't going to be there when he got home, which was fine. He wasn't sure how he would have reacted if she had been. It would be his first time seeing her since they'd broken up, but also since he'd…done whatever he'd done with Aronson.

Ryan figured that he probably should have been freaking out a little more about the fact that he was, apparently, at least slightly gay. There really wasn't any way around it. Making out with Aronson had been one thing, exchanging blowjobs was absolutely another. That was several steps significantly further along the Kinsey scale than he'd ever thought he would go. But he couldn't really freak out about it too much when it had felt that electric. That intense.

Sure, Aronson was still an asshole, they still butted heads at practice, especially when it came to Jesse Keen's ice time and deployment, but whatever he was like at the rink, Ryan couldn't get out of his head what he was like off it. What his mouth had felt like, the noises he'd made, the way his hair felt under Ryan's fingers.

Maybe this was what happened when you got old and lonely, that literally anyone who would touch you looked like a sure bet. But Ryan knew, with a kind of stunning certainty he couldn't entirely track, that it wasn't just Aronson's availability. It wasn't just Aronson's grudging willingness to blow him. Ryan was famous; Ryan was a Boston legend. If he had wanted to go out and pick up, he could have done it, no problem. He could've met women his age or probably even women his players' ages, if he'd been into that.

He had never really felt the urge to do that.

He'd always been so devoted to Shannon that he'd never even considered it, and then she'd ended their relationship, and then this thing with Aronson had just sort of—happened before he'd had a chance to even recover. The first time without his conscious intention or input, and the second, with the kind of curiosity that ached like a wound. He'd gotten a taste, a *hint*, and he had just had to know what it was like. And the answer had been…

Ryan's cell phone vibrated in his pocket, and he almost fell out of his chair with the shock of it. He'd been really stupidly lost in his thoughts, that was for sure. He managed to keep his balance, fish the phone out and answer. It was Murph, of course.

"Hey, buddy," Murph said. "Hadn't heard from you in a few days, so I just thought I'd check in and see how you were doing."

Ryan looked down at the papers scattered all over the desk, whiteboard ink smudging his fingers, his iPad warning him desperately that it was entering low-battery mode. He thought about sitting on that desk in the middle of the mess last night, about Aronson on his knees, mouth around Ryan's dick.

"Great, great," he said, and hoped his voice didn't sound too weird.

Of course, Murph knew him well enough that he wasn't fooled. "Really?"

"You've seen the games, right? We're doing great. Still .500 on the season."

"Sully, bud. I didn't mean the games."

Ryan exhaled. He had always told Murph everything. It felt strange and wrong to keep a secret from him, especially a secret this huge and life-changing. But it was still so uncertain and new and dangerous, it didn't feel right to tell anyone, even Murph. It wasn't just his secret, it was Aronson's, too. There was a lot on the line. He trusted Murph with his life, but he just—couldn't say it. Not yet. But he had to say something; the silence was stretching out, uncomfortable and pulled tight like an aging rubber band.

"It's been weird," he said, finally. "You know. Shannon dumping me like that. I'm going to get my shit tomorrow, whatever she hasn't thrown out already."

Murphy exhaled, too. Ryan could tell that Murph didn't believe him, but he trusted Ryan's judgment enough not to push. "Y'all should've stayed in Dallas."

"Of course you still blame all of this on moving to New Hampshire," Ryan said, so fond it ached.

"Was I right, though, or was I right?"

"Probably. I don't know. I don't know if I'll ever get a chance to talk to her again outside of a courtroom, but I think that probably uh… Dallas wouldn't have helped."

"Probably not," Murph admitted. "Still. Wish you guys had lived down here. It'd be good to see you again."

"You and Tara are welcome to visit anytime you want. I'll get you tickets. Although you'll probably want to stay in a hotel. I, uh. Well, right now my apartment's just an air mattress."

"Jesus, that's the most divorced-guy thing I think you've ever said. What are you eating, ramen packets?"

"I can cook," Ryan said, stung. "And besides, we still have catered meals after games at the rink."

Murph's booming laugh cheered him up immeasurably. He could almost picture the way Murph would've brushed his hand through his hair, pushing it out of his eyes. "Well, we'll have to take you up on it, one of these days. Once you get a little more settled. Maybe we'll bring the kids. They'd love to see Uncle Ryan again."

"Yeah, sure," Ryan said. "Let me know in advance, we can bring them to a morning skate, too. I'm sure the boys would humor them."

"You're the best," Murph said. He had the kind of vehement sincerity that would have embarrassed Ryan, if it had come from anyone else. But that was Murph. They'd grown up together. He felt the same way.

They chatted a little bit about what they had been up to as well, and Ryan realized, belatedly, that despite his best intentions, he had probably been talking too often about Aronson. About Aronson as a person, not just a coworker. It was an uncomfortable thought, particularly because Murph usually noticed those things. "Okay, I gotta get back to it. Are you satisfied I'm not withering away into dust, *Mom*?"

"There's still something weird going on and I'm gonna get to the bottom of it. But for now, yeah."

Ryan hung up before he could say anything else that might give him away.

In a way, he was glad that they had the next few days off. Things with Aronson had been understandably fucking weird. They'd gotten through the practice without incident, but Ryan was aware he hadn't been up to his own usual standards. He'd been awkward and distracted, too self-aware of where he was skating, mostly talking with Petey and Heidi.

"The face-offs," Heidi said, skating up to him, "are *grim*."

"You want me to see if I can get Conroy to hire a face-off coach?" Ryan said, only half joking. Andy Chernoff, the Beacons' owner, had deep pockets, and Conroy had indicated to Ryan that as long as it was a reasonable request in service of player development, he would entertain it.

"I can work with them," she said, rolling her shoulders, "but it's going to be a seasons-long assignment, at this point. We're seeing some improvement working on the drills in a game-like simulation, but… Williams gets beat clean, a lot."

"What do you think the issue is?"

"Could be experience. Could be—he's got to learn how to use his size a little more forcefully. It's not a problem on the ice. Just getting the timing right in the dot."

Heidi was a machine when it came to face-offs: you could drop a puck in front of her and no matter how you tried to angle it, she was almost always able to sweep it back clean. She had a way of positioning her knee just right, so that a linesman wouldn't kick her out. But the way she balanced allowed her to get a head start muscling into the circle. Ryan had always been happy he hadn't had to worry about them in a game simulation, although he'd taken many against Murph when they were just fucking around at practice. Murph had always enjoyed shoving him down on the ice.

The face-off talk was a good distraction, but he was still aware of Aronson, where he was off working with the power-play unit. It didn't help that Aronson kept watching him without doing it obviously, from the corner of his eye. Every time Ryan caught him at it, he could feel his whole skin prickle, like the rink had suddenly dropped another twenty degrees. It was ridiculous, and Ryan had never been so happy to get the hell out of the rink before.

I-95 was a nightmare usually, but it felt even worse when he was kind of dreading the destination. It also felt worse driving an insanely cumbersome truck. There wasn't any reason to suspect that Shannon would be waiting there when he got home, but the part of him that was able to anticipate plays on the ice felt off anyway, the hair prickling at the back of his neck. On the ice it had always meant a goal coming. Now, it just spelled impending disaster.

He'd lucked out, though, because the U-Haul had Bluetooth. It was a little childish, but he scrolled through his saved albums and put on *Nevermind*, an album that he'd loved so much as an angsty teenager that he'd worn out several tape versions of it. With the windows rolled down to the chilly November air and the familiar riffs of "Smells Like Teen Spirit" blaring from the speakers, he felt like he could finally exhale, at least a little.

The feeling didn't last long. It slipped away faster and

faster the closer he got to Newfields. Then it was like the walls closed in again, the familiar tightening in his chest of going back to a home that had never really felt like home. It was funny, the way he felt like that in Boston and at the house he'd owned with his ex for so many years. He wondered, briefly, whether he'd ever have a place that felt comfortable to return to. Someplace *his*.

The house looked exactly the same as he'd left it. Either Shannon was mowing the lawn, or she had hired someone to keep up with the upkeep; it looked as immaculate as ever. She had put in new window boxes with professionally designed plant arrangements, a riot of red leaves and knobby sticks and whimsical shapes. Ryan had never seen the point of anything like that—half of the arrangement wasn't even planted in the box; it was just shoved in there with stakes. He'd never said *no* to them—he had made enough money over the course of his career that he rarely said no to anything Shannon wanted—but once he'd offered his opinion, Shannon had never asked again.

He parked the van in the driveway and thought he'd have to ask Shannon to hold on to some of his workshop equipment a little longer. That would require a house of his own, and he had no idea when that would be possible or even really feasible. Right now, even furnishing a two-bedroom apartment seemed almost insurmountable.

Shannon opened the front door and Ryan almost tripped over his own two feet, right there in the driveway.

It was the first time he'd seen her in person since the morning of his birthday, and he was almost relieved that he still found her incredibly attractive—so he definitely wasn't 100% gay. Her face had more stress lines than it had had when they'd met, but she was still a beautiful woman—a few inches taller than he was, with curly black hair she usually wore swept up in a bun. She had really striking light blue eyes that looked right through you and she'd always dressed in a way that really accentuated her face and her body.

"Hello, Ryan." She couldn't quite meet him in the eye.

"Hi…uh, you know, I wasn't expecting you to…well, be here at all, really."

"I know. I was thinking about it, though, and it's been a while since we were able to actually talk, and I didn't know if you were going to bring anyone to help you pack."

"Murph's still in Dallas. And you know I wasn't going to ask any of my brothers."

"Yes." She took a deep breath, one that visibly moved her shoulders up, and exhaled, long and slow. "Look—do you want to come in? We can have lunch, and then we can start packing."

Ryan didn't know how he felt right in that moment. He'd never felt the betrayal that he thought he'd have felt when she ended things. He didn't resent her. He felt wary, unsure of what was coming next, but not any of the things you probably should've felt in a situation like this. "Yeah, okay."

It was even weirder going back into the house. It still had the same smell that he associated with being home, but it didn't feel like home anymore. Shannon had already done a few things to change it up: she'd taken down the small amount of hockey memorabilia she'd permitted upstairs; she'd hung up a few new pieces of art. There were a few amateurish ceramic bowls and sculptures on display on the coffee table. She'd been burning an unfamiliar candle, on top of the familiar smell of the house layered a fir and pine winter scent.

In the kitchen, Shannon had already set up lunch. She'd made something she used to make for him all of the time during his playing days: poached chicken salads with quinoa and chickpeas and a thick, herby yogurt dressing. The same way she always had, there was a little pitcher of ice water with slices of lemon and lime in it, some of the herbs left over from the salad muddled in the bottom. It was all so familiar that he felt a brief pang of missing her, missing *this*, before he remembered what he was there to do.

"Ryan—" she started, right at the same time that he said, "Shannon."

"You go first," she said, after a second.

"Look, Shan, I just wanted to—I don't know. I wanted to let you know I don't have any hard feelings about the way things ended. And that I'm sorry I fucked things up so bad. I knew you wanted a life without hockey, but I'm just not ready to give it up. I *can't* give it up. And that's not fair to you. And it wasn't fair to expect you to be okay with it. I just—I love you, but I did a really shitty job of showing that, especially these last few years."

Shannon stood for a minute with her arms crossed over her chest, like she was hugging herself. She laughed, short and a little sour. "I thought a lot about getting an apology like that from you over the years. It's weird that I'm getting it now and I'm still mostly just relieved that we're done. Is that weird?"

"No," Ryan said, and he was surprised to find that it was true.

She took a step forward and picked up the plates, setting them out on the table. "Jesus, Ry. We got married *so* young, you know?"

"Yeah, I do, I was there," he said dryly, and she laughed again, more genuine this time. "Maybe we should've waited. Maybe you would've realized that you didn't actually want to marry a hockey player after all. Do you regret it?"

"Sometimes," Shannon said, slowly. As she spoke, she spooned out the salad on the plates, poured him some water. "Sometimes I think I could've had more years doing things I loved without fighting with you about hockey all of the time. But maybe I wouldn't appreciate where we are now as much as I do without that."

"Look at you, getting philosophical on me. You know I'm just a hockey player, right?"

"Stop," she said sharply. "You might be a hockey player, Ryan, and you might be a fucking idiot when it comes to anything involving emotional intelligence, but you're not *stupid.* You're probably one of the smartest people I know. That's what made this so frustrating over the years."

Ryan stared at her. "Shannon, seriously?"

"I'm being serious, Ryan. I don't know anyone who studies that damn *game* as seriously as you do. I don't know anyone who'd be up at all hours of the night reading about neuroplasticity or fucking Sun Tzu. I think part of this whole problem is just you didn't—I don't think you know what you would have been capable of *without* hockey. And you never wanted to, I get it. That's fine. But it's just—it makes me so sad, sometimes, thinking about what we could have had."

Ryan thought about it, too. He knew Shannon had

wanted kids, at one point, but it had never worked out. He knew Shannon had wanted to get more involved in art education: he'd encouraged her to take classes, but he didn't have the vocabulary or the time to talk to her about it at home. Somewhere, in some parallel universe, there were a Ryan and Shannon sitting in this same house, while the kids were running around upstairs screaming, talking about a new class she was directing or—but it wasn't a parallel universe. It was this one. Here he and Shannon were, in their forties, looking down the barrel of a no-fault divorce.

"I'm sorry," he said. "And I do mean that."

"It's okay…and maybe it's weird to say, but I do mean that, too. It might have taken us a hell of a lot to get here, but I'm not… I was angry when I first kicked you out. But I've been working with someone on this and I'm learning to, like…let it go. You know?"

Ryan last year would have made a joke like, *Sure, Elsa*. Ryan this year said, "I'm really proud of you, Shan," and meant it.

Shannon swallowed and looked away, busying herself with pushing him a plate. "Yeah, well. We've both grown up a little, at least."

They ate the lunch without talking about heavy topics, just logistics about Ryan's workshop and some of the things he would need to leave by necessity. It was like a weight was lifted off his shoulders, knowing things weren't as fraught, knowing he no longer had to worry about her dumping his shit on the curb for the trash men or giving it away. She helped him pack some of the more portable stuff: his clothes shoved in trash bags, his memorabilia wrapped up in newspaper, his books stacked in plastic bins she'd bought for him.

It wasn't easy work, with just the two of them: a lot of trips out into the cold, with Ryan's arms stretched as wide as they could to hold the bins.

When they were finally finished, a few hours later, they paused at the doorway. Shannon looked at him with the kind of expression he might have been able to decipher, once, but couldn't now. She looked sad and relieved and longing all at the same time, and she held out her arms to him. The embrace was familiar and not familiar as well: her hair smelled the same as it always had; her body felt the same in his arms, the way they couldn't quite see eye to eye, no matter how he arranged himself. She hugged him tightly, so hard he could feel his ribs creak under the force of it.

It felt final. It felt like the goodbye he hadn't been able to get from her, the day she'd kicked him out.

"I'm glad we did this," she said, as she released him.

"It was fucking weird."

"Yes, it was. But I—I didn't want you to hate me."

He felt very tired, suddenly, ran a hand through his sweaty hair to get it off of his forehead and out of his eyes. "I could never hate you, Shan. You've been like—we grew up together. You were my whole life for decades. We just—"

"Grew into different people."

"Yeah."

"We still have the court date in December, you know."

"Yeah, I know. It's a date," Ryan said, flashing quick finger guns at her, and she groaned in exaggerated disgust.

"Jesus, I forgot what shitty dad humor you have sometimes."

"But Shan—you're okay? It's okay? That we're doing this?"

"Yeah," she said. The smile was still a bit sad. "I really think we're both going to be so much happier when this is done. And that's all I want. I never wanted to hate you. I just didn't want to be miserable anymore." Impulsively, she leaned forward and kissed him on the cheek, then stepped back just as abruptly. "Drive carefully, okay?"

"You know me," Ryan said, "I'm always careful."

As he was driving home, his listen-through of "Little Fury Things" was interrupted by the phone ringing. Against his better judgment, he answered. "Hello, Dad."

"Where the hell are *you*? Where are you driving to?"

"I'm driving back from Newfields."

"Newfields? Why the hell were you there? Did you come to your senses and take Shannon back?"

"Dad… I was picking up some of my things."

"Divorced," Dad was muttering. He sounded like he'd been drinking, his voice thick and a little slurred. "Never thought a boy of mine would ever get *divorced*. How're you ever going to show your face in the parish again?"

Ryan desperately wanted to say something about marrying a girl who was younger than your own fucking kids before your wife was even cold in her grave, but he had to be the bigger person when it came to Dad. Trying to fight with him just meant getting deeper into the muck and the mud yourself. You might win the argument, but you'd feel just as disgusting afterward. Instead, he said, "I haven't been to church in over five years, Dad."

"Maybe that's your problem," Dad said, gearing up

to rant again. The irony was, of course, that Dad himself only ever went when one of his boys was getting married, or a grandchild was being baptized or having First Communion.

"Goodbye, Dad," Ryan said, and hung up.

It hit him all of a sudden, as he was driving. The grief and pain of losing Shannon, or more accurately, the marriage that had taken up the majority of his adult life. The stretched-tight tension he hadn't even realized he was feeling, being the mature and responsible and adult one, seeing his ex-wife and refusing to take his father's bait. Ryan didn't pull over on the side of the road, but he thought about it, thought about banging his head down on the steering wheel and seeing how that would feel.

It had been a long time since he remembered crying. He hadn't even cried, not really, when his mother had died. He wasn't actually going to do it now, but he thought that maybe if he was the kind of guy who cried, this would be the moment he did it.

Instead of any of that, another idea formed in his head, impossible to dislodge. It was a terrible idea, but it had some real appeal. Ryan kept driving, took a deep breath, touched his finger against the little text message icon on the car interface.

CHAPTER SEVEN

November

Aronson, the text message from Sullivan said, way too late to make any kind of question as to what the point of the text was. It was only by chance that they had each other saved as contacts: Sullivan had come in with grand plans of building a camaraderie among the coaching staff, and Eric had promptly spit in his face about it. There were a few texts in the chain that they had with Petey and Heidi, but this was the first direct message he'd ever received.

What do you want?

Where do you live.

What?

Where do you live. Come on. Give me your address.

For a second, Eric stared at his phone. Sullivan wasn't the kind of person to pull stupid pranks, but it was still a weird request. What's wrong with you? he asked, instead.

Just give me your fucking address, man. I've had a long day and I'm going to stop by.

YOU'RE going to stop by? MY house?

Yeah. Are you scared I'm gonna piss on your stoop or something? I'm house trained.

It was one of the things Eric had considered, but he wasn't about to tell Sullivan that. *No.* He hesitated for a second. He still wasn't sure what the hell was going on with the extracurricular activities. He still wasn't sure how the hell he felt about it, other than annoyed that he was apparently fucking easy for it. He was annoyed he was even considering this.

He sent his address.

Was that so hard? Sullivan asked.

I'm going to rescind the invite if you can't behave.

Sullivan wrote, LOL, and Eric had to stop to count to ten, pinch the bridge of his nose and move on.

Eric looked around at his apartment. It wasn't as depressing as some places. He only had a galley kitchen, but he used it. He'd taken the time to actually hang some art, and he had some plants in the window he hadn't killed yet. He had real furniture that wasn't from IKEA. It had made many trips with him over the years, but it was still intact.

It had been a long time since he'd invited anyone he was sleeping with back here. It had been a long time since he'd had anyone except Petey over, and Petey didn't give a shit if his coffee table was covered in papers and books that Eric always started with the intention of finishing. Petey didn't care if there were pots and pans drying on the counter. Who was he kidding: Sullivan probably wouldn't care about that, either. Eric racked his brain, trying to remember when he had changed his sheets last.

Maybe that was optimistic. Given the way the last few times had gone, the odds of Sully actually seeing his sheets were not certain.

In the end Eric settled for picking up the dirty clothes from the floor of his bedroom and throwing them in the laundry basket, kicking it into his closet and shutting the door. That'd have to do.

By the time he actually got a text that said open your door, it was even later. Later than he would normally be considering having someone over. He opened the door and said, "You couldn't just find someone else to bother?"

Sullivan didn't say anything at first, just frowned at him until Eric took a step back, letting him over the threshold.

"Look," Sullivan said. He dropped his winter coat on Eric's floor. He looked exhausted, dark circles under his eyes, the T-shirt he was wearing under his jacket still stained and smudged from whatever he'd been doing before he got there. He took a deep, ragged breath, like if he didn't plow on with what he was saying, he'd never get it out. "I don't want to talk, I don't want to think, I don't want you to be fucking *nice* to me. I don't want to have to be mature, I just—I just—"

Eric stared at him. This was probably the least Sully conversation he could ever remember having. For the first time, he didn't have that cheerful, cocky self-assurance he usually had, the aura of a guy who was used to the world giving him everything he wanted. Eric thought about asking him what he really wanted. Instead, it was like his body reacted without his brain's input. He leaned down to kiss him, and Sully's mouth opened immediately, eagerly, under his.

"You want me to be mean?" he asked, pulling away, trying not to laugh at the frustrated little noise that came out of Sully's mouth. He put one hand against his chest, walking him backward toward the couch.

"Yeah, I—" Sully licked his lips. They were dry and chapped, a little red like he'd been chewing on them. Eric wondered what the hell he'd been doing on their day off that had him acting like this.

"Well. What if I don't want to give you what you want?" Eric said, and pushed him down on the couch. "What if I decide I'm gonna treat you *so* nicely—"

"Aronson," Sully snapped, from where Eric had pushed him sprawled on the couch, "I swear to god, can you turn it the fuck off for *twenty minutes*?"

Eric choked on his own laugh, but more of them bubbled up behind. "Twenty minutes? Jesus, what kind of sex have you been having?"

Sully's whole face was red, although whether it was humiliation or fury, Eric couldn't tell. "Lately? Just on the desk at work. And twenty minutes was being generous."

"Wow," Eric said, moving forward, "don't recall any complaints from you at the time, actually. It was mostly a lot of *come on* and *oh my god* and *please*, eh?" When he got down on the couch to straddle Sully, trapping him in place, it took him a second to gauge whether it was the right move. Sully was built like a barrel, but Eric was a lot bigger. That didn't stop Sully at all from trying to angle his head up for another kiss, but Eric pushed him back down. "Maybe I'll just make you wait?"

Underneath him, Sully was already squirming, although there wasn't much room to move. Eric could feel every movement of his body, his muscular legs shifting underneath Eric's thighs, his heart beating a million times a minute against Eric's chest, his dick already hard.

"You wouldn't," he managed, his voice a little strangled.

Eric shifted his arm up, his forearm pressing just so against Sully's neck. He could feel the Adam's apple bob. Sully's little gulp of surprise. Of *nervousness*. "You don't know me at all. I can be really fucking patient. And somehow, I get the idea that you're not very good at that, either."

Sully didn't answer immediately, just looked up, mouth twitching like he wasn't sure whether he wanted to scowl or to smile. When Eric pressed his forearm down again, Sully said, his voice a little strangled, "Do you know how long it took me to crack a major league roster? I'm real patient."

Instead of arguing, Eric shifted down. Even with the wrist against his neck, Sully kissed him eagerly, mouth open and sloppy, even though his breath felt ragged and strained. He was shifting again, seeking some kind of friction, movement from Eric, anything. His hand had moved around to try to grab Eric's ass. As soon as he did it, Eric stopped moving. He pulled his mouth back.

Sully's eyes flew open, the scowl back again. "Come *on*," he said.

"You're a terrible fucking liar," Eric said, unable to

hide the laugh in the words, using his free hand to grab Sully's wrist and pin it back against the couch.

Sully held himself still, almost ostentatiously so, like he was making a point of it. Even with the renewed effort, he was trembling, with excitement or nerves, Eric couldn't tell. For a second, the doubt: was he moving too fast, assuming too much? It was pretty clear that Sully had never fucked around with a man before, however queer he might've been. It was pretty clear that he was enjoying it, but it was still… Well. Sully was a big boy. If he wanted Eric to stop, he could say it.

Instead of worrying further, Eric lost himself in the push and pull. The teasing, the promise of more pulled away just when Sully started to get *into* it. Eric could feel the pulse in Sully's wrist, hammering under his grip. Eric could feel Sully gasping into his mouth, trying to angle his head for a more bruising kiss. Eric could feel every inch of him, hard and straining upward, more and more frustrated the longer Eric let things go without slipping a hand down his pants, without *really* doing more than holding him down so he couldn't pursue the touch he clearly wanted desperately.

Eventually, Sully broke, his voice a raspy growl. "This is—god, you're such an asshole."

"You wanted me to be mean," Eric said, a little singsong.

"Yeah, I didn't mean *torture* me, I—"

"Jesus, you even talk too much in bed? I should have fucking guessed."

"This is the *couch*."

Eric pulled back, looked down at Sully, measuring. He took the pressure off of his throat. "Do you want to move it to the bed?"

Sully blinked. His whiskey-brown eyes were a little hazy, distracted. He looked stupid as hell and Eric had the brief animal satisfaction of knowing he'd done that. "Considering the way my knees felt at practice after the last time, yeah. Move it to the bed."

Eric's own knees creaked a little when he shifted out of Sully's lap and moved himself off of the couch. When he looked down at Sully, he had his eyes closed for a second, like he was trying to gather his wits before he stood. He followed Eric into the bedroom without any further smart-ass remarks, though, and Eric was briefly glad he'd thought to clean up.

Sully sat right down on Eric's bed like he owned it, looked up at him with the kind of challenge in his eye he always had at practice if they were demonstrating a drill and Sully especially wanted to put him in his place. "Get naked," he said, and pointed one finger at Eric's pants, which, admittedly, were not doing a whole lot to hide how into this he was, either.

"Oh, you're giving the orders now?" Eric asked, amused. "Pretty bossy, Sully. 'Be mean to me.' 'Move it to the bed.' 'Get naked.' I'm getting some mixed signals, I think."

Sully said, "Oh my *god*, you're insufferable," and in one quick movement, yanked his sweater and undershirt up over his head, and just as quickly, pulled his pants and underwear down and kicked them off.

Eric had seen him naked before, in the showers at the rink. But it was different there: you couldn't look too long or too hard, and Eric had spent years of his playing career being normal about it in the locker rooms.

Today, he had the ability to look at Sully all he wanted to, the compact body formed and shaped especially for the sport: the barrel torso and the layer of fat over a core that Eric knew felt hard as a rock underneath, the absurdly muscular legs that seemed almost too big for the rest of his body. His broad shoulders and thick neck.

And his face, handsome and charming and *stupid*, the laugh lines at the corners of his eyes and mouth, the twitching smile that always seemed to tug the corner of his lips up, the strong jaw and stubborn chin. The warm brown eyes with short, lush eyelashes that were currently staring back up at Eric, focused only on him.

His dick—thick and hard, already leaking, gripped in one calloused hand.

"Are you just going to stare at me," Sully said, for the first time sounding a little uncertain, "or are we going to get this show on the road?"

"What'd I say about being patient?" Eric asked, and Sully groaned and said, *"Still?"*

Still clothed, Eric got down on the bed, took one hand to Sully's chest and pushed him down. "You wanted me to be mean," he reminded him.

"I thought you were going to—I don't know, talk to me the way you do in practice, or push me around, I didn't think you were going to—" He was twisting again under Eric's body, one leg hooked over Eric's to keep him from escaping. "I really didn't think…"

Eric shook his head. "Again, I wanna know what kind of sex you were having." He stopped, when something in Sully's eyes shuttered, started closing down. That wasn't what he wanted. It was only fun if both of them were into it. "Okay, fine. You said you didn't want to think? Don't think."

It turned out that Sully liked it when Eric held his wrists down, when he had to try to push back against his full body weight to arch himself up into a kiss. And he could, for a time, lift Eric up. It wasn't quite the same as the bench press, with the force pushing back down and the particular angle, but he had that smug little smile when he did it that made Eric want to *humiliate* him.

It wasn't hard. All he had to do was shift one hand down to take Sully's dick in his hand, and he surrendered almost immediately, his body twisting pinioned between the two points of contact.

It was intense, how badly Sully wanted it, how roughly Eric could touch him and he'd still be panting for it. It wasn't quite a wrestling match. Eric's bed wasn't big enough for that, and neither of them were fully young enough for it, but Sully managed to turn the tables, climbing on top of him, a heavy weight seated on his hips as he bullied Eric back against the headboard.

"Take off your *clothes*," Sully demanded, grinding against him, and Eric couldn't help laughing.

"I really think," he managed, "you gotta make up your mind what you want out of this."

Sully, his hands tugging at Eric's shirt, looked him straight in the eye and said, "I think I made that pretty clear. I want *you*. I want everything."

Eric, mouth dry, did not ask *are you sure*, because it was pretty fucking clear that Sully was. Maybe they'd been heading toward this the whole time anyway. Maybe it had been inevitable, the first time he'd leaned down angrily, attacked Sully's mouth with his own because he hadn't known anything else to say to express his frustration. It was funny, now, that he almost couldn't remember why he'd been so furious, not when he had Sully in his bed, annoying and persistent and trying to pull Eric's pants off without actually letting him up to move.

Eric had to shove him down into the bed before he could actually get his pants and shirt off, laughing again when Sully took the opportunity to stare at him, too. He wasn't sure what he was seeing. Especially after he'd stopped playing, Eric wasn't anything special, tall and more lanky than built.

But for a guy who'd apparently waited until middle age to figure out that he was into other men, Sully was certainly enthusiastic about looking, and he was certainly enthusiastic about touching. He was enthusiastic when Eric pushed his head down and said, "Suck my dick, then," and he was enthusiastic when Eric got a hand in his hair to tug at it.

Eric was honestly obsessed with the sounds he made, the gasp when Eric yanked him back up so he could kiss him, the choked-off noise of surprise when Eric pushed him back down. It was that Sully just liked everything so fucking much, no matter what Eric did, even when Eric hadn't touched his dick at all, he was still achingly hard, gripping himself with one hand like if he didn't, he was going to come right then and there.

"Fuck, you really like that," Eric said, which was stupid and obvious and also made Sully groan around his dick, so it was worth it. "God, that's—yeah. Like that." Eric held out as long as he could bear it, but at a certain point, if Sully wanted *everything*… He pulled Sully's head up, trying to bite back another laugh at the offended noise Sully made when he did.

"I don't want to come before we actually fuck," Eric said, and Sully groaned again, and said, "You're *killing* me."

Eric tried to collect his ragged wits, tried to think of all of the ways he should explain things to someone who'd clearly never done this with a man before. "Do you have any preferences or—"

Sully shrugged. He looked ridiculous, his hair an insane bird's nest, his mouth wet with spit and pre-come, his lips red and swollen. His dick slick and wet from where he'd been grasping it while Eric fucked his mouth.

"You're the one with the experience," he said. "I'm willing to learn new things."

It turned out that Sully couldn't shut up if his life depended on it. He couldn't stop laughing when Eric slid one slicked-up finger inside of him, and when Eric said, "What the hell is so funny?" Sully said, "I'm just, uhhh, oh, thinking of prostate exams, how awkward it is, you know—" and Eric, who was at once so fucking horny it actually hurt him and so fucking in awe of Sully's ability to just say anything that came into his head, said, "Well, I'm clearly not doing this the right way if you're still thinking about that."

It turned out that it took a little while and some careful stroking and a few more fingers before Eric said, "Are you still thinking about the doctor's office?"

Sully, on his stomach on the bed, shifting restlessly against Eric's sheets, his hands fisted in the blankets, managed, "What?"

"That's what I thought," Eric said, smugly.

By the time they were actually ready to attempt it, Sully was sweating, red-faced, the flush visible down his neck. "I've, uh—kind of done this before. Once. Shannon was trying to spice things up in the bedroom and I said I'd let her, but then I couldn't stop laughing the whole time…"

Eric stared at him, disbelieving. It was just such a ridiculous thing to say, but there was Sully, his pupils huge and his hair insane and his body swaying into Eric's, just talking and talking and talking like it wasn't completely insane. He was just so fucking ridiculous. He was a Cup champion and an MVP and all of that stupid shit, and he was a divorced middle-aged man who had no idea what the fuck he was doing, and he had shown up at Eric's door and basically begged Eric to fuck him. He had told Eric that he wanted *him*. It was just—

"I'll tell you what," Eric said, pushing him over on the bed. "If you're laughing like *that* once we get started, I'll…" He didn't know what to offer. They were already here, in bed, Sully was already on his hands and knees, waiting, while Eric fumbled around with the condom package. "It won't be like that."

"Okay," Sully said, a little strangled, when he felt Eric pressing against him.

Eric couldn't help touching him while he was doing it, tracing the lines of the muscle bunched along his shoulders and back, how tense he was, how warm his skin was. Learning the texture of it, the scrapes and scars he'd picked up from a lifetime of playing hockey.

"Relax," Eric said, "come on. Just relax. Remember when I said I'd treat you nicely?"

Sully sounded startled when he laughed, a little puff of a chuckle that escaped before he could stop it. His head hung down and Eric rested his hand on his neck, right at the hairline. Sully said, "I'm fine. It's fine."

It was more than fine, actually. By the time Sully had relaxed enough that Eric felt comfortable moving on, it felt like they'd been frozen in place like that for an insanely long amount of time. He hadn't really done this in a while; he'd been busy at the beginning of the season and then Sully had basically fallen into his lap. Sully, who was tense under his hands, who was waiting for something, as Eric shifted his hips, moving so slowly it was almost painful.

Underneath Eric's body, Sully started shifting back against him, like he was testing how it felt, seeing what he could take.

"Shit," Sully mumbled.

"See?"

"Are you going to—to make me wait again?"

Eric thought about it, thought about drawing it out until Sully lost it and started trying to order him around again, frustrated and furious. It was an appealing thought, but if he didn't start moving, he was going to explode, and not in a sexy way.

"No," he said. "I'm not going to make you wait."

He didn't.

It took Sully a few minutes to get the rhythm of it, to relax enough to really let himself go, but once he did, Eric was a fucking goner. It was insane to feel the heat of Sully's body, the strength of it underneath Eric's, the way his shoulders and back and ass felt under Eric's hands. He was making these noises whenever Eric thrust, half-incomprehensible words of encouragement and half-incoherent groans of appreciation.

For all of the competition they had coaching and on the ice, Sully was pretty fucking easy in bed, shuddered when Eric dug his teeth into his shoulder, moved his head when Eric yanked it at an angle to kiss.

It felt like forever; it couldn't have really been that

long. Eric could feel himself getting close, the drag up and down his spine, everything in him tightening. He pulled out and the noise of loss that Sully made almost ended him right then and there. He took a second to breathe through his nose, get himself under control, and pushed Sully back down on the bed, on his back. After everything they'd done, Sully was loose and relaxed enough that Eric could just push back in with a sigh, could watch as Sully's eyes fluttered shut again.

Sully was panting, now, his hands grasping at Eric's shoulders like he had to hold on to something or he was going to fly away. "Fuck," he gasped, "Aronson, come on, harder, I'm—" And then he opened his eyes, looked up at Eric's face, and the crooked grin was back. He was laughing, that unrestrained, stupid, joyful laugh of his that was so annoying during practices and felt so different in bed, with Sully's furnace of a body pinned under Eric's.

"What's so *funny*," Eric managed, shifting around so he could press his forearm on Sully's throat again. That, it seemed, was the right move.

"It just feels—this is what I wanted," Sully said, still grinning like a loon, even while he was gasping and twisting and sweating, "not to think. Fuck. *Yeah*, like that," and then his whole face screwed up in an objectively dumb-as-fuck expression, and he came, hot and wet against Eric's abs.

It didn't take Eric long after, the kind of orgasm that knocked him flat on top of Sully's sweaty body. When he opened his eyes, slowly gathered himself up to pull out, he caught Sully's tiny wince of discomfort.

"Sorry."

"It's fine. I'm just—well. Shannon and I didn't really make it that far the last time."

"Jesus Christ—"

"Sorry, I probably shouldn't…that was…fuck, Aronson. That was something."

Eric couldn't think of anything to say. Sully sat up in his bed, slowly. His body was marked up with Eric's teeth, from his fingers digging into Sully's skin. He stretched, slowly, like he was testing out all of his limbs to make sure they still worked. He looked up and Eric couldn't really decipher the expression in his eyes, just that they were still wide and a little crazy and darker than they usually looked.

Sully said, "Thank you. For, you know." He gestured around to the crumpled sheets, the sticky mess.

Eric snorted. "Yeah, such a hardship." He groaned, pulling himself into a sitting position. "You can clean up first, if you want."

He sat in silence in the bed, listening to Sully in the bathroom, the splash of the sink and the toilet flushing. He wondered, again, why Sully had turned up here looking like a truck had run him over. It wasn't any of his business to wonder or to care about that.

Sully emerged, still naked, from Eric's bathroom and started picking up his clothes from the floor. "I'll, uh, see you at work tomorrow," he said, awkwardly hop-stepping into his pants.

"Do you want me to see you out?" Eric asked, a little sarcastically.

"Nah," Sully said, "I know where the door is."

"Okay," Eric said, and wondered whether this was the full, real Ryan Sullivan experience. It was not what he had been expecting. But it was almost as annoying.

II.
WINTER

CHAPTER EIGHT

December

The thing about the end of November and into December, Ryan was finding, was that the team's results had evened out from .500 to slightly below it. Despite any coaching work that he and Aronson and Petey and Heidi managed to drum into the youth, he still had an entire roster full of underperforming veterans, and he was starting to find that no matter what he did in the practices, they were still essentially the same players. There were a few, like Emil Härmälä, who had discovered new levels of backchecking that they'd never had before. But then there were others, like Jesse Keen, who simply could not seem to put together the lessons that Ryan was desperately trying to teach them.

Sometimes, when he watched Keen in the neutral zone making blind passes to no one, Ryan wanted to drop the determinedly positive face that he presented at practices and even on the bench, and scream. Unhinge his jaw and let loose with the full stable of curses in five languages that he'd picked up over the course of twenty years in the league.

"You're gonna have to do something about him," Aronson said, for the umpteenth time, as they sat in an all-hands coaching meeting going over tape. The game had been particularly egregious: a stupid penalty that Keen had taken had led to the game-winning goal against.

"He'll sit the next game, but there's not a whole lot more that I can do," Ryan said. "I can bump him down the lineup, but then he's just going to be someone else's problem and our fourth line is going to get caved in even worse."

"Waive Jesse Keen, waive Jesse Keen," Petey sang, in the tune and rhythm of "Carol of the Bells."

"While I do not agree with goyische holiday shit this early in December," Aronson said, "Petey's right. You *have* to make them face some consequences, Sully, or they don't have any incentive to get better."

What Ryan didn't say, immediately, is that they were probably right. What he also didn't say was that he wasn't ready to give up on his coaching philosophy, which was still relatively new. He'd put a lot of thought and care into it. Waiving a veteran was a pretty harsh move. While Keen had a one-way contract and would make the same in the major or minor leagues, it was still a statement that wouldn't go over well. For a man who hadn't sniffed the minors in at least a decade, it would be a blow, and Ryan couldn't tell how liked in the room Keen was, whether there would be ripple effects or not.

"He'll sit for now," he said, "and we'll see if that lights a fire under his ass."

"The man is wearing heatproof underwear," Heidi muttered, and Petey laughed, but everyone fell silent and moved on to the next issue once Ryan shot them a look that said: we're doing it.

The other thing about the end of November and December, Ryan was finding, was that road games were a great opportunity to experiment. Specifically, with fucking around with Aronson.

He was actually kind of shocked how easy it was, to follow Aronson back to his room after games; to drag Aronson back to Ryan's room. He was shocked how easy it was to learn things he never thought he'd like but actually liked *a lot*. He was shocked that Aronson didn't seem to mind if Ryan couldn't stop talking or couldn't stop laughing; he seemed to think it was funny. Which was something, even if he didn't actually like it and just wasn't saying anything.

He was shocked how easy it was to accept that maybe, his entire life, he just hadn't realized that he was queer until Eric Aronson pushed him up against a whiteboard.

Ryan's life had had weirder things happen, but that was probably up there.

The road trips and travel had been a good excuse not to go home for Thanksgiving. There weren't games on the day of the holiday, but Ryan had begged off, saying he was tired and had preparation for the game the day after.

He had ignored the barrage of text messages from his brothers and from Dad, all of them talking shit about how he thought he was so important now that he was back in the major leagues again, and he wasn't even *playing*, he was just coaching. Ryan read every single one of them—he never had read receipts on because he didn't like to give anyone the satisfaction—and sighed. He was definitely going to have to go home for Christmas. And that wasn't even counting his divorce hearing, right smack in the middle of the month.

Even phone calls with Murph had gotten awkward. Whenever Ryan started talking about the team, it all looped back to Aronson, and he could hear Murph starting to check out. As much as he tried not to, it happened anyway. It was like any small space left in his brain that wasn't occupied with hockey had suddenly been filled with Aronson: the way he frowned and the way he smiled, the way his body felt under Ryan's and inside of it, the way it was so easy to piss him off and get a reaction out of him.

Aronson, though: he had turned out to be exactly the kind of distraction Ryan hadn't known he needed. Sure, he was still an obnoxious little shit in practice, especially now. They had a kind of competition going, who could shoulder-check who accidentally the most times without anyone noticing, and Ryan was winning. And then they were on a western road trip in the beginning of December—Los Angeles and San Jose and Vancouver—and it was even easier not to think about what was waiting for him later in the month.

They landed in Los Angeles, where they'd be staying for the game against the Blades and the Arsenal. The first night, the coaches—with the exception of Heidi, who didn't always travel with the team because sometimes she was working with their minor league affiliate in Providence—went out to dinner. Ryan didn't remember much of the conversation because all he could think about was Aronson, about what they could do after the check was cleared and they made it back to the hotel.

The thing was that Ryan had thought he knew about sex. He'd been having it for over thirty years at this point, but the thing was that he was learning he didn't know much at all. The thing was that Aronson was constantly surprising him. It wasn't just that he seemed to understand instinctively how to make Ryan do and say absolutely insane things, with his tongue and his hands and his dick. It wasn't just that he seemed to be driven equally as insane by the things that Ryan did to him even when they were fumbling and awkward.

Somehow, it just worked.

"Do you ever think that you've… I don't know. Kind of lost your mind or something?" Ryan asked. He was lying on his back where he'd collapsed after pulling out, still disgusting and sweaty and red-faced.

Aronson was sprawled on his stomach, eyes half-closed. Ryan took a second to admire the way he looked like that, the funny hockey proportions gone to seed—his broad shoulders and muscular ass and incongruously lanky body. Some hockey guys waxed; Aronson was hairy from his neck down to his ankles. His curls were dark with sweat and without his glasses, he looked younger, somehow, less intimidating.

"Pretty much every day," Aronson mumbled. "Only explanation I can come up with for you, anyway."

Maybe earlier in the year Ryan would have been upset by that, or even a little stung. But the more he took a pit stop to the end of the evening in Aronson's bed, the more he was starting to realize that Aronson was more bark than bite. He reached out, experimentally, ran his hand down the length of Aronson's back. Aronson didn't pull away, just opened one eye and looked at Ryan a little warily, like he wasn't sure what he was doing.

"I'm not gonna be able to go again," he said.

"I can't, either," Ryan said, surprised. "I don't know, I just—wanted to touch you."

Aronson gave him another one of those looks, not quite suspicious, but definitely measuring. There was something going on behind his eyes that Ryan couldn't decipher. His back felt tense under Ryan's fingers, so he took them away. It felt like the weird kind of precipice moment where whatever was going on between them could nosedive very sharply south, depending on the way Aronson responded. Instead, he rolled over onto his back, looked up at Ryan with a wry smirk twisting the corner of his mouth up.

"You're kind of a slut for any kind of physical affection, huh."

"What?" Ryan demanded, stung, and kind of—embarrassed. He wasn't sure what it was about this whole thing—whether it was having sex with another man, whether it was just Aronson—that always made him feel so off-balance, but sometimes, he felt like a teenager again, awkward and unsure.

"Like this," Aronson said, sitting up. He ran his hands down Ryan's sides, and Ryan shivered but didn't pull away. He couldn't pull away. Aronson's hands made their way farther down, tracing his thighs, warm against Ryan's skin. "See? You fucking *love* this."

Ryan thought about retorting, *It's been a while since anyone actually enjoyed touching me*, but that sounded even worse than whatever Aronson was probably thinking. So he just shut the fuck up and let Aronson touch him.

Aronson's face had started out with that mocking little smirk, but the longer it went on, the more Ryan's body swayed unconsciously into his hands, the more his expression changed. Ryan had lost track of the time; lost track of how long Aronson had been touching him. It didn't matter. By the time Aronson's fingers closed around his dick—hard, again, which seemed impossible—the noise Ryan made, an involuntary gasp, sounded completely unlike him.

"See?" Aronson said, again. "God, you…you really…" His voice didn't sound mocking anymore, though. It was rough and ragged, and when Ryan finally opened his eyes again, Aronson was staring at him, like he could take Ryan apart just by looking.

"I thought you said you wouldn't be able to go again," Ryan managed, before Aronson's mouth came down on his again, and then neither of them was talking at all anymore.

It was really like his body, which had had very limited, unexciting sex for the past five years or more, had suddenly developed a mind of its own. Like a tree withering away in a drought turning greedily into a rainstorm.

Against all of his own logical thoughts or desires, there he was, in Aronson's room again after the games. And there Aronson was, letting him in, even while he was saying shit like, "This doesn't change *anything* at work, this doesn't change *anything* about the way I feel about you."

"And what's that?" Ryan asked, trapped between the wall and Aronson's body, his legs hooked behind Aronson's back. Since the first time they'd done this, it was like Aronson secretly enjoyed making the point that despite Ryan's muscle and history and awards, Aronson could manhandle him easily. Not that Ryan was complaining.

"You annoy the shit out of me," Aronson said, teeth digging into the dip of Ryan's neck, right against the muscle. "You're the most annoying, frustrating little—"

"Okay," Ryan agreed, the hand he had fisted in Aronson's hair yanking his head back up. That was going to leave a bruise tomorrow. "You're also pretty fucking terrible," he managed, although it came out a lot fonder than he'd intended it to sound. "You really have to—have to stop that, someone's going to ask questions—"

"You'd like that, wouldn't you?" Aronson asked, dumping him onto the fluffy hotel comforter, and Ryan had to admit that, secretly, he had a point.

The next day, the boys lost to the Blades, which wasn't surprising: the Beacons were rebuilding, and the Blades were nearly done. Ryan was going to need to tell them to watch it around the net. There was a fine line between battling for the puck, and slashing at the goalie's glove so hard that one of the Blades' big forwards lost his mind about it and the Beacons earned costly fighting *and* instigator penalties.

Ryan just had to move on to the next one the same way he always did. This would be Anaheim, which should have been a *gimme*. There weren't any sure things in this league, though: even the lowliest team in the standings could defeat a Cup champion, given the right bounces. There would be time to go over video with the team before the game, the specific small things they would need to tighten up, the things that Ryan had studied in Anaheim's play that would be easy to exploit.

Meanwhile, by the time he got back to the hotel, he was exhausted, but too amped up to sleep. He could feel the anticipation shiver through him, knowing that

Aronson was probably going to open the door if Ryan knocked.

Aronson did, one eyebrow raised. Even without his glasses to emphasize how high the eyebrow had gone, it was still a ridiculously sardonic expression. He was already stripped down to his boxers and undershirt, and Ryan, for some reason, couldn't stop staring at the dark curls of hair visible over the neckline. It was especially difficult now that Ryan knew what it felt like, soft under his fingers.

"Can I help you, Sullivan?"

Even now, it felt ridiculous to say it out loud, but he was tired enough that he didn't want to beat around the bush or play games. "Fuck me. I mean, you should, that is. Fuck me."

Aronson looked at him for a long, silent moment, the corner of his mouth twitching like he couldn't decide whether he wanted to smile or frown. It was funny, how they'd gotten physical in a moment of anger, but once they'd actually started doing this regularly, it was like Aronson couldn't keep up the pretense for real. He'd say one thing and his body would say something completely different. Ryan wasn't sure what he actually felt about all of it, but at least Aronson wasn't unwilling, anyway.

Aronson took a step back from the door and flourished an equally sarcastic gesture at the bed, and Ryan stepped over the threshold and into the room proper, chin lifted. Aronson wouldn't embarrass *him* out of this.

"That an order?" Aronson asked.

"What do you think?" Ryan said, stripping off his shirt.

Aronson followed him into the room proper, shaking his head. "You're ridiculous, you know that, right?"

"What do you mean?" Ryan demanded, kicking off his pants.

"Just…everything about you," Aronson said, almost a little bemused, as he stepped into Ryan's space and pushed him back toward the bed.

Ryan let him do it, fell back against the duvet without much of a protest, Aronson crouched over him. Ryan looked up at him, searching over his face: the dark brown eyes, the full mouth that could so easily turn Ryan into a quivering mess, the shadowed hint of a beard, the sharp jaw and stubborn chin. Aronson's face was all angles, and Ryan had the irresistible urge to touch it. There was nothing to stop him, so he did, fingers brushing over Aronson's stubbled jaw.

"I'm tired," Ryan said. "Make it quick."

Aronson made a noise that was somewhere between a snort and a laugh. "Jesus, you're bossy tonight."

"I'm *tired*," Ryan reminded him, "and I still have to go back to my own room after this, you know."

Aronson's mouth did that little twitchy motion again, like he wasn't sure how annoyed he actually was. He didn't say anything right away, just took Ryan's dick in his hand, and said, "Well, you better get it up, then, old man."

It was pretty embarrassing how fast Ryan's body obliged, and he could feel the hot flush of excited shame in his cheeks and ears. Even when they were rushing through the preamble of sex, Ryan still marveled at how different it felt from the last few times he'd slept with Shannon. They had felt emotionless and distant. This was anything but. Every small touch of Aronson's fingers on his skin, every grip of Aronson's hands on his biceps or hip, felt new and revelatory. Every dig of Aronson's teeth against his lower lip was something Ryan wanted to study and commit to memory.

Ryan urged him on, and Aronson obliged, hands rough on Ryan's skin, fingers rough in Ryan's body. It was different than it had been the first time, when Aronson had been so fucking determined to treat him nicely even though it was the opposite of what Ryan wanted. It was like now that Aronson knew Ryan could handle it, he was trying to test Ryan's limits instead. To see when he'd say *stop* or if he'd tap out.

Well, the joke was on him, because Ryan fucking loved all of it.

"Come on," Ryan managed, voice strained. It was really too fast, what they were doing, and it hurt, and Ryan didn't care about that one fucking bit. *"Fuck me."*

Aronson, somehow, managed to look skeptical. He was on his knees, crouched above Ryan's body, two big fingers in Ryan's ass. It felt incredible; it felt like too much. "Fuck you? You barely seem like you can handle this."

"I want to see what it feels like," Ryan said, fingers wrapped around Aronson's free arm just in case he decided to pull away. "Before I'm really ready."

"I've asked this before and I'll ask this again: Sullivan, what is *wrong* with you?"

"Nothing," Ryan panted. "I'm just competitive. You know this."

Aronson's mouth twitched again but he didn't answer, just leaned down to kiss Ryan again, twisting his fingers. For a long moment Ryan couldn't speak at all, and when he did, it was half phrases and unfinished sentences, ragged and wanting: "Come on, come on, come on, do it, please—"

In the end Aronson had to compromise. It wasn't as slow as he seemed to want but it also wasn't as fast as Ryan wanted. They were trapped in a close, humid limbo, a tangle of limbs and lips and teeth. It still felt electric, and Ryan was sweating with the effort of taking it, trying to breathe through it, trying to relax. Aronson pushing inch by steady inch, filling him.

It was strange, how a month ago Ryan would never in his wildest imagination have guessed he'd be in this position. On his back, wrists pinned down to the pillow, stuck on the knife's edge between pain and pleasure. Equally strange how much he just did not fucking *care* about anything except how good it was going to feel, once he could convince Aronson that he wasn't made of glass.

"Insane," Aronson mumbled into his mouth, "like you want a good grade in fucking. Where the hell did you come from?"

Ryan thought about telling him, *from Southie, what did you think*, but he was too busy shifting back against Aronson's body, trying to force him to go deeper. Move faster. He thought that maybe Aronson was going to say something again, but they'd fallen into the rhythm of it now, and the only sound in the room was skin on skin and uneven breaths.

And then Aronson began moving, really moving, in earnest, and Ryan wasn't thinking about much at all anymore.

Ryan was finding that regularly getting the conscious thought railed out of his head had an effect on his day-to-day. It was a lot easier to ignore texts from his father and brothers when he wasn't just sitting around doing nothing after work. It was a lot easier to remain calm in practice when Aronson was being a dick when Ryan knew that afterward, he could just push Aronson's head down and make him suck Ryan's dick.

"What are you smiling about?" Aronson grumbled, back in Boston again, while they were waiting for the guys to finish one of the skating drills.

"Just thinking," Ryan said cheerfully.

"About *what*."

"Something to be said for the killing-them-with-kindness approach."

Aronson shot him a suspicious look, and Ryan did his best to remain blank-faced.

Even with the distraction Aronson provided, the final divorce hearing still snuck up on him before he was ready. The whole process had been relatively painless, considering. His agent had found him a well-respected divorce lawyer; they'd had the conferences where they discussed what Ryan wanted out of the whole process—which was a fair division of assets and nothing more than that. He didn't want to spend any time fighting with Shannon about it. And now he was driving back to New Hampshire so that the judge could finalize everything.

It would probably be the last time he'd see Shannon for quite a while after, and he wasn't sure how he felt about the whole thing. She had seemed relieved to close the chapter of their lives together, and he had to admit he was also somewhat relieved to be done. But it still felt strange, to be heading in there in one of his game-day suits, his hair carefully combed, and his collar and tie arranged so that the hickey Aronson had left behind wouldn't be visible in the courtroom.

The actual divorce hearing went by in a blur; if you had asked him to tell you any details, he would not have been able to recall a single one except for the way Shannon looked, sitting at the opposite table with her lawyer, elegant and composed. Her shoulders relaxed when the judge told them that he had reviewed their paperwork, the submissions of the attorneys, and would be issuing an order in accordance with the recommendations. Ryan's ears rang, a little, an echo.

Afterward, Shannon crossed the aisle. Behind them, their lawyers had their heads together, talking over some point about the split of assets. Shannon ignored them, came up to hug him. It wasn't as hard or bone-crushing a hug as the one she'd given him in Newfields, but when she pulled away, she still looked a bit sad. "This is it, huh?"

"This is it," Ryan said. "You're officially a free woman."

"About that..." Shannon looked down at her shoes, twisting one of the many rings she always wore. "I just wanted to be honest with you. Since we've been handling all of this so—well. I'm seeing someone. I have been for a few months now."

"What?" Ryan said, surprised. He'd half considered the possibility before, but never seriously. He wondered if the news would have come as a blow, if life hadn't fallen into place the way it had.

"I didn't want to hurt your feelings, it truly wasn't personal, it just sort of happened. He's an artist and a sculptor, and we met at a pottery class he was running, and he's very kind and—"

"Shannon, you don't have to feel bad about that. It's

fine. I'm just really happy you're happy, you know? You deserve that."

She stopped short, surprised. "Well, that's—that's very mature, Ryan."

"I, uh, met someone, too."

Shannon's mouth dropped open. *"What?"*

"It's pretty new, so."

"Well, that's great," Shannon said, slowly, like she was still trying to process it. She didn't sound upset, at least. "What's she like?"

Ryan took a deep breath. The judge had gone back into the robing room behind the bench; the attorneys were still talking about whatever it was attorneys talked about when they didn't want to gut opposing counsel with a fountain pen, when they weren't exactly friends but knew each other well anyway.

It was probably a stupid idea to say anything, but he'd never liked hiding things from Shannon, and she had been up-front with him. He didn't want to think about how it would feel if she reacted badly, so instead he said, all in a rush, "He's kind of an asshole, sometimes, but it works for me. I guess."

Shannon stared at him again. "That's—that's great, Ryan. Is this—is he someone I'll be able to meet at some point?"

Ryan shifted, a little uncomfortable. "I don't know if it's really like that, right now. I don't know if you and I are really like that right now. Or ever. But if we're being honest, I wanted to be honest." He didn't know if it would ever really be like that. If he wanted it to be like that. He also didn't know how to explain it to her. Whether there was even a label he could use. He said in a rush, realizing how it must have sounded, "I'm not—

it's not like I never loved you, like I was never attracted to you. This thing with him—it sort of just happened. I'm learning a lot of things about myself, you know? It's been pretty weird."

"I—I can imagine," Shannon said. She was still looking at him like she'd never seen him before. "You know. This explains a lot of shit about Murph."

"Murph?" Ryan said, blinking. "This has nothing to do with Murph. What are you talking about? Murph and Tara have been married for years, the same way we were."

"Oh, *Ryan...* I think, maybe, you still have a little learning to do." Ryan stared at her, but she didn't explain any further. "Okay, well, I'm meeting Jackson for lunch, so I should probably start packing things up here."

"All right, Shannon."

Shannon reached out and touched his cheek. "Ryan, I'm just sorry this all didn't work out. You're a good man. I hope this—whatever you're figuring out is making you happy, too."

And just like that, his marriage was over.

The news as Eric was getting his morning coffee ready seemed more and more dire these days. The lawsuit against the Railers for their role in covering up the assault on an anonymous player had been proceeding through the courts. Eric wasn't familiar with the way the American court system worked, really, but the team had hired an independent investigator to look into allegations that the front office and even the coaching staff had been aware of what happened. The report was going to come out any day now, or at least, had been about to come out any day now for the last few months. Privately,

Eric wondered whether they'd ever release their findings. It seemed like the kind of thing the team would do its best to squash.

Today, the other dire thing was that he was getting his coffee ready in Ryan Sullivan's apartment, and it turned out that Sully did not have any proper coffee-making equipment at all. He had a $20 Mr. Coffee and a single-serving Keurig machine both taking up space on his counter, and it looked like he'd never used the Mr. Coffee in his entire time staying here.

"You know this shit is terrible for the environment, right?" Eric called, fiddling with the flippy top of the Keurig.

"I never use it," Sully mumbled, still burrowed deeply in the covers where Eric had left him. The apartment was small enough that Eric could hear him, even muffled by the blankets, even in the kitchen. "I just go to Dunkin'."

"Of course you do," Eric said, pinching the bridge of his nose.

"What's wrong with Dunkin'?"

"If you wanna drink vaguely coffee-flavored *water* that's mostly cream and sugar, there's nothing wrong with it."

"Jesus, I didn't know I was fucking a coffee snob."

"It's not being snobby, it's called having *one* taste bud, Sully."

"Fuck off, it's too early for this."

It was, of course, a little early. And they had been up late last night. Late enough that when they were finished, Sully had rolled over and wrapped his arms around Eric's body, closed his eyes and muttered into

Eric's chest hair, "Come on, it's ass o'clock, you can stay over for *once*, it's not gonna fucking kill you."

Eric had felt his heart beating too loudly in his own ears, knocking against his ribs. It was probably loud enough that Sully could have heard it, too. This felt like something he shouldn't have been doing, but the bed was warm, and he was so fucking relaxed and loose and comfortable, that he'd said, "Fine, *fine*."

He'd woken up in the morning to the light streaming through Sully's blind-less window and Sully's arm slung over his waist still and his phone buzzing on the floor next to Sully's bed and thought: *fuck*.

By the time he'd spoken to his mom and jury-rigged passable coffee in the percolator, Sully had stumbled into the kitchen, wearing only his boxers. He yawned hugely, stretching one arm a little, like it was aching, and he wanted to test it. Eric tried not to stare at him when he did it, at the way his stomach and shoulder muscles shifted, the way the boxers rode up his thighs. It was just his fucking luck that he had developed some kind of temporary derangement about Ryan Sullivan, where every stupid thing he did made Eric want to shove him against a wall.

"Do you do that every morning?" Sully asked.

"What?"

"Talk to your mom?"

"Most mornings," Eric said, warily prepared to get defensive about it.

"That's really sweet," Sully said, and smiled at him, still sleepy-eyed, hair messy.

"You tell anyone about that, I'll fucking kill you." To cover his discomfort, he turned away, so he could pour them both cups of coffee.

"Your secret's safe with me," Sully said, and Eric heard him opening some cabinets, and the fridge. "It *is* sweet, though. Does she still live in Canada?"

"The only way she's leaving Montreal is in a coffin," Eric muttered. "Born and raised there. Loves it. I offered to move her out close to me, since she's kind of frail these days, and she refused—*what* are you doing to that coffee?"

"Making it drinkable," Sully said, as he dumped heaping teaspoons full of sugar into the cup, followed by long glugs of hazelnut-flavored creamer.

"Oh my god. Jesus, Sully, you do this *every morning*?"

"I go to Dunkin' every morning, usually. But someone insisted on making coffee here."

Eric reached out and gripped his shoulders, and said, "Ryan Sullivan, I'm going to fix you. Somehow. I'm going to teach you how to be better."

Instead of answering or trying to twist out of his grip, Sully went up on his tiptoes and kissed Eric on the mouth. It was disgusting. He tasted like morning breath and artificial hazelnut and sugar, and somehow, Eric was still kissing him back anyway, his hands slipping down to grip Sully by the biceps.

"Oh," Sully said, with a little sigh as he pulled away, "you want breakfast? We have time. I have eggs."

"You really missed your calling as a lawyer. Very convincing argument, right there."

Sully shoved him hard into the cabinets, a little painful when his spine and ass hit the knobs, and said, "Do you want something to eat or not?"

"Fine," Eric said, "feed me."

He tried not to stare, but it was kind of a treat watching Sully cook in his boxers, the shift of muscle, the way his head bent low in concentration. Eric sat on the kitchen table, his legs swinging, arms crossed over his chest, and waited. "You missed practice yesterday," he said, after a long pause, broken only by the sound of butter sizzling in the pan, the clank of a fork against ceramic, the faint hiss when Sully poured the eggs in.

"Yeah, uh, I was in New Hampshire for a court hearing," Sully said. He didn't turn to look at Eric, and his shoulders sagged a little.

"A court hearing?"

Another one of those shrugs that rolled across Sully's entire body. "My divorce was finalized. It was a pretty easy divorce as far as those things go, but since we had the assets to divide up and we'd been married for so long, so we still had to..."

"Oh," Eric said, not entirely sure what you said when a guy you'd been sleeping with for a month told you that his divorce had just been finalized. Eric had known, vaguely, that Sully had been married at some point, but he'd never worn a ring since he'd been coaching. He'd also remembered, vaguely, that Sully had mentioned to Petey that his wife had kicked him out of the house. And Eric just...hadn't thought about it after that. "Are you...okay?"

Sully looked over his shoulder at Eric, and his eyes were dancing with the kind of mirth that seemed out of place for such a heavy topic. "Am I okay with my marriage to the girl I met at eighteen and married at twenty and spent most of my adult life with ending? Actually, yeah? She seems a lot happier already and that's...mostly what I wanted for her. I loved—love?—her, you know? It really wasn't her fault that she hated hockey so much, and I..."

Eric looked around the kitchen and living area of Sully's relatively compact apartment, which was piled high with hockey equipment, hockey memorabilia, hockey books and various papers from work, which were all about hockey. "You are basically hockey in hobbit form."

"Yeah," Sully said, and shrugged. "It was about as amicable a divorce as I think I could've hoped for. She kept the house I hated. She's seeing some sculptor from her pottery classes already."

"Good for her," Eric said, surprised.

"Yeah," Sully said. The whole time they'd been talking, he'd been constantly stirring the eggs, pulling the pan on and off the heat. "I told her I—well, that I was seeing a man."

"You *what*?"

"I didn't tell her about *you*. Don't worry. But I told her I was, uh, figuring some things out about myself, you know."

"That's...bold."

"I never could lie to her. And it's not anything I'm ashamed of. It just is. You want toast?"

Eric stared at him. He had spent so many years hiding shit from his parents, afraid that they'd think less of him, afraid of disappointing them, afraid their religious practice wouldn't end up being compatible with who he was as a person. He'd never even gotten a chance to come out to his dad before he'd passed. And here was Sully, just some middle-aged townie from Boston, who'd figured out he was queer for approximately two fucking weeks, and he was already coming out to his ex-wife like it was no big deal.

"Sometimes you, uh, really surprise me."

"Sometimes?" Sully said, sliding a plate of eggs and toast across the table at him. "Shit, I gotta start working harder."

They ate in silence, and Eric kept looking sideways at him. The thing was that Sully wasn't classically handsome. As a younger guy, he'd been almost *cute*, with his stubborn chin and big brown eyes. He'd managed to edge his way toward distinction with the silver hair and the hint of a beard that he never fully grew in, but he was just magnetic. The draw was his charm, the stupid earnestness bleeding in every sentence, the way his eyes on you felt like everything else in the room faded out.

It was like that even here, eating eggs in his shitty apartment kitchen.

Sully was saying something, and Eric said, "What?"

"I said, we have some pretty intense ground to cover in practice today. I already texted Petey about some of the defense drills, but for the power play, I really need you to get the drills moving at as high a speed as you can get them going."

"You got it, boss," Eric said, and saluted him with a piece of toast.

They left for practice separately, because it would have looked pretty suspicious if they hadn't, and Eric tried to get his head on straight. Things were shifting in ways that he didn't fully understand, ways that felt like tiny pebbles underfoot that could rapidly become a cliff collapse if he didn't watch his step. Except there was no clear path before him and no easy guidance as to where to walk.

At the practice facility, Petey was already on the ice, doing slow figure eights and blaring some kind of prog rock band Eric didn't recognize on his tinny phone speakers. He felt a little guilty, briefly, that he hadn't been there as early to tease Petey about his shitty taste in music the way he usually would have.

When Eric pushed out onto the ice, Petey gave him a lazy wave. "Hello, stranger. Ain't often seen you around these parts."

Eric felt a chill down his spine that had nothing to do with the fact that he was at ice level. "What do you mean?"

Petey smiled his inscrutable smile, and said, "Glad you and the boss are getting along. Things were getting a little uncomfortable before you worked your shit out."

"We didn't work anything out," Eric insisted, lamely, lying through his teeth.

Petey didn't answer, and Eric didn't have a chance to argue with that serene smile, as the team and Sully both started to come down the tunnel toward the ice. The power play practice might have been a success, but the vague sense of unease was still present. The sense that something dangerous was about to happen. He just didn't have any fucking clue *what* that was.

"Really, do you want me to get you a step stool?" Aronson asked Ryan, midgame.

Ryan, perched on top of the bench so he could get a better view of exactly how badly the Beacons were getting crushed by the Toronto Justice, sighed. It was one of those games where no matter what adjustments he tried to make on the fly, nothing was really working. He had probably been shown on the broadcast at least once hiding his face in his hand when a bad defensive-zone giveaway had immediately ended up in the back of Davey's net.

"I can see fine from up here," he said. "Not like there's much to see."

Aronson surveyed the ice: it was the last few minutes of the second period, and they were down three goals. It wasn't impossible to mount a comeback, but it wasn't likely, especially because all four lines had been struggling with successful zone entries. Or zone exits. In all three zones.

Ryan felt like he was vibrating out of his skin. He *hated* losing so fucking much, even when he wasn't the one on the ice anymore. He had known going into it that the Beacons were rebuilding, that the team was not good on paper and in practice might have been worse with regressions and underperformances.

Knowing and experiencing it were two different things, especially because he had to keep it cool and keep his philosophy firmly in practice. He was focusing on the positive, encouraging, helping the players grow. He was *not* ripping them apart or tearing them down.

But Ryan hated losing.

And watching Laurent Martel take a stupid penalty right at the end of the period, which meant they would be starting the third on the kill again? Ryan thought that maybe the top of his head was just going to explode.

Mercifully, the horn sounded to end the period, and the players filed back toward the locker room to rest, refuel and, depending on their preferences, have their gear changed or dried. The coaches followed after.

Aronson said, "Is this it? The game that's going to break the illustrious Ryan Sullivan?"

"We still have a whole damn period to play," Ryan said to him. "We can come back and win it."

Aronson pushed his glasses up his nose and gave Ryan

one of those looks, sardonic and judging, that used to piss him off but now mostly made him squirm a little uncomfortably, knowing what that usually preceded. "You don't really believe that."

"No, but I'm sure as hell going to try to convince *them* of it," Ryan said, and pushed the doors to the locker room open.

It was only during the worst games that the coach went immediately into the locker room between periods. The team would know, immediately, that they'd fucked up.

Whenever he gave speeches like this Ryan could never remember what he said afterward. It was like he entered into some sort of a fugue state, passionately expounding on the fact that they needed to play smart and stay out of the box, that they needed to anticipate the play better and think about where they were positioning themselves off the puck. Things just came out of his mouth without his brain's conscious input.

All he could see were the faces of the players immediately in front of him. Williams's serious determination. Cook's smile. Martel's scowl.

At the end of it, he exhaled and said, "It's a rebuilding year. But I know you hate losing as much as I do, and I've seen you play with more effort than we've been putting in tonight. Let's go out for the third and keep it tight and give them hell. All right. Thanks, boys."

"I can always bag skate them," Aronson said, as they and Petey left the players to finish changing.

"Not very chill of you, Roney," Petey said.

Ryan shook his head. "Absolutely not. We'll switch up the practices, keep them moving, but it has to stay fun and it has to stay motivating."

"Optimism is a disease," Aronson said, shaking his head. But on the bench, it was different.

Ryan wasn't sure exactly when things had shifted, but he wasn't complaining. Somehow, in between the hotel rooms and apartments and the rest of it, working with Aronson on the bench had gotten—easier.

They still had their tactical disagreements, especially about the power play, but since the first night against Colorado, when Aronson had directly contradicted his requests, things had settled. Ryan had to admit that, maybe, he was also more open to listening…but there was only so much they could do with the roster. If he split up Cook and Williams, then instead of one line that could score, he had zero lines that could score. And there weren't many other options for shuffling the lines around.

The Beacons mounted a spirited comeback in the third, mostly on Williams's back. He seemed determined to single-handedly win it, from the thread-needle passes to set Cook up for one-timers to his own drive to the net to shovel in a rebound. Ultimately, it wasn't enough.

Ryan pulled Davey with three minutes to go to try to get them the extra goal and maybe push it to overtime, but the empty netter sealed their fate instead. Losing 4-2 wasn't as bad as getting shut out 3-0, technically, but it felt the same.

Ryan had to face the media after every game, and he always tried to keep it the same tone: even, never too high, never too low. He didn't call out individual players. But there were always pointed questions he couldn't entirely talk his way out of.

"Sully, what do you think about the fact that there

just isn't any secondary scoring on this team?" someone asked from the scrum.

Ryan couldn't lie and say that they were playing the right way 5v5, because the numbers were quite clear that they weren't, whether you were looking at publicly available stats or the Beacons' own internal numbers. But he tried not to throw anyone under the bus as his usual philosophy.

Instead, he exhaled, and said, "We just have to get back to playing the right way, keeping track of the little things, taking care of the team. It's easy to get complacent across the season, and I know that the next game, after these practices, we're gonna clean this shit—sorry, excuse my language—up."

Whether anyone bought it—media or players—was anyone's best guess.

Later that night, Ryan found himself on his knees at the side of Aronson's bed, Aronson's legs bracketing him in, one of Aronson's hands in his hair. He was gasping; he still wasn't so great at controlling his breathing, but he was always *determined* to go for it 100%.

"Taking care of the team," Aronson said. He had that particular tone of voice he had sometimes when Ryan had really gotten to him, taut and kind of trembly, like he didn't want Ryan to know how much it had affected him. "You're always fucking saying that."

"It's important," Ryan managed, after pulling off. His own voice was throaty, rough. Aronson hadn't been easy on him. "The little things. Watching out for the guys. It's always been important; I've always said that."

"You have. And you're right. It's important. It's just…" Aronson said, that little sly smirk twitching the corner of his mouth up. "I bet you liked taking care of the team. Eh?"

Ryan blinked, shifted his weight so he wasn't leaning forward. He wouldn't be able to do this much longer; his knees were already screaming. "Wait, are you trying to dirty talk me about my fucking *media availability*?"

"I'm not trying, bud."

"This is insane," Ryan said, his hands gripping Aronson's thighs.

"Taking care of the team…one player at a time," Aronson said, his voice a mocking singsong.

"Oh my god—"

If it was anyone else, Ryan probably would have felt—embarrassed, or humiliated. But Aronson was so clearly enjoying this, his dark brown eyes dancing, like it was a joke he was letting Ryan in on, that Ryan just leaned down and bit him on the thigh instead, teeth digging in. Aronson hissed but didn't pull away, put his hand in Ryan's hair and pushed him back down.

"I'm here. I'm here right now. Take care of me."

Ryan, his mouth otherwise occupied, couldn't answer. Not with words.

After they were finished, Ryan pressed his fingers against the deep red mark he'd left on Aronson's thigh. "The media availabilities really get you going, seriously?"

"The things that come out of your mouth," Aronson said with a satisfied sigh, "and the things that go into your mouth. Just a talent, you know."

By the time the holiday break rolled around, Ryan had been so busy and distracted with practices and games and travel and having what seemed to him like a ridiculous amount of sex that he almost forgot he had agreed to go home to his parents' for Christmas. The text from Chelsea, reminding him, felt like falling through the sheet ice on a pond in the winter.

The Sullivans were nominally Catholic, in that the family had emigrated from Ireland generations ago and belonged to the same South Boston parish since. They had all been raised with a vague sense of constant guilt, a lot of noisy family events, and set foot in church approximately twice a year. Ryan, once he moved out for college, stopped going at all, eager to shed as much of that baggage as he could.

Dad, on the other hand, had gotten more religious as the years had dragged on, but in a way that meant that he didn't have to attend church any more than he normally did. The lectures had increased, and the strict adherence to family rituals around the big holidays like Christmas and Easter, but that was about the extent of it.

Ryan had always hated Christmas, even when Shannon was there to soften some of the worst of it. This would be the first year he would have to go alone, without his mother or his wife. Briefly, he imagined what it would have been like to drag Aronson along. The mental image of his father and Aronson having to have a conversation was almost worth the fact that it would likely end with someone bleeding. Aronson wasn't the kind of person to put up with anyone's bullshit, and Dad—well, Dad had a lot of bullshit to offer.

Petey had gone home to his family in Vancouver; Heidi and her wife, Melissa, and their adorable baby were having a quiet holiday at home. And Ryan had to just get the fuck over it and suffer through.

By the time he got there, everyone was already present.

The thin driveway along the side of the house was already packed, the Sullivan & Sons Construction truck backed into the far end of the drive by his brothers' cars. They were always trying to one-up each other there, too. Jimmy had just upgraded to a new BMW, so Eddie had bought a Porsche.

The house was festooned with multicolored lights, and the noise from inside already carried out to the street. It was one of those cold, crisp nights where Ryan would really have rather just gone for a run along the Charles. Or jumped off a bridge. Pretty much be anywhere, doing anything, other than this.

He took a deep breath, squared his shoulders, and went in.

Almost immediately, Kevin grabbed him by the arm and said, "Well, look who it is, the head coach of the second-to-last-place team in the Atlantic Division."

"You guys angling for that lottery pick after all, huh?" Mark demanded.

Ryan counted to ten internally and said, "Merry Christmas to you, too."

It went downhill from there. His brothers all seemed delighted that the team had been slumping and were eager to tell him. Kevin, especially, went on at great length about the power play and how *he* would have fixed it.

"You'd just tell them to shoot more?" Ryan asked, incredulous.

"You can't get too fancy passing constantly," Kevin said, chest puffing out a little, "you just have to get the pucks on net."

Sometimes when they got like this Ryan thought about all of the things he could have said: that the only reason they were so critical was because they had wanted what he had so fucking badly and had never had the talent or determination to get there. They had all played pro hockey at some level, at least for a few seasons, but Ryan was the only one who had made the North American major league. Eddie would talk your ear off at length about his time in Sweden. Kevin had played a few seasons with the Beacons' minor league affiliate. And Mark had done his time in the league below the minors.

But the fact was, Ryan was the only one who had *made* it.

It didn't matter if he had. Ryan might have been a Hall of Famer with the kind of illustrious career his brothers could only dream of, but listening to his family talk, you'd have thought he was some kind of draft bust. He never said anything when they chirped him. It was just like fighting with Dad—not only were you outnumbered, it left you feeling dirty afterward.

Ryan tried to spend as much of his time playing with his little nieces and nephews and talking hockey with the older ones as he could. Eddie's oldest daughter was trying out for her high school team and wanted his opinion on whether she should consider switching out her curve to try to get a little more power on her shot. Mark's middle son wanted his advice about which colleges he should be considering if he really wanted to push for the major leagues one day.

He even spent some time in the kitchen with Andrea and the other wives while they were helping to get the dinner ready. They were all perfectly pleasant women, even if they had almost nothing to talk about.

But he couldn't avoid his father forever. Dad had

made his way out of the lounger and into the kitchen, where he immediately began his reign of terror, poking his nose around to see the progress on the various parts of the meal while Chelsea tried to run interference. Dad saw Ryan right around that time, and his eyes narrowed.

"You're too good to say hello when you come into my home now?"

"I was catching up with everyone," Ryan said, lamely.

"You come in and greet your *father* before you run to hide in the kitchen."

"Mark—" Chelsea started, but fell silent when Dad whipped his head around to glare at her.

That was how these things always went: fighting with him just got him angrier. There wasn't an easy way to win without going nuclear, and no one was willing to see how far it would take to get there. And now that Ryan had already pissed him off, there wasn't going to be an easy recovery.

It was funny: he had been so fucking competitive on the ice, never backing down from a challenge no matter how much bigger the other player was, but when it came to his dad, he always felt like he was five years old again, listening to him screaming in the car on the way home from a mites game where Ryan hadn't back-checked hard enough, and the puck had ended up in the net.

He hated feeling small. And the only place he ever felt small was at home.

By the time dinner rolled around, Ryan had already fielded questions and critiques from his brothers and from Dad, eaten some food that didn't have much taste and had probably far too much to drink. It didn't help that at Dad's house people were always shoving beers into your hands, and it also didn't help that that was one of the only ways to make the evening tolerable.

He sat silently at his place, wedged in between Andrea and Madison, and pushed his food around on the plate with a fork. Suddenly, he wasn't very hungry. At the head of the table, Dad was ranting on about how soft the league was nowadays, particularly this whole Railers lawsuit business. In *his* day, players were men, and they handled that shit themselves. And probably that guy was lying anyway, just looking for a payout, like all of those other—

Ryan pushed his chair back. He stood up. Dad yelled after him, "Where the hell do you think you're going, son?"

But Ryan, walking faster and faster and faster toward the door, wasn't listening anymore.

When he had lived at home, Eric's family always celebrated what his dad had jokingly called "Jewish Christmas," which consisted of Chinese takeout and watching a movie at home. He'd always enjoyed those evenings, even though his and his father's taste in movies couldn't have been more different.

Specifically, because Eric didn't like movies very much and it didn't matter whether it was an art house film or a blockbuster, he had a hard time sitting through them. Joseph Aronson, on the other hand, had owned an insanely large Criterion collection that grew every year. Those were the movies they watched together. It had become kind of a tradition that Eric would pretend he didn't understand what was going on with the plot, while his father got increasingly frustrated every time until he realized that Eric was winding him up.

His father had been dead for a few years now, and

Eric worked such crazy hours, even on the holidays, that he couldn't always go home to his mom. But he still made the sacrifice and watched some boring old movie while eating takeout, and he thought about Dad and all of the time they'd had together and the time they wouldn't be able to have together anymore.

It was kind of a weird comfort, knowing that Dad had had a happy life, that he had been in love with Mom up until the end. But it also still nagged at him, in the back of his head, that there were things about Eric he hadn't ever been able to know before his death.

Aronson, Sully texted him.

Eric frowned at his phone. Isn't this like your big holiday?

Yeah, and it sucks.

Well, it's only like eight o'clock. You have a lot of time to go.

Sort of yes, sort of no. I'm outside your apartment building.

You're what?

I'm outside your apartment building and I'm freezing my balls off. Can you let me in?

Eric set the phone down. This was not what he had expected. Sure, they had been fucking around for a little while now and he had even stayed over Sully's apartment a few times, but this was...well, Christmas was a big fucking deal. And he didn't know why Sully wouldn't have been with his family, why he would have ended up on *Eric's* doorstep of all places.

He said, I'll be right down, paused the TV and got up.

Sully was, indeed, outside the apartment building. He wore a too-thin coat, the kind of coat that you grabbed if you were driving somewhere and weren't planning to be outside very long. He looked a little drunk and his eyes were red like he'd been rubbing at them. He was shivering and Eric wondered whether he'd walked there. Where he'd walked from. Basically, he looked fucking *miserable*.

Sully's eyes fixed on Eric like he was an anchor in a very rough sea, and he said, "Can I come in? Please?"

"Uh, yeah, sure. Come on up?"

"Thanks. Sorry. I didn't mean to—I don't know, what do you even do on Christmas?"

"Well," Eric said, gesturing for Sully to go up the stairs first. "You may have heard of my people's longstanding tradition of Chinese food and a movie. I already finished dinner, but I was watching something. If you, you know. Are interested."

"Thanks," Sully said, once they were inside Eric's apartment. He was still shivering, and he looked so fucking pathetic, like a cat that had been pulled out of a pond.

"Uh," Eric said, unsure of how to handle this. He'd seen Sully a lot of ways since they'd started working together: inspiring and confident and bitchy and completely undone, but he hadn't ever seen him like this, and he didn't know how to react. "Did you walk all the way over here in that jacket?"

"I just—you don't really know anything about my family, right?" They were still standing in the middle of Eric's living room, just looking at each other. "I don't really know how to explain it, but I fucking… I *hate* going back there. They're just the worst kind of asshole and there's *five* of them. But it's not even that. It's just—it doesn't matter what I've done. Even now. After all of these years. How I've proven all of them fucking *wrong*—"

Sully took a step forward, and his mouth was turned down, furious and intent. His hands were fists at his sides. He was shaking, although whether it was with anger or the cold, Eric couldn't tell. "I hate listening to that bullshit. And I hate feeling small, Eric. I fucking *hate it*."

At any other time, Eric would've made a joke about how much Sully liked when Eric pushed him around, but his body was moving for him. He took Sully's hands in his. They were icy as hell. "Jesus, you're cold."

"I left my car there," Sully mumbled, but he didn't pull away when Eric tried rubbing the warmth back into them. "I just had to…go. I don't know. I couldn't do it tonight." He looked up again. In the dim light of Eric's living room, his eyes were wide and dark. "I just—wanted to be somewhere else."

Eric realized belatedly that he was still holding Sully's hands in his. "Well, you're here now," he managed, before Sully was kissing him, pressing himself up against Eric's body. Eric wasn't sure which one of them started moving backward, but they were falling onto the couch, Eric first, Sully on top of him; Eric yelped in shock when Sully got his icy hands under Eric's shirt.

"You little *shit*!"

"Warm them up," Sully mumbled into his neck. His

hands stroked Eric's sides, and Eric shuddered. "Warm *me* up."

"I don't really have a choice about this, do I?" Eric demanded, squirming as he tried to get away. Behind them, the TV started playing again and Eric shifted again, realizing he'd sat on the remote.

Distracted, Sully's head whipped around. "What the hell are you *watching*?"

"Uh…it's *Inherit the Wind*."

"You mean the one about the Scopes monkey trial?"

"Yeah, you know it?"

"That's an interesting choice of holiday viewing."

"It was my dad. He always liked old movies, and this was one of his favorites. He's been gone for a little while now, but I like to keep the tradition going." Sully's hands were slowly warming up against Eric's skin, but he shivered anyway. "I really hate movies. But I have a lot of…a lot of good memories of them, with him."

Sully had pulled back a little. He looked down at Eric with an inscrutable expression. "You really love your parents, huh."

"They're good people," Eric said, embarrassed.

Sully had pulled his hand out from beneath Eric's shirt. Instead, his fingers traced down the line of Eric's wrist, over his sweater. "I left home as early as I could to get away from that. And then my mother died when I was away at college. And my dad, well. I don't have a lot of fond memories of him. So it's just nice that you love them so much. It's not what you'd think about you at all. At least not when first meeting you."

"What would you think about me?" Eric said. He had meant it to come out sarcastic, but his voice was weirdly quiet instead. How fucking weird was it that he actually cared what Sully thought about him?

"You're kind of an asshole at first, but you're also kind of a big softy, aren't you? You really *do* care."

"Oh, spare me," Eric said, with an exaggerated groan, and then he had to immediately lift his hand up to swat Sully's attempt at pinching his nose away. "All right, that's it, I'm cross-checking you into the boards the next time we're on the ice."

Sully shifted around in Eric's lap, and Eric bit back a small groan. Sully was grinning, the kind of shark-toothed smile that he had during drills, sometimes, when he knew that he was really wearing the team out. "That's exactly what I mean. You don't want anyone to know what you're really like. But now *I* know."

"You wouldn't—"

"No," Sully said, and leaned down to kiss him. His skin had warmed to the temperature of Eric's apartment, finally, and his kiss was eager and hungry. Eric didn't want to think too long about the fact that Sully had wanted to be anywhere except his family's house, and that the first place he had thought to go was Eric's. "Hey. You've got a perfectly good movie and a perfectly good tradition going, huh?"

"You *really* want to watch Spencer Tracy cross-examine an old fundamentalist?" Eric said doubtfully, finger brushing the line that demarcated Sully's hair and his neck. "We could just fuck."

"We can do that later. I want to see the movie."

And like many things that Sully did, Eric found himself giving in. Sully shifted off his lap and wormed his way under Eric's arm, and surprisingly enough, it wasn't actually all that bad to just sit like that. Now that the shaking had subsided and he was fully acclimated to a room with heating, holding Sully was like having a miniature furnace tucked against his body.

There wasn't much left in the movie, just the final climactic scenes. The guilty verdict, Cates's allocution, the sentence of $100, Jennings's collapse. Sully watched anyway. Eric realized he'd had a hand tangled in Sully's hair and moved it away. By the time Spencer Tracy had started ripping into Gene Kelly's cynicism, it felt much later than it was.

Nobody to mourn you, no one to give a damn. We are all alone.

"Jesus," Sully mumbled into Eric's side, as Gene Kelly asked who else would defend his right to be lonely, "some cheerful holiday viewing."

"Mm," Eric agreed. It hit him, right then, that *he* specifically wasn't alone, for the first holiday in quite some time. The realization was a little shocking. "Hey," he said, shifted so he could tip Sully's chin up with two fingers. "Do you want to come to bed?"

Sully smiled, slow and sleepy. "Thought you'd never ask."

Somehow, the sex was different this time, too, just as slow and sleepy as Sully's smile. Eric could barely get his clothes off because Sully wouldn't stop kissing him, wouldn't stop touching him. For all of the desperation in his voice when he'd first shown up on Eric's doorstep, that seemed to have faded away, replaced with the sort of confidence and surety that Eric recognized from his playing days.

Eric let him do it, let him take his time exploring what their bodies could do together. The force of that admiration, the intense study that Sully had about everything in his life turned just on him. It was a lot. But instead of being overwhelming, it was just *good.*

For once, Eric didn't feel the need to tease him or push him. He didn't have to do that. That wasn't what this was about, as weird as that seemed. It had been a damn long time since he'd had sex like this, and part of him didn't even know how to react.

"Can I—" Sully asked, eventually.

"Can you what?"

"Fuck you? I really want to."

Eric exhaled. They'd switched it up often enough already. He genuinely didn't have strong preferences about positions; he enjoyed Sully pretty much any way that they did it. It felt different tonight, though, and he didn't know why. It felt bigger to say "yes," and it felt almost vulnerable to let Sully do this now. But Sully had shown up on Eric's doorstep and Sully had trusted Eric with his family and Sully was slowly opening Eric up like a goddamn textbook.

Sully, kneeling over him, said, "You good?"

"Get it over with," Eric said, pulling him back down into a kiss.

"Wow," Sully mumbled around his tongue and his teeth, "not a very enthusiastic endorsement, huh—"

"Fuck me, you gigantic baby. Do you want me to tell you how good at it you are?" Sully's ears went a bit pink, and Eric laughed. "Shit, you do?"

The thing was. Once they actually started, once they got into the rhythm of it. Eric was having a hard time stringing together his thoughts, coming up with anything to say except "Fuck, Sully, like that, like that, like that—" and having a hard time doing anything except grabbing onto any part of Sully that he could reach.

Inside of him Sully felt overwhelming, thick and almost uncomfortably full, but so fucking good. Above him, Sully's serious face, pained and twisted like he was trying so hard to hold himself back, sweat beading his forehead, in and out of focus whenever he managed to coordinate himself to smash a sloppy kiss against Eric's mouth. Eric reached up again and touched his cheek.

"What—what?" Sully managed.

"You're very good at fucking me," Eric said, and Sully came with a stupid little groan.

His whole body seized up, collapsed on top of Eric, and he gasped, "Oh my god, I'm sorry, I didn't—"

"It's fine, it's fine," Eric said, wincing a little as Sully pulled out. He pushed himself up into a sitting position, even though his whole body was still trembling on the edge. "You can make it up to me."

Sully didn't answer, just looked up at him with a question in his eyes. He went down easily enough when Eric pushed a hand at his chest, then flinched when Eric shifted and straddled his thighs. "What are you—"

"Jerking off on you, obviously."

Sully's eyes, still a bit post-sex sleepy, opened wide with surprise, but he didn't pull away. He licked his lips, watched while Eric took himself in hand. Even though he was spent, his gaze was still so fucking hungry that Eric knew he wasn't going to be able to last long.

He didn't. He forced his eyes open when he came; watched his come striping Sully's broad chest. Sully's little exhale when he did it was irresistible and before Eric could spend too much time thinking about it, he had leaned forward and they were kissing again, the kind of slow, devouring kiss that annihilated all thought from his head, even the exhaustion from the late night and getting thoroughly fucked.

Eventually, Sully pulled away and said, "That was pretty hot, but, uh, it's getting kind of disgusting now—let me up."

Instead of answering, Eric smeared his hand through the mess on Sully's chest, ignoring his yelp of dismay and disgust, the sudden shift of his muscle as he tried to use a wrestling throw to toss Eric right off of the bed. The element of surprise worked in his favor.

Eric, in a heap on the floor, said, "I deserved that."

Sully's face, peering over the edge of the bed. "Never a dull moment with you, huh?"

By the time they had cleaned up and gotten back in bed, Sully was smiling, his eyes closed. "Thank you. For all of this. It's probably the best Christmas I've had in a while."

To cover his discomfort, Eric said, "Well, you're welcome to come over and fuck me anytime."

"I'll keep that offer in mind, Eric," Sully mumbled, and then he was asleep.

Eric lay in bed, staring at the ceiling for a long time after that. Something had changed and he wasn't sure how he felt about it. Didn't even know if he knew how to describe it. Didn't know if he even wanted to. Eventually, he fell asleep like that, listening to Sully shifting around in the bed, closer and closer to Eric's body.

CHAPTER NINE

New Year's Eve—January

It was funny, Ryan thought, as New Year's Eve snuck up on them, how insanely quickly his life had changed. Turned completely upside down. This time last year he'd been at home, coaching peewee hockey with a wife who resented him for it, ignoring the fact that she resented him for it.

This year, he was on the bench for a matinee game in Las Vegas as the head coach of his childhood hockey team and the assistant coach standing next to him had just spent a few choice seconds whispering behind his hand all of the things he wanted to do to Ryan after the game.

Ryan had managed, pretty admirably, he thought, to keep a straight face.

"Eat some bad airport sushi before the game?" Petey asked.

Okay, maybe he wasn't doing such a great job at that.

The coaching had been a pretty insane seesaw too. They'd had so many rough games where the team got blown out 6-1 or 5-0 or in one particularly memorable case, 10-1. Ryan had tried various ways to reset: intense practices that were not bag skates but about accountability, fun practices that engaged the brain, shuffling the lines repeatedly, rotating the unlucky thirteenth forward or seventh defenseman...pretty much everything that he could do except sitting down particular veterans on the bench and ripping them new assholes.

And then today, at a matinee game, the boys were decimating the Vegas Aces, who were consistently near the top of the Pacific Division. It was like a completely different team had shown up and Ryan felt the familiar pressure headache building up behind his eyes. The tantalizing glimpse of what he *could* have once everything started clicking. The thing that would always be just out of reach until he could start shedding roster deadweight, the kids started coming into their own and the team finally learned consistency.

It wasn't anything they could count on actually lasting. Not this season. Not when injuries made things unpredictable, not when the roster would inevitably regress, because that's what he had to work with. But he would have to enjoy it while he could, on the afternoon before the new year. He could enjoy watching the team play disciplined, crisp hockey, not even letting the antics of Vegas's resident rat, Leo Cohen, get to them. The game-winning goal was scored with Cohen in the penalty box, spitting mad.

After the game was over, Ryan faced the media with the usual questions. In the back of the room, he could see Petey and Eric watching him, Petey with sleepy eyes and Eric with sharper interest.

"Are you getting frustrated with Jesse Keen, Sully?"

He had to be careful with questions like these, the ones that were so pointed you knew that the reporter had a specific column in mind already and it was probably something like *Coach Sullivan Finally Loses Patience with Veteran Forward.*

"I'm not getting frustrated, no," Ryan said, shaking his head. "I would like to continue seeing a consistent effort from everyone on the team, and that includes Keener, but this will come with time."

"Considering we are almost into the new year, do you think that we are maybe running out of time?"

Ryan shrugged. He rubbed his face as he considered the question, fingers dragging down his chin, and realized belatedly that he was echoing something that Eric had done to him the night before—gripped his chin and forced him to look. In the back of the room, Eric had that smirk on his face, like he'd realized exactly what Ryan was doing, too, and Ryan could feel the back of his neck turning red.

"Uh," he said, trying to keep his composure. "To be blunt, this is a rebuilding year. Obviously, we would all like to make the playoffs, but we have to be realistic about what the team is and what state it is in right now. I'm happy with the performances we are getting from the younger players."

The questions were cut off, thankfully, after a few more minutes, and Ryan excused himself. He stood in the hallway alone for a few seconds before the guys started coming out of the locker room and heading back to the bus. He took the time to wish them all a happy new year, to check in and see what their plans were, whether any of them had any issues with the accommodations. To Cook and Williams especially, he said, "I know we're in Vegas tonight, but try not to go too crazy."

Williams laughed and said, "Coach, I'm headed back to my hotel room to crash. If Caleb wants to worry about American drinking ages, that's on him."

"You said we were going to play *Call of Duty*," Cook groused, "come on, old man, it was a *matinee game*," and Ryan shook his head. The league was certainly a different place than it had been when he'd been coming up if the boys were spending more time in their hotel room playing video games than going out on the town.

It was late, but the coaches had agreed to go out for dinner together to celebrate the new year and the progress they'd made. Heidi hadn't come on the trip with them, because her wife's birthday was New Year's Day and she'd asked to stay home. Ryan had let Petey make the reservations and it seemed like maybe he'd picked the spot solely based on the name, which was Peyote. He wouldn't have put it past Petey, who had exactly that kind of sense of humor. The restaurant itself was bright and trendy and very pink. Eric took a picture of the table setup, rolling his eyes just a little. It was a feast of the seven fishes kind of meal, though, and the food was good, so Ryan didn't complain.

Petey didn't drink, but he toasted the two of them with his sparkling water. "To the two of you finally figuring shit out," he said. "Sometimes felt like I needed to come to work in bomb squad gear just in case."

"Laying it on a bit thick," Eric drawled, knocking back his little champagne flute.

"Not at all. Sully, you can tell him he's wrong."

"He doesn't listen to me," Ryan said, taking another bite of the last dish, which was uni ice cream with a golden corn puff. It wasn't something he would ever have seen himself eating when he'd been growing up in

Southie, but there were a lot of things he was currently doing that thirteen-year-old Ryan probably would have stared at, goggle-eyed.

"No?" Petey asked.

"Not at all."

"Hmm."

By the time they were done with dinner and had taken a cab back to the Strip, it was almost midnight; Petey had already broken off from the group to go, as he put it, explore the streets as an anonymous celebrant.

"Petey, are you gonna be okay?" Eric asked.

"I'll be fine. I like to do this. Spend the night alone. Let the adventures come to me."

"Adventures?"

"Don't worry. Whatever happens, I'll be on the plane tomorrow."

Neither of them could convince him to stay, and, instead, walked together back toward the hotel. Ryan caught Eric doing it again, from the corner of his eye: ducking down to pick up a smooth white pebble from a gravel garden.

"Eric?"

"Yeah, bud."

"What are you doing?"

"What?" Eric asked. He looked a little guilty, slipping the rock into his pocket.

"I noticed you do that in every city we've been in. Take a rock or a pebble or something. What are you saving them for?"

The Vegas Strip was chaotic on New Year's Eve, even before the actual new year rolled around, with neon and flashing lights everywhere; people spilling in and out of the casinos and restaurants. With all of the chaos, Ryan only had eyes for Eric, handsome in his rumpled suit and messy hair. Eric pushed his glasses a little farther up his nose and sighed.

"It's a Jewish custom, kind of...to put stones or pebbles on the graves of family members. These are for my father."

"You pick one up in every city we go to?"

"That's the thing. It's not really a *mitzvah* in the traditional sense. It's just a custom. You can do it however you want, but I always felt like... I never got to spend as much time at home as they would have liked, and they never really got to travel with me. So this is my way of bringing the places I've gone to him. I go back to the cemetery whenever I'm in Montreal, and I talk to him about them."

Ryan was warm and a little tipsy and very full from the meal, and there was a lump in his throat he couldn't entirely describe. "What do the stones on the grave symbolize?"

"It's just—I don't know. There are all kinds of interpretations. That it's keeping the soul in the world or keeping demons out. Sometimes it's just practical. They last longer than flowers. Or just a reminder that we've been there."

"That's really...that's really nice." They were still walking, their arms bumping. Ryan wondered what would have happened if he'd hooked his arm through Eric's.

Eric glanced sideways at him. "Thank you."

"I never really visit my mom's grave."

"No?"

"I feel guilty," Ryan said, the words coming out in a rush. "I never used to go home; you know? And I wasn't there for her. I knew she hadn't been feeling well, but I didn't know she had been that sick. I didn't get to spend more time…"

"I think once you get old enough, we all have our regrets with our parents. I never told my parents the truth about me, and I think about that every day. That he died not knowing who I really am. It just feels really shitty. They were so proud of me, but they don't really know me at all, in some ways."

When he had first taken the job and Eric had been such an asshole about it, Ryan would never have guessed that they would have had so much in common. Not in the obvious ways, of course—thank god Eric's parents didn't sound anything like Ryan's dad—but the regrets, and the secrets, and the losses. Eric *understood.* He felt warm again, from his chest down to his toes, the warmth of knowing that he was talking to someone who got it.

It must have been New Year's: the fireworks were loud and sudden, and Ryan jumped before he could catch himself. Eric was laughing at him, cracking up: his eyes almost closed when he was really amused, and Ryan wanted to grab him and shake him and probably also kiss him. They couldn't do any of that in public. Instead, Ryan gave him a little shove in the arm, and Eric, still grinning, shoved back.

"My room or yours?" Ryan said.

"Sully," Eric said, "surprise me."

Eric woke up on January 1 in Ryan Sullivan's hotel room, with the man himself draped over Eric's back like a barnacle and a mild hangover.

"Ow," Eric said, fumbling one hand over the side table to reach for his glasses.

"Mmf," Sully mumbled into his shoulder. For someone who was always at the rink early and insisted on everyone else getting there early too, he sure as hell hated mornings.

Eric tried to shift around so that he could look at Sully head-on, but it was difficult, because Sully was still stubbornly asleep, his face pressed against Eric's shoulder.

"We gotta make it down to breakfast, mon chum," Eric said, before he could stop himself.

Fuck, he had to be more careful about that. It was the kind of phrase that had two meanings, and he definitely didn't think that Sully knew either of them, but there was no need to complicate things when they hadn't discussed expectations or their relationship. No need except for the fact that waking up on New Year's Day in a forcible embrace *did* things to his stupid head.

Sully didn't seem to notice or realize, so Eric was safe to skate by on another day of refusing to define what was going on here beyond *I'm sleeping with my coworker and also spending most of my spare time with him outside of work, but that's fine, because we're both very busy and also don't have any interests besides hockey.*

He watched Sully demolishing a plate of hotel buffet breakfast with amusement, watched the boys drift down from their bedrooms, in varying degrees of exhausted or hungover or chipper, with amusement. His own headache subsided gradually after he chugged three cups of coffee in quick succession. It wasn't very good coffee, but it did the trick.

By the time they were all packed up and headed back to the airport, Petey had made his mysterious return and Eric was feeling much more like himself. Better than himself. The last few New Year's Eves he could remember, he had spent alone, and woke up in the morning with the knowledge that he was getting older, and opportunities of all kinds were slipping through his fingers. This year just having Sully's solid body in the bed with him had been grounding in a way he had never expected.

The good mood only lasted as long as the wait to get on the plane. Jesse Keen stood next to him on the tarmac, scowling.

"What's up, Keener?" Eric asked, a little wary. He knew the problem, of course. No veteran was happy about being healthy scratched or about the media digging in for quotes about how the coach was disappointed in him. Sully had been working with him extra, the way he always did with the scratches, but the sting wouldn't be easily wiped away.

"Am I gonna be able to play the next game or is it all gonna be the affirmative action line again?"

Eric could feel the cold fury that he'd always felt when he'd heard shit like that on the ice settle in. "Excuse me, what did you say to me?"

"I said am I gonna be able to play the next game or is it all gonna be the affirmative action line again?"

"Keen, beyond the fact that Williams and Sinclair are important parts of our top line *and* the only line that's regularly scoring any points? You can't *say* things like that. Not to me. I won't stand for it."

"What the hell, Aronson? You're old-school; you of all people should understand."

"I of all—do you have any idea who the hell I am and where I come from?" He was speaking quietly, so the rest of the team wouldn't hear him, but he felt like he was screaming it. He felt like he wanted to be screaming it, wanted to do all of the shit he would have done as a young man. All of those options would have ended in violence.

Keen must have realized his mistake as the words were coming out of Eric's mouth, but it was too late to take it back. His whole face shuttered, and for a second, it seemed like he was going to double down. "You're from Montreal."

"I'm a middle-aged retired fuck," Eric said shortly, "and I was one of the few Jewish players in the league. What kind of shit do you think I heard from opponents? On the ice?"

Keen stared at him, wordless.

"Yeah, you forgot that, eh? Well, don't fucking forget it again, Keen. Sully might be preaching patience and understanding, but I'm not that kind of a guy."

"Right," Keen said. He turned away.

On the plane back to Boston, Sully looked at Petey, already passed out in the chair across from them, and back at Eric. He frowned and reached forward, his fingers resting against Eric's wrist for a second. "What's wrong?"

"What kind of a guy do you think I am?" Eric asked.

"What?" Sully's broad, handsome face looked confused. "What do you mean?"

"You knew me as a player. You knew me on the ice, the kind of reputation I had. What kind of a guy do you think I am?"

The plane was always a little chaotic; guys chattering loudly in the back, other guys with their headphones on, the tinny music audible over it. Some of them snoring. Petey was, the noise like a buzz saw. Even so, Eric kept his voice down, and Sully echoed his volume. "I'm not entirely following. As a player? I thought you were kind of an asshole, I guess. You weren't *dirty*, not like some of those guys were. But you sure as hell had that temper."

"Okay," Eric said, leaning back in his chair.

"That wasn't the answer you wanted, huh?"

"I mean was I—do I look like the kind of guy who'd say something shitty? On the ice?"

Sully started laughing, and his face when he did it lit up, his stupid, loud laugh that Eric liked so much. "Eric, you don't remember calling me an Oompa Loompa?"

"…I did?"

"Come on, seriously? It was my fifth year in the league or something. I had to ask a teammate if you actually meant *me*."

"Ryan Sullivan."

"Eric Aronson."

"That's not what I meant. Like, would you have assumed I was the kind of guy who'd say something racist."

"I mean, no? I knew you were Jewish, and you never—you just seemed like the kind of guy who'd chirp or try to get under someone's skin. I thought you were an asshole, I never thought you were a racist asshole."

"Okay," Eric said, but he still felt ill at ease, like his skin was too tight.

Sully was still watching him, brown eyes shrewd. "Just because someone made a stupid assumption doesn't mean the rest of us thought that."

"Okay."

Sully's hand, briefly, on his knee. "We can talk about it later. Once we get home."

"Yeah?"

"I have thoughts," Sully said.

And Eric, because he was a weak fucking bastard, said, "Okay."

Since he'd moved in, Ryan's apartment was pretty bare-bones. He'd had the time to furnish and decorate it, but not the inclination. It was a lot of effort and energy he didn't possess. Not after the end of a day when he had a game or travel or any number of other responsibilities. It was fine, but sometimes going home was kind of depressing. Acknowledging the piles of books he didn't have time to read, the boxes of stuff he'd brought home with him from New Hampshire that he didn't have time to unpack, felt like too much.

Instead of finding time to deal with it, Ryan spent a lot of time at Eric's apartment instead. This wasn't an ideal solution, either: Eric's apartment was one step above a studio, and particularly on the way back from roadies, with Ryan's suitcase spilling over everywhere on the floor of the bedroom, it got a little cramped.

Ryan liked watching Eric move around in it, though. He'd been here for long enough that he had bought everything he needed and knew where everything was. He moved with the ease that those things brought to him, even in the small galley kitchen, the minuscule bathroom. Only Ryan's presence threw him off his game, but he'd started adjusting to that, too, pivoting around him while he cooked or making space for him on the couch that was really too small for two former hockey players.

"So what exactly happened to make you have that crisis of conscience?" Ryan asked, once they had settled down a little and had some water and Eric had placed an order for Thai delivery. He listened while Eric briefly described the encounter with Keen, watched while his face darkened.

It was rare that Ryan really saw Eric *angry* these days, and it reminded him that the man had depths that he had barely plumbed. The way his eyes got dark and hot, the way it was like all of that tension and power crackled through his body, an energy he barely held in check.

Ryan hadn't been lying when he'd said that he hadn't thought of Eric as a dirty player during their playing days, but he had definitely been aware of that temper, that capacity for violence barely held in check. It was part of the game—deeply woven into the fabric of the game—but that had never been the kind of player that Ryan was. He had seen it in other players with a kind of fascination and envy. Had vaguely remembered Eric's numerous suspensions, all the while knowing that that would never happen to him.

Ryan had won the Sportsmanship Award twice, and it wasn't because he was such a nice fucking guy. It was because he had been a superstar who regularly got the shit kicked out of him, but also rarely took penalties. There was a distinction.

"What thoughts did you have?" Eric asked, after they had gone over the basics. He was leaning against the kitchen counter, his arms crossed over his chest. He looked very different in this context, barefoot, rumpled from the plane, glasses slipping down his nose.

"There's a certain kind of guy who really regrets the fact that things are changing, you know? Especially guys like Keen. He came up right around the time when things weren't like they were for us, but it was close enough that I think he really regrets he wasn't around for the worst of it."

"Maybe," Eric said, shortly. "It just…we were both products of a different era, but I never—I talked shit on the ice, sure, but I never *said* shit like that. It just fucks me up, Sully, you know? I played the way I did because of who I was. Because of all of the shit I had to prove. If people were going to give me crap, I was going to make sure they regretted ever looking at me funny. And it's the same way now. I didn't get this job because of who I was. Or maybe you got the job because of who you were, but…"

Ryan took a step forward. "You really wanted this, huh?"

"I've been working my whole fucking life to prove people wrong. This was the next part of that. I'm *going* to be a head coach one day. I might not have the Cup, I might not have the hardware, but I'm fucking good at what I do, and I'm going to show all of them."

Ryan had thought about what it would mean to come into a team where the coaches had been employed before him and been passed over for the promotion, but in a general sense. He hadn't really thought about what it would mean for Eric, even after all of this time. "I didn't know. I'm sorry."

Eric just looked at him from under the sardonic line of his eyebrows, the corner of his mouth twitching. "At this point, Sullivan? It's fine. I resented the hell out of you at first, and I still think you're too fucking nice, but it's…we're fine now. Whatever the hell we're doing."

"You'll be a head coach one day. I don't doubt it. Hell, depending on the way the rest of this year goes, you might even be a head coach as soon as next year."

Eric laughed, then, a dry chuckle. "Sully, you're a fool if you think they're not going to offer you an extension, no matter what the team's record is."

"You don't know that—"

"With the way Cook's playing? With the way Williams is playing? With the way all of our baby d-men have stepped up to eat twenty-five minutes a night? I remember how miserable they were last year under Leclerc. It's so different now. You're getting your extension."

"Turn that same confidence on yourself. If an opportunity comes up—you know, like, I won't hold you back."

Eric's phone buzzed and he glanced down at it. "Food's here," he said, and fled, like that alone would be an excuse to avoid having to talk about what Ryan had just said. By the time he had returned, Ryan was sitting on the couch, still thinking about it.

"You really think your reputation is preventing you from getting these opportunities?"

"Maybe not all of it," Eric said, sitting down next to him, "but at least some of it's definitely got something to do with the fact that I've had so many suspensions and teams think that says something deeper about *me*."

Under Ryan's hand, Eric's thigh was warm and muscular and solid. "I just feel like once people get to know you, they'll understand. That that's not who you really are. They just have to talk to you, and I feel like you'd convince them."

Eric raised one eyebrow, pushed his glasses back up the bridge of his nose. "I just have to plead my case, huh? All right, Department of Player Safety."

"You had the hearings, right? It's not like you didn't have the opportunity to try before."

"Are you kidding?" The snort was disparaging. "Like any of them actually listened to what I had to say."

Before he could even think about what he was doing, Ryan found himself sitting up straight, posture ramrod formal. He took his hand away from Eric's leg, raised his own eyebrows and said, "This is an in-person hearing for Eric Aronson to discuss potential consequences as a result of the biting incident committed on the ice against"—Ryan racked his brain, trying to remember the actual details of Eric's incidents—"Jason Martin of the Vancouver Vanguard."

Eric stared at him. "You're serious."

"This incident occurred on the ice during a game. Words were exchanged during the course of play, and the two grabbed hold of each other, wrestling briefly, before Aronson took Martin down to the ice—"

"You can't be serious."

"I would caution the player to avoid interruptions," Ryan said severely, "as that shows he is not taking the process seriously. This is an opportunity to be heard."

He could see the line of Eric's full mouth, pressed thin in an expression of disbelief, twitch. The emotions that flickered across his face went in quick succession: confusion, annoyance, amusement and finally they settled into that sardonic smile, like Eric had decided he was going to play along, however stupid Ryan's game happened to be.

"My apologies, Senior Vice President," he said, "I'm taking this very seriously, actually."

"Good," Ryan said. He lifted his chin. "Because this is the major leagues, and we are representatives of the sport. Incidents of this nature are not—"

"Excuse me," Eric interrupted. "Do I get to say anything in my own defense?"

"You are a repeat offender who is familiar with the process. If you continue interrupting, then I will have to take that into account when deciding on your punishment."

"Okay. Please finish, Senior Vice President." Eric's mouth was still twitching, like he was trying so fucking hard not to laugh but was finding it very difficult. His face was admirably straight as he inclined his head slightly to the side, waiting for Ryan to continue.

"Before I was so rudely interrupted," Ryan said, "we were going over the facts leading up to this hearing. Once Martin is down on the ice, their bare hands are in each other's faces and words are continuing to be exchanged, and it appears that Aronson bites down on Martin's hand with force."

Eric was still watching him. His hands were folded in his lap as he sat there, the very picture of a contrite schoolboy. "If you—"

"Silence, please," Ryan said sharply. "We will need to review the video before you can present your defense." He realized, belatedly, that he had no video to review, and pulled up YouTube on his phone. He typed in *Eric Aronson biting fight Vancouver* and found a clip someone had uploaded. They watched it with the sound off, Eric's dark brown eyes searching, like he was remembering exactly what had led up to it.

"Excuse me, Senior Vice President," Eric said, when they were done. He had moved a little closer on the couch while they were watching, and Ryan could feel the heat of Eric's body against his thigh. It was objectively insane, the way Eric's physical proximity could do that to him: like there was some kind of invisible magnetic force between them that he was minutely attuned to. "Can I present my defense?"

"Yes," Ryan said, and swallowed hard. He wasn't really doing a very good job of being an intimidating authority figure; he was trying to concentrate on the role he'd chosen for himself, but all he could do was watch Eric's hands, the way he had twined his fingers together to crack his knuckles. The way he knew those same fingers felt, bruising against his body or twisting inside of him.

"My defense," Eric said, leaning in. His voice was low and throaty, the kind of voice anyone else would have used when you were flirting with a woman in a bar. "My defense is that he liked it."

"That's—that's not a defense," Ryan said. He lifted his chin up again. "I need you to take this seriously, Mr. Aronson. You are a repeat offender, and you are facing a stiff suspension."

"Stiff, huh?" Eric asked. His mouth was twitching again, just the corner. His eyes were dancing. "I can provide physical evidence."

"This is highly…highly irregular," Ryan managed. Eric's hand was on his thigh, now, gripping hard enough that Ryan could feel his fingers digging in. If he was really committing to the bit, he would have knocked his hand away, he would have said that there wasn't physical evidence to offer, that everything was on video.

"I can be very persuasive when I need to be. Come on, Senior Vice President. It's in the CBA that I'm allowed to present evidence in my own defense at DOPS hearings. Are you going to violate the CBA?" His hand crept higher up Ryan's thigh. An inch or two to the side, and he'd be cupping Ryan's balls, at this rate.

"You may present your case," Ryan said. His voice sounded thick and a little strangled, but it was hard to make it come out normally when Eric was looking at him like that, like he was hungry, like he wanted to devour every little bit of Ryan right then and there. "But be quick about it. We have other hearings lined up this afternoon."

"I really need to take my time to convince you," Eric said. He took Ryan's hand in his own and turned it over so that it was facing palm-up. Weirdly enough, Ryan's hand felt sweaty, and he could hear his heart pounding in his ears. Eric didn't look away from him when he leaned forward and pressed his mouth against it. Lips first, then his teeth.

"I don't like this," Ryan said, sharply. "I don't think he would have liked this, either."

"I'm just getting started," Eric murmured against Ryan's skin. And unfortunately it turned out that he was right. It also turned out that Ryan's palm was fucking ticklish, and his whole body jerked in response when Eric kept moving, his tongue teasing against the skin, his teeth nipping to follow it. The palm first, and then his fingers; tongue teasing around Ryan's thumb.

"I—this isn't biting," Ryan said, his voice cracking. "This is another offense entirely."

"Okay. We'll move on to the main part of the case."

"Mr. Aronson," Ryan started, desperately trying to get things back under control, and failing just as miserably when Eric shifted forward to straddle his thighs and trap him in place, when he leaned forward, his mouth against Ryan's neck. His breath was hot and humid in the small space between, and Ryan's entire body jerked in shocked reflex when he pressed his teeth against the tender skin below Ryan's ear. "Shit. Oh—*oh*," he gasped. Whatever Eric's mouth was doing felt like Ryan had touched a live wire, like a current ran through his whole goddamn spine.

"Exhibit A," Eric said. His tongue was hot and wet against Ryan's overheated skin, and Ryan shifted uncomfortably underneath him, already kind of hard. He was teasing Ryan, now, his mouth never staying long enough in one spot for it to feel truly satisfying. "I think I'm beginning to convince you."

"This isn't—this isn't biting."

"You really want to know, huh?" Eric asked. Ryan couldn't see his eyes from this angle, but his voice was soft and dangerous, and neither of them was laughing anymore. "Do you think, Senior Vice President, that maybe this whole hearing was a pretense—I think you fucking *wanted* it—"

Eric's teeth dug in suddenly, sharp, the pressure not that bad at first but steadily building the longer he worried Ryan's skin between his teeth. It was exquisitely painful, and Ryan squirmed underneath the pressure, unable to hold himself still. He could hear his breath in his own ears, the ragged, harsh noise of it. His hands moved again without his own conscious volition, scrabbling at Eric's back for purchase.

"Yes?" Eric asked when he let go. His thumb rubbed against the bite, wet with his own spit, and Ryan could already feel how tender it was, how it would probably bruise tomorrow.

Ryan couldn't say anything at first. His brain was running a million miles a minute but couldn't focus on anything except the way it had felt when Eric hurt him like that. "What was Exhibit B?" he asked, finally. "We have to be thorough in this hearing. I need to know all of the evidence for and against you."

"I can be thorough," Eric said, and the laughter was back in his voice. He tugged at the hem of Ryan's shirt, like he wanted to lift it up, and Ryan went with it. It was chilly in the apartment, once he was shirtless, and he could feel his nipples pebbling, from the cold and from the force of Eric's eyes on him. "Do you demand a hands-on demonstration from everyone in these hearings?"

"I—" Ryan managed. Eric was kissing his neck again, working his way down. He whimpered when Eric's teeth dug painfully against the muscle and tendon of his shoulder, pressing down. It hurt so fucking bad, but it was also like something was lighting up under the skin with every second Eric did it, like the part of him that had always pressed his fingers against his bruises was suddenly putting two and two together. "I—need to be fair. And—and thorough. I…"

"Who would've thought that the Head of Player Safety's such a little slut?"

"I'm not a—I'm tough but fair," Ryan said, his voice cracking again when Eric twisted his nipple, sharp and sudden and surprising. "I have to be, when all of you insist on, on breaking the rules."

“Well. If you have more hearings this afternoon. Maybe I better get back to work convincing you. Maybe I better leave some marks so that the guys who are here after me know.”

Ryan wondered if it was possible to be so turned on that your entire body burst, just exploded into a cloud of bloody mist and viscera. “I think maybe you should do that,” he managed. He wondered how he looked right now, his neck bitten and bruised from Eric’s teeth and wet with Eric’s spit, his hair messed up from Eric’s hands, his whole body flushed red from how much he fucking *wanted* this. His eyes felt huge and wide and crazed and—

Eric wasn’t talking anymore. His mouth trailed down Ryan’s chest, and his teeth dug into skin again, unexpected and painful. Ryan’s body tried to curl into and curl away from it: Jesus, his chest was going to be a mess tomorrow, too, the way Eric was torturing him.

“Excuse you,” he gasped, “this wasn’t where the bite occurred on the ice.”

“I’m giving you the full experience,” Eric mumbled into his skin. His tongue flicked against Ryan’s nipple, then his teeth. “I told you: this is so the other hearings, so they all know who had *you* before them. Who left *you* looking like a fucking—”

“Like what?” Ryan asked, squirming underneath him, increasingly desperate.

“Like a fucking mess. Like you fucking begged for it,” Eric said. He’d slid off Ryan’s lap so he could reach his chest more easily, and he was on the floor between Ryan’s legs. His eyes were wide and dark when he looked up at Ryan again, his mouth red and swollen, and on instinct, Ryan reached out and took his glasses off, set them gently on the side table.

"I have to beg now?" Ryan demanded. "That's not—how you treat the Head of the Department of Player Safety."

"I think that's how the Head of the Department of Player Safety wants to be treated," Eric said, palming Ryan's dick through his sweatpants. "I think maybe the Head of the Department of Player Safety better let me know exactly what he wants, because I'm just a repeat offender, and I want to make sure I'm not going to get an unfair suspension."

Ryan froze. Eric wasn't touching him anymore, and he felt the lack of hands or mouth or *anything* on his body like a physical ache. But he also didn't want to beg—there was being easy for it and there was giving in immediately. Eric ran one finger down his inner thigh and Ryan shuddered. Just the light touch, the hint of what he *could* have, set his heart knocking against his ribs again.

"Bite me again," he said, after a long pause. "My thighs."

The look Eric gave him then, heated and hungry and all-consuming, was almost too much, but Ryan couldn't look away. At least he couldn't until Eric did what he'd asked, tugged his sweats down while Ryan shifted his hips eagerly to help him along. It was almost worse than anything on his neck, the sensitive skin on the inner thigh and the hard muscle he couldn't help clenching against the pain. It was almost better because Eric's hot breath was so close to his dick, because his hands were gripping Ryan's legs so tightly he couldn't have squirmed away even if he wanted to.

"Okay," he managed, "okay, okay, okay, please, you've made your point. He liked it—I like it—I—"

"I didn't show you Exhibit C," Eric said. His unruly hair was even messier where Ryan had been clutching it, his eyes equally wild when he pressed his hands against the bruises he'd left behind on Ryan's legs and Ryan shuddered helplessly under the force of it.

"Wh—what's Exhibit C?"

It turned out that Exhibit C was Eric spitting in his palm and wrapping his warm fingers around Ryan's dick. He wasn't laughing anymore, watching Ryan's hips jerking up into his hand, listening to Ryan's desperate, panting breath. "This doesn't—this isn't a mitigating factor," Ryan gasped, one of Eric's fingers teasing the entrance of his ass. "You still, you're still going to get a f-five-game suspension."

"Oh?" Eric asked. His voice sounded just as breathless, although he was preoccupied, alternating between digging his teeth into Ryan's thigh muscle and pressing wet, sloppy kisses along his abs, and torturing him with his hands. "What do I have to do to lessen my punishment, Senior Vice President? The playoffs are coming up and we're fighting for a wildcard spot."

"I'm—" Ryan said, twisting on his fingers, his whole body shuddering, "I'm offended you'd imply—imply I could be bought—"

"Who said anything about buying?" Eric said, licking his lips.

"What are you...what are you gonna do?"

"I thought," Eric said, stroking one hand along Ryan's thigh, the other gripped just too loose to be satisfying around his erection. "I thought we should see how you look on my dick. I think probably that's what you've been angling for this whole time, huh?"

"I… I…"

"It's okay if you want it," Eric murmured. His voice was gentle, coaxing. "You've got a really stressful, busy job, I think maybe you should just let me…"

It was so fucking ridiculous and it felt so good that he almost broke, but Ryan was so determined to keep a straight face, to remain committed to the bit, even as Eric let go of him, shuffled on his knees over to where he'd dropped his suitcase that had his bathroom kit and the lube and condoms, fumbling eagerly through it until he could return to Ryan's side.

"What do you want?" he asked Ryan.

Ryan looked at the condom in his hand and looked at Eric's face and shuddered again. "I want you to—to fuck me raw. I want you to leave it so everyone after you knows what I've—what you did."

Eric froze; the stillness itself felt like a slap. For the first time, he broke the scene, and said, "Ryan… you're sure?"

"There hasn't been anyone else," Ryan mumbled. He could feel his face heating up, which was ridiculous. His whole chest felt red, and it wasn't just because he had the imprints of Eric's teeth pressed along it. "Not for a little while now. If you're okay with it. I really wanna feel it. Feel *you*."

"Jesus fucking Christ," Eric said, almost reverently. "Okay. Well. If that's what the Head of the Department of Player Safety wants…"

Ryan hadn't been sure what to expect at all when he'd offered, but somehow, the reality blew it out of the water anyway. By the time he'd relaxed enough to try, by the time Eric lifted Ryan into his lap, he felt like he was going to shake out of his skin anyway, so keyed up by the game they'd been playing, by the way Eric had been touching him, by *everything*, that he thought it would have been insanely intense no matter what they were doing. But it was different without a condom, too. It did feel more, more of everything, electric and hot and vulnerable. With every stroke and drag and thrust he felt every single inch of Eric inside of him, and it drove all of the conscious thought out of his head. All he could do was move, all he could do was chase the orgasm that was almost, *almost—*

He looked down at Eric, sitting with his back against the headboard, eyes closed, fingers grabbing Ryan's ass and moving him exactly the way he wanted it, and for a second the breath caught in his throat. It was objectively insane, that they were doing this; it was objectively insane that it worked.

Eric opened his eyes and saw Ryan watching him and said, "Is—is the Head of the Department of Player Safety—satisfied?"

"You feel—" Ryan said, and swallowed hard. "I'm so close. You have to come inside of me. Mr. Aronson—you have to—Eric—"

Eric swore, something in French Ryan didn't understand. He shifted his hips, angling up, and all Ryan could do was hang on. It wasn't even that it was faster, but the steady, punishing force of it was too much. Ryan could feel his whole body tensing up, and then the release, obliterating. By the time his dick was desperately trying to empty itself all over Eric's bare stomach, Eric was still moving, and it was almost too much to bear. Ryan was determined—*determined*—to do this, so even though he was shuddering and overstimulated, he ground down on Eric until he could feel him tense and come, his head dropping down to rest on Ryan's abused shoulder.

He could feel it inside of him, too, messy and wet and somehow, exactly what he had wanted, as objectively disgusting as it should have been.

"Two games," he gasped. "I'm reducing your suspension to two games."

"You're…you're unbelievable," Eric managed, mouth pressed up against Ryan's sweaty skin. "*God*, Ryan."

It took them a while to recover, but eventually it dawned on Ryan that their food had been sitting, forgotten, on the kitchen table. Eventually, they had to move, Ryan wincing when Eric slowly pulled out.

"That's what you wanted, though," Eric said, lips twitching with suppressed laughter again.

"Yeah, I know," Ryan said, "but you weren't complaining either, Mr. I'm Leaving Marks for All Those Other Guys."

"You better go get yourself cleaned up," Eric said, smirking, and Ryan could tell he was *enjoying it*, from the way he stretched and looked over the damage he'd done to Ryan's body. It felt like a secret Ryan would have to keep, but one that he'd treasure, turning it over and over again in his mind. The way that Eric looked at him just in that moment. Fond and hungry and satisfied. "Before you get that all over the floor."

"Disgusting, Aronson."

"Mmm. You begged for it, remember?"

He did. He shivered again, thinking about it.

"How the hell have you managed to boss an entire team of guys around all these years?" Eric asked, groaning, as he hauled himself to his feet. "When you're this easy."

"It's just with you," Ryan said, a little embarrassed. He turned away quickly, before he could see too much of Eric's face. He didn't know what he would find there, and he was almost afraid to look.

And then there was the food, and the bathroom, and he was distracted.

CHAPTER TEN

January

In the morning, Ryan woke up to the sound of Eric moving around in the kitchen and, specifically, the sound of a teakettle whistling. He sat up in the crumpled sheets and blankets and thought, briefly, about what they'd done yesterday. He felt embarrassed for approximately five seconds before curiosity drove him out of bed and into the apartment's living area.

Eric was doing something complicated with the kettle and what looked like a glass vase of some kind, ringed by a wooden clasp where the neck narrowed. He was wearing only his boxers and Ryan took a second to admire the way he looked, the shift of muscle in the long line of his back.

Eric glanced over his shoulder when he heard Ryan come into the kitchen. "Morning, lazy."

"Lazy?" Ryan demanded, glancing at the clock. It said *5:00 a.m.* "I'll have you know that I'm planning to go for a run in a minute."

"After last night?" Eric asked, his eyebrows raised above the line of his glasses. "Clearly, I need to fuck you harder next time. Also. Maybe put some pants on before you go."

Ryan looked down at his naked body and shrugged. He managed to resist the urge to press his fingers against the bruised imprints Eric's teeth had left behind, but it was a close one. It wouldn't have done to inflate Eric's head further, especially when he was clearly still smirking about how intensely he'd upended Ryan's world last night. Instead, Ryan looked suspiciously at the glass vase and asked, "What are you doing?"

"I'm making you some decent fucking coffee for once," Eric said. He was pouring the kettle over the wide mouth of the vase, a little bit at a time, and waiting before pouring again. Ryan, who had never had that kind of patience for anything in his life that didn't involve hockey, stared. "With the *good* shit and my Chemex."

"Oh..." Ryan said, doubtfully. "You know I'm not gonna be able to taste the difference, Eric."

"That's just because you've never tried it. You're so used to drinking sugar milk, of course you won't be able to taste the difference. But I'm going to make you *the* best coffee and you're going to try and it and I'm going to *train* you to like it."

Ryan stared at him. "Eric...buddy...the thought is a nice one. But there's a reason I like my coffee the way I like it. It's what I grew up with."

"Come on," Eric said. His voice had that coaxing edge that it had had when they were fucking around yesterday, when he'd murmured, *It's okay if you want it.* Ryan could feel himself getting a little hard, remembering, and Eric laughed when he noticed. "You'll like it, Ryan, I promise."

"If I *don't* like it?"

"I'll buy you Dunkin' Donuts coffee every day for a week."

"Isn't that against your moral code?"

"Yes," Eric said, and his eyebrows rose above his glasses again. "So that's how you know I'm serious about this coffee. It's Ethiopian and it has notes of milk chocolate, Concord grape and cherry."

Ryan, who had never been able to taste anything except coffee when drinking coffee, looked doubtfully at the Chemex. "Can I put sugar in it?"

"No."

"Milk?"

"No!"

He watched Eric pouring the mug of coffee for him with a small amount of trepidation. The fact that Eric *cared* enough to do this was, weirdly, the thing that stuck with him. Ryan knew he wasn't going to like the coffee. He already knew he wasn't going to be able to taste chocolate or grape or cherry or whatever it was that Eric was going on about. Ryan hadn't even tried drinking black coffee in decades, and there was a reason for it.

But Eric *cared* about coffee, and he had enough space in his morning to try to make sure that Ryan cared about it, too. Ryan realized, with a sinking feeling, that he was enough of a fool to actually drink this shit.

Eric held out the mug to him, and the hopeful look was out of character for him. Ryan took a deep breath and blew on the hot coffee until some of the steam rising had cleared away, and took one small, careful sip. It was still hot enough to burn the first layer off of his tongue, but even then, it tasted like black coffee. It wasn't as bitter as some coffee he'd had; he'd have to give Eric that. But it still tasted like—well, bitter bean water.

Eric was still watching him.

"Take one of your little pictures, it'll last longer."

Eric just looked at him, one eyebrow raised.

"Sorry," Ryan said, "it just tastes like coffee to me."

"Try some more," Eric said, crowding forward so that he trapped Ryan against the counter, without much space to escape unless he scooted sideways.

"Oh, is this a threat now?"

"Yes," Eric said, his arms bracketing Ryan in.

Careful not to spill the mug of coffee between them, Ryan went up on the tips of his toes to press his mouth against Eric's, morning coffee breath and all. For a second Eric resisted, like he was going to keep arguing, but then his body relaxed into the kiss and his hand came up to take the mug away from Ryan and set it on the counter behind them. That was all the cue Ryan needed to grab the sides of Eric's face with his hands, half an attempt at distracting him from making Ryan drink the rest of the coffee, half just eager, as always, to touch him.

"I thought you said you were going for a run," Eric mumbled into Ryan's mouth.

"I am. You just have to let go of me."

"Hmm," Eric said. He didn't let go.

Ryan's back dug uncomfortably against the edge of the kitchen counter, but somehow, his inclination wasn't to try to push free. It was nice, being in the kitchen in the morning together, even with the shitty coffee a constant threat behind him. It was nice, to have Eric's hands teasing him and Eric's breath hot against the shell of his ear.

It was—nice.

"I can cut it a little short," Ryan said breathlessly, and Eric laughed and replied, "You're always a little short."

"I'm going to kick your fucking ass at practice, you know that, right?"

"Can't wait," Eric said, and then Ryan wasn't thinking about the coffee or the practice anymore.

Eric was the kind of guy who didn't trust it when all of the parts of his life seemed to be going well. He wasn't the kind of person whose life worked out like that, not without more strife and struggle. His mom was in good health as far as he could tell. The team was still in its holding pattern of playing a decent game offset by a real fucking stinker, which was frustrating, but was about as good as he could expect given the quality of the roster. And things with Ryan had been—

The thing was that Eric didn't even know how to describe the situation with Ryan. They hadn't ever really talked about what they were doing and Eric, to his immense confusion, couldn't bring himself to ask. Forty-two years of bluntly saying whatever the hell he wanted to whoever the hell he wanted to say it to hadn't prepared him for the experience of waking up in the morning next to a short-as-fuck hockey savant from Boston and wanting nothing more than to tease a stupid smile out of him.

Every morning when he talked to his mother and she tried and failed to set him up with various women in her huge extended circle of acquaintances, he thought about telling her that he was seeing someone. That he was seeing a man, specifically. That he was seeing a divorced goy without children. And then, of course, the words froze on his tongue. He couldn't tell his mother about Ryan any more than he could ask Ryan to define what the hell they were doing.

It was fine. It was all fine. Everything was working, everything was running smoothly, he just couldn't actually put definitions or limits or labels on anything. And that was fine, too, because for the first time in a very long time, he was able to actually enjoy something sort of like a relationship.

He was able to enjoy shit like looking at Ryan's body for days following the role-playing incident and seeing the physical marks that he'd left behind. The signs that Ryan was his, even if he wasn't able to actually say it.

The kind of marks that had caused some raised eyebrows in the locker room before and after practice, but no one had been willing to say shit to Ryan about them. Eric had just looked at them instead, willing himself not to get hard thinking about it, knowing he could go back to his apartment and press them later, make Ryan squirm and sigh and demand whatever he wanted out of Eric instead.

The kind of marks that were still there almost a week later, although they were faded to the purple-yellow stage of bruising that meant they'd soon be gone, and Eric pressed his fingers against them in the shower that morning while Ryan looked at him reproachfully.

"They're almost gone, Eric, you've made your point."

"Should I make it again?" Eric asked, only half joking.

"No," Ryan said, severely, "I don't want more bruises this week. Murph's visiting with the kids today and it's already pretty ridiculous that I look like this."

"He is?" Eric tried to remember if Ryan had mentioned the visit before but came up blank. "I don't think you said anything about it."

"We'd been talking about it for a while," Ryan said, squinting against the spray of the shower. He still had fluffy soap bubbles clinging to his body, and Eric ran his finger through the ones on his chest, just to watch him shudder. "And he had some free time with their schedule and a school in-service day, so I told him to just come up."

"So I'll get to meet the famous Murph?" Eric asked. It was half-teasing but half…he didn't even know. There was really no reason he should feel the way that he did about it. There was really no reason he shouldn't even be able to describe the way he felt about it.

"Of course," Ryan said, like he was surprised Eric would even ask. "I told them to come to practice. And that we could all go out for dinner later on, if they wanted."

"Wait, we?"

"Of course you're invited, too," Ryan said impatiently, pushing him out of the stream of water so he could rinse himself off. "And Petey and Heidi and her wife, if they want to come."

"Uh…huh," Eric said. It took him a second to try to wrap his head around everything that was going on here. "Well. That should be interesting."

"Behave yourself," Ryan said severely, frowning up at Eric. He looked about as threatening as a naked man in the shower *could* look, but he also looked a bit like a drowned kitten. Eric resisted the urge to ruffle his wet hair. "Murph's one of my oldest and best friends, and I want to…make a good impression. With the team, with practice, with everything."

"I'll be on my best behavior. Promise," Eric said,

and the smile Ryan gave him was both blinding and exactly the kind of evidence that Eric was in fucking trouble. He let Ryan lean up to kiss him, let himself forget, with the heat of that kiss, exactly how much of a disaster this had the potential to become. Exactly why he was the kind of guy who shouldn't have trusted when it seemed like things had been too easy.

He felt ill at ease on the way into the practice facility for morning skate. They still left separately and arrived separately, and for the first time, it really hit him what that meant. As Eric was getting changed to head out onto the ice, he heard the commotion that indicated that not only had Murphy arrived, but his children as well.

Eric took a deep breath and turned around to face the music.

When he'd been playing, Sean Murphy wasn't the kind of player that he spent a lot of time thinking about. Sure, he had been a superstar in his own right, he was the captain of the Desperadoes, and he was a threat every time he stepped on the ice. But personally, beyond the stupid chirping that Eric had directed at anyone he squared off against, he hadn't spared one single thought regarding him.

It turned out that, years later and up close, Murphy was still a big guy. He was a little taller than Eric and even though he'd gone to seed a bit, he was still just as burly as he'd been during their playing days, and he looked… Well, the only way to describe him was that he looked like a guy from Boston. Like a guy who'd be an extra in the background of some Martin Scorsese flick about Boston cops and mobsters, or maybe an extra in a Dropkick Murphys video. He had a shock of red hair that was only partially gray, a face that was more freckle than it wasn't and a smile as wide as the Charles.

He grabbed Ryan in a bear hug that lifted him right off his feet, hooting an incoherent greeting of joy and excitement, and Ryan was hugging him back, his fists pounding against Murphy's shoulder blades as he yelled, "It's been too fucking long, brother," and Murphy said into his shoulder, "*Too* fucking long."

Eric hung back while Ryan and Murphy yelled excitedly at each other, occasionally pausing so that they could hug again, and he shook his head: it was like being around Murphy emphasized Ryan's accent tenfold. It was a reminder that they both came from the same place and that Eric didn't belong there at all.

The rest of the team and the coaching staff were all hanging around, watching, and Petey shot a sideways glance at him. "Ol' Murph's really larger than life, isn't he?"

"You can say that again," Eric agreed.

By that time, Ryan had grabbed Murphy by the bicep and dragged him over. Eric already felt snappish and on edge, like he'd rather just pick a fight with Murphy and get it over with than wait for anything else to happen. But Ryan was smiling so widely and so fucking happily that Eric bit his tongue and let him talk. "Murph, this is my coaching staff—Heids, Petey and Eric."

Murphy turned a somewhat suspicious green gaze on him when Ryan said *Eric*, like he was expecting something different from what he was actually seeing. "It's nice to meet you," he boomed. "Mason and Sophia are waiting out in the hallway since Sully said everyone was still changing, but I couldn't wait."

"It's really fucking good to have you here, buddy,"

Ryan was saying, still hanging on to Murphy's arm like he couldn't believe he was real. "I'm excited as hell to show you everything we've worked toward over the last half a year or so. The staff is just one of those things. We've finally got it clicking."

"Must be nice to be the one in charge, finally," Murphy said, his eyes dancing. "All of those years we had to bite our tongues, eh? And now *you're* the head coach."

"It's a collaborative process," Ryan was saying, shaking his head. He'd finally let go of Murphy's arm, and he was smiling at Eric instead. He must not have realized he was doing it, but his fingers rubbed at the bruise Eric had left on his neck, getting some kind of subliminal comfort out of pressing against it. "Some of us got off to a bit of a rough start, but we're all on the same page now, and it's been really—really nice to work with these guys."

"And you," Murphy said, turning to look Eric over with more attention. His glance flicked from Ryan's neck and back. "*You've* come a long way since the biting days, huh?"

"The biting days were because I didn't appreciate being called a fucking kike, Murphy," Eric said shortly.

The abrupt silence after he said it was awkward and felt like it went on a long time, until Ryan took a deep breath and said, "Murph, Eric might have been a scrappy player back in the day, but he's been a great and levelheaded addition to the coaching staff. All of us have grown and changed since those days, right?"

"Sure," Murph said, agreeably, and Eric frowned at him, just so he'd know exactly what Eric thought about him.

It wasn't much better on the ice. They were doing

small-area drills again, with a heavy focus on 5v5 situations because there was only so much they could do special teams work without the even-strength game slipping. Murph's kids were admittedly very cute, small, violently redheaded versions of him, and both of them played hockey. Sophia was a goalie, but she could skate and hold her own with her brother, easily.

Ryan ran the practice, but he also took the time to goof off with them, "checking" Mason into the boards and grabbing Sophia's hands and spinning her around and around and around. It was, Eric thought, very grudgingly, very fucking cute. Of course Ryan was *also* good with children, on top of everything else. He tried not to let himself get too distracted, watching them, because he still had a practice to run as well. But it was difficult, when Ryan was so clearly bursting at the seams with pride and joy, both showing off his team and showing off Murph, his best and oldest friend.

The small-area drills were easy to show off to their greatest effect, because the guys loved them. It wasn't just that they were closer to game simulations than endless repetition drills, but Ryan made them fun, and switched them up often enough that they had to keep on their toes. The specific drill they were running today involved both the forwards and the defensemen, focusing on gap control and puck battles, but only within a tiny, proscribed area. The players could tag in as necessary.

Maybe because Murphy and his kids were there, maybe not, but the pace and intensity seemed to have been kicked up a notch. Eric, who wasn't in awe of anyone, was still aware that for a lot of the younger players, having *Sean Murphy* watching them play was probably a big deal. As big of a deal as it was to have Ryan Sullivan as their head coach.

Eric took a break by the bench, squirting Gatorade into his mouth, when he heard the sound of someone skating toward him, the *snick* of blades stopping on the ice. He turned around to find Murphy in front of him, broad frame barely shoved into his Desperadoes-branded sweats.

"Aronson."

"Murphy."

"Sully talks about you a lot," Murphy said. His voice lacked inflection, but it was the kind of forced casual tone that said more than anything else.

"Yeah?"

"Yeah. He talks about you…pretty much constantly."

They stared at each other in silence for a second. Murphy looked away first. "We work together," Eric said, unnecessarily.

"Uh-huh," Murphy said. "I don't—look, Aronson. I'm not assuming shit about you. About him. But I want you to know that I've got my eye on you."

"Really."

"Yeah. And if you do anything to, I don't know…" Murphy said. For someone who was always smiling, the expression he had on his face now seemed highly out of character. He wasn't smiling at all. He didn't have any expression at all: he just looked Eric straight in the eye, so serious that Eric felt for a second like he was actually facing the Department of Player Safety again, and not in a sexy way. "Anything at all to make him unhappy. I just want you to know that I'm fucking watching. And I'm not going to be happy about that."

"Funny," Eric said, and smiled.

"Come on, Sully," Murph said. He laughed, although there wasn't much amusement in it. "We've been friends for how long? I know you. Whenever we talk anymore, he's all you talk about. And I saw the way he looks at you. I saw the—your neck."

Ryan stared at him. He shouldn't have been surprised that Murph had figured it out. Not really. Murph was the man who knew him best of anyone. He'd known that Ryan was going to propose to Shannon before Ryan had even figured it out himself. From the very first day they'd met, Murph had just *gotten* him. But still, this was so outside of Ryan's own experience, that part of him had thought that maybe it wouldn't be so obvious to Murph, either.

He exhaled. It felt strange to say it out loud, to acknowledge it at all. Especially to Murph. But he couldn't lie to him. It just felt wrong.

"I don't know," he said finally. "We haven't actually talked about it at all."

Murph couldn't look him in the eye. "Okay," he said.

"Okay?"

"I gotta…you know. Process it. You're…?"

"Sleeping with him? Yeah."

"Okay."

Ryan kicked a pebble by his shoe tip, watched it spin out across the pavement. "Is that all?"

"Are you—what? Gay?"

He snorted. "No. I don't know. I loved Shannon, you know? That was real. I never even thought about being…you know. With a man. Until he kissed me. I never thought about it at all, and it's bizarre, but somehow it just—it just works."

He was starting to realize that coming out, even in

this limited way, wasn't just a one-time thing. He hadn't been nervous with Shannon, but today…it felt like picking at a scab and waiting for the wound to start bleeding again. He knew he had to look at Murph, but it was difficult to do it. It wasn't that he was embarrassed about the whole thing with Eric—it had actually felt like a huge weight off of his shoulders to acknowledge it to anyone. It felt *real*. But Murph had sounded so upset about it that Ryan worried about what was coming next. He had never had any indication that Murph was homophobic or bigoted in any way, but this was not what he had expected. He hadn't expected Murph to look the way he did, almost like he was nauseous.

"Do you have a problem with it?" Ryan asked, finally. "Me? And him?"

"Not the way you're worrying," Murph said, again, with one of those short, humorless laughs. He looked up, finally, and for a second he looked so young and lost that Ryan was reminded of their first training camp together in Dallas, the first night they'd gotten fucked up down there together and Murph had confided in him that he was scared about being sent down, that he was scared he wouldn't live up to his draft pedigree, and Ryan had held him while he puked and said, *You're going to be a fucking Hall of Famer, Murph, I know it.*

And here they were, both of them Hall of Famers, and Murph was saying, "I never really had a way to put it into words, especially because of the way our lives ended up going, but now I—I don't know, Sully. Do you ever think about what could have happened? What could have been?"

Ryan's ears were ringing. It felt like he'd been slammed into the boards with a high hit. "What?"

"Us. Do you ever think about it. If we'd… I don't know."

"What?" Ryan said, again, stupidly.

Murph ran his hand through his hair. He looked like he was torn between laughter and tears, his face twisted up with the kind of emotion that Ryan had never seen from him. Murph was always smiling; Murph was the kind of guy who should always be smiling. "Ryan, you fucking idiot, I'm trying to tell you that this whole thing—you and Aronson—it made me think about things. About us, about the way we used to be together, about the way I've—and you know what? You're *it* for me. You always have been. I just didn't know how to put it in words until we were married to other people. Until now."

Ryan wondered if it was possible to have to go through concussion protocol without anyone having touched him. He felt concussed, like the world was spinning and he was going to lose the entire dinner he'd eaten. All he could say was the same thing he had been saying. "What?"

"Ryan," Murph was saying. There was an urgency in his voice that hadn't been there before. "Can you please…say something besides that?"

"I just—I don't know what to say. What does this even mean? You're married. You and Tara have been married for years. You have kids! The *kids are here*, Murph, I'm seeing someone, I—what does this *mean*? What?"

The air between them was vibrating with tension, the kind of sympathetic ache that had never been there before. Murph had always been easy. The easiest thing in Ryan's life, the one thing that had always been predictable, that had always made sense. And now everything was wrong, and he had to look back on their years together in a completely different light. Because Murph was being honest and Shannon had been right.

The friendship he'd had with Murph wasn't a regular friendship at all. It had never been. Right from the beginning when they'd battled each other along the boards in elementary school and Murph had laughed after knocking Ryan on his ass and Ryan had thought, right then and there, that he would do almost anything to make Murph look at him again. There had always been something else, simmering beneath the surface, and they'd both been too blind or too frightened by what it meant to look at it directly. It was easy not to look at it, in a sport as straight as hockey, when girls were so easy to meet and everyone got married so young.

Murph, who was looking at the ground again, saying, "I don't know what it means. I love Tara. I love my kids. I have a good life with them in Dallas, you know? I'm not…discounting that. I'm not expecting anything beyond that."

"I mean—I have the Beacons, and Eric, I wouldn't…"

"I know. I wouldn't expect you to. That's the thing, Sully, you know I'm like… I'm really fucking proud of you, for everything you've done, for everything you're doing. This team. The staff. You're really building something here. I should have told you earlier, before I—Jesus, Sully. I didn't even mean to do this tonight. Ever. You were just looking at me with those fucking big eyes and I…"

Any other time, Ryan would have embraced him, would have pulled him into a bear hug and hung on until he felt better. That was the thing about Murph; he had huge arms and he gave the best hugs, the kind of hugs that made everything else feel secondary. He couldn't do that now. "Murph… I don't want to lose our friendship. I *can't* lose our friendship. You're the most important person in the world to me. You always have been—nothing's changed about that."

"I'll always be your friend," Murph said. He looked sideways at Ryan, like facing him head-on was too painful. Headlights too bright to see. "I can't lose that either. I'm sorry I did this. I shouldn't have said anything."

"No, you should have. We've always been honest with each other, and I…this is too big not to…"

"I just…need some time to think about it. I need some space; I just need to…" Murph looked stricken again and Ryan had to fight the urge to hug him again. "Look, can you settle the tab for me? I think I'm just—I'm just gonna go back to the hotel. I just…have to go."

"Yes," Ryan said, "of course, I was going to treat everyone anyway, I… Sean?"

"Yes, Ryan."

"I'm sorry. For everything. I didn't know. I never, I never knew."

"How the fuck would either of us have known?" Murph asked, and he smiled. It was a sad, sickly smile.

Before Ryan could react, Murph had moved forward with all of the speed his big frame still possessed and thrown his arms around him. It was a bone-crushing hug, the kind of hug that lifted Ryan right off of his feet. Ryan took the opportunity to bury his face in Murph's chest, because it would probably be the last time for a very long time, if he ever had the chance to do it again. Even now, Murph still smelled exactly the same as Ryan remembered, the kind of familiar sense memory that shot him right back to all of those hours spent on buses and planes and in locker rooms together, how close they'd been, all of the time, without ever knowing.

And then Murph set him back down on the ground, and it was over. They stood there, a few inches apart, staring at each other. Murph said, "If he hurts you, I'll kill him," and before Ryan could say, *Eric would never do that*, Murph had turned and fled. Ryan watched him go, weaving through the evening crowds, watched him until he couldn't see him anymore. He was shaking, from the cold and from adrenaline, and for a second, he wished he smoked cigarettes or weed or *anything* that he could use to settle his fucking nerves.

Eventually, he realized that he had to go back inside. He walked up the steps and had to make the conscious decision to do each one.

"Are you okay?" Eric asked, concerned, when he sat back down at the table. "Where the hell is Murphy?"

Ryan didn't know what he must have looked like. Probably like he'd seen a ghost. In a way, he had. "Uh. I'll tell you later. After all of this. We should…" Everyone was staring at him now. "Let's get the check, eh? My treat."

And Ryan smiled, and took a deep breath, and prepared to go back to playing the part of the gracious host. Like his whole world hadn't been flipped on end. Somehow, Eric's hand on his thigh under the table, warm and comforting, was the only thing that got him through it. Somehow, he got through it. But he was a different person when it was done.

The fact that Murphy had disappeared before they'd even settled the bill was strange enough, Eric thought. Ryan smiling that fixed and fake-looking smile was stranger. He was by nature the kind of man who smiled often, but it was always genuine, always the kind of smile that reached his eyes. This one looked like he was a second away from screaming. Eric had thought about asking what was going on, but something told him that until they were alone, it would be better not to ask.

Even though Murph had driven the three of them to the restaurant, Eric and Ryan ended up walking back alone. Ryan was silent the entire time, distracted, and that too was unusual, since Ryan usually never shut the fuck up.

He was silent still when they went up the stairs to Eric's apartment, when he headed into the bedroom without saying anything else. Eric took the time to hang up their coats and do a quick run-through of the apartment to make sure there wasn't anything that needed to be put away, and then followed him in.

He found Ryan on the floor of the bedroom, leaning against the bed. His knees were pulled up to his chest and his chin was resting on them. He looked a million miles away, like he was anywhere but here.

Eric sat down next to him. "Ryan?"

"Yeah."

"You, uh…want to talk about it?"

Ryan laughed, although the sound was a little wet. He turned his head so he could press his face against Eric's shoulder. It was such a catlike gesture that Eric would have laughed, if they were in any other kind of situation.

"Murph's in love with me."

Eric exhaled. "Yeah, I, ah. Had kind of figured that out, too."

"Everyone knew but me," Ryan said, and laughed again.

"You okay?"

"No. Of course not. He's my best friend, Eric. He's been my best friend since I was eighteen years old." Ryan let Eric slip an arm around his shoulders. Leaned into the embrace. "He wanted some space."

Eric could feel the future stretching out like carnival taffy, pulled so thin it was about to snap. There were a number of ways this could go and none of them made him feel particularly confident. It was kind of insane, he thought, to realize how much whatever happened next meant to him. How much he didn't want Ryan to say what Eric thought he might say. "What do *you* want?"

"I don't know. I guess I need some space, too. To process this. It's just…he's always been the one thing in my life I could trust to be there, always. And now…"

The thought coalesced in his head. Thinking about it ached, like he'd been slammed into the boards without being able to tense up for it first. But even if it hurt, there were certain things that were the right thing to do. Before he could stop himself, Eric was saying, "You know. If you're in love with him, then I'd understand if you wanted to stop doing this, if you wanted to—"

Ryan's head whipped up to stare at him. "No! I don't want to stop doing this. I mean, shit, I don't know what I'm doing. I love Murph, I've always loved Murph. I don't think…maybe I was in love with him once, and I probably never realized it. But I'm here for a reason, Eric. I know we haven't fucking talked about anything we're doing and that's fine. We don't have to. But I don't want to throw this away."

The invisible weight on his shoulders lifted and Eric exhaled. "Okay. Well. I'm…shit, I'm no good with fucking words like this. I'm sorry, buddy. This can't be easy."

"It's a little better now," Ryan said. "Can we—can you kiss me?"

Eric kissed him. He didn't want to think about the relief behind it, the desperation. It was enough, for now, that they were here.

CHAPTER ELEVEN

February

Murph's visit at the end of January had really fucked Ryan up, he realized later. It was funny: the divorce with Shannon hadn't affected him nearly so much. They hadn't spoken in the months since the final divorce hearing, and he barely even thought about her. He went a week without talking to Murph, and it felt like the world as he knew it had ended.

He wasn't his usual self at the numerous charity events the coaching staff had to attend, he wasn't charming the season-ticket holders in the same way. He wasn't as sharp on the bench, and he wasn't as intense in practices. Eric and Petey were able to cover for him, to a certain extent, but once February rolled around Ryan realized that he really had to get it the fuck together. He couldn't let his personal life affect his work life that way: if he did, he would never be able to do the job the way he needed to do it, especially because his father was lurking at the edges of the team, like a scavenger biting at his ankles and waiting to steal the scraps of garbage.

"Who are you texting?" Eric asked, his voice a sleepy

mumble, as he rolled over and pressed his face against Ryan's ribs.

"My fucking dad. Guess who wants free tickets for him and Chelsea and my brothers?"

Eric's eyes opened fully, and he propped himself up on his elbow. His expression was measured, searching. Even without his glasses, he always had a kind of raven-like air when he looked at you that way, like some kind of big, overgrown bird with prey in its sights. "You know that Conroy will just give you the tickets if you ask for them."

"That's the thing. I don't want to ask him. My family is…you give an inch, they take a mile, and then some. If I give him the tickets he's just going to keep asking."

"So just say no, then."

Ryan didn't laugh, but the noise that escaped was a sort of pained chuckle that was close enough. "I *am* saying no. Mark Sullivan never accepts no as an answer. That was the first lesson he taught me as a boy."

Eric flopped back down in the bed and closed his eyes. Ryan fought the sudden and inexplicable urge to run his fingers through Eric's unruly hair, which had grown a little longer as the season went on. Eric said, "I'll tell him to fuck off for you. Gladly."

"Ha. Mental image is nice, but man, would that backfire. Then I'd never hear the end of it about someone else fighting my battles. No. Sorry to keep you awake. This is just something I need to handle on my own."

"It's fine, mon pitchounet." Eric's muffled voice drifted off, and he was asleep again.

Ryan looked at his phone again. Dad had said, *It's the least you can do considering all of the shit I've done for you over the years.* He sighed and rubbed his hand over his eyes. He really had to just put all of it into the background, concentrate solely on the team, which was in another losing skid. He locked his phone and lay back down in the bed, turned over on his side to look down at Eric. In his sleep, he did look younger, more peaceful, in a way that he never did on the ice. And he just let Ryan see him like that without even thinking about it anymore.

Ryan closed his eyes, although it took him a long time to sleep.

They lost on Valentine's Day, and even Ryan could tell that the season was really starting to wear on Williams. He might have been the team's number-one center, but he was still young, and going against top lines that had learned to game-plan for him every night for twenty minutes was starting to wear on him. It was the kind of night when everyone blew their defensive responsibilities, when they went down 3-0 in the first and Davey had to come in cold in the second to relieve the starter.

In the locker room after, Ryan made sure to go over to talk to Williams, let him know that it wasn't his fault. "We're expecting a lot out of you, Willy, and you've more than risen to the challenge. You know a night like this doesn't change that."

"I should be better," Williams said, raising one eyebrow. Like it was a challenge to pep-talk him into accepting this.

"We can all be better. We're going to work on it. But that's what it comes down to, in the end. You can only work on the things you can control. The roster is what it is, and you're a load-bearing beam, buddy. It's not fair to you, but that's what it is."

Williams exhaled. Around them, the rest of the team was still noisy and chaotic, stripping out of wet gear, checking to see who'd lost the most money on the board, chirping each other. Williams never participated in the worst of it. He wasn't that kind of a kid.

He looked back up at Ryan, his dark eyes shrewd. "They're going to blame me."

"The reporters?"

"Yeah."

"I won't let them. But even if they did, you know you can't let it get to you too much."

Williams nodded. "I'm working on it."

"Good kid," Ryan said, and squeezed his shoulder. "If you want to come to the office to review tape tomorrow before morning skate, we'll all be there. We can talk about that one goal against in the third."

"I'd like that, Coach," Williams said, and finally smiled.

Ryan watched him go and thought about the way he accepted the weight of the world onto his shoulders, the way Ryan had always done as a younger man. That was a leader: that was the kind of kid you wanted as the backbone of your team going years forward. He was lucky, to be coaching, and to have a few of them so early in his own career. The team was a good group, and Williams was the fulcrum.

The questions from the press started immediately after the game: "Are you disappointed in the team, Sully?"

He was frustrated. He couldn't lie; it killed him watching the team dig themselves into a hole with mistakes that he had tried so hard to drill out of them. But he never threw individual players under the bus and wasn't about to start now. "I'm disappointed in some of the lapses. But a young team, it's like potty-training toddlers, you know? They might piss on the carpet because they're having too much fun to remember to go, and it's up to the parent to teach them. It doesn't mean that you don't love him. You just have to work with him."

Afterward, Petey clapped him on the back. "All-time metaphor with that one, man," he said cheerfully. "Don't worry. We'll get out the training pants and get those defensemen using 'em this weekend."

"Thank you, Peter," Ryan said dryly.

"You ain't the only one with metaphors, Coach," Petey said, with all of the immense satisfaction that only he could manage.

It was late by the time they finished with the media availabilities and talking to the players who had been particularly disappointing and getting ready to head home. It wasn't even a question that he would head back to Eric's afterward, and it was late enough that Ryan risked just getting into Eric's car with him.

"Hey," Eric said, as he was circling his block looking for a spot, "I wanted to, uh…tell you something."

"What?"

"I'm going home to Montreal for the All-Star weekend. I do every year, but since we've been spending so much time together, I wanted to warn you. I know I probably waited too long to do it, I just—there was so much other shit going on."

It was weird, like a shadow of the way he'd felt when Murph had made his confession. Felt it like a physical blow, a hand pushing hard against his chest. "Oh. Yeah.

That makes sense. Of course you don't get to see your mom very often, that really makes sense that you'd want to go home and visit her."

He wasn't sure why it felt so bad, but it was probably the prospect of the whole weekend alone. Ryan *liked* being around other people, even if his family was shitty; it was part of the reason he'd gotten into coaching. He was always around other people that way.

The way the All-Star breaks worked, the guys who would be playing went, and the rest of the team would be scattered, too. Williams had been picked by the league, and Cook had won the fan vote, so they would be gone. Some of the rest of the team would go to show support for their buddies. Some of them would go home, like Eric was planning to do, to visit their families. And some of them, like Laurent Martel, loudly proclaimed their intensions to do absolutely nothing except enjoy a quiet beer and play some video games. There weren't any practices and there weren't any team events.

He'd probably have to spend most of the weekend dodging his family.

Eric parallel parked his car at about 40 mph, something he did regularly and that always shocked Ryan when he did. When he turned off the ignition, he looked sideways at Ryan. His eyes were uncharacteristically nervous. "Unless."

"Unless what?"

"It's kind of last minute, I know. I've had my tickets booked since they announced the dates, but…if you wanted to come with me?"

Ryan stared at him. "Come with you? Like, to your mother's home?"

"You don't have to if you don't want to," Eric said.

He wasn't looking Ryan in the eye anymore. "I know it's kind of a weird thing to ask."

It was risky, but Ryan's body was moving without his brain's input. He leaned across the center console and took Eric's chin in his hand. It was a quick kiss, a messy clash of mouth on mouth, and Eric made a surprised noise into it.

"Shit, of course I'll go," Ryan said.

Eric pulled away. The corner of his mouth tipped up in a smile, for once, no sarcasm hinted in it. "You'll like it, I promise. I have so many places to show you. You're going to love the food. My mother will—well. She'll like you."

"You told her about me?" Ryan asked, momentarily stunned.

"Not yet. I didn't want to do it unless I knew *you* wanted to do it, but I'm going to do it tonight. Okay?"

"Uh, sure, okay," Ryan said, still trying to process the conversation. "Eric…thank you?"

"Yeah, well. Let's see how the conversation goes first before you start thanking me," he muttered.

"Hey. With everything I've heard about your mom, I'm sure it'll be fine. Shit, I have to start packing."

Eric laughed and turned the car on again. "So maybe we should head back to your place instead?"

"Guess so," Ryan said, feeling the weight of that shitty weekend lifting already.

He hadn't really been expecting anything for Valentine's Day, but this meant more than any gift or card or dinner could have. Eric had given him something he couldn't have even imagined asking for. He exhaled, pressed his fingers against the cold glass of the window and, for a second, wondered at how quickly his life had changed in just a few months.

Eric still couldn't entirely believe that he had done it. Was doing it. His hand wasn't shaking when he called his mother, but it felt like it should be. Part of him still thought that maybe it might have been easier to just show up with Ryan, let her figure it out on her own. He knew she would have been fine, probably, but that wasn't fair to Ryan.

Ryan, who had become important enough to him that Eric was breaking years of his own personal rules for the first time. Ryan, who was currently in his bedroom, playing Soundgarden on his tinny phone speaker while he packed his weekend bag. Eric could hear him singing along, his shitty, enthusiastic voice carrying.

"Éric!" she said when she picked up, delighted. "You missed your last call."

"I'm sorry, 'Man, I've been busy. And I'll see you very soon, you know."

"I do. I'm looking forward to it. It's been so long, tateleh."

"I was actually calling to talk to you about the visit."

You couldn't put one past Rosa Aronson: as soon as the words were out of his mouth, her tone sharpened audibly. She wasn't worried, necessarily, but she was focused in. "Is anything wrong? You don't need to cancel, do you?"

"No, no, nothing like that." He was shocked how calm his voice sounded. "I'm seeing someone—I have been for several months now—and I wanted to bring him home to meet you."

In the long pause that followed, Eric died several painful deaths.

Finally, she said, "My boy, you have been seeing someone for *several months* and you are only just now *telling your mother about it*?"

"Maman, you heard me say he was a man, right?" With all of the fear that had built up about telling her, about wondering whether his mother's age and tradition would have led her to disown him, it was almost a comical situation that the thing she was most upset about was that he had someone in his life and hadn't told her. Of course it would be just his luck that his elderly mother had misheard him, now, when he'd finally gotten up the stones to tell her.

"Of course I heard that," she said impatiently, "my hearing aid is working just fine. But you have been seeing this man for months and you have not *told* me? When I have been worrying about you being alone for so long? My darling, did you really think I would..."

"I really didn't know, 'Man," Eric said. The shame felt thick in his mouth, cloying and dirty. Not of who he was, but that he hadn't trusted her to accept him. The heavy regret of wondering, now, whether his father would have been the same. "I didn't know what to think. I'm sorry."

There was another long pause. "No, tateleh. *I'm* sorry. We should talk about this when you come home, but first...of course you should absolutely bring your boyfriend. I want to know about him first. What is his name? Is he Jewish? Does he have children...?" The hope in her voice was almost painful.

He thought: *boyfriend?* His brain immediately

skipped over the word. “Thank you, ’Man. He’s not Jewish. He doesn’t have kids. His name is Ryan.”

“Ryan—*Éric*, you *didn’t*.”

He had to laugh. Once again, in everything, his mother wasn’t worried about the fact that Ryan was a man, but that Ryan was his boss. She wasn’t wrong. “You’ll understand when you meet him, ’Man,” he said, finally. “He’s really…something.”

“Yes,” she said dryly, “considering the way you used to complain about him, he certainly must be. All right, Éric. We’ll talk about this when the two of you arrive. Do you have any dinners you’d like me to make?”

“’Man, I don’t want you making *any* dinners, I want you to rest. I’ll take you out—”

“The usual, then,” she cut him off. “I love you, tateleh. You know that, right?”

“Yes,” Eric said, although for the first time in many years, he was able to say it without qualifications. He hung up and looked at the phone screen for a second. His head was spinning, but he felt like laughing, like running into the bedroom and picking Ryan up and twirling him around in a fucking circle. The knowledge that Ryan would probably let him do it and laugh about it. Things certainly had changed over the last few months. He was still trying to play catch-up with his own life.

In the bedroom, Ryan was zipping his bag. He looked up, smiled and asked, “How’d it go?”

“We’re good,” Eric said, because it was easier than trying to explain anything else. “You’re going to have to help me bully her into going out to dinner instead of cooking, though.”

"Eric Aronson, I am not *bullying* your elderly mother into *anything*—"

"Just wait," Eric said. It was strange; his mouth was smiling without his brain's conscious input. "You'll understand when you meet her."

"I'm looking forward to it," Ryan said.

Flying into YUL had been bittersweet over the years. It was such a familiar airport, one he'd spent so much time in. Sweet to see his parents; bitter to leave them. And then, after his father had died, a whole other layer of regret and the knowledge that time was slipping by faster than he could do anything about it. Walking through the arrivals hall with Ryan at his shoulder, talking a mile a minute about the time that the baggage claim at YUL had lost the entire Desperadoes' gear and Murph had threatened to go down there and sort it out himself, felt different than anything he'd been through here before.

"It's nothing special," Eric warned him, as they got into a taxi to head to his mother's house.

"Shut up. It's where you grew up; of course it's special."

The thing was that it wasn't a very impressive house. Eric had grown up solidly lower middle class, and the house reflected that. It was an older building, a long brick rectangle with a sloped roof on top, a skinny yard in front and a shallow yard in back. There were a few equally skinny, stubborn trees on that block, and he had spent many hours in the street shooting pucks and orange balls at the beaten-up net his parents had to replace too frequently. It had been a happy place for him, close enough to walk to the synagogue he attended with his parents, not too far from his billet when he had gone away to play in Boisbriand for juniors.

He knew he shouldn't have been nervous about Ryan meeting his mother, because Ryan always made a good impression on everyone. His mother was excited to meet him. There was no need to worry about it. But he was evidently doing a piss-poor enough job hiding it that Ryan looked over and said, "Hey, it's going to be fine, you know?"

"Logically, I know this," Eric said, exhaling.

"Okay, well, logically or not, it's going to be *fine*," Ryan said, following Eric up the concrete path to the door.

When Eric's mother answered the door, she immediately threw her arms around him and held on tight. He hugged her back, trying not to think about how frail she felt these days when he remembered her from his youth as an imposing and solid physical presence. Her grip was just as tight as it had always been, though, and her eyes were just as bright when she looked up at him and said, "I'm glad you're here." She took a step back, her smile a little intimidating. "And you… I've heard a lot about you, Mr. Sullivan."

"Sully, please," he said, holding out his hand, "or Ryan. It's a pleasure to meet you, Mrs. Aronson."

Instead of taking his hand, she threw her arms around him in the same bear hug she'd subjected Eric to. "Then you'd better call me Rosa, Ryan."

Eric exhaled: he shouldn't have worried. It was clear that Ryan was going to be fine here. He knew his mother, the way she opened her home to his friends, the way she lived to feed guests and make them feel welcome. There had been nothing to worry about. And yet, seeing the physical evidence of it…for a second, he let himself stop thinking about it and just enjoy the novelty of watching Ryan Sullivan and his mother, chatting away like they had known each other for years.

Ryan hadn't known what to expect when he'd agreed to come home to Montreal with Eric. He hadn't known what to expect from Eric's mother, beyond the fact that Eric had said he'd told her who Ryan was to him and that it had gone much better than he'd expected. He'd been to Montreal before over the years—had actually had his bachelor party there, been dragged through the strip clubs on St. Catherine by his older brothers and gotten incredibly, painfully sick in an alleyway after. He'd been there for games, which had always been a little more intense than usual for him: even though he played in Dallas, he'd grown up a Beacons fan, and he'd still nursed that little rivalry deep in his heart.

This was completely different. This wasn't even coming to Montreal as a tourist. This was…well, it was important that he made a good impression. This was meeting the mother of someone who had, in a fairly short time, become pretty important to him.

Whenever Ryan stopped to think about everything that had happened to him over the last year or so, he almost felt like his head was spinning, dizzy and off-balance. It wasn't *bad*, it was just objectively somewhat insane.

Ryan hadn't known at all what to expect from Rosa Aronson, but he could see the ways she was both like and completely unlike her son. She was much smaller than Eric, but still taller than Ryan, and however frail she was, she had the air of someone who would only be stopped by force. Her thick-framed glasses mirrored Eric's, and her snow-white hair was a hint of what might be in his future, once the salt overtook the pepper.

Where Eric had been grumpy and closed-off and combative, she was immediately warm and welcoming, throwing her arms around Ryan in a tight hug. But he could see she had the same sharp sense of humor, the same mean little glimmer in her eye that promised a cut to the quick if you weren't on your toes.

Eric's childhood home was so different from Ryan's. It wasn't as big, but it felt warmer, cluttered with books and papers and full of family photographs. Ryan surreptitiously snuck glances at the pictures of Eric and his parents from his childhood: they had had him later in life, and Eric's father was the spitting image of Eric to the point that it was a little eerie, like looking at the same face from years in the past.

"You look so much like your dad," Ryan said to Eric, while Rosa was puttering around in the kitchen, getting their lunch ready. Eric had tried to argue with her that he would do it and she had both shut him down firmly, and banished both of them to the living room so they wouldn't get in her way.

"Everyone always says that," Eric said, looking down at the same photograph Ryan had picked up. In it, Eric was about thirteen years old, and he and his parents were at the beach. He had been tall even then, gangly and awkward. "I don't see it."

"Really?"

"Maybe I don't want to see it," he admitted. "My dad was special, you know? There was only one of him. It doesn't seem right that people tell me that."

"I dunno, Eric," Ryan said, looking down at the picture again. "You're also pretty special."

"Shut up," Eric muttered, clearly embarrassed, and Ryan relented. "Anyway, now you know what I meant about Maman being stubborn as fuck."

"Again…" Ryan said, trying to hide his smile and definitely failing, "I wonder who else in this room has that particular quality."

"That goes for both of us, you know. Not just me."

"Probably," Ryan said, and slipped his arm around Eric's waist. "It's just nice, though. Seeing where you came from. Seeing parts of them in your face."

"Who knew you were such a romantic?" Eric drawled, but Ryan could tell from the little crinkle at the edge of his eye that he was smiling.

"Boys!" Rosa called from the kitchen. "Lunch is ready."

It turned out that lunch was Montreal-style bagels with cream cheese, lox, and all of the fixings, which included everything from thick slices of red onion and tomato and cucumber to dill that Rosa had hand-shredded, and capers. She had bought a few other things from the deli: whitefish and fruit salad and little chocolate pastries called rugelach.

"So you see," Rosa said severely to Eric, in her heavily accented English for Ryan's benefit, "I wasn't actually *cooking*, I was *assembling.* And now we have time for you to tell me about yourself, Ryan."

Ryan told her while they each assembled their bagels, although it was a bit of a sanitized version. He told her about growing up in Boston with older brothers who were all taller than him and a father who liked to play them all off against each other, about how he was the only one who had actually made it in the major leagues. He told her about marrying too soon and divorcing too late, about accepting the head coach's job on a hope and a prayer and not having expected anything that came after.

Rosa was a good listener. She asked questions occasionally but didn't push, and she kept her warm, dark brown eyes, filmed a little with cataracts, focused on his face the whole time. It was a disconcertingly direct stare, the same one Eric had, Ryan thought, a little hysterically. But it wasn't uncomfortable, being the focus of her attention. He could tell that she was interested in *him*.

"Do I get the embarrassing stories about Eric, or do I have to wait a few days for those?" Ryan asked. He was at the point in a meal where he was full but still had some food on his plate: he pushed around a bit of whitefish salad with his knife.

"Maybe you'll be surprised to hear this, but Eric was a very good boy," Rosa said, and laughed. "He loved his books when he was growing up, and he was a real bookworm until he got seriously into hockey. The worst thing he ever did was fighting, and usually he had some sort of a reason for it, and I couldn't be too angry."

"You were a bad influence," Eric said, looking down with a smile.

"Well, if a boy throws a penny at you, he deserves to get a punch in the nose."

Ryan frowned. He thought, briefly, of all of the stupid shit his brothers had thought was so hilarious as kids, the shit he knew they did even at practice, to their own teammates. The shit his father had even encouraged. It wasn't a stretch to think that those kinds of things would have happened to Eric, even outside of

Boston. "I'm sorry. I never had to deal with anything like that growing up, I—can't really imagine."

Eric shrugged. "It was a fact of life. They stopped doing it once they realized that even if I lost the fight, they weren't getting out of it unscathed."

"So you came by the reputation honestly, even before hockey?" Ryan asked, shaking his head, to Rosa's laughter.

"Sorry," Eric muttered, after lunch, as they were washing up the dishes and Rosa was putting some of the leftovers into the fridge, "she's been like this with everyone I've ever brought home. Grills them like crazy."

"I don't mind. It's nice that she's interested. And brought home?"

"Well, you know. I dated women too, for a long time, almost exclusively…but it's also been a long time since anyone's met Maman."

"Oh," Ryan said, because he didn't entirely trust himself to say anything else.

They spent another hour or so hanging out in the living room with Rosa, who had made coffee and insisted on bringing it out in what she called "the nice mugs," which were a set of vintage-y-looking white coffee cups printed with gold butterflies and flowers.

"You're really getting the star treatment, you know," Eric whispered out of the corner of his mouth to Ryan when Rosa went back into the kitchen for more rugelach. "She doesn't bring those out for just anyone. Guess you have to make the Hockey Hall of Fame first."

"Stop," Ryan demanded, embarrassed. "You didn't tell her all of th[illegible], did you?"

"She looked it up herself when you first got the job. She knows how to get on the internet and everything."

"Jesus," Ryan said, hiding his face in his hand.

"Don't worry," Eric said, "she was probably just looking up your advanced stats. Nothing embarrassing."

After lunch was over, Eric took Ryan on a walking tour of the old neighborhood. It was pretty much what it had looked like on the drive in: pleasant and residential, with an abundance of trees and bushes. They walked past the synagogue where he'd grown up attending, with its beautifully landscaped grounds and its various memorial plaques and statues. They mostly walked in silence; Ryan enjoyed looking around and taking it all in. It was easy to imagine Eric as a child sitting on those steps, his nose buried in a book, his glasses slipping down his nose, or Eric being bar mitzvah'd, which he had explained was like being accepted as an adult in the community and had involved leading an entire service by himself.

When Eric wasn't looking, Ryan slipped a pebble from the synagogue grounds into his pocket. He could feel it there, smooth and round, pressing against his thigh.

"Like I said," Eric said, as they were walking home, "it's nothing special, but I had a happy childhood here."

"Stop being so self-deprecating. Like seriously, Eric, I grew up in Boston."

Eric laughed. "I made myself forget." He mock-shuddered, looking disgusted. *"Boston."*

Later that evening, Rosa brought out dinner, to Eric's protests and Rosa's insistence that all she'd had to do was cut some vegetables. She had made a roasted chicken and some vegetable side dishes: roasted asparagus and something that involved potatoes and carrots, heavy on the ginger, cumin, and cinnamon.

It was nice to have a home-cooked meal and eat dinner in a household where there wasn't tension overwhelming everything at the dinner table; Ryan could relax and listen to Eric and Rosa teasing each other or Eric catching her up on the way the season had been going or Eric smiling at her or Eric throwing him under the bus with a sly remark that would immediately prompt a question from Rosa when he hadn't been paying attention.

After they'd done Rosa's dishes, again, Eric kissed Rosa on the forehead and said something in French to her that Ryan didn't understand but was apparently the indication that they were finished with dinner and going to take Ryan's bags up to Eric's room.

He hadn't been sure what to expect there, either. His own bedroom at his parents' house had long been converted into Chelsea's craft room. There was still a twin bed shoved in the corner, but it was buried under rolls of patterned fabric, and the vast majority of the rest of the space was devoted to scrapbooking and yarn and other supplies. He felt like that was probably one extreme, and the other was the typical hockey bedroom that hadn't been touched since the guy went away to juniors, and the only thing that had ever changed was accumulating more and more hockey memorabilia.

It turned out that Eric's room was neither of those things. It was clear that he came home often enough to actually care about the way that it was updated, and even though it was small and only had the space for a double bed, it wasn't cluttered with childhood artifacts or his parents' discarded items that hadn't fit anywhere else. It had the same Spartan style that his apartment had, with a lot of gray and navy blue, and as always, books piled up everywhere. Ryan immediately gravitated toward a stack of them, a little jump in his stomach when he saw the overlap: they both had copies of *The Art of War*, Marcus Aurelius, and *Henry V*, alongside the more obviously work-oriented tomes.

"You have good taste in books," Ryan said, thumbing through the well-worn and hand-annotated copy of *The Art of War*.

"I'm glad you approve," Eric said, dryly.

"So I'm allowed to sleep in here?"

"Ryan, I'm forty-two years old. Yes, you're allowed to sleep in the room with me."

"Pretty sure it wouldn't be the same at my dad's," Ryan said, and set the book back down on the stack.

"Well, luckily, you're not in Boston anymore, Dorothy."

"Ouch, that was terrible."

"What are you going to do about it?"

What Ryan did about it was cross the room to take Eric's shirt in his fists and pull him closer so that he could tug him down into a kiss. Eric's mouth opened easily under his, hot and giving, and Eric's hands grabbed Ryan's ass to pull him closer against the long line of his body.

"That's a good start," Eric said, a little breathless, "but really, I know you're capable of a lot more than that."

"It's just—I don't know, it's kind of weird in here," Ryan said, laughing a little nervously. "It's your childhood bedroom. Your mom's downstairs."

"Considering you started this," Eric said, his hand

worming its way under Ryan's shirt, "I think maybe you're kind of into that."

"Into what? Sneaking around in your parents' house?" Ryan asked, teasing at first, then sucking in his breath sharply when Eric tweaked his nipple. "Not in the least. I'm not—"

"Not what?"

"Not into the exhibitionism—"

"Hmm, the guy who blew me in his office with the door unlocked, not into the exhibitionism?"

Ryan looked up at Eric, how fucking delighted he always was to needle him into discomfort, the way Ryan *liked* it. Well, two could play at that game, couldn't they? He lowered his gaze, pulling out of Eric's hold, and said, "Are you *sure* it's okay to do this? Your parents aren't going to come home in the middle of things, are they?"

Eric's hands on his biceps flexed, squeezing tighter for a moment. "Ryan fucking Sullivan."

"What?" Ryan asked, innocent as anything. "I have to be careful; my parents would *kill* me if they knew I was here."

"How do you keep talking me into this shit?" Eric grumbled, but he didn't sound terribly annoyed about it.

"Because you only have so many opportunities to make out with me," Ryan said, refusing to break character, "and you said your parents wouldn't be back until late, so this is the perfect time to sneak me into your bedroom."

Eric looked at him over the frame of his glasses, and there was a second where Ryan wasn't sure whether he was actually going to go for it or not. And then his face shifted, and he was smiling, just a little mean. He moved forward and his hands on Ryan's hips were warm; Ryan could almost feel the heat of them through his clothes. "I think that was just because *someone* was pretty eager to get sneaked into my bedroom and fucked up—" Eric walked him back toward the bed. "Or fucked?"

Ryan's calves hit the edge of the bed, and he let Eric push him down onto it. It wasn't a hard push, but Ryan also wasn't fighting with it. He shifted backward so that Eric could move forward, between his legs. "But I've never done anything like this before," he said, looking up again.

Eric's eyes were laughing, but the curl of his mouth was a little mocking. "Oh really? That blowjob at school says otherwise. You like to pretend you're so innocent, such a good, well-behaved boy, but you're…anything except that, huh?"

"You make me do stupid things," Ryan said, voice lowered to a throaty whisper, "against my better judgment. Like being here—" Eric was close enough to touch, so Ryan took advantage of the proximity, pulling him forward by the belt and leaning up into the kiss.

"You're fucking ridiculous, you know that?" Eric mumbled into it.

"You're enjoying it," Ryan retorted, and got the answer he was looking for when he started to unbuckle Eric's belt and try to get his hand down his pants.

"You know, for someone who claims he's never done this before, you're awfully—awfully sure about—"

"I'm a fast learner. You know that."

"Yeah, you're a fucking teacher's pet, is what you are—"

Ryan ran his hand slowly up Eric's dick, very satisfied with the drawn-out noise of protest it got him when he stopped moving. "Well. You should tell me what you like. So I can learn."

"We have to be quiet, though, just in case my parents come home early."

"I can be quiet," Ryan insisted.

"You were pretty loud last time," Eric said, smirking, and Ryan could feel the tips of his ears turning a bit red, thinking about a completely imaginary encounter, about how it might've been if they had been doing this as teenagers, awkward and fumbling and eager.

"Tell me what you like," he insisted.

"Spit in your hand when you jerk me off," Eric said, his voice a little rough, "and once you do that, you can—a little harder. Faster."

Ryan did what he was told and the groan that he ripped out of Eric's throat when he shoved his hand back down his pants was worth all of it. Eric's body bracketed him in on the bed, close enough that he could lunge up to kiss him, although it knocked them both off-balance, landed them sprawled in the bed with Eric on top of him. From there it was messy and awkward and stupid, Ryan unwilling to stop touching him but trying to get his pants off at the same time, Eric trying to help but preoccupied with fucking Ryan's mouth with his tongue, and Ryan yelped again when Eric stopped kissing him, only to nip at his earlobe.

"Shh," Eric said, pressing his hand over Ryan's mouth. "We have to be quiet, remember?"

Ryan thought about digging his teeth into Eric's palm, or licking him, but it was weirdly exciting to have Eric's hand there, pressing down. In the end he settled for shifting the angle of his hand, being able to watch Eric's eyes close when he did it.

By the time Eric had managed to kick off his pants and get Ryan's off too, they were both hard and straining, and Ryan could hear his own ragged breath panting into Eric's mouth. "Come on," he said, the laughter bubbling up in his throat, still marveling that something that was basically a mutual hand job could feel like this, "come on, Aronson, make me come, *come on*—"

Eric's breathless amusement was audible when he said, "Not doing a very convincing job of playing a good boy, Sully. Always thought once I got you in bed you'd be like this—"

"Shh," Ryan demanded. "We have to be quiet in case your parents come home, *remember*?"

Ryan couldn't remember the last time he'd ever had sex like this. When he was actually a teenager, sneaking girls into his parents' home, they had never been anyone he'd been seriously interested in. When he and Shannon had gotten together, they'd both been young as hell and had never tried anything particularly wild—that had only come later, when they'd been trying to save their failing marriage. It was something else altogether to fall into bed with Eric, a grown man who might have been discovering what he liked, but felt sure as hell about it, and comfortable enough to mess around, comfortable enough to laugh about it.

He looked up at Eric, the glasses slipping down, smudged from Ryan's nose bumping against the lenses, and felt his chest constrict with the force of his fondness, with everything that had happened to him over the last six months. If he stopped to look at it too long, it was overwhelming. So instead, he concentrated on the way Eric's hands and mouth made him feel and lost himself in the kiss.

Afterward, when they'd both come and before they'd managed to get out of bed to clean up, Eric propped himself up on one elbow and looked down at Ryan with a disbelieving expression. He'd lost his glasses halfway through and his lower lip was still a little red where Ryan had worried it. His chest was still sticky-looking where Ryan had come all over it.

"I really don't know how you talk me into this shit."

"No?" Ryan asked, still panting a little. "Because from where I'm sitting, you didn't require a whole lot of talking."

"Easy as hell for you, I guess," Eric said, then groaned as he hauled himself to his feet. "I let you talk me into this even though we have to go out into the hall to get to the bathroom."

"Better move fast," Ryan said, unable to stop the stupid smile from tipping the corner of his mouth up. "Don't want your mom to see."

Instead of answering, Eric leaned forward and kissed him. It was a different kiss than the ones they'd shared just a few moments ago, fond and almost sweet, over before it began. "Watch it," he said, as he pulled away. "I'm not getting dragged into this again."

"Mm," Ryan agreed, and lay back down. He wasn't going to think about it. There wasn't any reason to.

Eric hadn't been sure what to expect when he'd invited Ryan to come home with him, but it was going better than he'd ever expected.

Ryan and his mother had hit it off immediately, which didn't surprise him. Ryan was charming, and the kind of blinding, intense earnestness that had made Eric hate him in the beginning translated to most people falling in love with him a little bit, in some form or another. His mother wasn't immune to Ryan's charm either, especially when he insisted on helping with the dishes and asked her interested questions about her late husband and her childhood growing up in Côte Saint-Luc. It was a huge relief, really. Eric had hoped that Rosa would like Ryan as much as he did, and it was a weight off of his shoulders that she seemed to.

Rosa hadn't minded that Ryan was sleeping in Eric's room, and she greeted them every morning with coffee and a bone-cracking hug for each of them. Eric knew that she was thinking about how he would be gone soon; he tried not to think of it, either. It was a strange little reprieve, like a pocket universe, at his mother's house with Ryan.

They'd spent their time in Montreal pretty busy. It was strange, walking around with Ryan; he was clearly recognized more often than not, but probably due to the Boston connection, only a few people approached him. No one asked what they were doing there together; no one looked at them askance, although both of them were very conscious of how and where they touched.

Eric had taken Ryan to some of the museums and a few of his favorite restaurants, in Mile End and Rosemont and Little Italy. They had the poutine at Ma Poule Mouillée before Eric dragged him up to the summit of Mont-Royal, to look down over the city and the sparkling lights of the buildings and streets. It was really a beautiful city; Eric thought maybe one of the most beautiful cities in the world. He took a picture of the skyline. He didn't post often on his Instagram, but it was a nice place to catalog moments that he didn't want to forget. And Ryan wasn't in the shot, so none of his old friends would ask any uncomfortable questions before he was ready.

"It's a nice view, isn't it?" he asked, when he was done.

"I won't argue with that," Ryan said, pulling his coat a little closer around himself.

"You're cold—we can head down, if you want."

"It's okay." Ryan smiled when he looked up. "It's been nice, up here with you. Seeing the city the way you see it. It really is beautiful."

And Eric, overwhelmed again with all of the stupid things that he could have said, looked back out over the city and thought about what he would have to do on his last day. Instead, he checked his phone and whistled. "Hey, did you see? Our boys Cook and Williams are tearing it up at the All-Star game. Cook's got a hat trick. And guess who assisted on each one?"

"I'm glad the boys are having fun," Ryan said, and laughed. "I remember the first time I went it was a good time, and then after that, it was just…kind of a drag. I didn't get to have the same vacation everyone else did."

"You just have to rub in your multi-All-Star status every chance you get," Eric said, rolling his eyes, although he was finding that he didn't have the same kind of bitterness about it anymore. Maybe it was because now he knew Ryan, knew that he wasn't arrogant about it. Or maybe it was knowing that despite all of the hardware, Ryan still crawled into Eric's bed every night, got eagerly down on his knees for him.

On their last day in Montreal, they were in the bathroom. It was a small bathroom, and they had to step around each other to brush their teeth and shower in any kind of reasonable space. Eric spat some toothpaste into the sink and said, "Hey, if you want to hang out with my mom alone, or explore the city for a bit this morning, you're welcome to do whatever you want."

Ryan's gray head, wet from the shower, immediately popped around the side of the curtain. "Why? What are you doing?"

"Well, I, ah, have to go to the cemetery to visit my dad. It's not a particularly fun trip. So I understand if you'd rather do something else."

"Are you kidding? Of course I want to be there for you. Unless…you don't want me there?"

Eric sighed. "It's not that I don't want you there. Not at all. I just didn't want you to feel at all obligated."

"Well, trust me, you fucking idiot, I want to be there."

"All right," Eric said. He felt, unaccountably, relieved.

Joseph Aronson was buried at Baron de Hirsch, which was a reasonably annoying bus ride away from his parents' house. The stones felt heavy in his coat pockets as they sat, Ryan's thigh pressed against his in the seat next to him. Eric watched the familiar streets rolling by and it felt different, knowing he wasn't going to be alone there this time. Rosa didn't make the trip often herself anymore, but Ryan was undeniably there, a warm, solid presence.

The cemetery itself was nondescript, bordered by a low stone wall and sandwiched in between the residential neighborhood of ugly condo buildings that had sprung up around it. It was crowded, with rows and rows of utilitarian headstones stretching out to fill the entirety of the land. Some of the graves had beds of red and white flowers planted on them; some were just grass. All of them were stacked neatly head to toe. No sense in wasting space, when there wasn't much of it.

Eric knew immediately where to walk to find his father's marker. Ryan trailed along after him, like he didn't want to get too close and make Eric uncomfortable. On instinct, Eric reached out and took his hand, briefly, even though it was risky. "It means a lot that you're here, so don't feel, I don't know. Weird. Okay?"

"Got it," Ryan said, and smiled, a little uncertain.

When they got to the gravesite, Eric took a few minutes to clear away some leaves and branches that had blown up against the stone that the cemetery workers hadn't gotten to yet. He brushed his hand over the top of it, although there wasn't any dirt to be found there. It had been over thirty days since he'd been to the cemetery, so he went through the blessing you said when you were coming home again. He finished, murmuring, "Baruch et adonai m'chayeh hemetim."

And then there wasn't anything for it but to begin, the way he always started, in French, "Hello, Papa… I've really missed you."

As he placed the stones on the grave, he went through each of the cities they'd visited, told Papa a little bit about the games. He talked about how the team had been struggling but they'd figured out the power play, a little bit; he talked about how proud he was of the boys for pushing through it even when the games were tough; he talked about how Ryan had come to visit, too. He couldn't bring himself to look behind him to see what Ryan's face was doing, so he kept his eyes firmly forward instead. The stones formed a little row on top of the grave, and when that filled up, Eric crouched down on the cold ground, laid them at the bottom as well.

He knew Ryan was listening and he knew Ryan could probably only understand about a third of what he was saying. That was probably for the best, because Eric had started telling his dad about Ryan, too.

"I wasn't really sure what to expect, 'Pa, but it's been really good for me. I don't even really know how to describe what it all means. It's been a lonely few years, wondering whether I'd ever be able to bring someone home to meet Maman, and now here we are, and he's meeting you, too, in a way. I wish I'd been honest with you before the end. I should have trusted you, and I will always regret that I didn't. So this is the best I can do now. He is…well, he's funny and smart and kind even when I don't fucking deserve it. He's good with the boys. He's patient with the worst of them. Maman likes him; he was so kind to her. He's been an open book with me since the beginning, and things are—they're just really good. In a way I never thought I'd be able to have. And he wanted to come here with me to see you, and it means so much to me that he understands what it means, and I think maybe—"

Eric caught himself. Ryan was standing off to the side, so that he wasn't intruding on Eric's private moment, but close enough that he could still hear. Eric knew that he didn't speak French fluently, but that didn't mean he hadn't picked up a few more words than Eric had suspected. And besides, *je l'aime* wasn't difficult to translate.

Because that was the tricky thing. It had crept up on him, quietly and gradually. But it was true. Eric did love him, and it was probably the stupidest thing he could've done. Ryan was his boss; Ryan hadn't signed an extension yet, despite being in constant conversation with

Joe Conroy about the state of the team and what they could expect for next year; Ryan was newly divorced and had known he was queer for all of fifteen minutes while Eric had been struggling with what that meant for him as a professional hockey player for almost his entire adult life.

There were so many reasons why it was stupid, and why it wouldn't work out, and why he was better off either saying nothing, or ending things right now.

But he also didn't want to lose whatever they had, as undefined as it was. He hadn't wanted that before he'd realized he was in love with Ryan Sullivan, and it was even harder to think of it after.

"Hey, Eric?" Ryan asked, and Eric realized he'd been silent, staring at his father's grave, for probably too long. "Are you okay?"

"Yeah, uh. My knees can't really handle this anymore."

Ryan held out his hand and Eric looked up at him and his handsome, open face, and realized, once again, what a fool he'd been not to realize before this. He took Ryan's hand, let himself be pulled to his feet.

"Goodbye for now, Papa. I won't be so long next time," Eric said, his hand on the cold stone.

And together, they left for home.

CHAPTER TWELVE

February

The weekend in Montreal had flown by faster than Ryan had even thought might be possible, and it had been even better than he'd thought possible. Rosa Aronson was as different from his father as you could imagine, and Eric had been so visibly happy to be at home with her again that Ryan still got a little reflective glow of it in his chest whenever he thought about it.

That had been the strangest thing to realize about Eric: that under the fighting and the sarcasm and the abrupt rudeness, he was really just a guy who loved his parents more than anything and lived for hockey and was game for whatever stupid ideas Ryan came up with in bed. That he had the same little unhealed wound of regret when it came to his father that Ryan had about his own mother. That they had nothing in common at all in many ways but also everything in common in the ways that really mattered.

It was almost a shock going back to work and dealing with the realities of being the head coach of a major league hockey team. Part of Ryan's brain was still in Montreal, waking up next to Eric in the bed that was technically too small, or walking in Mont Royal, or helping Rosa wash the dishes. Instead of any of that, Ryan was right back in the swing of leading practices, handling the media afterward, planning strategies and managing the lineup.

The first practice after the break proved to be kind of a mess. It was clear that Cook and Williams were exhausted, and also that several of the other members of the team had been using the time off from work to party it up. Keen and Martel both showed up at the practice facility with dark bags under their eyes, looking a little green around the gills, and Ryan bit back a frustrated sigh when he noticed.

Before he could say anything, though, Ryan chanced to look up at the yellow bleachers that stretched along the inner wall of the practice facility and froze in place. The practices were open to the public, and there were usually fans lining the stands to watch the team working through the drills. Usually, it wasn't a problem; everyone knew the rules, and no one interrupted or distracted the players.

The person who had caught Ryan's notice wasn't doing anything either, not really. But it was just like his father to show up where he wasn't wanted, to make a point that your own wishes didn't mean shit when compared to what Mark Sullivan wanted. You could establish as many boundaries as you wanted, and it didn't matter if you couldn't actually get away from him.

Dad noticed that Ryan had seen him, and although Ryan couldn't make out the details of his face this far away, he did cross his arms over his chest, which was the kind of self-satisfied gesture that Ryan knew was probably reflected in a smirk.

Petey noticed something was wrong first. "What're you looking at, Coach?"

"Unwanted visitor," Ryan said grimly, as he waited at the red line to start the latest drill.

Petey's gaze traveled up to the stands, but obviously he didn't recognize Ryan's dad. "Oh yeah?"

"I guess I never told him he *couldn't* come, but I'd hoped the fact I wouldn't get him free tickets was enough of a goddamn clue for him to know he wasn't welcome."

He never knew what to expect when his father showed up to things like this. When Ryan was younger, it had usually meant being loudly heckled if he wasn't playing up to his father's standards or screamed at in the car if they had lost the game. Things had changed a little bit now that Ryan was an adult—his father never yelled at him the same way—but there was a part of Ryan that always curled up in an instinctive recoil when his dad turned the force of his disapproval on him. It was unfuckingcanny, really. Thirty years later and it still made Ryan feel like a kid again.

Ryan contemplated skating off the ice and stomping up the bleachers, skates and all. Telling his dad to get the hell out, what kind of a stunt did he think he was pulling. But that was unnecessary conflict. His dad wasn't *doing* anything, except sitting there, knowing that his presence would be bothering Ryan.

Ryan swallowed hard and turned back to the practice at hand. "All right, boys. We're going to be working on special teams today. Black team's on penalty kill first; gold team's power play. We'll do each drill from both sides. I especially want to see attention to detail—once again, we're working on making the right pass, not too many, not too few. You're going to need to make these reads in a split second, same as you would in the games."

"Yes, Coach," the team chorused, although he could see Keen in the back rolling his eyes.

The practice went on: Eric was using a tablet to video the players so he could immediately show them what they were doing, good or bad; it was a funny little extension of his penchant for taking pictures. It was a fast-paced practice and Ryan should have been satisfied with it, but he couldn't relax enough to pay attention.

Maybe it was his father's presence that made him feel so unsettled, maybe it was just the sour notes ruining what had been one of the best weekends of his recent memory, but Ryan had a brief moment of rage that shivered through him. As a player he'd always been a tenacious, gritty competitor, but it was fueled by his love of the game, not his fury. This was different. For a second, he felt like his skin was too tight for his body, like he might explode. He took a deep breath and counted to ten. He exhaled on another count.

"Keen, is there anything you'd like to share with the class?" Ryan said. It wasn't the tone of voice he liked to take with the boys: even with the healthy scratches, he usually strove for patience. This clipped snap wasn't anything close.

"Just that we've been doing these drills for fucking ever and the power play still sucks. Like, no offense, Coach. But it does."

Ryan thought about the way Eric always pinched his nose when he was trying not to say something he'd regret, and wondered whether that would help. He turned a flat stare on Keen. "While some of that is strategy,

Keen, it's also on execution. Which is why we have returned, once again, to doing the drills. It's not your concern, particularly, as you are not going to be on either power play unit this game."

Keen's chin lifted and his eyes were briefly mutinous. Ryan could feel the tension of the moment in the silence on the ice. He had the room and had had it since the beginning of the year when he had come in and given them his pitch. That hadn't changed, even though they'd gone through a roller coaster of a season with a few hot streaks here and there followed by abject blowouts, a season marred by injuries and roster shuffling. He had the room, but that didn't mean the boys weren't waiting to see how he would deal with something like this.

Keen stared back at him, but eventually, looked away first. As soon as he broke eye contact, some of the tension broke too, and everyone moved into position to start running through the drills.

Ryan always did the drills with the team, and he usually liked skating hard through them, whistle clenched between his teeth, stick in his hands as he passed and shot with the rest of them. Sometimes, the coaches would have their own little side-game going, who could get the most shots on net, who could skate the drill the cleanest among all of the suited-up players on the ice. It made things *fun*.

Today wasn't like that, though. It didn't matter what he did, he was constantly aware of his father at the corner of his peripheral vision, watching. Probably judging. Since Ryan had become the head coach of the Beacons, his father had often offered unsolicited advice in voice mails and text messages that Ryan tried to ignore. Ryan was well aware of what Mark Sullivan thought about his coaching style, and it wasn't positive. Having him there felt like an itch between his shoulder blades, just out of reach, building and building until it was almost painful.

"Ryan?" Eric said, during a lull in the activity. "You okay?"

"My dad," Ryan said, jerking his chin up in the direction of the stands.

Eric looked up, a slow, level look. Ryan didn't have to say anything more; Eric immediately understood the situation. "Ah."

The drill was a good one, even if Ryan was working distracted and out of sorts. He wondered whether anyone could tell by his face. The boys were skating hard, and each time he blew the whistle short and sharp to bring new players out into the drill area, it all went smoothly. When he blew three blasts of the whistle to indicate that the black and gold teams were to switch their positions, he realized that Eric wasn't on the ice anymore. For a second, Ryan stopped skating himself, wondering whether he'd hurt himself somehow.

It took a minute before he could see Eric's gangly frame, still in skates, stomping his way up the stairs of the bleachers. Which was—*what* the fuck. He was going to ruin his blades.

Eric wasn't just headed up the stands, he was making a beeline for Ryan's father. And then he stood there, looming over him. Ryan couldn't hear what they were saying, or even really see his father's facial expression, but judging by the agitated hand gestures that flashed around the side of Eric's body, whatever Eric had told him was not what he wanted to hear.

Disoriented, Ryan blew the whistle again to signal a change. Not everyone had noticed something was wrong, of course, but Williams, who was waiting for his turn, skated up to him. "Is everything okay, Coach?"

"Uh, yeah," Ryan said. "Sorry, just distracted."

"What's Coach Aronson doing?"

Eric's back was still facing the ice, but he hadn't moved. Whatever he was saying to Ryan's father was still ongoing. Mark Sullivan stood, and for a second, Ryan wondered whether he was going to try to hit him. Even in his playing days, Mark had been known as a rat, the kind of guy who wouldn't wait to ask you if you wanted to go before the gloves were coming off. He was older now, achier and heavier, but that didn't mean he didn't still have a temper.

Eric could handle himself, of course, but Ryan still didn't want him to have to.

"He's talking to my father."

"Your *dad*?"

Ryan chuckled, although it wasn't a noise with much amusement behind it. "Yes. You knew I'm a local boy, of course. He was bound to turn up for practices at some point."

Williams's dark, thoughtful gaze had turned back up to the bleachers, where Eric was still speaking with Ryan's father. His father had raised his voice, but his words were still indistinct beneath the noise of the practice. All Ryan could hear was a garbled, furious insistence that he had every right to be here in a public facility. Eric, on the other hand, was still speaking quietly enough that his response was lost in the noise.

His father scowled at Eric and flipped him both middle fingers, said "*Fuck* you" loudly enough that the sound carried down to the ice. Everyone froze, watching in silence as he stomped down the line of seats, broad body shaking with fury as he made his way toward the exit. Eric followed behind him, and as they both came into a closer view, Ryan could finally see their faces clearly. Eric and his satisfied smirk, Dad's face mottled red with fury.

It was awkward. The kind of public scene his father's wife despised. Chelsea hadn't come, of course, but Ryan could imagine her face draining of color while Dad ranted at her once he got back. She always nodded and agreed with him, but that didn't mean anything. Dad was great at steamrolling people into acquiescence.

Eric shot him a brief thumbs-up, then looked at the team and said, "What are you lot looking at? Back to fucking work, boys."

When Eric had made his way down to the ice, Ryan asked, "What the *hell* did you say to him?"

"Just told him that he wasn't welcome here today, and that if he wanted to make a scene, I was more than happy to provide him with one." Eric's smile was a little crooked, and not for the first time, Ryan regretted the fact that he couldn't kiss him whenever he wanted. "Surprising how far a few polite words can get you after all. Should've tried that one during my playing days."

He had shocked a laugh out of Ryan, a short bark, and Keen's head whipped around to glare at them. Ryan ignored him. "You didn't have to do all of that, Eric. Thank you. But I was fine with him here."

Eric just looked at him, head cocked a little to the side. He did look very much like a crow in that moment, his bright, dark eyes seeing right through Ryan. "Maybe you were, maybe you weren't. But I took care of it for you anyway." There was an awkward little pause, like he'd swallowed off something else he was going to say.

"Don't worry about it. I don't know if he'll be back, but we'll all be here if he is. He's a real asshole, huh?"

"You have no idea. One of my first hockey memories is him pounding the glass so hard after I took a penalty, he shattered it."

"Holy shit, Ryan."

"Yeah, well. Now you know why I'm so focused on making sure everyone gets along. What'd you call it the first week? My kumbaya shit?"

"We've both come a long way since then, I think," Eric said, and patted him on the shoulder.

"You're right," Ryan said. All of a sudden, he knew with certainty something that had been wheeling around in the back of his head. They were up against the cap limit, and some of the veterans were underperforming. There were a few prospects in Providence that he wanted to give a chance, wanted to see how they could do after the trade deadline. He'd been avoiding it, knowing the conflict that would result. But now? He knew. "I want to talk to Conroy about waiving Keen."

Eric whistled. *"Finally."*

"It's time," Ryan said, watching the players running through the drills again. While they had been talking, Petey and Heidi had stepped in smoothly to take over, make sure things were still running. "He's been a real disruption in practice. And his effort on the ice…well, the less said about that, the better."

"You don't have to convince me," Eric said, laughing. "I was on board from the beginning. But I'm just—this is a big step for you, buddy."

"It's the right one." Strangely enough, he knew, as he said it, that it was true, with all of the certainty he always felt when he knew he'd made a good play, something that was going to end up in the back of the net. "All right. I'll get Conroy on the phone after practice, and I'll see what he thinks."

"Are you kidding?" Eric teased. "His homegrown coaching prodigy? The only question he's gonna have is how fast can he get that guy on a bus to Providence."

Ryan's stomach still felt unsettled: the vague sense of shame that he still hadn't been able to confront his father himself, the flare of heat in his chest when Eric had just done it for him anyway, the tingling nerves up and down his spine of figuring out how that phone call was going to go. He shoved all of it down. He didn't have time for this. He had a practice to run. Taking a deep breath, Ryan blew the whistle to stop the drill, and said, "All right, now we are going to talk about gap coverage on the penalty kill…"

And he had Eric and Petey and Heidi behind him.

The main takeaway that Eric had had from the Montreal trip—besides the fact that he'd somehow fallen in love with Ryan Sullivan—was that Maman also fucking *loved* Ryan. And not only that, she was all too eager to team up with him to find out all kinds of embarrassing stories about Eric's childhood. He smiled, a little, thinking about the two of them at Maman's kitchen table, Ryan listening eagerly as she told him a story about how during Eric's bar mitzvah, he'd corrected the rabbi in front of the entire congregation about a particular point in the Torah portion Eric had been reading.

"You were a little know-it-all even then, huh?" Ryan had asked.

"Little? I was already six feet tall," Eric had retorted.

He'd grinned. "Unfortunately, you'll never get anywhere near there."

Ryan had flushed, although it was the half-pleased way that he always did these days, when Eric teased him. Because they both knew how much they enjoyed the size difference, how it worked in bed. Neither of them could say that in front of Eric's mother, but they'd known it, and as soon as Eric had been able to get him upstairs and into his room, he'd showed him.

As practice wound down, Eric thought about Mark Sullivan's furious face, the way he'd spat venomous words back at Eric when Eric had asked him to leave. Ryan hadn't asked him to do it, of course. Ryan would never have asked for anything like that. His default manner of dealing with his family was avoidance, the same way that his default manner of dealing with Keen and some of the more useless veterans had also boiled down to it.

Eric had been happy to step in between them. But that didn't mean that knowing exactly what a vile person Sullivan was made him feel any better. He thought about Ryan as a boy, growing up in that household. Thought about Ryan's broad smile and bright brown eyes and the way he was so fucking *earnest* about everything. Thought about Mark Sullivan trying to crush that earnestness underfoot. No wonder Ryan never wanted to go home.

The coaching staff had gone into Ryan's office after the practice, listening on speaker while he spoke to Conroy about Keen and the request for waiver. Conroy hadn't been surprised, and Ryan had been short and to the point. When the call had ended, they went to tell Keen, before it was confirmed with the league.

Predictably, he reacted badly. "You're *waiving* me? You're fucking kidding."

"You should be glad that Sully is a more patient man than I am," Eric said shortly. "Or you would have been sent down to Providence in December."

"You had a chance to change your attitude and your play," Ryan added, because of course he was always so reasonable about it. "The closer we're getting to the trade deadline, the more roster flexibility I'm going to need, especially with call-ups. Unfortunately, Jesse, you are the odd man out on this one."

Keen spat on the floor of the locker room. He muttered something under his breath that sounded awfully like *fuck all of you*. And with that, he turned around and stalked out of the practice facility.

Ryan drove Eric back to his apartment, silent and out of sorts. Eric thought about the language Mark Sullivan had snarled at him and the hot fury that had risen in his chest. He hadn't told Ryan about what his father had said. There was no need to upset him. But it had been an internal triumph that Eric hadn't let himself be baited into doing something stupid. He'd been polite and he'd been steely and eventually, he had won.

"Ryan," Eric said, sliding his hand sideways to grip Ryan's thigh. The muscle was tense under his hands, even sitting in the car. "Are you okay?"

Ryan's brown eyes were troubled, his mouth, almost always smiling, turned down at the corner. "Should I have said something to my dad? I don't like the idea of you fighting my battles for me."

"You didn't have to say anything to him if you didn't want to."

Ryan flicked the turn signal on, his eyes checking the right-of-way. It was convenient; he didn't have to look directly at Eric while he was driving. "It's just—you saw a little bit of how he is. When he gets angry, he won't stop fighting until he's just fucking destroyed everything in his path. I learned really early on that it was just easier not to engage. And honestly, it's the only way I've ever been able to have a relationship with any of them."

"Ryan," Eric said quietly, "you know them best. And you know…you may not have been a fighter, but you were *always* tough to play against. Don't forget that now, when things are complicated."

"Thanks," Ryan replied, except he still sounded out of sorts. Frustrated.

"Maybe it just wasn't the right time."

"When will it be? When will it ever be? Jesus, Eric, what if I'm always a coward like this?"

"It's not cowardly. Trust me. If you think what you got with me was a scene, you can only imagine what it would have been like if you'd confronted him today. He probably would've blown a gasket."

"Oh, he wouldn't've left, that's for sure," Ryan said, and sighed. He turned on the radio—of course, it was already tuned to 98.5, the sports-talk station. They drove in silence, listening to the hosts of the show chatter on about the happenings in the league.

"And this is just in, following an investigation by the law firm of Johnson Brown & Williams, the final report on the Railers' handling of the sexual abuse allegations during their Cup run decades ago has been returned. We have not been able to read the contents of the report, but it appears that the entire front office, along with Richard Terrance, the Railers' longtime head coach, have been fired."

"Holy shit," Ryan said, and glanced sideways at Eric for the first time. "If they got rid of *Terrance*—that's huge."

"He must have known," Eric said grimly. "He must have known and never done anything."

Ryan's face reflected exactly what Eric felt: horror and disgust and worry. "And in the middle of the season like this, too. It must have been *really* bad."

"It's really hard to imagine that anyone could treat one of the boys like that," Eric muttered. "It makes me just—furious, thinking about it."

"It would never happen here," Ryan said firmly. "Not like that. You can trust me on that one."

"I do trust you to do the right thing. Quite a lot, you know."

Ryan's face was red when he glanced sideways again before turning his attention back on the road. They made the rest of the trip in silence, both lost in their own thoughts about the news.

III.

SPRING

CHAPTER THIRTEEN

March

By the time March rolled around, Ryan really felt like he was hitting his stride as a head coach. There wasn't much he could do about the fact that the team wasn't going to finish particularly high in the standings. Injuries had ravaged the regular lineup: Travis Sinclair was out for the rest of the season after a shoulder surgery that couldn't have been put off any longer; Davey had to sit a few weeks with a sprained MCL; and Laurent Martel had gotten a nasty concussion in a stupid and useless fight. He was still dealing with post-concussion symptoms. Ryan had had to call up some guys from Providence, which wouldn't be a bad thing on a rebuilding team normally, but it wasn't the ideal time of the season to be trying to integrate new players into the system.

It was easier to deal with the media, too. They were still asking, especially after hard losses, how he felt about the team's record and where they were at this point in the season. They weren't mathematically eliminated from the playoffs just yet, but they would have to win almost all of their remaining games to make it.

The same way that he had for months now, Ryan answered patiently, "The way this season is going, I'm not looking at the standings, I'm really not. What I've been trying to do is to build a culture, which is one where we are playing the right way and doing the right things on the ice, a culture where anyone who's called up knows what we're looking for from them and the system we want to play. In that sense I'm very satisfied with the way that the team is playing. I can't do much about the injuries, and I can't do much about the fact that the roster is where it is at this point in the season."

On the bench it was easier, too. While Ryan still got caught up in the flow of the game, he didn't feel like he was missing as much as he had been at the beginning of the season. It was easier to manage line changes, easier to keep track of who was going where, and although they still took the occasional sloppy bench minors, overall, he felt like he had it handled.

He felt satisfied with the way that Heidi was handling the skills aspect of the practices: the younger players had all taken the strides that he'd hoped they would, and even some of the older players had improved their underlying numbers. Emil Härmälä actually had a positive Corsi for percent, which had never happened in his entire career; Cook had gotten him a cake that said "69% CF (nice)" and had smashed a piece of it in Härmälä's face like they were at a wedding. Petey had gotten the PK under control and even though there was still the occasional sloppy in-zone coverage, overall, they were taking care of the zone.

Since Keen had been sent down to Providence, he'd been playing with a chip on his shoulder, but he was a point-per-game player, and even better, Ryan didn't have to worry about him grumbling in the locker room about his usage or upsetting Eric.

Everything was going well, for the most part. So why did he still feel so unsettled and anxious? Ryan had never been an anxious person as a player. He'd had a clear goal to work toward and the stubborn drive to get there, no matter what. There wasn't any reason it shouldn't have been the same as a head coach.

"What's going on, Coach?" Heidi asked, during a lull in the practice, while the boys were stretching it out, or goofing off in the distance, firing shots at a protesting Davey. He wasn't a particularly big goalie, but when even a baby in forty pounds of pads stopped you in your tracks on a breakaway, it was going to hurt like hell. "You seem a bit out of sorts."

"Joe Conroy offered me an extension last week," Ryan said slowly. He kept his voice down so Eric wouldn't hear. That was another thing he didn't completely understand yet, either. Why he felt so weird about telling him.

"But that's amazing!" Heidi exclaimed, then dropped her voice when Ryan shushed her. "What? Why? Aren't you happy? Would've thought you'd be thrilled to stay."

"Sometimes I wonder why I ever left coaching peewee hockey, to be honest."

Heidi laughed and rolled her shoulders. "I'm sure those are the days when we get blown out 7-2."

"Thankfully, those days aren't happening so often anymore," Ryan said. "But… I don't know. All of you have the one-year contracts too, so I know I should take it so I can give you all some job security if I can, but I don't know if it's the right choice for me."

Heidi stared at him, uncomprehending. "Why not?"

"Am I really the best person to coach this team? Or

should I be giving someone with more experience the chance? Would it be better to try to get further away from—from home, you know? There's just a lot of variables. Don't get me wrong, Heids. I love coaching, and I love this team. I just took the job kind of impulsively, and now that things have calmed down, I just want to make sure I'm doing the right thing for everyone else."

"I can't speak for Petey and Roney, obviously," Heidi said, a small, concerned frown twisting her mouth down. "But Sully, as far as my experience? You've been the best coach I could've hoped for. You gave me the opportunity and I, for one, am gonna be fighting to hold on to it. I'd understand if you didn't sign the extension, but I'm pretty sure I speak for all of us when I say we'd like you to stay."

Ryan wanted to tell her thank you, but all he could think about was his father showing up at practice, the stupid distraction that it had become; his own inability to stand up and say *get the hell out of my practice facility*. Mark Sullivan was the kind of guy who was going to die at age 102 out of sheer spite, so it wasn't like that was going to get any better in the meantime. It was one thing to worry vaguely about it before accepting the job, another entirely to know exactly what he was in for if he couldn't figure out how to grow a pair.

"It has been really rewarding," Ryan admitted. That was an understatement; he didn't have the words to describe what coaching the team had meant to him, what seeing Cook and Williams grow into players he could be proud of had meant to him, what meeting Eric had meant to him. If he didn't sign the contract, he'd have to give all of that up. "I don't really *want* to go."

"So stay," Heidi said, like it was simple.

Maybe it was.

Eric wasn't expecting the call when it came. It was a day just like any other day. He woke up with Ryan's stubbly cheek pressed up against his back, pushed him away without rancor and sat up in bed. They showered together and Ryan complained again about Eric's undrinkable coffee, although by now, Eric had made concessions and started keeping hazelnut creamer in the fridge, even though he shuddered reflexively every time he saw it. They left the apartment together, and Ryan vibrated in place for a second like he was half-ready to go up on his toes and try to kiss Eric right there, in public.

"See you at the rink, Coach," Eric said dryly, the same way he always did.

On the drive to the practice facility for morning skate, Eric's phone rang. It wasn't a familiar number or area code, but for some reason he answered it anyway instead of ignoring it. "Hello?"

"Is this Eric Aronson?"

"Yes," he said, half-suspicious and half-terrified that something had happened to Maman, even though it wasn't a Montreal number. He considered whether he should pull over to the side of the road to continue the conversation.

"Eric, I'm very happy to have reached you. This is Paul Clifton."

At that point, Eric did pull over to the side of the road.

Paul Clifton had recently been hired as the new general manager of the Long Island Railers, after the dust had settled from the initial bloodbath. He was another longtime hockey man, although he had spent most of his career playing in Edmonton. The kind of old-school enforcer that you never saw in the league these days. The end of his career had overlapped the beginning of Eric's, although Eric couldn't remember anything particularly memorable about playing him. He'd been an assistant GM in Tampa before the Railers had poached him, so he had experience—he wasn't all brawn.

Eric ran through any number of things he could have said, including *how the hell did you get my number.* What he settled on was: "Can I help you, Mr. Clifton?"

Clifton chuckled; his deep voice amused. "Just Paul or Clifton, please. Mr. Clifton makes me think of my father, and he's been dead for years."

Eric laughed, too, a little uncertainly, and waited for Clifton to go on.

"I'm sure you can probably guess why I'm calling you, Aronson."

The thought had been forming in his head, but he was superstitious enough that speaking it before he was ready felt like it would just be drawing the attention of the ayin ha'ra. Instead, he took a deep breath, his hands white-knuckled on the steering wheel. "Why don't you tell me?"

"As you know, there was recently a complete overhaul of both the front office and the coaching staff. While we have our former assistant serving in a temporary capacity right now, we'd like to offer you the opportunity to interview for the head coach's spot."

Eric's head was full of static. He'd been working for this for so fucking long, and he'd been *wanting* it for even longer. He'd thought maybe it might've been the time when Leclerc got fired, but that hadn't been in the cards. He wasn't even upset about Ryan being hired anymore, not when it had ended like this. But the offer…this wasn't the way he thought it would've happened, bittersweet and almost tainted.

He was a practical man. There were only thirty-two positions. This opportunity wouldn't come knocking again, maybe not ever. Eric exhaled. At his left, he could see the traffic zipping by on the interstate, no one aware of all of the noise in his head. "Thank you very much for the opportunity," he said. "When would you like me to come down for an interview?"

"I've looked at the schedules, and I think this Friday would be most convenient, if you're available."

Eric flipped through his mental calendar. The team was playing back-to-back home games for the next two days, so they would be late nights. It was a little under four hours on the Acela. He wondered, for a second, whether he could convince Ryan to come with him, whether they could make a weekend out of it. But that wasn't possible. Not only did he not want to tell Ryan about it immediately, they had practices on Saturday that neither of them could miss to go swanning about New York.

"I'm available, so long as Conroy doesn't shut it down," he said. He'd make it work. He'd have to talk to Joe Conroy, but he'd make it work. "I'll let you know if it's going to be an issue with the Beacons."

And then he'd have to talk to Ryan.

After hanging up with Clifton, he called Conroy to work out the details.

"I don't know whether I want to take the position," he said, because he was being honest. Conroy had always been up-front with him, and Eric wasn't the kind of guy to bullshit. "But I'd appreciate if you would allow me the opportunity to interview."

"Of course we won't stand in your way if you have the opportunity for a head coach's position," Conroy said easily. "We'll miss you behind our bench, of course. But I won't prevent you from pursuing a promotion of this nature."

"Thank you, Joe," Eric said. "Can you not tell R—Sully about this yet? Like I said, I don't know if I want to take this position, so I don't want to…make things weird on the bench."

"Whatever you want." Even though he agreed, Eric could almost hear his eyebrows shooting up.

Eric hung up and drove the rest of the way to work.

It wasn't much time to prepare for an interview, but that was almost better. He couldn't overthink things, even if he tried. Today he just had to concentrate on the practice and the game and then on figuring out how he was going to explain his absence to Ryan. They didn't win the game, which was frustrating; even one of Ryan's ten minutes of frantic tape-watching before throwing together a speech for the boys hadn't had its usual effect. It had been one of those games where they played down to the opposition; for whatever reason, the Beacons had never played well against Detroit.

When it was all over, they were the last two men in the rink, which was how it ended sometimes. Ryan was an incurable romantic who sometimes liked to stay behind and look out at the ice, pristine again after the Zamboni had finished with it, at the empty arena rising above them. Eric, it turned out, had not even realized he'd had a part of him who could appreciate something like that until Ryan had woken it in him. It was funny. He'd been doing this so long, as a player and as a coach, and he'd never actually just *looked* at it that way. In a way, it almost felt like being in the sanctuary at synagogue. The same kind of religious awe.

"Hey," Eric said.

"Hmm?" Ryan asked. He looked over his shoulder with a smile.

"You're gonna have to stay at your apartment on Friday."

Ryan blinked. His eyes didn't narrow, exactly, but the smile faded. "What's up? Is everything okay?"

"Oh, it's fine. It's fine. It's nothing about you, I just have some business to take care of, and I might not be home at a reasonable hour, depending on how things go."

Ryan's eyebrows went up. And up again. "Uh-huh," he said. "Are you sure everything's okay?"

Eric thought about just *telling* him, but there wasn't any need to rock the boat if it wasn't an absolutely sure thing that he was going to get the job anyway. So he smiled, and said, "I'll tell you as soon as I get everything settled. Trust me, okay?"

"You know I trust you," Ryan said, "I just wish… I don't know. This seems like something pretty big. You know I'm not going to get weird about whatever it is, right? You can trust me too, you know that?"

"I do trust you," Eric said. Even to his own ears, it sounded lame and toothless. "This is just something I need to take care of on my own. I promise I'll talk to you as soon as I have more information."

"Okay," Ryan said. His eyes looked a little darker in the shadows of the tunnel.

Slowly, the lights in the rest of the arena were flickering off with the loud pops that always surprised Eric, even when he was expecting them. "I promise, Ryan."

"Okay," he said, again. "So we're not going to see each other tonight?"

"No," Eric said, regretfully. Tonight was the kind of night it would've been nice to get railed until he forgot his own name, but he was going to do the responsible thing and update his résumé and prepare for the interview. Ryan laughed, suddenly, and Eric said, "What?"

"It's been kind of a while since we haven't."

With a little shock down his spine, Eric realized how right he was. Ruefully, a little dangerously, he leaned forward and kissed Ryan quickly on the mouth, a press only, just to see his eyes fly wide open in shock. "I'm sorry. I'll see you on Saturday, mon pitchounet."

"You called me that once before—what does it even mean?"

"It's stupid," Eric said, more than a little embarrassed. "A nonsense endearment. My little pitcher."

"Little p—"

"Mon chum, we don't have the time to start this right now."

"Yeah, yeah," Ryan muttered, and shrugged. "All right. You go. I'm still thinking."

It wasn't easy to leave him, standing there in the empty, dark rink, but Eric did it.

It probably wasn't the most efficient way to get down to Long Island. Eric could have flown and then taken a cab, but the hassle of getting in and out of the airports didn't seem worth it, especially because he despised both LaGuardia and JFK. He could have driven, but then he would have lost the opportunity to prepare for the interview in silence in transit, because he would have had to deal with New York drivers. Really the only option was to take the train into Penn Station, and from there, to catch a cab to Floral Park, where the Railers' business offices were located. The trip would be slightly over five hours, and he had to leave at the ass-crack of dawn to make it on time.

Eric bought his train tickets, looked over his résumé one last time, ate three melatonin gummies and did his best not to look at his phone as he tried desperately to pass out. He woke up in the morning and resigned himself to Dunkin' Donuts coffee from South Station. As he was buying it, he thought about how Ryan would have loved rubbing it in and felt a momentary twinge of guilt that he had to push down.

His mother called while he was boarding the train, and immediately figured out that something was up.

"It's nothing, Maman," Eric told her, relieved that probably no one around him was Francophone.

"Why do you sound like you're in a train station?"

"I see your hearing aids are calibrated properly," Eric said, a little sour. "I've been offered an interview for a head coaching position."

"Oh, *tateleh*!" Maman exclaimed. "That's wonderful! You've worked so hard for—wait. You sound unsure."

"I'm not a hundred percent positive that *this* team is going to be the right fit for me, but even beyond that… I'm not really sure, you know. What to do about Ryan."

"You haven't talked to him about it? *Éric!*"

"I know, Maman, I know, I just… I don't even know if it's going to pan out. I didn't want to upset him. I'll deal with it once I know for sure, one way or another.

It's just hard. I've been working for this for so long, but Ryan is—I kind of fell in love with him, Maman."

She sighed. "Nothing is ever easy for you, is it?"

Eric laughed. "I'm too much of an asshole for things to come easy, you know that."

"Éric," she scolded, "no you aren't. You're a good man, and Ryan knows it. You should really just talk to him *honestly*."

"I'm going to. After the interview."

"I hope it's not too late," his mother said severely, and then sighed. "You will do well in this interview, keynahora."

"We'll see. Look, 'Man, I have to go," Eric said, and immediately headed toward the back of the train, where he knew he could probably find a window seat.

Eric had always liked train stations, from the old-school ticker board in Philadelphia to the soaring glass ceilings in Penn Station. There was something about the echo and the noise, the ebb and flow of commuters in and out, that felt strangely soothing. It was easy to disappear into the crowd, one of a million other people going about their business.

He didn't have time to appreciate it today; as soon as he disembarked, his briefcase slung over his shoulder, he had to head out to catch a cab. No use taking chances with New York traffic. Strangely enough, now that he was here, he felt the calm certainty he always felt knowing that soon he would be out on the ice, that the fight he was dreading would be finished soon.

The Railers' front office was an unassuming, modern building with copper siding, tucked into a residential neighborhood of Long Island. He stood outside, looking up, and thought about how shitty it had felt when

Joe Conroy had told him they were going in a different direction. He felt the vague twist of nausea in his stomach and stamped it out viciously.

Eric went up the stairs, where he was greeted at the front desk by the administrative assistant, who then took him to the elevator. The interview room was about what he had been expecting, the kind of featureless conference room decorated in Railers gear that could be easily reconfigured into any position needed. Clifton was there. The owner, Bennett Norris, an older, grumpier businessman who'd made his millions in the beer distribution business, wasn't. That was either a good sign or a bad one: that he'd made up his mind already or was leaving the entirety of the decision to Clifton.

"Good afternoon," Eric said, extending his hand for the shake. He remembered belatedly that he should've said *Clifton* or *Paul*, but there was nothing for it now.

"Good afternoon, Aronson," Clifton said, with another one of the warm chuckles that had characterized their conversation on the phone. "It's a pleasure to meet you. Why don't you sit down, and we can get started talking about what I expect out of the next head coach of the Long Island Railers, and you can tell me how you envision your own coaching position."

As they sat down at the table, Eric couldn't help raising his eyebrows. "Do you want to see my résumé?" He had it, still, tucked in the black folder in his briefcase.

Clifton laughed again. "I don't need to see your résumé, Aronson. You can leave it with me if you like, but the reason I reached out to you is specifically because I liked what you had to offer. From your experience as a player, to your time coaching in Boston."

"Uh-huh," Eric said, a little suspiciously, because *that* sounded almost too good to be true.

It turned out that what Clifton was looking for was typical: the sort of modern coach who could both relate to the players on a very basic level of past experience, but who was willing to look forward to the future of the game, to work with an analytics staff to identify areas for improvement and to try to bring a more unpredictable element to their tactics. They wanted someone to work with the younger players at a developmental level, but also ensure that the older players weren't getting bored or left behind.

"And what would you be looking for, if you accepted a job with this organization?" Clifton was asking.

Eric thought about it for a moment, but he was talking before he could fully organize his thoughts, fully articulate it. "I want a coaching staff that I could work with collaboratively. Staff with no deadweight, everyone offering their opinion. I want to be able to have free rein with the practices to do some unorthodox things. Small-area drills, experimental game simulations, that sort of thing. I want to be able to hire a skills coach and someone to work with the boys with mental strength training as well. I want—" For a second, Eric swallowed, hard. What he was describing was basically the situation he had in Boston with Ryan. And it was the kind of situation that he had no idea whether he'd be able to recreate somewhere else. He wouldn't have Petey's aggressive chill or Heidi's keen insight into details. And most of all, Ryan's...everything.

He realized, belatedly, that he had stopped talking. "It's a lot to ask, I know."

"Not really," Clifton said, steepling his fingers.

"We have the budget to get you extra coaching staff, if you aren't happy with the skills coaches we have already. You'd have input into the hiring, as well. I'd want to make sure you could get along with and trust your staff."

"Of course," Eric said. His stomach felt uneasy, nauseous. "Being able to trust your staff is paramount."

The interview went on for quite some time. Clifton asked him about the on-ice incidents he had had as a player and Eric answered honestly: he didn't put up with bullshit from anyone, let alone someone using slurs. "But one of the things I'm most proud of is that in my old age, I don't need to fight anymore, at least not as a first resort. I've reined in my temper. And I think that has served me well in this position." He thought, briefly, about blowing up at Ryan in the office. The first argument that had led to pushing him against a whiteboard and everything that had come from it.

Get it together, he told himself.

"And what about the whole Player A lawsuit?" Eric asked, as the interview was winding down. "How is the team planning to handle this?"

Clifton's face grew solemn. "We're handling it. We're fully cooperating with the investigation, and as you're aware from the interview, everyone who was involved in the decisions that led to the cover-up has been released from their employment with the organization. We are fully committed to building up a new and transparent front office and management style, one that is devoted to ensuring the safety and security of our players as well as all of our employees."

"What are your concrete plans about this?" Eric asked. "If this were to happen again. If a player were to, say, report to me that he had been assaulted, and I reported to you."

"We would have procedures in place to handle such things," Clifton said smoothly. "The lawyers are working on all of that right now."

Eric could feel himself frowning, and tried to rein it in. "What about 'going to the police to report a crime'?"

"Obviously, that is the end goal," Clifton said, smiling again. "But you know how front offices are. It's a lot of red tape and following the appropriate channels of communication."

The thing was that Eric wanted this job so fucking much. In theory. He had wanted this job for years; he had been furious when Ryan had stolen it right from under his fingers. But this was not what he'd wanted to hear. This was more of the same, this was corporate speak for *we're not going to do the right thing until we can be sure that we're covering our asses.*

Eric had never been in a situation like Player A had been, and he didn't know how he would have reacted, if he'd been trying to crack a major league roster at the time. He knew the desperation, the fear, the knowledge that you had to do *anything*, including playing through injuries, so you wouldn't lose your spot. And now that he was a coach, he knew that it was his job to help protect those specific guys, the guys like him. The hungry, desperate ones. The ones who were vulnerable.

"But you'd take it to the police?" he pressed.

"Of course," Clifton said.

While Eric wasn't entirely sure if he believed it, it was the sort of thing that he couldn't argue too much in a job interview. They ran through the last pleasantries, the last few questions, the jovial reminiscing about their playing days and what it used to be like in the league and how fast things had been changing recently.

Finally, Clifton said, "I'll be blunt with you, Aronson. This is basically your job to lose. I just need you to give me an answer in the next two weeks whether you'll accept or not."

"Thank you, sir," Eric said, swallowing hard around the lump in his throat. "I will have to talk to Ry—Coach Sullivan and the rest of the staff, and I'll get back to you as soon as I can."

They ended on a handshake, and then the assistant came back in to escort Eric to the door. He had a lot to think about on the train ride home.

Ryan wasn't sure what to make of the fact that Eric was gone all of Friday. It wasn't that they missed him at practice, exactly—Heidi was more than capable of stepping in to work with the forwards in his absence. But Ryan felt it, like a hole in his chest, if he was going to be melodramatic. The whole practice felt off-balance to him; he caught himself constantly turning like he was expecting Eric to be there, for the stupidest things. To ask him what he thought about Cook's board battle or Williams's edge work or any of it. To needle him about the way he'd get grumpy when one of the boys showered him in snow. To tease him about where they'd go for dinner after.

It was *one practice*; there was no need to act like some ridiculous teenaged boy, mooning after the girl of his dreams. But there was the nagging little fear in the back of his head. It was unusual that Eric would miss practice or a game for any reason. So that basically meant it would probably have been a job offer. And if he didn't want to tell Ryan about it yet, that meant it was probably something serious, something he was considering accepting.

Ryan tried his best to concentrate on the practice, but his head felt like there was a thunderstorm brewing in there. He wasn't upset. He was happy for Eric. They'd never talked about what they were doing, but he'd started to...he didn't even know what he was hoping for. It had felt real and solid and like something when Eric had took him home to Montreal. But if he was going to be leaving Boston, Ryan also couldn't expect that things would just continue that way. It was one thing to keep them up when they were working together, in the same city, when it was easy. It was another thing to commit to something long-distance.

Either way he was going to have to talk to Eric, finally.

That opportunity came sooner than he was expecting. Ryan was already home at his sad little apartment, making himself dinner, when Eric texted, Can you let me in? Ryan checked the stove burners he had on under his griddle to make sure that nothing would catch fire if he accidentally got locked out of his apartment and went downstairs to do just that.

When he opened the door, he found Eric on the doorstep, bedraggled from the steady rain that had been falling that evening, droplets misting his glasses. He had a black leather briefcase tucked under his arm, and his coat was billowing a little in the wind. When he saw Ryan, he took a step forward and grabbed him by the shoulders and leaned down to kiss him.

Ryan made a surprised noise into his mouth, especially because now he was getting rained on too, especially because they were basically in public, but went with it, still swept up in the emotions of realizing that they might have to end this soon. Eric kissed with the kind of desperation that Ryan felt, like he knew things were changing faster than they had been ready for, like he didn't want it to happen any more than Ryan did.

When they finally pulled apart, Eric's glasses were a smudgy mess of rain and nose-prints, and he was breathing a little raggedly. Ryan said, "Uh, you know, you can come in where it's not raining."

Eric laughed, although there was a hint of uncertainty to it. "Yes. Of course."

"I'm making cheesesteaks," Ryan said, "if you, ah, want one. If you can eat one?"

"That sounds perfect right about now," Eric said, and followed him up. "I don't really keep kosher, you know."

The cheesesteaks were something that Ryan had eaten in Philadelphia in his playing days, and he'd gotten kind of obsessed with recreating them at home. They weren't exactly clean eating, but sometimes you just wanted a gigantic portion of meat and onions and cheese on some bread that, by the time you were finished with it, was practically falling apart under the weight of the filling. He'd gotten pretty close—the key was freezing the meat before you started trying to slice it—but the bread was always a struggle. For some reason, the right kind of rolls just weren't available outside of Philly. He made do.

Eric leaned against the counter in his narrow galley kitchen while Ryan worked. He'd already done most of the prep, so now it was just a matter of cooking the meat and onions on the grill and laying the cheese on top toward the end, toasting the rolls just a bit in the fat left behind. He watched Eric from the corner of his eye, waiting for him to talk. He'd taken off his coat and wiped his glasses off with a cloth, but his curly hair was still a little damp, and he kept rubbing the back of his neck uneasily.

"Can you just tell me what's going on?" Ryan said, finally, as he was chopping up the meat straight on the griddle.

"I had an interview today." He didn't sound happy about it, his voice tight and stretched. "I was offered a head coaching position."

Ryan's stomach dropped. He shoveled meat onto the roll and looked up, forcing himself to smile. It wasn't hard, and it was the hardest thing he'd ever done. "Eric, Jesus, that's amazing. Congratulations, buddy. I'm, I'm sorry I don't have anything special we can drink to celebrate."

"Well," Eric said, mouth twisted down. He couldn't look Ryan in the eye. "I'm not sure if I'm going to take the job."

"What?" Ryan said. It was like whiplash, a little. The pride and the fear and the relief. "Why not?"

"Well. As you might've already guessed considering the vacancies around the league, it was the Railers."

Ryan stared at him. "Oh. *Ohhh*, Jesus."

"Yeah. So. I asked them about what they'd do if a player reported something similar again, and I wasn't very encouraged by the answer. It was just corporate bullshit for doing the bare minimum to cover their asses. I was—not thrilled by it."

The meat steamed in the buns, but Ryan suddenly didn't feel very hungry. "Eric, I…look, no one deserves that position more than you. And I think if you want it, you should take it. You've worked so fucking hard for it, and this kind of chance doesn't come up very often. You know better than anyone."

"Yeah," Eric said, shortly. He pulled one of the plates toward him but didn't eat, either. "I just…morally, I'm not sure if I can do it. And I heard their owner on the radio on the train ride home, ranting about how unfairly the organization was being treated in the press. It's just…it's the chance of a lifetime. But I don't know if I can take it, Ry. I just don't know."

The dinner forgotten, Ryan took a step forward, and wormed his way into an embrace. Even now, it was almost shocking how easy it was to fit their bodies together, considering Eric's height advantage and the way Ryan's face ended up buried somewhere in his chest when Eric's arms tightened and pulled him in closer. "The thing is, Eric. You're like…a really good person. I *know* you. And I know if you took that position and anything happened, the guys would trust you, and *I* would trust you to do the right thing, no matter what the team wanted."

"That's. Probably kinder than I deserve," Eric said, voice muffled by Ryan's hair. "I appreciate you saying that, probably more than you know. But I don't know…"

"I think that if you want the job," Ryan said, hating himself for how fucking sad he felt saying it, "you should take it. Like I said. No one deserves that more than you do. And I want to see you—I want to see you behind the bench where you belong."

Eric mumbled something again that sounded like *I am behind the bench*, but Ryan couldn't hear it clearly over the pounding of his heart in his own ears. "I have some time to think about it. So I'm going to think about it. Okay?"

"Yeah. This isn't the kind of decision you should make right away," Ryan managed. "But I want you to know, like, whatever you do. I'll support you in it."

"Thank you," Eric said again, and kissed the top of his head, a gesture that was so ridiculous that Ryan tried to swat him away. "Hey. I'm starving. Let's eat, and then we can talk about like—anything other than this. Please?"

"Whatever you want, buddy," Ryan said, and sighed as he untangled himself from the embrace. "I can be a very good distraction."

Eric, laughing, kissed him again, but Ryan didn't feel any better after it.

Eric had a hard time falling asleep, even after a pretty intense orgasm. He lay awake in Ryan's bed instead, alternating between staring at the ceiling in the shadows of the room and looking back down at Ryan's face. Eric liked to see how slack and relaxed Ryan was in sleep, because awake, he was constantly in motion, constantly on edge, constantly smiling or talking or getting his stupid nose into everyone's business.

Given everything that Eric had learned about him since they'd started sleeping together, it wasn't surprising at all that he was a cuddler in bed, either: he spent most of the night trying to squirm his way closer to Eric, who inevitably ended up pushed to the very edge of the bed by the time the sun started peeking through the blinds.

Looking at Ryan was a more pleasant occupation than trying to figure out what the hell he was going to do about the job the Railers had offered him. He hoped Ryan was right: that he was a good person who'd be able to do the right thing if it came down to it. He'd been a fighter his whole life, and that hadn't changed now that he wasn't putting on the gear and pads anymore. But there was a difference between knowing that you wanted to do the right thing and doing it in practice.

Surely, the other coaches hadn't *wanted* to actively cover up that kind of abuse. Maybe they had been lulled into complacency by the possibility of the playoffs, by the desire not to get fired and keep their jobs, by the knowledge that someone else would handle it. It was easy to pass off responsibility if someone told you it would be handled. Who was to say the same thing wouldn't happen to him?

Ryan's simple, easy confidence in him still warmed his chest like almost no other compliment or honor he'd ever received. But he still couldn't entirely believe it.

Even beyond that, there were the optics of it. He didn't want to accept the job and come in to be the Band-Aid, the distraction. He could potentially be the first Jewish head coach in the league in over a hundred years, and that would certainly be a talking point that they could use rather than the ongoing lawsuits. Accepting the job would be an implicit approval of anything the organization did, because there were probably non-disparagement clauses in the contract.

But then there was the fact that he desperately wanted the job. He wanted to have the opportunity to build something long-term, something successful, something that was his. He wanted to prove everyone wrong who'd ever looked at him and called him a goon, everyone who thought he couldn't do it, everyone who jokingly mentioned his long, long slate of penalty minutes, his lack of hardware or a Cup. Eric knew, deep within himself, that if he had the chance, he could run with it. He could do it. Maybe not the next year or the year after that, but eventually.

Every time he thought about the pros and cons, he ended up right back where he started. He wanted the job. He didn't know if he could live with himself for taking *this* job. He truly wasn't naive enough to think that the fact that he was a good person, or tried to be a good person, would be enough to counter systemic, organizational rot.

But other people did it every day. Other people compromised their morals to get where they needed to go. You couldn't get ahead in the world without being a little ruthless, a little selfish. Right?

Ryan grumbled in his sleep, turning over on his side and pushing himself even more insistently against Eric's body. He always ran hot, and Eric was normally the kind of guy who liked his space in bed. He'd gotten used to Ryan this way, somehow.

Ryan wasn't ruthless or selfish. He wasn't a pushover; there was a spine in there, but he cared about the boys, as a group and individually. He worked with the healthy scratches long after everyone else had left the ice. He had apologized to Eric when he'd realized what the situation had been. He waited almost the entire season to waive a guy who was barely trying, just because he wanted to draw out the best in him another way.

The shitty thing about the whole situation was that Eric knew he had a clear choice, and it wasn't the easy one. He just had to get up the stones to make the call.

He ran his hand down Ryan's arm, wondering what the hell life would be like without him in it. It was funny how he'd wormed his way in there, in such a short amount of time, intertwined himself in every aspect of Eric's day-to-day, like it was nothing. There weren't many people out there like Ryan Sullivan, and that was probably a good thing. Eric wasn't sure if the world could actually handle more than one of them.

He closed his eyes and tried to sleep. He had a lot of work to do in the morning.

CHAPTER FOURTEEN

March

They didn't talk about it when Ryan got down on his knees to blow Eric in the shower in the morning, and they didn't talk about it when Ryan made him breakfast afterward. Ryan didn't want to push too much. He knew it was a big decision and Eric probably needed the space to think through it all on his own. Ryan had a lot of things to think about, too, but they were nebulous, unformed thoughts knocking around in his head like ghosts.

It was the rare Saturday where they didn't have a game or travel or any practices scheduled in the morning, the kind of day that felt like a holy grail. On a normal morning, Ryan assumed that they probably would've spent the day together. Maybe they would have gone out to lunch or walked around the Commons or another park. The spring weather wasn't warm, exactly, but the bitterness of the winter was starting to fade along with the new plants unfurling in the sunlight.

But it wasn't a normal day. He watched Eric eat his eggs and toast with his usual single-minded focus, and said, "So are you gonna take some time to go back to your apartment and figure this out?"

"Yes," Eric said. He sounded grateful, and he looked exhausted, the dark circles that he always had under his eyes standing out a little starker this morning. He wasn't wearing his glasses yet, and his chin was shadowed with the hint of the stubble that had already started growing in overnight. "I have to think some things through and make some plans and some phone calls, probably."

"Okay," Ryan said, trying not to let any hint of emotion bleed through into his voice. He didn't want Eric to feel like he couldn't take the job, just because Ryan would miss the hell out of him. Just because Ryan had, what? Fallen in love with him?

Oh, shit. Ryan *had* fallen in love with him.

Somehow, in between dealing with the team and his divorce and arguing and sleeping together and meeting their families, Ryan had fallen in love with Eric Aronson.

He wanted to laugh. It was so fucking ridiculous, the whole situation. Part of him wanted to cry, because he'd only realized it right as things were potentially ending. And he couldn't even tell Eric now, because he didn't want him to feel obligated to turn the job down, to stay in Boston with Ryan, when he had all of the opportunities in the world elsewhere.

Ryan swallowed hard; of course Eric noticed. He raised his eyebrows. "You okay?"

"Yeah," Ryan said, "yeah, I'm fine."

Eric was still looking at him with that searching, questioning look he had sometimes, the one that made players in full hockey gear wilt on the bench when they'd fucked up. Ryan had a different reaction, of course: getting half-hard, visible through the boxers. His body's stupid, automatic response broke the tension.

Instead of asking him another question, Eric laughed and said, “Oh, I see how it is.”

Ryan lifted his chin, and said, “Well, what are you going to do about it?”

What Eric did about it was exactly what Ryan wanted, and by the time they were ready to say goodbye for the day, Ryan felt lazy and sated and, if not exactly better about the whole situation, then at least distracted. He was probably going to have to deep-clean the kitchen counter later, but it was worth it.

After Eric left, Ryan settled in for what he planned to be a quiet day, cleaning his apartment, going over tape and taking notes, and watching scouting reports from the staff for the next game they were playing, on the road in St. Louis. He was wiping down the counter again when his phone buzzed in his pocket, and he took it out to see who was calling. And then his stomach sank, because of course it was his fucking father.

Ryan should have just let it ring. He should have sent it straight to voice mail. He already felt like an exposed nerve, there was no way that any of it was going to go well.

“Ryan,” his dad said as soon as he picked up, “we need to fucking talk about the way you’ve been handling things.”

Ryan closed his eyes, rubbed his eyelid with his thumb. “Oh, we do, huh?”

“I’m not happy with you. At all. And neither is anyone else in the family. I know you have the day off. You *will* come for lunch.”

He couldn’t help it: he laughed, which was exactly the wrong thing to do. He could almost hear his father vibrating with rage on the other line. "Is that an order, Dad?"

"Yes," Mark Sullivan said, and hung up.

Ryan looked at his phone. He could do what he had always done, which was avoid the confrontation. What was his father really going to do if he just didn't show up? Rage impotently at home. Or probably find some kind of a way to show up later, either at practice or the games, and make everything awful again.

The thing Ryan was learning, the older he got, was that some problems could be solved with kindness. Some problems could be solved with patience. But the really thorny ones, the really deep, long-standing ones…running away from them forever wasn't going to fucking cut it. Especially because Eric wasn't always going to be there to fight his battles for him.

Ryan took a deep breath and went to get ready for that goddamn lunch.

For such an unassuming house, it was funny how deep-seated the feeling of dread in his stomach always was when he started walking up the sidewalk to the front stoop. It was like somehow the front face of the home personified everything he hated about going home, the way the shutters and door looked like a leering face. Some indie director could probably make an excellent horror film about that house, Ryan thought, as he rang the doorbell.

"You're in for it now," Chelsea said, when she answered. She looked the way she always did when Dad was in a mood: harried and worried and drawn. For the first time in a long time, Ryan wondered whether she regretted marrying Mark Sr. so young. Whether she ever thought about trying to leave. She'd been barely out of college when they got married, and the career in fashion design she'd been trying to pursue had abruptly ended.

Ryan exhaled, suddenly feeling very tired. "Yeah, I got that impression from the phone call."

"I tried to tell him how busy you are," she said, as he followed her through the hall to the kitchen, "but you know how he gets when he's in a mood."

"Yes, I do," Ryan agreed. "What's for lunch, Chels?"

"Subs from Olympic. I'm sorry. I tried to tell him you like that one specific grinder, but…"

"He's making a point. Don't worry, I won't be staying long."

"Oh, god. Ryan, please, don't…"

"I'm sorry, I just don't think that this is going to go very well. You know."

"Shit," Chelsea muttered.

"Sorry," Ryan said, again.

She sighed. "It's fine. I should have expected this when he was going on about inviting you. The two of you have always been oil and water."

Ryan had always thought this was an interesting way of saying that his father was an asshole and Ryan had done his best to avoid him, but he supposed that when you were living in a house like his father's, you had to tell yourself stories to make it tolerable. Ryan had certainly done enough of it before he had been able to escape to college.

Even though the lunch was already set up in the kitchen—Chelsea always made a point of arranging meals on the actual plates and setting a table, even if it was the kind of casual takeout that you could eat straight from the wrapper—Dad was still where he always was, holding court in the living room in his recliner. At least none of Ryan's brothers were over today; he wasn't sure whether he'd have the spine to say the things he had to say if they were all there watching him. As it was, his stomach was doing nervous little flip-flops, the same way it had before each of the drafts he'd attended and never been chosen.

"Ryan," Dad said, when he saw Ryan enter the room. "Sit down, boy. We're going to have a little talk about the way you've been treating your family."

"How have I been treating the family?" Ryan asked. Even now, it was easy to keep the emotion out of the words. His father wasn't interested in what Ryan had to say, he was only interested in the setup for the diatribe, which Ryan had clearly provided him.

And he went *off*.

It was the kind of rant that had spittle flecking his lips, face brilliant red like the thin capillaries running beneath the skin were in danger of bursting. Ryan let it wash over him like a tsunami, or an explosion. A shock wave.

Ryan barely even heard most of it, tuned in and out as Dad kept talking. "—and I put the fucking time and money into your training even though you were always a fucking runt, even though you had no chance at making it anywhere, *I* believed in you and pushed you to be better when no one else would—"

At this point in his life, Ryan wasn't even offended at the revisionist history: Dad hadn't ever actually supported him. He'd paid for the gear, sure. Driven Ryan to practices. Screamed at him whenever he hadn't backchecked hard enough or put the puck in the back of the net often enough. Ryan had learned the hard way how to be better than everyone else: it was partially to compensate for his size, but partially to get his dad off of his back. Dad would never see it that way. He would never have let Ryan quit, but he wanted the credit for the rest of it, too.

In past years, Ryan would have waited until Dad was finished ranting. He was half considering doing that, now, too, until his father's meandering train of thought had shifted from Ryan's failings to the way that the league itself was going down the shitter. He was working himself up more and more, and Ryan wiped his sleeve across his face to clear away the droplets of spit. Dad was standing now, looming over Ryan and ranting about Morin and Sato with the Constitution and Campbell and Walker with the Liberty, awful shit about how affirmative action was harming the quality of play and—

"Dad, you know the Cons won the Cup last season and Morin scored the game winner, right? You know Campbell almost single-handedly backstopped the Libs to *two* Cups, right?"

"Shut the fuck *up*," Dad said, his voice loud enough now that Ryan could hear Chelsea drop something in the kitchen. "You know as well as I do that the league is headed in the wrong direction. It's on your fucking staff, too, with that goddamn Jew on the bench—"

"Hey," Ryan said, sharply. "Stop it."

Dad stared at him like he'd never seen him before. "What did you just say to me?"

"I said *stop it*. Shut *up*, Dad."

"Where the *fuck* do you get off talking to me like that?" Dad demanded.

Ryan stood up, too. His father still loomed over him, even when Ryan was standing. He was about Eric's height, well over six feet. And he was imposing with the bulk of a life spent playing sports and then letting the underlying muscle go to seed. Ryan was the same as he'd always been, short and barrel shaped. No matter how strong he'd been, when his father stood like this, he always felt like a small child again, cowering in his mother's shadow, as if she could somehow protect him from the wrath he knew was coming. But he wasn't a child anymore. He was a grown man, and he would stand his ground.

"Because I'm fucking tired, Dad. Because you're a horrible fucking person and I'm tired of listening to you. That's what I came here to tell you. I'm through with this goddamn family unless you can get your shit together. Unless you can learn, somehow, to stop being such assholes. I truly don't believe you've got it in you to figure it out, so until then, leave me the fuck alone. Don't come to practices. Don't come to games. If you try to talk to me, I'll have you escorted out. If you try to call me, I'm going to block your number. I'm fucking *finished*, Dad. I'm tired. I'm goddamn disgusted. And if you ever, *ever* talk about Eric like that again, I'll make sure you never set foot in the Spectrum again."

Mark stared at Ryan like he'd never seen him before. His face was mottled red and white, like he would have gone pale if he hadn't been so apoplectically flushed with rage beforehand. For a second, Ryan thought that Mark was going to hit him, or try to. He tensed for the blow that never came.

That was the thing: he always knew, growing up, it could have been worse. Some of his friends had dads that used a belt on them after bad games. Dad had never done that. He'd never laid a hand on Ryan. He'd just yelled. Or stopped speaking to Ryan entirely. But ultimately, it had always been the guilt of knowing it could have been worse that kept him coming back.

It wasn't until now, until he was middle-aged himself, responsible for kids as young as he'd been once, that he was starting to realize just how truly vile his father had been.

How fucking sad his childhood had been.

"So that's it?" Mark snapped. "You're choosing that—that fucking *Aronson* over your own goddamn family."

"Yes," Ryan said. He felt, weirdly, calm. As calm as he'd ever felt before a big game. As calm as he'd been before Dallas retired his jersey or being inducted into the Hall of Fame. "And he's a better man than you could ever dream of being."

Mark lurched forward, and for another brief second, Ryan thought he was going to throw a punch, or try to push him back in the chair, or something insane. He didn't. He stood there, frozen and tense, panting with anger the same way a dog that had run too far and too fast would pant. Ryan could see his tongue through his open mouth, red and obscene.

"If you take one step out of this room, I'm going to disown you, boy," Mark growled.

"Good," Ryan said, simply. "I always stayed away from home, from you. I wasn't here for Mom when she got sick because I was fucking *scared* of you. But I'm not scared of you anymore. You can yell, you can disown me, you can do whatever you fucking want. But I'm telling you, right now, that this is a choice *I* am making. And you? You can go fuck yourself."

And he turned and left.

He could hear his father screaming at him as he left,

but it was just background noise, like any kind of television static.

"I'm sorry, Chelsea," Ryan said, as she trailed after him toward the door. "He's really going to be in a mood tonight."

"It's fine," she said, smiling tightly. There wasn't any humor behind the expression. "It was a long time coming, really. I'm…sorry, too, Ryan. About the way things went. You know what I mean, don't you?"

"Yes," Ryan said. "You know I don't blame you for any of it. Take care of yourself, okay? If you ever…you know. You've got my number."

Chelsea looked at him, her wide blue eyes as blank as a frozen-over lake. She was a beautiful woman still, even though living with his father had carved deep lines into her forehead and mouth that she'd tried to smooth out with Botox and fillers. "Don't worry about me," she said, and shrugged. "I'm used to it."

"You don't have to be, though."

Chelsea laughed then, and leaned forward and kissed him on the cheek. "You were always an idealist, you know. Go, Ryan. I'm sure you've got a million better places to be than Southie."

The feeling Ryan had when he shut the door behind him was like nothing he'd ever felt in years. A combination of fear—the finality of the way he had ended things with his father—and relief—the finality of the way he had ended things with his father. Somehow, it felt like he should have been shaking, but his footsteps were steady and his back straight as he walked back toward his car. It had been an awful confrontation, but he felt surer about himself, about *things* in general, than he had in years.

Instead of heading back to his apartment, he drove farther south, toward Roslindale. He hadn't been down that way in ages, mostly because he had no reason to. The only reason to visit was the Mt. Calvary Cemetery, where his mother was buried, and he hadn't been to visit her grave in years. He hadn't been exaggerating when he'd said that he hadn't come home because he'd been afraid of his father. And he'd avoided his mother's grave out of guilt for decades afterward. But if he was facing up to his fears, he had to face up to her, too.

The Mt. Calvary Cemetery was one of the few large Catholic cemeteries that were still active in the Boston area, and it wasn't anything particularly special. There were trees lining the fences and the roads that wound through the extensive grounds, but once you got inside, it was mostly just rows and rows of graves lining the flat ground, browning in the spring thaw. A stone chapel, door locked against intruders. Some larger, ostentatious stones.

Katherine Sullivan's grave wasn't anything like that. It was a simple, small headstone that listed her birth and death dates. It said, *BELOVED DAUGHTER, SISTER, WIFE, AND MOTHER.*

Ryan still remembered, like it was yesterday, standing by the graveside and listening to the way that the dirt sounded when it fell on top of the coffin. He had helped the cemetery workers shovel some of it in. It was the finality of the noise that had stuck with him, back then, the hollow patter of rocks and dirt on wood. He hadn't gone back since, and it looked like no one else had, either. The cost of the plot had included perpetual care, so the grass was weeded and mowed the same as any of the other graves.

But no one had left her flowers. No one had left anything.

As he'd walked, Ryan had his hands shoved in his coat pockets, and he felt his knuckle bump up against something flat and hard. He pulled it out, frowning, until he realized it was the pebble he'd picked up on the grounds of Eric's old synagogue in Montreal. It was round and flat and white, and he thought about Eric picking up pebbles in every city they stopped in, about Eric on his knees talking to his father at the gravesite.

Ryan took a deep breath and rested the pebble on top of his mother's stone. He crouched down to grave level, ran his hand over the top of the headstone. "Hi, Mom." It sounded stupid at first, to talk to a grave. Eric had done it as naturally as he did anything else, but he'd been doing it for years. Ryan's tongue felt awkward and ill at ease, but he forced himself to keep going anyway. "I'm really… I'm sorry I haven't been to visit you in a long time. I'm sorry I wasn't here for you before you died. I didn't know how sick you were. And that's not an excuse. I hope you understand why I stayed away then…and then after that, I just felt so fucking guilty. And that's also not an excuse."

His brothers had always looked more like their dad: big and burly and intimidating, blue-eyed and black-haired. Ryan had been the only one who resembled Katherine. They were both small, had the same warm brown eyes and stubborn cleft chins, the same smile, the same thick brown hair. Sometimes, Ryan wondered whether that was the reason his father had hated him so much, especially after she'd gotten sick. He remembered being called a sissy, a mama's boy, all kinds of ridiculous shit. In retrospect, it was so fucking stupid that his father—the man who had *married her*—viewed that as an insult. Because Ryan had loved her, so stupidly much.

"Uh. I'm back home now, maybe for good, if I sign this extension. I'm coaching the Beacons. I know you thought Shannon was right and that I should give up on hockey, but I've made a pretty good career out of it. I've had some really good memories. I met some really great people. Uh, and about that. Shannon divorced me, and I'm probably more okay with that than you ever would've guessed. We weren't right for each other, even if we both realized it too late. And I met someone else, and he's really…pretty fucking amazing. His name is Eric. I think you'd like him. Maybe. I hope. He's a good man, even if he pretends that he's not. He might be moving away soon, and things might be changing, and I don't know how to feel about any of it.

"But it's partially because of him that I got the courage to tell Dad to fuck off. And I did do that, did you know? Told Dad to his face to shut the fuck up and fuck off and I… I wasn't sure what to expect. I might not ever be able to go home again. But I'm okay with that. It's going to be pretty lonely here, if Eric ends up taking this job, but it was lonely before that, even when I did go home. You know I never really fit in there. For whatever reason. And I'm starting to accept that… maybe it's better for me that I didn't.

"So, uh, that's all the things I wanted to tell you. I have a really good thing with the team and with Eric. And I'm not sure how long it's all going to last. But I'm so fucking happy that I've had it, even for this short time. And I'm sorry I haven't been to visit more often.

I promise I'm going to be better from now on. I miss you so much."

He touched his fingers against the stone he'd placed on top of her grave, took a deep breath. "I love you, Mom."

Strangely, he felt better as he walked back to the car. Eric had the right idea, about the regular visits, about leaving the pebbles. He wondered what Eric was doing now. Whether he'd accepted the job. Whether he was putting in his two weeks' notice with Joe Conroy. Ryan could feel his shoulders hunch forward, defensively. He felt exhausted, like he'd been bag skating himself for hours.

It was time to go home.

Eric couldn't remember the last time he'd been so eager to talk to anyone as he was taking the stairs of Ryan's apartment two at a time. He'd piggybacked into the building on the heels of a girl who lived on the first floor and who'd obviously recognized him, which was an issue for another day. Right now, he had to talk to Ryan. Immediately. The apartment door was shut when Eric got there, and as he pounded his fist against it, he realized he probably should have called first to make sure that Ryan was home.

Ryan opened the door almost immediately anyway, his whiskey-brown eyes concerned. "Eric? What the hell are you doing?"

"Sorry, sorry, I was in such a hurry to talk to you about this, I didn't think to text."

"Actually, there's something I wanted to talk to you about, too."

They stood staring at each other in the doorway for a second. Ryan looked so fucking good to him, just then, in his ratty sweatshirt and joggers and his eyes red-rimmed, that it was difficult not to just grab him and push him back toward the bedroom.

Instead of doing any of that, Eric said, "You go first."

Ryan said, "Do you want to come in, though?"

It was strange how tentative it felt, crossing the threshold. He had no idea what to expect, coming from Ryan. Ryan held out his hand, and Eric took it. Ryan's fingers were cold, and Eric wondered where he'd been and what he'd been doing. But he didn't ask. Let Ryan drag him back toward the IKEA couch they'd bought out of sheer necessity and that Ryan had spent several hours putting together with only an Allen key and sheer stubbornness.

"Look," Ryan said, when they were sitting. "I love you. I'm not saying that because I want to hold you back or anything. I want you to have this job if you want it, *because* I love you. Like, I'm really kind of insanely in love with you, actually."

Eric could feel his heart pounding in his ears, the same way it always had when he was playing, when someone had said something shitty to him and he was so fucking furious about it that he felt at any minute that his head was going to explode. Except instead of fury, it was with an emotion that he couldn't entirely describe. Relief and happiness and sheer fucking disbelief. "You're in love with *me*?"

"Is that a problem?" Ryan demanded, like he was ready to fight about it, and Eric felt momentarily overwhelmed with all of the stupid shit that was going on in his head.

"No. No, kind of the opposite, actually," Eric said, his breath a little shaky. Ryan's hands were still in his, trembling a little. "So what I wanted to tell you was that I love you. And that's probably half of why I turned the job down."

"…you what?"

"I turned the job down. Partially because of you."

"Eric, no, that's not what I wanted you—really, if you want the job, I need you to take it. I'll be okay without you here. Don't give up this opportunity just for me."

Eric's chest was going to burst again, looking at Ryan's worried face and ridiculously earnest expression. This was how he always was, always had been: wearing his heart on his sleeve even while prepared for someone to stomp on it. "No, but that's exactly it. I want to stay because of you. There's the whole Railers thing. I'm not going to compromise my morals to get ahead in life, I've already decided that. But I want to stay here *with you.* We're building something special here together. And I don't want to give that up, not yet."

"Eric…" Ryan said, and his face was almost comical, how quickly the expressions cycled through it, confusion and acceptance and joy. He was smiling, now, so fucking wide that Eric could've easily stuck all five of his fingers in there. Not that he was going to do it, of course. Not yet. "You're really turning it down? For me?"

"For us." Ryan's fingers were gripping Eric's hands, so hard it hurt. "Like I said. I really think…not this season, not next season, maybe not even the season after that. But this is what kind of environment I want to coach in. These are the players I'm happy to know. I just want to build something special together. I *know* we can."

"I don't really know what to say," Ryan admitted, "except that I'm just really fucking happy. I thought I was going to lose you."

"You can't get rid of me that easily."

And then, before he could even think about it further, they were kissing. He wasn't sure whether he had leaned forward first or whether Ryan had, but it didn't matter. There was Ryan's mouth, familiar and warm and giving under his. There were Ryan's eyes, already closed, his eyelashes thick against his cheek. There were Ryan's hands, slipping up to take either side of Eric's face in his hold. There was Ryan's tongue, insistent and hot and wet against Eric's.

When they finally pulled away for air, Ryan said, "I told my dad to fuck off. It didn't go that great. But I did it."

Eric, who had been trying to figure out how he was going to maneuver Ryan back toward the bedroom, laughed. It wasn't what he'd been expecting, but it was just…they'd both grown so much, just from knowing each other.

"Look at you, baby," he drawled, "first you're waiving guys, then you're standing up to your dad? What got into you?"

"I just had, I don't know. Enough. There's a time and a place for it," Ryan said. He'd shifted closer on the couch, so he was practically sitting in Eric's lap. It was easy to gather him in for another kiss. "And anyway, there's something else I'd like to get into me."

"Smooth, Sullivan. Really smooth."

"Thanks, I thought so," Ryan said, his hand slipping underneath Eric's shirt to touch his abs, the hair trailing down them, to rest on his hip underneath the waistband of his sweats. "I'm serious, though. It's been a long fucking day and I want to—I don't know."

"You?" Eric asked. He was teasing, both the words

and the fact that he wasn't giving Ryan what he wanted, which was for Eric to touch him. He could feel Ryan practically vibrating waiting for the inevitable. "Ryan Sullivan, not knowing what he wants?"

Ryan flushed, which was both funny considering everything they'd done together since they hooked up the first time, and completely adorable. "I know what I want, I just don't know how to say it."

"Try," Eric said. He wasn't really teasing anymore. It was mostly because he couldn't hide the emotion in his voice, as embarrassing as *that* was. "If you want something, tell me."

"It's stupid, but I can't stop thinking about it, really. You know, we never actually ever talked about what this was. With us," Ryan said. He looked up at Eric, face serious, searching. "I know you're staying. And that's all I can ask for. But I want—more. Maybe it's a little fast, maybe it's not, but I've never been the kind of guy to not be sure of things. And I'm sure of this. I'm sure of *you*."

Still sitting in Eric's lap, Eric could feel Ryan's whole body tense, like he was expecting anything except the only thing Eric could do at this point in the cycle of knowing and falling in love with Ryan Sullivan, which was agree to give him anything he wanted.

"Are you asking me to be your boyfriend or something?" he managed, mostly because his mouth felt too dry, and his default reaction to these sorts of things was to make a joke of it.

"We're too old for that shit, Eric. But my something. Partner. I don't know."

"Partner?" Eric tested it out. It still sounded awkward and strange, but Ryan in his arms felt familiar and easy, and that was the important thing. "I'm giving you a hard time—yes, I know, I'm going to give you a really hard time in a minute—but if that's what you want, if that's what would make you happy? You can call me whatever you want. And I'll be there."

Ryan smiled suddenly, so broad and proud that Eric could see the flash of his teeth. This time, he did shove his fingers in there, choking back a laugh at the way Ryan's eyes flew open in shock, then lidded when he realized what Eric had done. Groaned when Ryan's hot tongue slid around the pads of his first two fingers, a parody of the way Ryan would have sucked his dick. Even that sent a jolt of pleasure right down his spine, all of his nerves tingling in awareness, like they were specially attuned to the tiniest movements Ryan made.

"You want to take this to the bedroom?" Eric asked, because he really didn't want to try fucking on Ryan's terrible IKEA couch.

"Mhm," Ryan said, the sound buzzing around Eric's fingers. He pulled away far enough so that he could actually talk again, shifted himself so he was sitting on the couch again and Eric could move freely. "And that's not the only thing I want."

"A hard time?"

"Holy shit, he pays attention," Ryan said, laughing. Despite the laugh, his eyes were huge, pupils dilated, and he licked his lips when he looked down and saw the outline of Eric's erection beneath the sweats. "A hard time. Fuck me until I can't remember my own name. You know the drill."

"Pretty tall order," Eric said, sliding off of the couch and holding out his hand. Ryan took it, so Eric pulled him to his feet. "Hope you're not disappointed if I can only get you to temporary paralysis, eh?"

"I'll withhold criticism until afterward," Ryan said, lifting his chin.

In Ryan's shitty little bedroom, with its low ceilings and dark windows and cramped furniture, Eric watched hungrily while Ryan stripped off his shirt and then shucked his pants and boxers, eyes hot and intent. It was kind of insane, how perfect he looked naked, like he could step back on the ice tomorrow and still hold his own against guys half his age. Short but solid. The gray hair spread across his chest, down his arms and thick thighs. And lower. Heavy balls and his thick cock, curving upward, hard just thinking about what Eric was going to do to him.

Goddamn, it was ridiculous that Eric got to see him like this, that no one else did anymore.

Eric followed suit, hastily wriggling out of his shirt and pants while Ryan pulled the blankets back on the bed. Somehow, his apartment always felt ten degrees colder than it did outside, at least until they warmed themselves up another way, and Eric was happy enough to pull them back up once the bed was shifting under the weight of both of their bodies.

It got desperate and messy very quickly, Ryan moaning when Eric dug his teeth into his shoulder; Ryan's hands scrabbling along his back; Ryan's mouth opening eagerly under Eric's; Ryan's dick leaking in Eric's hand; Ryan's breath panting raggedly in Eric's ear while Eric tried to keep it together long enough to say something coherent. He wasn't succeeding at all. His chest felt like it was going to burst right open and the words coming out of his mouth were an unorganized mess, a stream-of-consciousness narration about how good Ryan felt under him and also, unfortunately, how excited he was to continue coaching with him.

"Wait, what?" Ryan gasped. His mouth was hanging open, his eyes unfocused, and his hips were still making aborted little thrusts into Eric's fist. "Coaching? That's what you're going with?"

"Pretty sure you're into it," Eric mumbled into his neck. "I was looking into new papers about neuroplasticity yesterday…"

Ryan groaned again then, his eyes slipping shut. "Jesus, you know just what to say to me."

"I thought we could maybe switch up the positioning for the drills for the F1 facing a defensive-zone swarm—"

"Stop," Ryan said, his voice trembling on a laugh. "I think if you keep going like that I might actually come *while* you're doing it and I—I have to actually lead those drills at practice, Eric, *please*—"

"You'll have to figure out another way to shut me up, then," Eric said, his weight supported on his hands, his body bracketing Ryan in.

"Suck my dick, then."

"That's what you want?"

"Yes," Ryan breathed.

Eric obliged, pushing the blankets back again so he wouldn't get stuck underneath them. Ryan shivered in the chilly air of his bedroom, nipples tight and hard, and Eric couldn't resist pinching and twisting one of them before he shifted down Ryan's body. The little squawk of surprise and shock was absolutely worth it. So were Ryan's hands, twisting in Eric's curls, when he had gotten far enough down that Ryan could reach. Ryan's fingers, gripping tight, when Eric ran his tongue up the length of his cock, not quite taking it in his mouth.

"Come *on*," Ryan mumbled, impatient and demanding, hands trying to shove Eric's head down.

"When I'm ready," Eric said pleasantly, rewarded by the answering groan of frustration. But Ryan knew by now that he couldn't win these things, and he'd have to be patient, no matter how much he hated it. Eric could feel his fingers flexing, open and closed, as he tried desperately to hold himself back.

He'd already put his glasses on the little side table, so when he took Ryan in his mouth, he pressed his forehead up against Ryan's stomach to feel his abs flexing as he tried not to thrust up too far. It was funny: he'd had sex with a fair amount of men and women over the years, and it had never been like this. He'd never felt the stupid swoop in his stomach, waiting to see the reactions he could drag out of Ryan, with his tongue and with his mouth. It had never been this satisfying to reduce anyone to a groaning mess, to feel anyone's thighs clenched around his ears.

Maybe that's what falling in love got you.

He certainly wasn't complaining.

Neither was Ryan, head thrown back against the pillows, teeth digging into his lip, eyes screwed shut. He was mumbling incoherent encouragement and exhortation, his heels digging into Eric's spine. "Jesus," he gasped, "fuck, your mouth is insane, Eric, please—"

By the time that Eric had slicked up his fingers and gotten them worked inside of Ryan's body, clenched hot and tight around them, he couldn't even keep it together enough to tease. He felt like he had been infected with Ryan's earnestness, his honesty. All he could do was look down at him, the vulnerability of his flushed cheeks and glassy eyes, his ragged breathing and the way he kept saying, "Come on, come on, come on, *please*," in the cadence of a prayer, and know that it was reflected in his own face.

"How do you want to do this?" Eric managed.

"I don't care," Ryan panted, "I just wanna be able to kiss you when I come."

Eric's heart did another one of those stupid lurches. "Okay," he said, "get up here."

The way they fit together was familiar, but never anything he could take for granted. Ryan, in his lap, stubbly cheek against Eric's as he lowered himself down. It was too much and not enough, and it was Eric's turn to hold himself back, to do his best not to rush. It didn't take long: Ryan was so worked up from all of it, from the stupid shit Eric had been whispering in his ear, that it was almost easy.

"God," Ryan managed. His voice was strained, stretched almost as tight as he felt around Eric. "I love your cock."

Eric thought for a second about the first time he'd met Ryan as a colleague and not a player, his first instinctive reaction had been *goddamnit, he's hot* and the sort of furious hatred born of jealousy and frustration. And now, all he could think was *goddamnit, he's hot*, as he watched Ryan letting himself get adjusted to the way Eric felt inside of him, pressed his fingers down on Ryan's lower lip to watch the way it made his eyes go hot and dark.

"You damn sure take it like you love it," Eric muttered, and Ryan laughed, the sound more than a little breathless.

"I love it. I love you."

"Fuck. *Fuck.*"

It didn't take them that long after it. It wasn't skilled or elegant or anything except desperate, Ryan on top of him, sloppily catching his mouth in a kiss whenever he could reach. The shitty little bed slammed into the wall with the force of it, Ryan's hands braced on the headboard, leaving Eric free to explore his body with his hands. A touch he couldn't describe as anything except reverent, tracing the muscular lines of his back and his hip and his thighs and his ass. And finally, stroking his dick, urging him on.

Ryan did kiss him when he came, tongue fucking Eric's mouth and his hands grasping desperately at his shoulders, like that could pull him deeper, closer.

Eric watched him in the aftermath, eyes closed and face flushed, the sweat beading his forehead. He was trembling on the edge, too, but… "Can I keep going?"

"Whatever…whatever you want," Ryan said, on a long, satisfied sigh, and then a yelp when Eric, in one movement, pushed him down on the bed and fell on top of him, still deep inside. His eyes flew open when Eric thrust again, and he shook underneath him, the aftershocks of the orgasm, the overstimulation of Eric fucking him through it, ignoring the sticky mess smeared on his stomach. His dick, still hard and wet, twitched again where it was trapped between them. "Oh, Jesus, Eric. *Eric—*"

That was what did it, eventually, the desperation, the pleasure edging on pain in his voice, throaty and wrecked. Eric couldn't look at him when he came, couldn't look at anything. His head was buried somewhere in Ryan's neck, eyes closed, Ryan's fingers digging into the meat of his shoulder.

It took him a while to open his eyes. When he did, it took him another while before he finally gathered up the coordination to pull out and roll off of Ryan's limp body. Ryan, who stretched again and said, "I need to get up but Jesus Christ, I don't wanna move." Ryan, who turned his face to push it against Eric's shoulder like a cat. "Carry me."

Eric snorted and said, "No, can't move," because he couldn't put together the coherent thought to say anything more than that.

"Mm," Ryan agreed. "I fucked it right out of you."

By the time they did get out of bed and cleaned up, Eric had no idea how late it was. He was bone-tired in a way that he wasn't usually these days, but it was good. As soon as Ryan came back to bed, they could pass out, and that would be that.

When Ryan did get back in bed, he immediately rolled over and wormed his way under Eric's arm. "I told you."

"You told me what?" Eric asked, sleepily.

"You're a good man. I knew you'd do the right thing. I always trusted you to."

Eric thought about it for a long moment. "I wanted to earn that trust."

"You did, Eric," Ryan murmured into his shoulder. "And now…sleep."

Eric slept, a better sleep than he'd had in years.

IV.
THE OFFSEASON

CHAPTER FIFTEEN

April–July

The closer they got to the end of the season, the less meaningful the games became. The Beacons had been mathematically eliminated from the playoffs in the end of March, which Ryan had been expecting. Despite his best efforts, the team just hadn't had it, and they'd been ravaged with injuries the second half of the year. The guys took it about as well as he could have hoped for, and they kept fighting even though technically, they had nothing to fight for except their pride in the logo on the sweater.

"Hey, Coach?" Williams said, after one of the losses. It had been a backbreaker: close enough to a win that it hurt just that much more.

"Yes, Willy?" Ryan said, backtracking just enough so that he wasn't yelling over his shoulder to talk. "What's up?"

"I just want you to know that next year is going to be better."

"Is it?"

"Yeah," Williams said. He had come out of the dressing room to tell Ryan this, and he was still half-undressed in his underlayer and shorts, face shining with sweat.

"You couldn't wait five minutes?" Ryan asked, amused.

"No, I wanted to tell you before I lost the thought. It's just like—we didn't play very well this year. But we're going to come in next year and I'm gonna make sure everyone is working hard. We can move on from 5 on 5 and concentrate on special teams. Losing, it just…it sucks so much, Coach. I fucking hate it so much. I know we'll probably have a top-five draft pick this year, and that's what the team needs, but next year… I just want you to know I'm going to be ready."

"Thanks, Willy," Ryan said, running a hand through his hair. "You know how much I appreciate your contributions to the team. I just want you to try to enjoy your summer a little bit, too, eh? Take a vacation? See your family? Hang out with your friends?"

"I've got the whole summer for that," Williams said, rolling his eyes. "This loss just…for some reason this one really bugs me. And it's *not* going to be like that next year."

"All right," Ryan agreed. "But, you know, I also want you to take a vacation."

"That an order, Coach?"

"Yes," Ryan said, and held out his fist for their handshake.

He stayed late that night to go over tape with the rest of his staff, although at this point it was a futile effort. It reminded him a little of his first days in Dallas with Murph, when the team had been a disaster waiting to happen every night, but the players had put in a ridiculous effort anyway. Murph had always hated to lose, and he and Ryan had been responsible for a number of rallying locker room speeches even when the older players had basically given up.

Ryan sighed. He wondered what Murph was doing. Whether he was okay.

"You good, Ryan?" Eric asked him, as they were finally ready to pack up for the night and head home.

"You go on without me," Ryan said, after a second. "I have a few things I want to take care of here first."

Eric's eyebrows went up, but he didn't argue. He hesitated and said, "All right. See you tomorrow, then."

They would meet up later, of course, but there was the need, even now, to be careful. By the time Ryan was alone, it was almost one in the morning and he was exhausted, but took the time to neaten up the papers scattered over his desk, wipe the whiteboard clean of his notes and diagrams. His mind was full of jumbled, scattered thoughts that didn't quite connect. Memories of his time in Dallas and memories he was building here. Crashing in Murph's hotel room after a night out with the team and waking up spooned up against Murph's broad back. Waking up in hotel rooms with Eric now. The look in Murph's eye when Ryan had scored the game-winning goal of the Cup-clinching game, the way they'd embraced afterward and it had felt like—

Before he could really think about it, Ryan pulled out his phone and called Murph. He wasn't sure whether Murph would actually pick up. Not only had they not spoken since the disastrous dinner in Back Bay, it was still pretty late. The phone rang a few times but just when Ryan was about to hastily end the call, Murph answered.

"Hey," Ryan said, uneasy.

"Sully."

Ryan listened to him breathing in silence for what had

to have been at least a minute, trying to think of what to say. “I didn’t really plan this one out very well, huh?”

“You never did,” Murph said, and laughed. It was a little strained, but he didn’t hang up, so that was a step forward.

“I was thinking about a lot of stuff today. About when we won the Cup the first time. When I hugged you after.”

The noise Murph made sounded like someone had punched him in the gut, a sharp and sudden exhale. “Yeah, I…thought about that one a lot too, over the years.”

Even now, knowing what he knew about himself, Ryan almost couldn’t bring himself to ask. “Were you going to kiss me?”

Murph was silent again. “I was caught up in the moment, you know? It felt like the culmination of everything we’d been working for. And then you scored that beautiful fucking goal and won it for us, and it was just like a fairy tale, like everything was…but then I realized. Where we were. Who we were. I couldn’t. It was already too late. And then I just tried to tell myself it was a trick of the light, of the moment. Because what was the point?”

Ryan rubbed his eyes with his hands. “I think… I probably felt the same way. I just never recognized it for what it was. We were both already married. I mean, shit, I got married when I was practically still a kid. I never even thought we could’ve been anything except—”

“I know,” Murph said. He sighed, the noise especially loud in Ryan’s ear. “Like I said. I don’t blame you for the way things turned out. *I* didn’t realize until it was too late, and then I buried that shit for years until Aronson ripped the Band-Aid off. The way it was back then, how would we even have…? You know?"

"Yeah," Ryan said. "I just…are things ever going to be the same again?"

"The same? I don't see how they can ever be the *same*. But I've been thinking about it, Sully, and I think that maybe that doesn't have to be a bad thing. You're one of the most important people in my life, and I don't want to lose you. Maybe it's going to be hard, and maybe it's going to be weird, and maybe it'll take time…but I don't want to lose what you are in my life."

Ryan could feel his shoulders adjust, a physical weight off of them. "Yes," he said.

"Maybe it won't be the same. I don't know how long it's going to take. But we can leave the door open?"

"I'd really like that."

"Look, Sully, it's late, and Tara's gonna kill me when I wake her up when I get back to bed. But just keep that in mind. I love you, man. And we're always going to be friends. No matter what. Even if it's weird. And also if Aronson does one damn thing to hurt you, I'll kill him."

"He would never," Ryan said, out loud this time, and knowing with bone-deep certainty that it was true. "And I love you too, brother. Don't be a stranger this time, eh?"

"Yeah, yeah. And *you* sound like you're still at the Spectrum. Overachieving little freak. Go home, Sully. Get some sleep."

"Yeah, yeah," Ryan echoed, but he was smiling when he hung up.

Eric opened his eyes in a nondescript hotel room in the last week of the season, and realized that Ryan was already awake. The alarm hadn't gone off yet, but it didn't matter. Ryan had probably been up for a while at this rate, thinking so furiously that Eric could almost feel it physically.

"Ry," Eric said.

"Yeah?"

"What's wrong?" Even Eric's voice sounded strange in his own ears, sleepy and content in a way that it almost never had before, especially on the road. *Ryan fucking Sullivan.* Who would have thought?

"I was just thinking about my contract extension. And your contract extension. And Petey and Heidi's contract extensions. And the negotiations. And the… you know."

"What about it?" Eric asked, rolling over.

The room was still dim enough; the sun hadn't fully risen and only a sliver of light broke through the crack in the blackout curtains. Even in the dark, though, Eric knew Ryan's face by heart now, every familiar line and scar. Eric could see just enough, anyway. Ryan wasn't smiling, which meant—well, whatever it was must have been serious. He didn't smile even when Eric pressed his mouth against Ryan's shoulder.

"Just…we're going to stay, right? But what's that going to look like for us?"

"How do you mean?" Eric asked, his brain still racing to both wake up and catch up.

"Are we just going to keep this secret forever?"

Eric exhaled sharply and lay back against the pillows. "I hadn't thought about it." That wasn't entirely true: he had thought about it, and discarded the possibility. Hadn't even thought Ryan would be interested in telling anyone. His mother knew and that was all that really mattered to Eric.

"Because it's just… I don't know. I was thinking about how it would be nice to be able to move in together. To have a home that's ours. To not have to worry about sneaking around so much on the road, you know?"

"Yes…" Eric said, a little wary.

"It's just that you make me really fucking happy, Eric, and I don't know how it's going to feel if we're only gonna be able to do this halfway until we retire."

"Wow. Wow. You really know how to wake a guy up in the morning, huh?"

"Shut up," Ryan said, and punched him in the bicep, but it was with such a fond tone of voice that Eric couldn't resist rolling over on top of him, trapping Ryan's sturdy little body underneath his own.

"What were you thinking about?" Eric said, pressing a kiss against Ryan's eyelid.

"Stop," Ryan said, exasperated, blinking furiously, and Eric laughed and did it again. "You are *such* an asshole, Eric, Jesus—"

"I'm being serious, though," Eric said, his mouth at the hinge of Ryan's jaw now, trailing down his neck. "Tell me. What's your ideal future? What were you thinking about?"

"I just thought…" Ryan said, distracted, his whole body shuddering reflexively. "*Stop*, I can't think when you're doing that."

Eric shifted, caught Ryan's wrists in his hands. Looked down at Ryan pinioned beneath him and thought again how fucking lucky he was. "Okay. Sorry, mon pitchounet. What were you thinking?"

"Do you think it might be nice to be able to tell Petey and Heidi about us? And maybe the team?"

"Wait, you want to move in with me *and* you want to come out?" Eric said, his brain finally playing catch-up. "Tabarnak, you don't take things at half measures."

"Not completely. Not to everyone. Just in a way that matters. The people who matter to us. And as for living together…your apartment's awful. My apartment's awful. It'd be nice to finally have a *home*, you know? It feels sometimes like I haven't had one ever, really. And also, you know, it'd be way more efficient. We could carpool to practice together."

"And you want a home with me," Eric said slowly, ignoring that last part.

"Well, yeah." Ryan was blushing, his face an embarrassed, angry red that Eric could see even in the dim light of the hotel room, and it took everything he had not to lean down and kiss him senseless again. "I think I do."

"Okay."

"Okay what?"

"To all of it. Telling Heids and Petey. Getting the apartment. Whatever you want."

"What, really? Just like that? Seriously?"

"Look, Ry," Eric said. He could feel Ryan's pulse under his fingers, hammering nervously under the skin. "I've spent a lot of fucking years in the closet. I've lived with a lot of regrets. Am I maybe kind of terrified about what you're asking for? Hell yes, I am. But I'm more terrified of losing this. Losing you. Letting things go and regretting them later. Maybe it's time to…"

Ryan was looking up at him with a soft, fond expression, didn't struggle to get away even though Eric still had his arms pinned above his head. "To what?"

"Take something for myself. Live the way I'd like to. It's not sudden, Ryan. It's been years in the making. But you know what?"

"Hmm?"

"I don't think I'd have gotten here without you."

Ryan's eyes went wide and for the first time, he did struggle, trying to shift his head up. "Eric, come on, you can't say shit like that to me and not let me kiss you."

And Eric, laughing, gave in.

The end of the season came early, and it wasn't a surprise to anyone, least of all to Ryan. The Beacons had been more than a few points out of the last wildcard spot for quite some time, with the injuries stacking up and the youth still learning the ropes. They weren't last in the league the way some people had expected, and that was enough for him.

Ryan's meeting with Joe Conroy and the management group had gone well, too. They provided an updated version of his contract extension, which he was going to sign once the dust had settled. The negotiations for the staff had gone well, too, and he felt, overall, satisfied about how all of that was going, even if it wasn't news he wanted to discuss with the media. No matter his personal feelings, he was sure at least half of the questions would be about whether he was coming back next season.

The day that they cleaned out the locker rooms and met with management and for exit interviews was the day after their final game, which they had won, in a last-hurrah blowout to the tune of 8-2 against a Calgary team that was playing 11F 7D and limping into the playoffs without two of their stars. It had been good to end on a high note, he couldn't really ask for much more than that.

He spoke with each player individually, to thank them for their work over the season, and to tell them all of the things they had done well and that he would like them to work on for next year.

He spoke to Heidi and Petey after that, too, to tell them that he was going to be signing an extension and that he was planning to negotiate extensions for them as well. He'd also told them about Eric and been surprised by the reaction.

Heidi immediately threw her hands up in the air and said, "Of course."

"What do you mean, of course?" Ryan had asked.

"We had a little bet going," Petey said, with a sly, sideways smile. "I had money on the two of you figuring things out in the particular way you seemed to figure things out. Hughes here said there was no way you weren't anything but a hundred percent straight and oblivious."

Ryan felt himself flush red, and he glared at Eric, who was shaking with silent laughter. "What's so funny? This is *your* fault, too."

"Heidi was right about you being oblivious, that's for sure," Eric managed.

A little later, as they waited behind the door to the media room, Eric asked, "You ready to go out and face the vultures?"

"They're not so bad," Ryan said, with a straight face, and earned a snort of disdain. They were alone, for the moment, so he smoothed Eric's unruly hair down, said, "Really, you don't even think that."

"Could be worse. Could be Montreal."

"Don't let your mom hear you say that, buddy."

"I'd rather die." He smiled again and reached out to straighten Ryan's tie. "I think at this point you're keeping them waiting, Ry. Go on out there."

And Ryan went out to face the press.

The questions were about what he had expected. A lot of them centered on whether Ryan was planning to sign an extension; he sidestepped those and said that he had been working with the management group to discuss their options for next season and beyond, and that he would leave it at that.

There were questions about individual players' progress, which he was more than happy to answer. Overall, he was thrilled with most of them. Davey Kancheli had, despite his numbers, kept them in games they had no business being in. Cook and Williams had both proved that they were legitimate top-line players, and even if Sinclair was traded in the offseason, there was the possibility of finding another winger for them in the draft. No, he had no complaints.

The more creative questions required thoughtful answers, like what he'd liked about coaching in Boston—how passionate the city was about hockey, being close to home—and what he hadn't liked—how passionate the city was about hockey, being close to home. That one got a ripple of laughter through the crowd of reporters.

Kayla Lawrence asked, "Coach Sullivan, if you don't mind telling me what you've learned this season?"

"What I've learned?" Ryan asked. He looked up. While he'd been answering the questions, Eric must have come around the other side of the hall, and he was standing in the back of the room, behind where all of the reporters were sitting. He looked good, his arms crossed over his chest, beard shadowing his cheek and jaw, dressed in Beacons-branded sweats and quarter-zip. Eric was smiling, and Ryan couldn't believe, for a second, just how stupidly lucky he was.

"Just… I don't know. I've learned that there's a time to kill them with kindness and a time to put your foot down. That standing up for yourself isn't necessarily a bad thing. That meeting people at their level really is the best way of doing things. I've learned a lot more than that. About myself, about my staff, about my players. And what I ultimately learned, is I really, truly believe that we're building something special here. I can't say much more than that until the negotiations are finished, but it's just…everything about this team. About this year. It's been special."

"Thank you, Coach Sullivan," Lawrence said, lowering her recorder.

"We're good?" Ryan asked, glancing around at the other reporters. There was a murmur of assent. "Thank you, everyone. Have a good offseason."

And he took the steps down from the podium two at a time, down to where Eric was waiting for him.

Five Photographs from Eric Aronson's
Private Instagram

[Image Description: Posted on April 13. A photograph of Ryan Sullivan, dressed in a comfortable, ratty-looking set of sweats, clearly at ease with whoever is taking the photograph. He is sit-

ting at the kitchen table of his Allston apartment, which has the remnants of a dinner that hasn't been cleared away and wineglasses still half-filled with sparkling wine. He is holding up a signed contract and pen and smiling a big, cheesy smile with only the hint of an eye roll. End ID.]
[Caption Plain Text: fucking finally, buddy. End Plain Text.]

[Image Description: Posted on June 1. A photograph of a large, mostly empty living room. Sun streams through the big windows onto the brick accent wall and the original hardwood floors. There's a non-IKEA brand couch, both newer and better quality than anything either of them owned individually before, a TV stand complete with ridiculously large TV, a coffee table covered in books and a lot of boxes in varying states of being unpacked. End ID.]
[Caption Plain Text: if anyone wants to help us unpack I'll pay you in beer. End Plain Text.]

[Image Description: Posted on June 15. A selfie of Eric Aronson and Ryan Sullivan from the waist up. They are on a beach somewhere, shirtless. The clear blue ocean stretches out behind them. Ryan is smiling, huge and genuine, and Eric is scowling at the camera. Ryan is holding the phone to take the picture, and his other arm is slung over Eric's shoulders, although he has to reach up to do it. End ID.]
[Caption Plain Text: I hate relaxing. End Plain Text.]

[Image Description: Posted on June 25. A photograph of Rosa Aronson and Ryan Sullivan playing chess in her kitchen. The kitchen is warm-looking and cluttered with a variety of cooking implements on every single available counter surface; the walls behind the table are similarly covered in pictures. In the center of the pictures is a new photograph of Rosa, Ryan, and Eric together. Rosa and Ryan are sitting at the kitchen table, which is immaculate, both frowning intently at the chessboard. Rosa is winning. End ID.]
[Caption Plain Text: shut the fuck up. End Plain Text.]

[Video Description: Posted on July 15. A video of Ryan Sullivan and Eric Aronson skating at the Beacons' practice facility. The sun is bright through the big glass windows. They are both in full hockey gear, and it's a full-contact skate. They're both skating hard, and Ryan checks Eric into the boards. The sound of the impact is audible. Eric's laugh sounds very loud in the empty rink. He says, clearly, "You fucking *motherfucker*." End ID.]
[Caption Plain Text: good to be home. End Plain Text.]

* * * * *

ACKNOWLEDGMENTS

This book would not have been possible without the help of so many people. When I first sold *Game Misconduct* I never dreamed I would've been able to get the chance to write even more stories in this universe, but I am so thankful that I have had that opportunity.

Thank you to Deidre Knight, my agent, for your continued advice, guidance and advocacy.

Thank you to the entire Carina team—Stephanie Doig, Mackenzie Walton and everyone behind the scenes—for your belief in my screwed-up little guys and their stories, and for all of your hard work into turning my rough stories into something real.

Thank you to Cait, without whom this series would not have been written.

Thank you to everyone behind the scenes whose early reading, conversation and encouragement made this book a joy to write: my server buds; the Twitter crew (Aily and O. and Max and so many others, it thrills me to be able to write tailor-made to your various preferences). I've loved being able to share memes and thoughts and behind-the-scenes details. Thank you, too, to the friends I've made through these books and whose enthusiasm and early reads and friendship have been invaluable:

thank you to Bec and your playlists and your endless AUs; to Tia and your live updates and for being there for my first live hockey game in years; to Louisa for your conversation and amazing support and your continued advocacy for Murph.

Just: thanks. To all of you. More than you will probably ever know.

Turn the page to read an excerpt from *Goaltender Interference* by Ari Baran, the next book in the Penalty Box series.

CHAPTER ONE

July

Sometimes it felt like Aiden Campbell had closed his eyes at twenty-six and woke up thirty-six. One day he'd been a kid with a kid's body and energy and recovery time. And then the next, he had to be even more religious than he used to about stretching and yoga, or his body tied itself up in knots and ached when he lowered himself into bed.

Sometimes it did that anyway.

Normally, at this point in the offseason, Aiden would be headed to the gym, the same way he had done for countless mornings over the course of almost two decades. Or he'd be driving to Tarrytown to get some work in on the ice. Even in the summer, there was never much of a break.

Today, Aiden had nowhere to go, nowhere to be, nothing to do.

It was the first day of the offseason after the New York Liberty had been eliminated from the playoffs, but he couldn't even accurately call it the offseason anymore.

With the season over, Aiden was officially retired.

The decision hadn't really been deliberate. He'd been getting hurt a little more often these last few years, a groin pull here, a tear or a sprained ankle and a knee surgery there, the kinds of betrayals his body never used to make. When he'd have to wake up for morning skate, instead of feeling the thrum of excitement in his veins, he just felt tired.

Gabe Walker, his backup, took over the bulk of the starts.

When the last year of his contract came up and talks should have started, he'd put off reaching out to his agent for long enough that it started to get uncomfortable. He'd put it off until Caroline, because she was used to him, called and asked, "So do you want to make a decision, or is this your way of telling me you've done it already?"

Aiden thought about it. The pause went on longer than it should have. Finally he said, "Caroline, I think I'm done."

He didn't have many regrets. He'd brought two Cups back to New York. His home was decorated with individual awards. He'd been the backbone of the team for years. He was a lock for the Hall of Fame, first ballot or otherwise.

He'd known, in the very back of his mind, that it would be a good idea to make plans for the rest of his life. Consider the direction he wanted to take. Figure out where he was going from here. It had been too much. Instead, Aiden had boxed the thought up and put it away. The same way he boxed up every thought that he didn't want to consider, the things that were out of his control, the messy, unpleasant aspects of life he couldn't ignore. It was easier not to look at them.

He'd focused on the things he *could* control, which in this case turned out to be shepherding a team full of playoff virgins through the postseason. That had taken a lot of time and mental energy, and it had worked.

But now the playoffs were over.

It wasn't working anymore.

Aiden went downstairs to make himself breakfast in his white and shining kitchen. He had eaten basically the same thing every day for fifteen years, but he still took care in preparing it. The Routine was important, even if most of the Routine had been ripped away from him along with hockey itself.

Aiden took the toast out of the toaster.

Mom had been asking when he was coming home, but he didn't know when he wanted to do it. *If* he wanted to do it. He'd stopped going back to Winnipeg in the offseason about five years ago, after his last long-term boyfriend had broken up with him. That had been when his parents really started pressing him about whether he was happy, whether he was going to meet anyone, if he thought maybe one day he'd like a family of his own.

Instead of answering, he'd quietly shelved his plans to buy an offseason residence in Manitoba and went all in on New York.

Aiden spread cashew butter on the toast and poured himself a cup of coffee.

Today was the first day of the rest of his life.

The Penalty Box series is available wherever books are sold, including Harlequin.com.